THE ARTIST OF AVEYRON

For Harriet & Bruce,
We're never too old to
build a new lifetime
friendship. Hope you enjoy!.
Tom Kuhn
9/17

T C Kuhn

ISBN: 1544952902
ISBN 13: 9781544952901

OTHER NOVELS BY T.C. KUHN:
THE STONE BREAKERS
VOICES UPON THE WIND
RED EARTH SKY
A DARK WINGED SHADOW
THE CORN MAIDEN'S GIFT
CHILDREN OF THE CIRCLE
THE KIMONO SONG
PLACE OF THE MISTY SKY

Visit the author's website: www.peopleofthestone.com to check out the author's BLOG and for email contact information. The BLOG deals with current topics in Native American prehistory, archeology, and anthropology in general, and more expansively with related or current topics and specific subjects, often of a controversial nature, addressed in his books.

COVER ART AND LAYOUT BY JOSH ROSE
(rose@elephantroommedia.com)

THE LEGACY

AD 2016

The drive down from Paris seemed unusually long this time. But then it had been several years since Jason last made the tiring trip. The circumstances, however, were much different—and much happier—on that occasion than on this one. At that time he and Marie had been excited to make the nearly day long drive to introduce their new daughter Angélique to the part of Marie's family who still lived in the distant valley and small villages of Marie's childhood. On this occasion, though, they were making the journey for the much less happy purpose of allowing his wife, and now their daughter as well, to close an important part of their shared past. It was a past Jason had never felt a part of in the same way his wife, and then his daughter, clung to and remained attached over the years that separated them from the tiny valley. It remained a place Jason had barely come to know or understand except in a very basic way, mostly because he had been there on only two previous occasions.

As he glanced over at where Marie was dozing in the seat beside him he happened to look up into the rear view mirror and saw Angélique staring out the window at the seemingly endless, perfectly manicured fields and wooded hillsides zooming past as they sped south along the busy *autoroute*. For a brief instant, Jason wondered what his daughter was thinking and smiled at that realization, before quickly refocusing on the road ahead. She was eight years old and at an age where he felt he could no longer make that easy determination and anticipate what her next words or actions might be. Those words and actions were generally more a reflection of her mother's influence than his most of the time anyway, he mused with little concern over that realization. Just then, as he glanced again at the image of the flashing red hair bobbing back and forth while his daughter silently mouthed the words to some familiar tune, he wondered how the coming days might change each of these two important women in his life and how they might also affect him in ways he could not yet imagine.

As on most of those occasions in the past when he was back in France with Marie, and now with their daughter as well, Jason felt strangely out of place and at a distinct disadvantage when dealing with events that might influence their tightly knit little family in some way he could not anticipate. This feeling of inadequacy was never more apparent to him than on those two trips when he had come with Marie to the Aveyron Valley, where his wife always seemed in some undefinable way to be a different person than the one he felt so close to at other times. Perhaps it was just their vastly different backgrounds, or possibly it was something far deeper he could never mentally latch on to; but that old feeling had been growing in him steadily since they left Paris earlier that morning.

Jason had met Marie nearly eleven years before, when he was on his first major job assignment with the large company he worked for at the time. He had not been out of business school long at that point and was eager to accept the position to become the company's "man" in Paris. At that time the offer surprisingly came his way mainly because he spoke a little French and had no family to burden his expense account. As such, he could live in Paris for less money than more senior executives, who might have wanted the desirable posting for themselves—or so he was told later. His company back then was in the specialty foods import business and their Paris account was becoming a fast growing part of their large American market at that time. He met Marie at one of the endless "mixers" and arranged get-togethers with clients he had suffered through those first, often awkward months in his new surroundings. Marie had been a liaison for an important man in a major French supplier his company was trying to woo into their sphere at the time. Much as Jason himself was then, she had been hired for her English skills and education—and her natural good looks, or so he suspected when they first met.

They were both younger than the usual crowd they were thrown into, and it seemed almost inevitable after a first, get-acquainted dinner together soon led to a dating relationship that eventually grew serious. When the end of his scheduled assignment approached over a year later, Jason thought of asking her to visit him in the States. However, he had instead found himself rather awkwardly proposing over what was to have been a parting dinner. Much to his surprise, or so it had seemed at that moment, Marie accepted with no hesitation. It took some time to get over the legal hurdles, but she eventually made it back to New York with him. He helped her get a less-important position with his company, and they lived there until a year or so after Angélique was born.

Then, with Marie's help and encouragement he struck out on his own to start a small company. It did much the same thing as he had been doing, but concentrated exclusively on importing specialty and luxury food items from France for the growing interest in such things in the States, especially after the world-wide recession began to abate somewhat. Their first trip back to France together with Angélique about a year after her birth enabled Jason, with Marie's old contacts, to meet a man with whom he soon formed a loose partnership, which helped get the new business off the ground and running with steady, if modest, success those first few years.

Unfortunately, in the last months that man had proven to be far less dependable—or honest, perhaps—than they were initially led to believe, and the new business was in more trouble than Jason was willing to admit to himself, to his wife, or to anyone else in recent weeks. When this unexpected trip became a necessity he hoped it might in some way provide the means or the opportunity to get a fresh start, or to at least improve his fortunes on this end of the business before they took a more desperate turn for the worse. Despite his growing business concerns, however, at the moment he knew he needed to be more focused on providing the support for his tiny family during what he knew might be the difficult and uncertain few days about to unfold.

Three weeks or so had passed since Marie received the message her grandmother had passed away and the old woman was leaving her the small, family farm in the south of France. Jason knew his wife had always been extremely close to her paternal grandmother, mainly because she had mostly grown up in the little valley and was just as often in the care of her grandmother as she was by her mother back then. However, despite some past hard times Marie had always remained fairly close to her mother, who still lived in Paris and with whom they had just spent the previous two days. Apparently the family farm was now coming to Marie through her father, who passed away some years before Jason had met her. There had also been an older brother; but he was killed in a car accident when Marie was barely a teenager. Jason learned later his wife's mother and her father's mother had apparently never gotten along well, as those things often went, especially after her brother's unexpected death. As a result, Marie often told her husband how much of the old woman's focus and affection had fallen upon her surviving grandchild for almost as long as Marie could remember.

Now, the last vestiges of that closeness in the form of the grandmother's farm, which must have been in his wife's family for many generations, was suddenly being dropped in their laps with all the normal headaches and possibilities such a bequest usually entailed. In this instance, however, the separation of several thousand miles made whatever outcome his wife might decide to pursue in the coming days one of growing uncertainty in the already distracted thoughts of a worried Jason. Just at that moment in his speculations about his growing dilemma, however, Marie stirred audibly and those wandering thoughts quickly disappeared. She sat up straight in the seat beside him, looked out the window, and asked.

"How long have I been napping? Shouldn't we be getting pretty close to our exit by now?"

"Probably another twenty or thirty minutes, if you still want to take the back way in along the river. Traffic has been a little slow as we start getting closer to Toulouse. I don't remember so many cars and big trucks on the roads the last time we were here."

Marie ignored his observation and immediately turned around to check on their daughter. Angélique smiled back at her and said she was thirsty. Marie reached for the water bottle in the holder between the seats, opened it, took a quick drink herself, and then handed it to Angélique. Then she turned to Jason.

"Well, that means another hour and a half maybe. I'm glad *Mama* packed those snacks for us. Can I get anybody something to eat—some cheese, or an apple maybe? I hope you two didn't try to get anything while I dozed. You should have woke me up after we passed Gourdon, or Cahors at the latest."

"I'm okay. You needed the sleep after the last couple of days, plus the jet lag. Angélique has been fine, counting cows and humming that little song she always does. We've both been fine—right, Sweetie?"

Angélique just smiled at her dad's grinning reflection in the rear view mirror and asked if she could have another one of the chocolate macarons she had eaten earlier. Marie reached for the bag between her feet and quickly replied to her daughter.

"*En francais, Cherie.* You know we always try to speak French when we're here."

Angélique moaned and repeated her question to her mother's satisfaction. Jason saw her looking up at the mirror, smiled, and just shrugged in mutual recognition. While his wife was dozing they had both easily slipped back into English in his brief conversations with his daughter. They were both ignoring this little "rule", which was established at his wife's insistence when she and Angélique came back to France without him for family visits every year since her birth. Marie was making certain their daughter was being raised in a bilingual environment. Despite a little personal inconvenience, however, it was also helping Jason maintain some of his skills in French, which would otherwise have begun eroding over the last few years, after they had improved dramatically during his nearly two year assignment in Paris. This little rule, moreover, did make some of his internet business communications a lot easier, as he was forced to admit to his wife on more than one occasion.

A couple of macarons later, they came to the exit they wanted about forty or so miles north of the city of Toulouse and headed off the fast-moving *autoroute* to continue on the narrower, country backroads that would take them to their destination in the lower Aveyron Valley. Jason glanced at his GPS and saw the desired location of the farm finally pop-into view for the first time just beyond the small town of Montricoux. Despite the long day of driving, Jason was once again struck by the beauty of his surroundings as he headed the rental car off into the countryside. The early fall skies of this part of southern France lived up to their reputation for clarity, and he was soon caught up in the scenery and excitement of getting near their destination, which Angélique was chattering about from the back seat. A glance over at his wife quickly gave him the impression that Marie was lost in some more serious reflection, however. Jason wondered what deeply embedded thoughts and memories of her grandmother and her own childhood might be flashing through her mind at the familiar sights for her they were by then encountering at nearly every turn in the road.

The sun was starting to dip low when they arrived at the final turnoff onto the gravel road that would soon lead them to the small, stone farmhouse and barn beneath the low ridge, which had now become a part of Jason's memories as well. A car parked just beside the driveway near the front of the house indicated the man Marie had contacted from Paris about their arrival was waiting for them as planned. Apparently, he was a cousin of hers of some sort and had been acting as a caretaker and all-around handyman for her grandmother in the last several years. The small farm was no longer a working one, and Jason could see none of the few ducks, chickens, dogs, or other animals he remembered from previous visits here were around and must have been taken elsewhere before or shortly after the old woman's passing.

Sad, he thought. Those sights and sounds had given the old place a touch of something warm and undefinable, which he could no longer sense in the somewhat overgrown and empty appearance of the otherwise picturesque little group of stone structures and unused fields. Their car had barely come to a full stop when a middle-aged man came through the front door of the house and walked over to greet Marie, who was already stepping out of the car, with a warm embrace.

"Bonjour, Jean-Pierre". Marie began in French, of course, and Jason quickly forced his thoughts to tune his ear to picking up the conversation. "I'm so glad to see you and to thank you for all you have done in the past month. I know *Mamie Béa* was always so grateful for what you and your family have done for her these

past few years. I can't thank you enough for your help. The place looks so good, and I'm glad you've found homes for all the animals. Angélique was hoping to see old *Matisse*, but I've told her he has a good home with you and maybe she could have a visit with him while we're here, ehh."

The man smiled and walked over to help Angélique out of the car to tell her the old dog would undoubtedly be excited to see her again and that his wife would love to have them all over for supper in the next day or so. Jason greeted the man with a warm handshake and began unloading their luggage, while the other three soon disappeared into the small, stone house. He looked around before heading that way himself with the first load of bags and wondered once more just what his wife might decide to do now they were finally here. They had spoken only a couple of times in the last two weeks about what her possible future plans might be for the farm. Each time he quickly determined she was wavering considerably about selling, renting, or maybe keeping it for a seasonal residence for themselves, if they decided to expand their business in France. That particular option was something Jason was increasingly hesitant to begin discussing with Marie given his own uncertainties about the future direction his business here might be taking.

Marie and Jean-Pierre were standing by the kitchen table talking when he entered and saw Angélique was already off exploring the small bedroom at the top of the stairs to the half, second story she remembered as being " hers" from their previous stays here. Jason and Marie had both tried to prepare her for the absence of her great-grandmother and the reasons for that absence after they received notice of the old woman's death. But neither of them could be certain yet how their daughter would react to her first experience with losing someone she had come to know and love. He could quickly see, however, the adaptability of youth would probably make their fears on that account up to now somewhat exaggerated. Jason knew Marie planned to take her soon to where *Mamie Béa*, as Angélique had also come to call her great-grandmother, was buried. It was something they were both hoping would allow for the conversation that might answer their daughter's as yet unasked questions in a more impactful setting. When Jason set down the bags inside the door, Marie turned to him with a smile and said.

"Look, dear. Clarisse has sent over this wonderful cassoulet for supper, with all the extras, and Jean-Pierre has brought us some wine from his own little vineyard. Wasn't that thoughtful? Really, Jean-Pierre, it's too kind, and you must thank Clarisse for all of us. You've both done so much already."

"That's what family is for, Marie. You know, everyone around here loved Béatrice, and there was a wonderful turnout for the funeral. I know you'll have some folks dropping by to offer their condolences and assistance as soon as they know you are all here. How long do you think you will be staying?"

"We've made no real plans yet. We've got the car for two weeks, but that can be changed easily enough." She glanced over at Jason with a smile. It was the first time he had heard her hint they might need to extend their stay. "I imagine there will be some things to tidy up with the lawyer up in Cassaude who wrote to me about the property, once we figure out what we want to do with it. I'd certainly like to get your input on that as well, Jean-Pierre. Maybe we can talk some about it tomorrow evening when we come over for dinner. It will be so good to see Clarisse again."

"Yes, we'll be expecting you about 1800 or so. She wanted to have Etienne and Hélène, also; but I told her it might be a bit too hectic to have all the grandchildren there so soon after you've arrived. I'm sure Jason and Angélique will be tired after that long trip down from Paris. By the way, Jason, I've left you a couple of bottles of red from my own vines. The 2015 is good with the cassoulet, but you should save the 2013 for something special. Everyone says it was my best vintage ever, and I think I agree. Too bad I have so few producing vines these days. I tried to get Béatrice to let me start some of my best cuttings over here to replace the ones she had let rot away. But she always said she didn't want all the worry and bother over it anymore, and there was never any point in arguing with her once her mind was set on something. You know, Marie, your grandfather used to produce some nice little wines right here. The sunlight for the vines is much better than over at my place and there's more good soil on that long slope up behind the barn. It's something you really should consider—if you decide to hang on to the farm," he winked.

"By the way, there are some jams, eggs, and a few things for breakfast in the refrigerator. Clarisse sent a couple of extra baguettes as well for your breakfast. Call us if there is anything else you need in the meantime." He was about to turn and leave, when his face lit up with the recognition of something he had forgotten. He reached into his shirt pocket, pulled out a small envelope, and extended it to Marie.

"I almost forgot this. Béatrice gave it to me two days before she passed away. She made me promise to give it to you personally, no matter what. She said it was very important you have it as soon as you returned, whenever that was. Sorry I didn't think of it right away. I guess I'd better be getting home before dark. You know how the roads are around here."

They both thanked Jean-Pierre again for his kindness and told him they would look forward to seeing him again the next evening. As soon as they heard his car heading away, they both sat down at the kitchen table and Jason began to look through the basket of food Clarisse had sent. He was about to get up to look for a corkscrew to open one of the wines, when he glanced over at where Marie was just running her thumb under the flap of the small, sealed envelope to open it. As soon as she did a tiny key fell out onto the table with a sharp click. She looked up at him; he sat back down to see what else was inside; and Marie pulled out a small, folded sheet of paper and began to read. When she was finished, she looked at him and responded in English for the first time since they got out of the car.

"It's in *Mamie Béa's* writing and it says there is a small trunk in the bottom of the big wardrobe in her bedroom. This must be the key to the trunk. It belonged to her grandmother, she says, and I should see what is inside when I come here after she has gone. That's all it says except this is important, that she wishes me a long and happy life, and that this is part of her legacy to me and Angélique."

"Wow! That sounds a bit mysterious, and maybe a little exciting. Let's call Angélique and get something to eat first. I'm famished. This food Jean-Pierre's wife sent looks a whole lot better than the last of the cheese and those macarons we polished off over an hour ago."

Marie agreed, laid down the letter, and got up to set the table. Jason headed back outside to get the rest of their luggage and other belongings from the car. By the time he had brought everything inside, Angélique was already at the table, and Marie was slicing some bread. He soon had the bottle of 2015 opened and one taste told him Jean-Pierre had a nice little wine there. But then he knew most small farmers in many parts of France maintained excellent family vineyards for their personal use. It was something he often thought about trying to figure out how to incorporate it into his business. However, he had never been able to come up with any kind of viable plan to put some larger, mutually profitable plan together. Still, there was opportunity here, he felt certain, but it would take someone far more competent than his current French partner to help get any ideas he might come up with off the ground. Of that Jason was certain as he set his glass down and poured one for Marie just as she dished a bowl of the still warm cassoulet and put it in front of him. They ate in silence until Jason, obviously thinking about the strange letter still resting on the table in front of Marie, turned to his wife and said.

"I don't recall you mentioning anything about this other grand-mother referred to in the letter. Do you know anything about her?"

"Actually, she was *Mamie Béa's* grandmother. She always just called her *"grand-mère Paulette"*, almost like she held her in some special status or something. But I always thought she was some legendary-like figure from her own past. The stories she used to tell about her seemed like they must have been made up to enter-tain me when I was a little girl and spent my summers here most years. Then, when my brother Jacques was killed in that awful ac-cident and *PaPa* got cancer so soon afterward, she didn't seem to speak so much about such things. I only remember she was some kind of dancer or entertainer and lived in Paris around the end of the nineteenth century before she came back here, got married, and taught school or something. I think the farm here actually came through her family, although I don't remember much about the circumstances, if *Mamie Béa* ever told me."

"Well, my curiosity is sure aroused. I for one am tired and was looking forward to going to bed early tonight; but maybe we should have a look at this trunk when we're finished eating."

Marie agreed, and as soon as they were finished and enjoyed the small lemon tarts Angélique had already found in the basket, everyone took their dishes to the sink. Marie led them to the bed-room behind the kitchen, which was to be hers and Jason's, and Jason saw the oversized, old walnut wardrobe he knew was so typi-cal of many of these ancient country houses in much of Europe. Marie opened it and began removing some quilts until she came to a trunk, which seemed to cover the entire bottom of the large armoire. It looked like an old railway trunk, although it was only about half the usual size. Jason groaned as he found the handles and began to remove it with some difficulty, until Marie pitched in and helped to place it on the floor between the foot of the bed and the wardrobe. The light wasn't great so they decided to carry it into the kitchen before opening it. The top of the trunk seemed to be covered with faded, old stickers from what must have been its owner's past travel experiences. Marie picked up the key, inserted it into the lock, and turned it with some difficulty until the simple mechanism gave, and the sturdy box was opened.

The first thing she removed was some faded clothing, which soon revealed itself to be the sort of costume a dancer might well have worn in the time period Marie had mentioned. Beneath that a stack of what seemed to be old theater pamphlets had been spread, and there was also a faded, yellowish photo of three women standing together. The one on the left was circled and all appeared to be wearing the same or a similar costume as the one they had just removed from the trunk. Marie stared at it for a moment and handed it to Jason, who took a quick look and put it behind him on the kitchen table where Angélique was sitting and watching the proceedings unfolding below her.

The next layer appeared to be some very old art instruction and drawing books. Included was a small, metal box full of pastel drawing pencils in various stages of use, from nearly new to worn down. There was also a large sketch pad, which Marie opened and began to carefully turn through. It was about half-filled with various drawings and sketches, obviously done by the same person. She looked up and said.

"*Mamie Béa* said that *grand-mère Paulette* was a teacher here a lot of her life. She must have been an art teacher. Look at these drawings. They're really quite good. I recognize that cliff at the mouth of the Gorge not far from here in this one, and that one is obviously the old church down in the village. Angélique, you'll like these pictures. You're always making drawings or sketching on your tablet. Here, look through these pencils. They're called *pastels,* Sweetheart. I'm sure *Mamie Béa* would have wanted you to have them."

Jason kept looking over his wife's shoulder as she turned through the sketch book until they got to the slightly faded, blank pages. Marie handed him the pad, which he simply put up on the table beside Angélique. Something else had already caught his wife's attention, and he wanted to see what might come out next. So far, he couldn't see why anyone would have made such a big deal of the contents of the old trunk.

Below the instruction books and sketch pad was what appeared to be a portfolio of some sort, similar to the ones artists still kept to carry their work around with them. Marie carefully removed it and undid the frayed ribbon that had once been used to bind it and protect the contents within. As soon as it was opened Marie began to remove the drawings, which were more finished this time. The colors were still amazingly bright and vibrant, even in the low kitchen light. The first drawings were landscapes, farm animals, and a couple of portraits of what might have been local people. There was one of a dog, which suddenly caught their daughter's eye. She squealed and blurted out.

"It looks just like *Matisse,* doesn't it, Mama."

Indeed, it did look like her grandmother's old dog, Marie answered as she looked at Jason with a strange, questioning look on her face. She spread out the remaining half dozen or so drawings and they saw what were obviously dancers depicted in various action poses. They were all dressed in similar costumes to the one that had first come out of the trunk. Suddenly, Marie stopped, pointed at first one and then another of these finished works, and said to Jason.

"Look, dear. These are all signed and dated. "The signature says: *Pa. Gambeau.* These are all dated from 1900. They're the only ones signed and dated, but it looks like the same person did them as did these other ones. I'll bet the "Pa." is Paulette, and I'll bet that Gambeau was her maiden name, before she came back here, married, and became a Poincare. That's the name *Mamie*

Béa's family line came through before she married my grandfather and they eventually moved back here to her family's farm. I know that for sure. I wonder why she wouldn't have signed and dated these other drawings, which could actually be later since they all appear to be of local things. These dancers are really very good. I can almost see them moving. They remind me of a lot of other art from that same time period around the turn of the last century in Paris. I took some art history in college, mostly at *Mamie Béa's* suggestion; although I was never very good at anything like drawing myself. Certainly not as good as you are already, Sweetie." She turned to Angélique, who was quietly sorting through the pastel pencils.

Marie and Jason then carefully began to slide the drawings back between the onion-skin papers that had divided them and replaced the lot into the portfolio binder, which had apparently protected them so well for the last one hundred years, at least. They were at the bottom of the trunk by then, but Jason had already noticed there was another, smaller portfolio resting beneath the larger one and was protected by what seemed to be some more old show bill pamphlets. There was also a small bundle of several letters, which were still in their envelopes and tied together by the same type of red ribbon that had apparently been used to bind both portfolio folders. Marie picked them up, glanced at the name on the outside, which appeared to be that of Paulette Poincare and the name of a village Jason did not recognize. Marie set the letters aside, pulled out the last portfolio, and slowly began to undue the ribbon. Inside was a single painting, similar in style and subject to the ones of the dancers they had just looked at it. Marie looked at it briefly, and then let out a gasp, as she turned to hand it to Jason. He noticed her hand was visibly shaking when he carefully slid his as she had just done under the painting to receive it.

"Oh my god, oh my god!"

That was all Marie could say as Jason looked at the painting, which was done on some sort of thin, hard surface, like wood possibly. The dancer was in an action pose and also appeared to be wearing the exact same costume Marie had removed from the trunk earlier. The painting was obviously very good, and the dancer might possibly be the ancestor whose trunk this once was. But beyond that Jason could not see why his wife had so suddenly gone pale or why her hands were still shaking. He stared back at her for a brief instant with that question on his face. She began to giggle, pointed at the lower right hand corner of the drawing, and said.

"Look at the signature, Jason. Look at the signature! This is unbelievable."

Jason looked where she was pointing and a lump suddenly surged up from his gut into his own throat. There in the lower right hand corner in plain, if somewhat crude script was the easily legible signature: *Henri de Toulouse-Lautrec*. Below the name was the date 1899.

"No, this can't possibly be the real thing, can it? I mean, I'm not that much of an art person, but I certainly visited enough museums from our days in Paris to know who this guy is. Are the dates right for your great-grandmother, or whatever she was, to have known this guy? It certainly appears to be a painting of this same woman in the photo. Jesus, what do you think this all means?"

"I have no idea, but I'm certainly going to find out. Let's look at these letters and see if they can tell us anything." Marie was trying to undo the ribbon on the letters without damaging either when Angélique, who had been looking over her father's shoulder at the painting, suddenly chimed in.

"Look, Mama. The lady in the picture has red hair—just like me."

Jason laughed and replied that, indeed, she did. Marie turned onto her knees from where she had been sitting, grabbed her daughter's cheeks in both hands, kissed her, laughed, and said.

"She certainly does, Sweetie, just like yours. Red hair runs in our family. Unfortunately, I must have got my dark brown from my mother's side. That's what *Mamie Béa* always teased me about."

Angélique resumed whatever she had been doing with the pencils and Jason focused on Marie who was slowly removing from its envelope the first letter of the four in the small bundle they had put aside. She began to read it, which took a couple of minutes since she needed to adjust her thoughts to the handwriting and the French phrases from an earlier century. When she was finished she looked up at Jason and spoke in the English they had all suddenly slipped into in the last minutes.

"Well, this is a letter to Grand-Mère Paulette dated in late 1900 and signed by someone calling himself *'your devoted Henri.'* The Henri signature looks identical to the one on the painting. It mostly talks about how happy he is to hear about the birth of her son and how he is glad she is continuing her artwork and has found a teaching position locally. He goes on about how bad his health has become and that he is working as fast as he can, because he believes his days are getting short. As I recall, Toulouse-Lautrec died around 1901, while he was in his late thirties I think. He led a very difficult life and had a pretty awful lifestyle, even by our modern standards. He was from close to here you know. In fact, the Toulouse-Lautrec Museum is over in Albi, about an hour's drive from here. I went there one summer when I was here. Jason, I think I'd better call over there tomorrow and see about getting all this stuff authenticated and get some idea about what we've stumbled into here. I'll bet those folks will sure be surprised to have this show up from right under their noses after all this time. I have a feeling our lives are about to change in ways we can't even imagine yet, and I don't just mean the money, which could be considerable.

"Imagine, *Mamie Béa* kept all this to herself for all those years. She must have known how important and valuable it all was and how much it could change our family's fortunes here in the valley and elsewhere; but she kept quiet about it. I wonder if she hadn't made some sort of promise to Grand- Mère Paulette about all this when she was younger herself. I think when she says in her note that it's now my legacy—and Angélique's as well—I guess it was her way of saying we should do what we think is best with it now. What do you think, dear?"

"Well, I trust your instincts completely, you know. This is your home, and it is your 'legacy' as you say. I suppose we should find out what we've got here first thing, no doubt. I mean what kind of money do you think we're talking about here anyway?"

"Who knows? Many thousands for sure, possibly millions, if it's all original, which it appears to be. Dollars or euros, who cares!"

She suddenly leaned over and kissed him full on the mouth, pulled back, threw up her hands and let out a happy yelp, which startled Angélique. They looked up at their daughter, who had apparently found one of the empty pages in the old sketchbook and was using the pencils to start a drawing. Marie was about to open and read another of the letters when Jason stood up to stretch his aching legs and knees and noticed the drawing their daughter was working on.

It was a surprisingly good sketch of a dog. He commented favorably on it, and Angélique replied it was a drawing of *Matisse,* and that *Oncle Jean-Pierre* had told her she would see her old friend the next day when they all came to his house. Jason stared at the drawing for another instant, turned to Marie, who was perusing the second letter by then, and commented.

"You know, dear, our Angélique is really quite the budding young talent. We should seriously see about getting her some art lessons when we get home."

Marie looked up from her reading and gazed off for a moment as if recalling something. Then she looked back up at her husband, and responded with a broad grin.

"Of course, dear, our little 'red-haired angel' is talented. *Mamie Béa* would often tell me when I stayed with her as a child: *You know, Marie, there's always been an artist in our family.*"

THE PAINTER

14,000 BC

"We will make our fires in this place. There will be shelter from the winds below that rock wall behind us, and there is clear water flowing over there from beyond those trees down to the stream we crossed before. The hunters can climb that piece of high ground in front of us to keep eyes on the passage we have just come through. Yes, this will be a good place to make our camp, until the herds move far beyond where our eyes and feet can follow them in the cold season."

There were immediate grunts of approval from some of the men standing close by the old man who had just made this pronouncement, one which many of them had been hoping to hear for the last two or three days. The women, who gathered behind the men as soon as the stop had been called, merely looked at each other, however. They mostly nodded in silent relief and began to lay down their burdens or step out of the heavy drags of furs and other belongings they had been pulling across the difficult landscape since more sunrises than any of them cared to recall. The

few young children in the band of about forty persons were immediately removed from whatever drag or pack they had been carried
on to be tended to by the older women. All the other women and
older children quickly set about the task of unloading the packs
and drags, from which everyone who was capable of carrying or
pulling something had already happily detached themselves at
the old man's much anticipated announcement calling the halt to
their long days of walking.

At such a moment when a more permanent camp was about to
be established each person knew what was expected of him or her.
There would be shelters to erect as soon as poles sufficient for the
task could be located. Younger boys and older girls were immediately sent out with instructions to look for appropriate pieces of
wood that could be found within sight of the new camping place.
Firewood was also an immediate concern, and the children knew
that the easiest pieces to gather would go quickly, thus making
their future efforts more time consuming if they did not immediately join those seeking to collect what was closest.

The oldest woman of the band, along with the wife of the chief
hunter, decided where the group's main fire was to be built soon
after the old man indicated this was to be their new home. Each of
these two women carried a hot coal from her last fire wrapped and
protected in a small, bark container, which she alone was responsible for maintaining while the people were on the move. Some of
the first wood brought in would be designated for the lighting of
the group's main fire, once these two women had dug out a place
and surrounded it with stones or earth. Everyone present would
gather for that ceremonial fire lighting and only then would the
individual wives or other fire keepers be able to ignite a piece of
wood from that blaze to carry to where their family fires would be
made. These fires would be located where their individual shelters
would be erected. Those positions would already have been determined for the women by their husband's status or relationship to

other male members in the band. The wives had all come from other bands, many of which were still related in some way to this group. However, their position in the larger band was mainly determined by the family into which they had married or otherwise been brought into the band.

Most of the male members of such small hunting bands were usually related by blood in some way. Often the band would be organized around a group of brothers or closely related cousins under the patriarchy of a single, senior male. In this instance, though, two such smaller bands had earlier come together for a short season of cooperative hunting, before splintering apart once more to face the coming season of cold and long darkness in separate camps. Those camps would be close enough to support one another in a time of crisis, but still far enough apart not to put a dangerous strain on the local resources of wood or small animals each would need to maintain itself through the longer cold season, when the hunters could not stray far from their home fires. The old man who had called a halt to their wandering was the senior member of the larger group of about twenty-five persons; while the leader of the smaller band was the eldest son of a cousin of the old man.

The old man's cousin and some of the older band's extended family had left some seasons past to form a new hunting band. Such splintering generally occurred when the band size exceeded thirty persons or even fewer. This seemed to be about the maximum number needed to keep enough adult hunters productive supporting all their families. It was also a number beyond which it was difficult to reduce the conflicts that inevitably resulted when too many adult males were forced into a cooperative situation— one which required nearly unanimous, consensus decision making if it was to succeed over time.

After the unpacking and the igniting of the band's fire, all the grown men gathered around the gray-bearded one who had chosen this spot as their temporary, new home to begin discussing the many tasks and assignments each of them would soon be looking to. Besides, this was a new camping place, one that no person in the band had ever known or used before. Indeed, this band was venturing farther to the south and the warmer lands that were said to exist there than at any time in their memories. All the men had previously noted the last cold seasons were longer and harsher than those that had come before. Many of the great beasts they followed and depended upon for their existence were already gradually beginning to move their grazing ranges in this direction, where the scant grasses they depended upon could be found in more abundance. By necessity, the two small bands were also forced to follow the herds farther south this season and this meant in the past full moon's walking they had been led into lands that were unfamiliar to them. As a result, the selection of a new campsite for the upcoming season of intense hunting of meat and gathering of furs was a decision of critical importance on the minds of the hunters and their families for many days. They were all openly relieved now that the old man had finally found a place that seemed to fit the many needs a band of such large size would require, even for a relatively short period of time.

Before the hunting, there would be new poles to gather and cut for the building of shelters and the making of the many new spears that would be needed. There were old trails to scout for signs of passing beasts—or other men—who may have recently passed through the same gap that led out of the steep-sided, narrow valley, which they had just passed through themselves; and any number of other necessary functions required to set up a camp that might last for two or three full moons. Two younger men quickly volunteered to climb the steep, round hill looming in front of where they would camp to assess the warning time the hunters would have to prepare for the coming of the herds, which would soon move past the waiting band not far below the terrace where the new camp was to be made.

Two other men said they would proceed along the base of the great stone wall below which they were halted and which marked the entrance to the narrow valley they had just passed through. They would look for signs of the sharp-edged stone that could frequently be found close by such a recognizable source. The hunters would require this critical material to make the many tools they would soon need to take and butcher the animals that would provide all their basic needs for the cold season about to descend upon them once more. It was this hard stone and its ability to be shaped into many useful finished forms which enabled the people to live in the same cold places as the vast herds and to follow the lifestyle of free-roaming hunters they had been pursuing since long before the memories of any of those among them.

It was an age-old triangle of dependency between the land, the beasts, and the stone—with the hunters at the center of the triangle. This critical dependency had made these many small bands of human hunters, who had spread themselves across the vast, often barren, terrain, the most powerful experimental instrument for change yet to appear during the many advances and withdrawals of the great sheets of moving ice and falling cold. These dramatic changes in climate were accompanied by the vast herds of furred animals with which these small bands shared this sometimes bleak, but sometimes equally spectacular, landscape.

One of the two men who had said he would go in search of new sources for the badly needed hard stones was the hunter called Taymak. The old man who led them was his uncle, the older brother of his father, who had passed from the light in a season still fresh in the memory of his son and the others who were close in blood to that skilled hunter. However, that man existed now only in their closely held memories and in the distant sky lights, from where he looked down through the darkness to guide his descendants who still walked in the world of living men.

None of those men objected when Taymak stepped forward to assume this first, necessary task. Besides being tired of walking themselves, most of the men quickly recognized that Taymak was the proper man to assume this important undertaking. Even among men of whom all possessed the requisite skills for working and shaping the hard stones into useful tools—skills they had learned by the time they had taken on the role of hunter within their band—Taymak was an acknowledged expert in the crafting of the best or most difficult to produce tools.

Beyond that, he was also known for the appealing appearance of all the useful things he manufactured and not just those of the sharp-edged stone, but those of bone, horn, and even wood as well. As such, it was not an uncommon thing for another man to ask him to provide some unusual carving in bone or some other material to decorate a special spear thrower or some other instrument a man might want to use to increase the power of his weapon over the beasts he pursued. Taymak had long been noted as a man who could study a beast—alive or dead—and then skillfully reproduce its appearance in some form on a piece of bone or carved on a bit of antler or soft stone. To possess such a likeness was believed to give a man some aspect of that animal's behavior, which a hunter might then add to his weapon or person. This allowed him to join his personal power with that of the beast and thus exercise that power in the taking of the animal, without offending the spirit of his prey, or others of its kind.

Such were some of the basic beliefs of these people, who often lived virtually within the midst of the great, moving herds of large animals they pursued across the usually barren or harsh landscapes. They had come to depend upon the beasts to the point they continually felt the need to assume some aspect of those animals' behavior, or even appearance. They strove to reach a unity of thought and action with their much larger quarry in order to anticipate their movements and know how best to take them with minimal risk to themselves, or to the continued survival of the herds upon which they depended for their own fragile existence. Countless generations of human hunters had learned to view the beasts not as adversaries but as co-inhabitants of an inhospitable land—one in which failure to know every detail about their fellow occupants could quickly lead to extinction for such small, roaming bands as these hunters had been forced by their difficult circumstances to become.

A man with the unique skills of the hunter Taymak would soon be seen as a "special" person among them, a person who had achieved a unique ability within a group where every man was responsible for his own well-being and that of his family. Mutually dependent action and cooperation was certainly of primary importance. However, any time a person revealed an unusual or unique talent within the group, that person was not discouraged from pursuing his "gift". But this was true only if it was seen as benefitting the group at large or as not being used by its possessor to elevate that person above his companions. Such an action might create stress or pressures within the otherwise egalitarian bands—which could then lead to one of those many forms of aberrant behavior that were still in their early stages of being revealed as dangerous to successful human group behavior and cohesion.

Taymak had come to be seen by the other members of his band as a man who could be looked to for guidance concerning the interpretation of what the beasts or the land revealed, without being someone who used that information to hold himself apart in the eyes of others. His family had been at the core of the band since beyond memory. He had brought a wife into it from a band where other men he knew had also obtained wives, and his son and daughter were by this time approaching the age when they were expected to become more essential members as well. He was a man in the prime of his years as a productive hunter and contributor to the important decisions the men faced in every season of their difficult existence.

However, when Taymak volunteered to be one of those who would go to look for sources of the sharp-edged stone close by the new camp, it was as much because of another, personal trait he had come to recognize in himself as much as his desire to be seen as doing something important at a critical time for his band. Taymak was increasingly coming to feel the need to be alone or away from his tightknit group of related families on any occasion he could manage without being seen as deliberately trying to avoid their nearly constant company. It was a need in him he could not adequately define or explain, and was also one that had begun to cause him some concern in the past seasons. This need to be alone to work on some carving in bone; or to etch pictures on a smoothed, dirt surface of the outline of some beast in motion; or even merely to stand and contemplate a piece of unusual landscape without knowing or even sensing why such a thing was important to him had started to take over his thoughts with increasing frequency as he grew older.

But on this occasion, he would have a companion on his short walk to initiate a process most of the hunters would begin in the days to come. It was that of becoming totally familiar with every aspect of their new surroundings in nearly every direction from their camp a man could walk and return from in the same passing of the light across the sky. Another, younger hunter he did not know well had also stepped forward at the old man's suggestion to say he wanted to go out to look for where the hard stones might be found. That young man was called Hiluk and was a hunter from the other, smaller band, which had come together with Taymak's group about a moon earlier to lend their power to the coming season of gathering meat and furs.

Taymak did not know him well but had no reason to object to the presence of another pair of sharp eyes, especially in a land with which neither man was familiar. He simply nodded in acceptance of the young hunter's offer when no other stepped forward at the old man's call or otherwise objected. Taymak merely walked over to him and said he would go to where his family was unpacking to set up their shelter to retrieve his extra spear and would meet the man by the main fire as soon as they could both get back to it. There was not much light left for this day, and both men knew their chances of finding anything of consequence so close by were not very good in any event.

Taymak headed for where his family was busily spreading out their belongings, some of which had remained packed for the many days they had walked south with only one or sometimes two night stops in anticipation of finding a more permanent camp. The first thing his wife spoke to him when he appeared to witness the final unpacking was they would be in desperate need of new furs for clothing, and hides for shelter against the coming cold to replace those which they were forced to leave behind or discard as too burdensome when their trek south first started. It was a common complaint among many of the wives, especially the younger ones, which other hunters would hear that first evening in the new camp. At least, Taymak replied, they were not as bad off as some, since both their son and daughter had been able to carry many of the family's more essential possessions on the long trail. When his wife saw her husband going through his trail pack, which he had dropped with the others when they halted, she immediately noticed he picked up his additional spear and some antler tools to put in the carrying bag that was nearly always draped across his shoulder.

"Will Taymak be going from the new camp so soon? We are in bad need of long poles to build the shelter. A fire alone will not keep the cold of the darkness from our bones this night."

"Yes, the old man has asked me to go with another from the small band to search for the sharp stones we are also in great need of now. I will look for any wood of a good size I can carry back. It will not be a long walking. There is much to do I can see here before the darkness. At least there will be a good moonlight to help, if I am late returning."

"Can I go, father? I can carry the poles, and my eyes are sharp on the trail, as you have told me many times."

The boy, a youth still some seasons from being named as a man, eagerly jumped up to ask his question—the hope for a positive reply from his father easily seen in his eyes. Taymak looked over at him, smiled, shook his head, and replied, which caused the boy to slump in unhappiness at his words.

"No, Duhann. I will not be away long. You must stay here and help your mother and sister. There may be poles close by you can find before other eager eyes spot them. There will also be wood to gather from near those trees over there for our first fire in this place." When Taymak saw the continuing disappointment in the boy's eyes, he paused, smiled, and relented somewhat. "But I will be starting in that direction also. You may walk with us as far as you can without losing sight of this place. Perhaps, we will find something of importance you can carry back with you when you return on your own. Come, we must go back to the main fire to meet the young man Hiluk before we can start."

The boy's demeanor changed completely at his father's last words. He dropped what was in his hand and looked to where he had laid the short spear he was allowed to carry only since the beginning of this journey. That act gave him a new status among the younger boys of the band, and Duhann was not about to be seen leaving the camp without his first "hunter's spear", as the untried boys proudly called these sharpened shafts. Taymak looked at his wife, Mawra, but simply shrugged and smiled in silent recognition of her obvious disapproval at his taking their son away from a more important task, at least as she saw it. But she knew Duhann was at an age where his every action was consumed by the excitement of his approaching manhood. She also understood fully with this change in his status her ability to exert much control over his behavior would soon be coming to an end.

As her husband and son quickly left to head for the main fire, Mawra hoped they might at least find some of the badly needed shelter poles close by, before others got to them first. She worried that once he was out of sight of camp Taymak, who seemed to want to spend more and more time away from her fire, even before this journey started, would not make it back before darkness fell. His strange behavior of late sometimes caused her to think maybe he no longer found her desirable in the same way he always had when they were both younger and before the children came to them. She was increasingly worried she was growing old in his eyes and perhaps this was the reason he seemed to be away from camp even more than the younger hunters often were. But then, when they were together, he still showed her the same warmth and affection which had drawn them close when they first came to the arrangement that had brought her to live with this group of mostly strangers far more seasons ago by now than she cared to remember. That thought gave her some quick comfort in the brief moment of doubt. She turned to where their daughter, her first born child, was sitting and staring at her as if to ask what they should do next, and said with no hint of her passing emotion in her voice.

"Come, Setha. Duhann will be with your father for a short walking. Perhaps, we should go together and look for wood for the fire before anything else is done. We have only the drag poles here, which is not enough to raise even a small shelter. Let us hope your brother can return with some more before the day passes much longer. Put that dried meat bag on your pack over there under the old furs. It is the last full one we have. We will go see what wood is close to the bottom of the rock wall or the edge of those trees below them. I see some of the other women and girls already heading for the small stream down below the slope. There will be easy wood there, and close; but it will not be as dry as what we might find higher up. Take that long cord from your drag and we will make a bundle to pull back with us. Then I will go to the old woman's fire to get a burning piece to start our own with, while you scoop out a hole where we spoke of before just in front of where I want to raise our shelter."

Mother and daughter soon left to head in nearly the same direction as her husband, son, and the other young hunter already moving more quickly ahead. Her tired legs were immediately feeling the effects of even the slight incline they were walking up after so many days on the hard trail pulling a heavy load. Mawra once again thought how the long seasons that had led her to this point in her life were truly weighing heavily upon her body. She looked over at her daughter, already somewhat rested, no doubt, more easily making her way up the long slope. She envied the girl her youth, and the exciting season of her life she was about to enter— that of her approaching womanhood. She knew it would not be long before some young hunter would come to her father to bargain for Setha in the same way Taymak once had for her. Mawra could only hope it would be someone as mutually acceptable for her daughter as her husband had been for her that day in her own past, which at least in that brief moment of happier reflection suddenly seemed not nearly so long ago as it had come to feel in her aching bones and more recent memories.

Taymak had already sent his son Duhann back to the site of the new camp with the two long poles they had picked up at the edge of the trees he was about to enter with the other young hunter who was accompanying him. That youth had also been most eager to leave when the three of them set out a short time earlier from where they met near the main fire, which by that time was starting to burn brightly enough to guide them back to the camp, if for some reason they could not return before the full darkness overtook them. That was certainly not Taymak's plan, in any event, as he told the younger man as soon as his son was sent back. He advised the youth there was no reason for them to extend their search very far on this first effort to scout the unfamiliar, surrounding lands. Besides, as he told him, if they kept the looming cliff wall close to them, there would be no need to worry if the trees growing in the direction they were headed became too dense and blocked out the fading light, which would force them to give up their search for the sharp-edged stone.

Besides, both men came from farther north and were not used to the more frequently seen, taller stands of expanding forest they were starting to encounter in the last days. Once they penetrated the first of the densely packed trees, which grew along the small stream of clear water descending from the higher slope they decided to follow, Taymak suggested they separate to proceed upstream on opposite sides of the fast moving water. That small rivulet of meltwater from some distant highlands was not much wider than a man was tall and could easily be crossed without getting one's feet wet.

Hiluk agreed to follow the down slope side, while Taymak wanted to search nearer to the base of the great rock face much farther up the slope. That decision would mean some more climbing for his tired legs; but he knew from experience this was the type of place where he might find a larger source for the dark grey or brown stone both men were seeking. Hiluk would have a better chance of spotting any washed away land from earlier times when the tiny stream might have carried more water and left behind pieces of the important stones, which might lead them later to sources higher up the slope or farther upstream into the base of the low hills just at the edge of their sight. Both men agreed to meet back at the point where they were separating before the last light disappeared to report what they had seen or found and then return to the camp together.

The climb up the slope to the base of the rock face proved steeper than Taymak had anticipated, and he was quite winded by the time he had gone as far as he deemed necessary to begin his search. He stopped for a few moments to recover his wind and to take in the magnificent vista that opened up before him when he turned around to look back down in the direction he had just come. Off in the distance he could just barely make out the camp, which was starting to take shape as more than one hide-covered shelter was already going up and the smoke of a couple of fires, probably made with wet wood he unhappily surmised, could easily be seen curling into the slightly overcast, late day sky.

He muttered under his breath how he hoped one of those fires was not made by his family. He was certain Mawra, and even Duhann, would have the good sense not to build a fire that would send smoke into the sky in an open place in strange lands, where no one could know if other, possibly unfriendly eyes might see it. He was somewhat surprised the old man would allow such a thing here. But then he knew all the people were tired from the long days of walking, and their aging leader must have many other important things on his mind as well just then.

After a few moments of familiarizing his eyes with the other sights and landmarks just then presenting themselves for the first time, Taymak thought this was, indeed, a most promising and even beautiful place for the people to camp, even if only for the next moon or two. Surely, the narrow gap they had just struggled through to reach this place would also be the main passage through which the important herds of beasts would soon seek their way to find the better cold season feeding grounds to the south. Their new camp would be ideally situated to take full advantage of those fast-moving herds when the watchful hunters reported they were finally on the move in this direction.

With his breathing back to normal once more, Taymak turned, picked up the single, thin spear shaft he laid down beside him earlier to wipe the sweat from his brow, and then began to walk in the direction he intended to follow close to the base of the towering rock wall. This point so high up the slope and close to the rock base was very steep. However, he knew because of his climb he would soon be gradually descending to where Hiluk would be making a slower climb as he followed the path of the small stream, which would also provide the people with the water they would need in the days ahead.

The light was beginning to fade and Taymak was about to conclude he must soon make it to the point he had earlier agreed to meet the young hunter for their return. He had already decided he might as well take the shortest way and finish the descent down to where he would undoubtedly run into the small stream and then follow it back to camp. He might even meet his companion somewhere on that same path back, since Hiluk should also have decided to reverse his course by this time as well. Taymak was still close to the base of the rock wall, which had diminished in height and would virtually disappear not far beyond this point. He was just rounding a detached piece of rock that jutted out and forced him to narrow his path to bring him closer to the edge to keep from taking a longer way down the slope. That would force him to climb back up to keep heading toward the end of the visible rock just up ahead. He decided earlier this point was to be the end of his search, and he would then go straight down the slope to find the little stream. To this point he had found nothing indicating a source of the sharp-edged stone was to be found along the gradually receding cliff base he was following.

Just as he rounded the stone jutting out into his path, he felt a sudden blast of cold air hit him in the face from somewhere farther up in the little cul-de-sac formed by this last, large stone and the point where the remains of the sloping cliff face disappeared totally into the earth. That was where the land began to flatten out just ahead and right at the spot he intended to end his search for the day. Taymak decided to turn aside for a moment to investigate this little indentation in the receding rock face to see from where this breath of air greeting his sudden appearance here was coming. The place narrowed quickly and came to an abrupt end only a few steps away. He could still feel the cold air upon his face but could not see why it should be hitting him here. There was not enough height left in the cliff above him to cause such a rush of wind over its edge and down the short gully formed between the exposed rocks where he now stood. He was about to turn to leave when he felt another, stronger rush of air upon him. When he stared more intently back in that direction he saw a narrow opening about waist high in the rocks. Taymak laid down his spear and walked the two or three steps over to kneel and inspect this hidden gash in the rock face.

At first glance he saw an opening just large enough for a man to pass through on his hands and knees, but only if he turned onto his side to squeeze through. It was quickly obvious this was the point from which the cold air was originating from somewhere in the darkness beyond. Taymak was tempted to stick his head through to try to judge how far this narrow passage went. However, he knew it was probably already past the time he should begin his journey back to the camp. He did not want to cause Hiluk, a man he did not know well enough to trust to wait long for him, to have to worry about where he might be. Still, he knew there was something here he must soon come back to investigate. These dark places in the earth were important images in the collective memories of his people, and for a man like Taymak in particular, this one might hold some significance, one which his mind was already beginning to grasp in those first, brief moments after stumbling upon it.

As a boy, not much older than his son Duhann, he had once accompanied his father and grandfather—a man who still walked in the light in those seasons—into one such dark place in the earth to witness the important ceremonies performed by torch and oil lamp light in the larger space at the end of one of these narrow passages. On the walls of the larger cave chamber formed there someone from the days when his grandfather had been a young man must have once painted the outlines of many of the beasts the people hunted. These were done in such a way they had almost seemed to the youth to come alive in the dancing light of the lamps and torches the men held up to reveal their black and red images. The older men chanted an ancient song that day to summon the spirits of these beasts and to ask them to come to the people that they might sustain themselves in the dark season to come.

The youthful Taymak was so struck by these images he had ever afterward given much thought to the skilled hands of those who must have produced them. As he matured in the following seasons, he gradually grew to feel he must also become a person who possessed such a skill. He often practiced drawing when he was alone, and then visualized and studied the beasts themselves, until he mastered this ability to create their forms on whatever surface he might choose. In that moment, as he knelt before the dark gash in the earth, Taymak's heart fairly raced with the prospect that here at last he might have found a place for which he had been unconsciously searching without even being fully aware of it. Here could be his own special place, one where he might allow the full expression of that skill finally to be put into the form he always hoped it might be. He had secretly held this thought since that distant day in the dark cave where he once stood with his father and grandfather and marveled at the sights appearing in front of his wide eyes, and his even wider imagination. Both those important men were now gone from his life. But the vision they both shared with him on that special day had always helped to keep their memories alive in the man who carried their blood and their heritage with him across the many seasons which had passed since that unforgettable experience.

Taymak was about to stand up to retrieve his spear and begin a quick descent to connect with the small stream that would lead him back to the new camp when a sudden thought occurred to him. Looking about quickly, he saw a small stone and picked it up. Then, he extended his arm all the way into the black gash in the rock face and flicked his wrist to cast the stone into the void to hear what might happen. Just as he hoped, the stone could easily be heard to bounce forward along an unseen, descending path until its sound soon vanished. Taymak grunted in satisfaction and then stood up to begin his search for Hiluk. In what seemed like a very short time, he discovered the downward angle of the rock wall he was following would lead him much closer to where the tiny stream passed through the small gap formed at the point the great cliff face disappeared into the land and where another, elevated, but dirt-covered portion of it emerged farther beyond. Soon he was walking as rapidly as he could along the noisy stream, headed back to where he hoped to encounter his youthful companion.

When he finally came to the place where the two men had separated earlier, he saw Hiluk seated on the remains of a fallen tree trunk, staring off in the direction from which Taymak was just then emerging. As soon as the young man saw him, he stood up to greet the older hunter for whom he had obviously been waiting for some time. Taymak smiled as he approached the silent youth and spoke by way of an apology for his obvious tardiness in returning to their rendezvous point.

"Has Hiluk been waiting long? The path up along the base of the rock wall was steeper and not as straight as I thought. I found nothing of any good stone there. What of your search?"

The young man reached into his fur covered pouch, which was slung across his shoulder, and pulled out three pieces of stone. He extended them to the older man and said.

"I found these close together some distance back up the stream, just beyond the place where it passes through the cut where the wall you must have followed ended and that hill over there beyond. I think these may have washed down from somewhere farther in that direction; but the light was growing too weak to follow longer. I decided to return here to wait for you. It would be good to look up there again when the new light is upon us and others can add their eyes to a search in that direction."

"Yes, these are good stones, broken from larger pieces in some distant season it is plain to see. It will not be hard to get others to search with us for more when they see these. But it grows dark quickly in this moon. Come, we must get through these trees and back into the open where the new camp is made before we lose the light. I must still try to find poles for my wife's shelter before we get back, or I will get no warm meat from her fire and only a cold back-side this night. I do not know about you, Hiluk, but this little walk after such a long day has made my insides growl like a hungry wolf at the thought of even some long dried meat upon which to chew."

Taymak laughed at his own remark, while his younger com-panion only smiled sheepishly out of respect for the older hunter without revealing what his own thoughts might have been at that moment concerning any new delay in getting back to camp. Hiluk had no wife waiting for him, only an aging mother and a father long past his best days as a hunter. During their mostly silent walk, Taymak stopped twice to cut and quickly trim two, thin saplings with the palm-sized, sharp-edged stone he carried in his shoulder bag. He deemed these two along with the ones Duhann had car-ried back earlier would be enough when added to the drag poles of the women to erect a shelter large enough to contain the family, at least until his wife might desire something more permanent.

The fires of the camp were clearly visible by the time the two men emerged from the low trees just where the small rivulet began a sharper turn away from them. From there it took a more direct route down to the larger stream farther below the little plateau between it and the rock wall where the old man had chosen to make the new camp. Both men quickly agreed to meet again at the main fire as soon as they went to their individual family places to take care of any needs that might have arisen in their absence. They knew they would be expected to give their report on what they had seen or found to the older hunters, who would most likely be assembled there to see what all the men who were sent out earlier would have to say.

Taymak found his family waiting for him close by the small fire just in front of where Mawra had done her best to erect the frame for their small, hide-covered shelter in his absence. As soon as she saw him approaching with the two much needed wooden shafts she said something to Setha and the girl stood up to relieve her father of his burden before he even took the opportunity to lay them down. Mawra said nothing but only smiled when she saw they were exactly what she would need to quickly finish the frame and begin the covering from the various hide pieces she and her daughter had already tied together and laid close by. She then extended to her husband a generous strip of dried meat, which she was keeping warm on the end of a sharpened stick at the edge of her fire. He smiled at her as he reached for it and casually commented it was good to see a warm fire—and one with no smoke rising from it—after such a long day. He began to chew as he laid down his spear, removed the spear throwing stick from the cord that held in the heavy, fur garment tied around his waist, slipped his shoulder bag off, and let it slowly drop to the ground. Then he looked at her and said.

"I must go to the old woman's fire, where the hunters will be waiting to hear what I have seen since I left the camp. It will not be a long talking this night. All are tired and eager for a full rest in the new camp. It will be good to sleep with no wind at our back-sides and no need to get up with the new light to be on the trail for another long day of walking. I will not be gone long. The old man spoke truly when he brought us here. The water over there that runs down to the stream below is the freshest I have tasted in many days, and is much closer. It will be good to rest here until the beasts come."

With that he looked at each member of his family in turn, smiled at them, and turned to leave. He had not gone far before all thee got up to begin the task of finishing the shelter while there was still enough light from the fire and the moonrise to put the last poles in place, before the three of them together could drape the assembled hide pieces over the sloping sides. This would provide the first true shelter from the cold and darkness any of them had enjoyed for many days. Mawra thought she would like to build a larger one as soon as she could when new hides were brought in by her husband, even if it might mean leaving some of these behind later when they took to the trail once more at the end of this hunt-ing season. She would begin to search for the proper poles she would need herself as soon as she could find the opportunity to go look for them in the days ahead. Till then, however, she knew there would be much to do to get ready for the making and drying of the meat and the countless other tasks that would fall upon her in the days immediately ahead for her small family.

As he walked the short distance to the main fire, Taymak decid-ed he would say nothing to the others of the opening in the rock he had discovered until there was an opportunity to return and investigate just what it meant by himself, or possibly with Duhann to assist him. Even then, if it chanced to be the type of place he hoped it could be, he would inform only the old man of what was there. His mind was still unclear about what he could, or should, do if his hopes were justified in the prospects of this being the place for which he had long searched. Was it one within which he could finally give the full expression of his growing desire—perhaps even his obsession—to paint the large animal images on such a surface; one that might bring about the same wondrous effect in others that were once produced on his own youthful mind?

These unclear thoughts were struggling to gain a place in his head when Taymak got close to the main fire where, as he anticipated, most of the adult men of the two bands were gathered and talking. However, as he came near and glanced about to see Hiluk was already in attendance, he quickly saw that some animated discussion was going on. There appeared to be some excitement clearly centered where the two men who had earlier gone up the steep hill were standing and what they were saying. That hill was not far off toward the center of where the widening valley opened, and they had wanted to see how it might serve them as a lookout point for the coming of the herds in the days ahead. Taymak quickened his pace to come close to the discussion. As soon as he did, it immediately became clear that some disturbing news must have been brought in by these two men. He cleared his head of all the wandering thoughts chasing each other through his mind and focused on what was happening. It was soon apparent all his plans might soon have to be given up in a way he could not have expected.

⇌ ⇋

Taymak lay awake far into the darkness that first night in the new camp while he pondered the troubling information the men had discussed around the main fire long after he told his family he would return. The two young hunters who climbed the steep hill that dominated the view of the entrance to the valley close by their new camp came back with news they had found evidence of a freshly made fire on top of the hill. They could not say when it was last used except they were certain it must have been since the last water had fallen from the sky. They had found the small fire with evidence of only two or three men, possibly watchers such as themselves, who may have stayed there for one or more nights. No one could know where they had gone or who they were. However, all the men knew that no members of either band had been this far south before, and the knowledge there might be larger groups of men close by, who may also wish to hunt this same desirable location in the days ahead, caused immediate concern and discussions by them.

Finally, the old man talked with two other senior members of both bands and informed the hunters that they would not abandon their new camp, but would increase their watchfulness and take every precaution in the days ahead. They would continue as planned until or unless these strangers made some effort to contact them. The women would stay in groups close by, and the smaller children would be kept in the camp at all times. When Taymak returned to his finished shelter he quietly informed Mawra of why he was so late in returning. She seemed concerned, but agreed to keep Setha close and to go with other women and the two older hunters who would remain in the camp when they moved beyond the far edges of the shelters. Still, none were to go into the trees or down to the river alone, and this included even the adult hunters as well.

The following morning the men went out as they had planned, except that several older hunters, who were still tired or suffered from old injuries which might hamper their movements, agreed to stay behind to help watch the camp. Much to the surprise of both his wife and son, Taymak excited the boy by telling him he would be accompanying his father that day. They were to go with four other men who were going to continue the search up the small stream for more signs of both the sharp-edged stone and other, smaller game that might be in the area. When they came to the place where Taymak knew he was closest to where the hole in the stone wall was, he told the others he and his son would go farther up to look above the trail and back on top of the stone cliffs to see what else might be discovered in that high place. Hiluk and the two younger hunters were surprised at his apparently sudden announcement. However, the elder hunter who was leading the party thought it was perhaps a good thing to do. Besides, no man could force another to do something in such an instance in any event—if that man seemed to express a good reason to the others for his decision.

Taymak said nothing as he led his son to the place that had continued to dominate his thoughts much of the long night before. On the way up the slope they stopped to pull fresh, sap-rich branches from two trees of a kind Taymak knew could be wrapped with the dried white bark that grew on other trees nearby. These would make torches which would burn for what he hoped would be a sufficient time to investigate what lay behind the dark gash at the base of the rock wall. Duhann was very curious about his father's unexpected actions; but he asked no questions and did as he was instructed to help in the preparation of the two torches. As soon as he was satisfied with what they had made, Taymak led his son out of the trees and up the slope to the place he had found the day before.

His heart was fairly racing when they found the spot. Duhann was very surprised when his father told him it was his intention to squeeze through the narrow opening from where the cold air still beckoned. They cleared away some loose stones and dirt, which seemed to widen the opening just enough for Taymak to more easily force himself through, if he took off his outer fur covering. Finally, he reached into his carrying bag, which he had already removed, and found the hard, heavy stone from which he sometimes ground bits to make the red powder the people used to mix with water to paint their arms and faces on special occasions, or to color their weapons before a hunt. He also took out the small piece of sharp-edged stone he could strike the edge of the harder stone with to produce sparks. Next, he removed a tiny amount of dried tree fungus he kept wrapped and dry in a small scrap of hide.

With this held firmly by his thumb close to the struck stone he could catch the spark he would need to ignite his torch. Duhann had already been set about the task of collecting some dried grass from nearby to wrap the outer portion of the torches. When that was done, Taymak struck several sparks from the hard stone until he captured one with the fungus. He quickly transferred the glowing spark to a wrapped torch and gently blew on it till the dried grass was in flames. As it burned down to ignite the slower burning and tar rich dried birch bark, he crawled close to the dark hole, turned to his wide-eyed son, and said.

"Duhann will stay here and listen for my voice. There is something I must look for in this dark place. If both torches burn out and I do not return, you must stay close here to listen for my words to guide me back with your own. If none are heard, and you have waited long past when the torches would burn, you are to return to the trail, find a place by its side, and wait for the other men to come past. Then Duhann, you must tell them all you have seen and done and bring them to this place as quickly as you can. Does my son understand all these words?"

The boy merely swallowed hard and nodded. There were many questions in his confused mind, but he sensed he would get no answers just then. His father merely smiled back at his silent nod and turned to begin to squeeze through the narrow opening—a burning torch in one hand and an unused one in the other. Moments later, all the youth could see as he stared into the blackness was the flickering light of the torch as it bounced off the rocks, until it gradually became only a faint glimmer, before disappearing entirely somewhere up ahead. Except for one loud groan from his father when he must have scraped his arm or leg against some rock in the near darkness, the boy heard nothing further.

Duhann waited in growing anxiety for what seemed to his youthful mind, which was not accustomed to showing patience even in the best of circumstances, like an interminable amount of time. Finally, he heard what he thought must be his father's voice somewhere off in the darkness. He could not make out the words, even when he stuck his upper body into the blackness as far as he dared. It almost seemed to him as if the voice was singing, which frightened him and caused him to pull back. Much to his relief, he soon after saw what he first thought was a glimmer of light, but which shortly became brighter as it came nearer to the narrow slit in the rock wall. A short time passed before he saw the crawling figure of his father approaching about a body's length beyond the opening. Moments later Taymak's head emerged as he squeezed back into the light. He was shivering in the sudden cold air he had begun to encounter on his way back, and the youth saw blood from a long scrape on his arm. However, there was a wide smile on his father's face as he crawled out, sat down next to his son, and dropped the faintly glowing remains of the second torch. He quickly reached for his heavy outer shirt, pulled it over his head, and then sighed deeply. At last, he turned to his son and spoke.

"I am happy you were still here, my son. It must have been a long wait. The torches burned much better than I hoped for. The air does not blow as hard inside as it does near this opening, and they did not go out as I had feared they might. Still, it is good to see the clear sky and feel the warm light again. It is a dark place, indeed, once the light from this opening is gone. But come, Duhann, we must leave this place now and climb around that corner there to search on top of the rock wall as I told the others we would do. We will go to where we can see back up the valley we came through in the last light. Perhaps, there will be a beast herd coming we can spy and tell the others of when we see them."

Taymak knew his son must have many questions about the strange actions of his father so far that morning. He finally told him while they were walking that he had only wanted to see what the dark place contained, because he had been in other such places when he was a youth no older than Duhann. Then he told his son he was to say nothing to anyone, even his mother or sister, about what they had just done, unless his father told him it was something he could speak of. To the boy's question about what he saw inside, Taymak only grunted an audible chuckle, rubbed his son's bare head, and answered with a broad smile that he had seen a special place and he would soon take him inside with him for Duhann to see it for himself. This reply seemed both to satisfy and arouse the boy's curiosity even more. However, to his question when this might be, his father merely replied with a small laugh he hoped it would be soon.

Then, he led the boy back around and up onto the flat plateau which formed the top of the great rock abutment that jutted out into the valley opening to squeeze it into the narrower passage through which the band had passed earlier—and through which they hoped the larger herds of migrating beasts would soon be forced to pass near to where their hunting camp was made. Once on top they explored along the edges and center until they came to the far end, where a spectacular view opened up in each of the three directions they could see. Unfortunately, and despite the clearer than usual midday light, neither could see any discernible specks or signs of movement off in the direction from whence the beast herds were expected to be approaching.

They were just about ready to return to where they might either meet the others on their return trip or, failing that, continue back along the now familiar little stream path to the camp, when something caught Taymak's eye. He quickly walked over and found the remains of two, stone-encircled fires not far from the edge where they had just been standing. He glanced about quickly and chided himself briefly for having been so careless after the warnings of the evening before. However, one look at the remains told him it must have been some time, perhaps even a full turning of the seasons, since these fires were made. Still, it gave him pause to think they had apparently come to a place that other men might already see as their own to protect from strangers in any way they saw fit.

He and Duhann looked about and picked up the chipped flakes from tools that had once been made by men sitting close to the fire. The boy found a nearly complete scraping tool a short distance away and his father rewarded him with a strong compliment about the sharpness of his eyes. Taymak placed the tool and a couple of potentially useful flakes in his carrying bag. Then father and son set off to wait for the others down by the little stream edge. They were not there long when the sound of the approaching men caught their attention. Taymak greeted the senior hunter, a man he had grown up with in the band and a friend from his youth. In reply to his question the man said they had walked far, seen good signs of many smaller beasts, and finally found a place where good-sized blocks of the sharp stone could be found or broken away near the base of a large, rock wall jutting out from the earth, where it covered the great stone of which it must be a part still buried beneath the dirt. Taymak informed them of the old fire places they found on top and showed the men the tool picked up by Duhann, who smiled broadly when his father stressed that it was his son who had found the tool.

However, neither party of hunters was able to report any sure sign the large beast herds were yet beginning to pass in this direction. This caused some small discussion of what it might mean, although no one gave voice to the others of his deeper concerns. Then, they all headed back to the new camp together. One of the men remarked his family's dried meat supplies were nearly gone and he planned to start hunting for fresh meat of any size when the next light came, perhaps back in this same direction. The other two young hunters agreed to go with him. Taymak knew he would also have to hunt in the coming days to replenish his family's dwindling stock as well. But he would not offer his services as a hunter to this or some other small party just yet. There was something he would have to do first, if the situation permitted.

That evening at the main fire all the men gathered again to hear what the various small groups who went out that day had found. Everyone was excited at the sight of the excellent quality of the stone the men found in the high grounds up the small stream less than a half day's walk from the camp. Except for the old fires Taymak saw, no one reported seeing any other clear signs of strangers. Nor did any of the scouting parties find any sign of the coming beasts, or that other herds had recently passed this way. The scraping tool Duhann found was passed around and examined by all the men. It was clearly a well-made tool they agreed and not much different from those most of the men frequently made for themselves. Two or three small hunting parties were organized to go out the following morning, but all were cautioned to be watchful and not to go beyond where they could return before the light faded into darkness.

After the others returned to their individual family fires, Taymak stayed behind to have a few words with the old man. He could see that his uncle was tired and he said only there was an important matter he wished to speak with him about when the light was new. They agreed to meet then by the fire, and Taymak returned to his shelter to make ready for what he hoped was a more restful night than the previous one. Mawra had some questions about how the day had gone and commented that Duhann had, rather strangely she thought, said little in response to her inquiries about it. Taymak only shrugged and smiled. She then mentioned their last bag of dried meat was half gone and casually asked when he planned to hunt for fresh meat. He replied there was something else he must attend to in the new light. However, on the following day he planned to go out with the other men to find some meat for their family's fire. Like the others, he told her, he was also growing tired of the dried meat and longed to savor the juicy taste of something fresh.

The next morning Taymak lingered by his wife's fire until all the hunters and others going out from the camp were gone. He promised Mawra he would take all of them up to where the small stream was so she and Setha could find new poles and other things they might need. He and Duhann would go along to watch and collect as much firewood as they could bundle and drag back to camp with the two women. They would spend as much time as the women needed. Then, he said he wanted to go down to the larger stream, where he had not yet walked, to look for some special stones that might be found there, if there was still light remaining. However, first he would go to the main fire to speak with his uncle about another important matter, he told her. Afterward, the family would take off together to see what they could find in the trees above the camp. He knew the eyes of the women would see things he had not noticed, or looked for—useful things they would want to bring back with them. It would still be a full day for all and their first one working together as a family unit in the new camp.

By the time Taymak walked to the main fire, he saw the old man sitting alone close by the freshly ignited blaze, which was always allowed to burn low during the darkness. He was warming his feet and obviously waiting for him. Most of the other adult men had left the camp to hunt or to do some other important task with their families, just as Taymak planned for later. He walked over and casually sat down by the elder, who merely nodded and said nothing, as he obviously waited to see what was on Taymak's mind that was important enough to keep him so close to the camp when all the other men had necessary things to do elsewhere. The younger man stared off into the distance for a few moments, sighed, and then spoke.

"Uncle, there is something I think might be important that should be told for your ears alone before it is spoken of to others.

It is about a place I found on our first day here, up over there near the base of the rock wall just where it slopes down and disappears into the earth. Do you recall in the long past seasons, when I was a boy and you and my father were young hunters not much older than I am now, when my grandfather and other men took us to a dark place in the earth? They led us through a passage of many rocks emerging from the ground and into a large space, wider and taller than any covered shelter. There, the light of our oil lamps and torches revealed the images of many great beasts that had once been painted on the walls of that place by some man, or men, long since forgotten. We sang ancient songs to the spirits of the beasts to call them to us, and it seemed to one who was not yet even called out as a man the very spirits of those beasts entered into my own there. From that day I have longed to return to such a place myself and paint the figures of the beasts in the same manner I saw then, that others might know these same strong feelings.

"Uncle, I have spent many seasons learning the skills to do this, and I believe those same ancient beasts spirits have drawn me to this place and shown to me at last how this is to be done. Up there beyond a narrow place in the rocks, I have crawled with torches to light my path and found just such a place as I have long dreamed upon."

With that Taymak fell silent, the rising emotion in his voice having forced him to pause and take a deep, cleansing breath of the cool morning air. The old man turned to look at him directly for the first time, thought for a moment, and then replied.

"For some seasons now, I have noticed a trouble growing in the spirit of Taymak. But I have said nothing; for it was not my place to do so, nor could I think clearly upon it without hearing his words to guide those thoughts. Many have spoken of my nephew's great skill and knowledge of how the many beasts are seen, and of his ability to carve their images on bone, or paint them on a man's body. Now, an old man can see clearly this skill has been sent to

Taymak in the way he has just spoken of—by the spirits of those ancient beast ancestors. This has always been a thing of great importance to our people, Taymak, and one that has been lost for many seasons, or so I had thought. It is true, and I do remember well the cave of which you speak from the days of your youth. But there were also others I visited as a young man myself, long before Taymak was brought into the light. We must go to this place you have found together that I might see it with my own eyes, and Taymak can show me what it is he would do with this great gift he has been given. We must prepare lamps and other... "

Before the old man could continue, shouts and a loud commotion could be heard coming from the open slope below the camp, which led off to the larger stream below. Both men stood up at the same instant to get a clearer view of what was happening. Immediately, they saw three women and a young girl running up the slope and shouting. When the women saw they had attracted the attention of those remaining in the camp, some of whom were starting to head toward them, they stopped yelling but continued to run until they reached the circle of shelters. They did not stop until they got to the main fire where the old man and Taymak were standing with three or four others by that time. The running women halted at last and the older one quickly looked at the old man and then said without even trying to catch her breath.

"Strangers! There are two strange men coming from down near the stream. We were gathering wood together and saw them coming. We dropped everything to run back. Look! Look, they are even now approaching up the slope down there."

She had stopped spilling out her warning and pointed back down the slope to refocus everyone's attention, which was on her, to two men slowly walking toward the camp. Both carried short throwing spears, but there were no spear throwers in their hands. Their clothing was not unusual, but they wore strange-looking, fur head coverings. One of the women wailed all the young men were gone from the camp, and these two must have been watching for just such an opportunity. However, before Taymak or anyone else could return to his shelter to retrieve his own spears and thrower, both the strangers came to a halt and squatted down just beyond the ring of shelters—and just outside the range of any well-aimed spear that might be hurled at them from within.

The women were in a panic and searching for their children to bring them close. The three older men still in the camp came to stand with Taymak and his uncle. Duhann then came running up just ahead of his mother and sister. Taymak smiled and beckoned him to stand beside him when he saw that his son carried his father's spear thrower and best throwing spear, along with his own short spear. After most of the people were gathered close and the buzz of questions and shouts for children to come close died down, the people turned to where the old men stood with the clear question of what they should do next on every face. When silence finally fell upon the gathering, the old man looked about for a moment as he gazed past where the strangers sat and off toward the trees scattered along the wider stream below the camp. When he saw no evidence of any more movement there, he turned to Taymak, who still stood next to him, and said in a calm voice loud enough for all to hear.

"Come, Taymak. Let us go to greet these men and see why it is they have come here."

Taymak stared intently at the faces of the two men squatting near the ground just in front of him. He and his uncle had walked toward where the strangers halted their approach to the camp, almost as if to be challenged—or greeted—in just the manner that was now happening. Taymak was told by the old man not to bring his spear, as a sign that these strangers were neither feared, nor had they created anger in the camp at their sudden appearance. As he gazed at the two faces peering silently back up at him, Taymak was surprised at how young both men were. Somehow, he was expecting them to be nearer to his age or perhaps even older. However, both these two appeared to be no older than the youthful Hiluk or several others of the youngest hunters in the camp. He could also not help but notice both young men seemed very uneasy, and their clothing was not in the best condition—nor were the two young strangers themselves in the best condition either.

The old man hesitated for a moment and then spoke slowly and plainly to ask them who they were and from where they came. The two seemed surprised by his words and quickly looked at each other, before the one leaned over and whispered into the other's ear. Then he looked back up at the two older men confronting them and spoke. Taymak tried hard to understand the man's words. However, most of them, even the ones that had familiar sounds, contained little meaning for him when he tried to understand them all together. When the man was finished, his uncle turned to him and spoke softly for Taymak's ears only.

"I can understand some of the words of this man's talk, but not many. They carry the sound of some words I have not heard spoken since I was a boy. I believe these men live in these southern lands and have for many seasons; but I can understand nothing of who their people might be from what they are saying. It would be good if Taymak could return to the camp and seek out the old woman who lives with the family of Kralaat. She was the wife of that man's father, and was brought into our band many seasons past from those who lived far to the south of our own people. She may be able to understand or speak the words of these men. I will stay here and try to find out more about them and why they have come here. Go quickly and find this woman."

Taymak turned away slowly and did as he was instructed. When he found the old woman, she was reluctant and even frightened at his request to go back down the slope with him to try to help speak with the strangers. However, she finally agreed and they soon returned to where the old man was now squatting himself opposite the two young men and continuing to speak to them and making signs with his hands to try to explain his words better and to draw some response from them in return. When he saw the woman, whom he had known since the forgotten days when she was first brought to live with this band, he explained to her the little he had already learned and asked her to try her best to speak with them and what questions she should try to ask, if she could. The two young men seemed to relax a little with the unexpected presence of the old woman. Still, it was obvious she was having some difficulty resulting from not having used her old speech for so many seasons when she began to address them. Their excitement grew quickly as she started to talk, however, and in a matter of a few moments a somewhat broken conversation was going on between the three of them.

Taymak squatted down beside his uncle to listen to what was transpiring and to pick up the occasional word or expression he thought he understood. It was obvious to him as he listened these two youths came from a people who must once have been close in some way to his own. However, how many turnings of the seasons may have passed since that separation had taken place the thoughtful hunter could not even begin to guess. He glanced at his uncle who was also listening intently and wondered what distant memories might be passing through the old man's thoughts as well. Finally, there was a pause in the difficult conversation and the old woman turned toward both men. She began to relate the story she had just heard. It was one that surprised both her attentive listeners.

"I do not understand all that was told to me; but the words are like those I remember from before I was taken as a girl and then traded as a wife into this band in a season long past. These two men come from a small band—at least I believe it must be so—that has camped not far from here for many seasons, over that way and beyond the river toward where the sky light goes to sleep with each darkness. Two moons past there was a bad shaking of the earth in the night. I believe this must be the same one that struck our own camp about then, just before we began this long walking to come to this place. Their band of four families was camped close under a rock wall when the shaking came. Many large stones rolled down from above and struck the place where most of the people were sleeping before any could run to the open space beyond. Most were lost in that moment, and two others gave up their spirits from bad hurts not long after. Only these men and four others remain of their band. But only these two are hunters. They lost all they possessed when the shaking ground came and none of them have had much meat to eat for many days. The others are two women, a boy, and an old man.

"They are in a hidden camp not far on the other side of the river down there. Their people always came here to hunt the large beasts in this season; but when they saw our fires they became fearful they would all starve and go to join their relatives in the forever darkness. When this light came, these two decided to come here and learn if we would stay long in this place, and if we might help them until they could try to move on to where they might find some other band of their people, who they believe are some days walk to the south. This is all I can understand of what they have spoken. Are there more words I should give them you would have me speak for you?"

With that she fell silent, as she waited for the old man to tell her what she should do next. He thought carefully for a few moments; smiled and nodded toward the two wide-eyed young men staring expectantly up at him; and then turned to Taymak squatting beside him and spoke quietly.

"I believe there is nothing to fear from these young men, or those they speak of who are hiding in some fireless camp beyond the stream over there. I believe as well their story must be truly spoken. We also felt the shaking of the earth in the moon they told of. It would truly have been a bad thing to have made our own fires under some rock wall, as these people did, at such a time. Look at these two. They have had little to eat for many days, it is easy to see. With only these young men to hunt for them, the four helpless ones they speak of must be suffering even more from cold and hunger. I think we must help these people. In return, they can show us much we do not know about these new lands, if they decide to stay with us until the beasts pass and we have made meat for the cold moons. It would be good to have two more young hunters, even if they bring more hungry mouths with them to our camp. What does Taymak say to these thoughts?"

Taymak quickly agreed with everything his uncle was saying. The old man turned to the woman and told her to tell these two they were welcome to come into the camp. They would be given some dried meat to eat and to take back to the others they had spoken of. But they were also to be told there was not much meat in the camp and the people had come to this place to hunt the beasts that must soon pass this way. These men were to be told they and the survivors of their band could stay with the people and add their spears to the coming hunt to share equally in what was taken. But if they chose to make their own camp or move on, there was little help the people could offer them now, until good hunting days came. Until then they could make fires here, and others would give old hides or help in the building of shelters, if they wished to stay. Those were the words the old man wished them to hear.

As soon as the woman gave these words to the two squatting men, they nodded to each other and stood up. Then they said something to the old woman to the effect that they would come into the camp, if they were to be made welcome. The old man smiled and motioned them to follow the three of them back up the slope, where all the people still in the camp were assembled to watch and speculate about what was being decided out of their hearing below. When the small group got to the main fire, the old man quickly explained to the others what had been said. There was relief on the faces of the women, and one or two said it was a terrible thing that must have happened to the relatives of these two strangers. At Taymak's urging, Setha returned to their shelter to bring back a couple of pieces of dried meat from their last bag, while others did the same or soon returned with a well-used piece of fur or other scrap of hide to give to the two men. Some spoke with concern about the probable condition of the child and the two women from the destroyed band based on what they were seeing of the appearance of these two young strangers.

Others, however, merely stood and stared at the young men, as if they were trying to decide what they could spare, if anything, of their own meager supplies. Perhaps, someone said, if the men not in the camp found good hunting this day, then it might be easier for them to share. The old woman explained this to the two men. She was also instructed to tell them it was alright if the other four survivors of their band wished to come to this camp later that day, or when the next sun arrived. The two men took the food and other offerings, nodded in gratitude for what was offered, spoke a few more words to the old woman, and then quickly left to disappear into the same trees they had emerged from earlier. The woman said to those standing nearby the men would deliver the offer to the others in the hidden camp, and they would appear in the next light, if they decided to remain in this place.

As soon as the strangers disappeared from view there was much talking and discussion about what the people should do, if they all decided to come here the next day. Finally, the old man explained to them the advantages, as he saw it, of taking in the refugees. True, it would be difficult to communicate with them if they decided to stay with the band through the hunting season. But after all, as he told them, their band was the real strangers here and not these poor survivors, who had always held this same piece of land as their own. Most likely, he said, they would soon choose to go south to find more of the people who spoke as they did, and there would be no need to fear them. Until then, they could be useful additions to the band, because they knew these lands so well. What he did not have to tell them was that young hunters—and marriageable women—were always in short supply in any growing band. Nor did he tell them since there would come a day after the taking in of the meat when this large band might split again for the cold season, the addition of these people on a permanent basis would not be an unwelcome thing for him to think about in the days to come.

Taymak returned with his family to their shelter to pick up the things they would need for their little gathering trip into the trees at the base of the stone rock wall. He could sense much of the tension in the camp about the possible threat of strange people in the area had been largely put aside by the events of the morning. By the time his family finished their gathering trip and brought the wood, bark, and other items they wanted to keep back with them the light was growing low in the overcast sky. The small amount of dried meat Mawra brought along for them to share had quickly been consumed and everyone was ready for something hot from the fire when they got back. All but two of the hunters who went out early had returned, and all had found some small success and reported that two men hunting together could take easy meat close by—at least until the smaller beasts discovered their peril from the new hunters in the area and moved farther away. Taymak told Mawra he would hunt early the next light with his cousin, who was someone he had known his whole life and with whom he often hunted. He promised the family fresh meat for the following evening's fire, and they all went to bed feeling better than at any time since they had left their familiar camping places to follow the old man to this strange, new land of forests and narrow valleys where none of them had ever been before.

Taymak, despite knowing full well he would have to hunt the next day—and perhaps for several others to follow before there was meat and new hides to satisfy the immediate needs of his family—was still very anxious to return to the dark place in the rock wall once more. He was even more eager and excited to show it to his uncle and explain to him what he wanted to do there and why he thought it was important to the people he complete his abiding desire to do this. He knew in the next days he would have to make one or more lamps from soft stone or fresh bone for which he could first reduce and then burn the fat of any animals he might take. It would be difficult to convince Mawra he must take some of this valuable commodity, which she would want to use for the preserving and packing of dried meat to use during the coming cold moons. However, Taymak knew he could not accomplish what he was envisioning doing in the cave with only the smoky light of even slow burning torches to guide his hand and keep his eyes clear.

The following two days turned out to be long but modestly successful ones for the two experienced hunters who went out both mornings together. The first day they went back up the small stream where others had experienced some success earlier. HIluk and another young man guided them to where they had seen fresh signs the day before of a small herd of six or eight short horned beasts. They tracked these bison, made a surround, and the four managed to bring down the smallest of the beasts and another, older animal, which could not run well enough to escape their well-aimed spears. The amount of meat was enough to last the four families it would feed for several days.

Taymak regretted not having brought Duhann along, as he told the boy he might, to help pack the meat and the split hide, which was his share, back to camp. As a result, the four hunters were forced to cache some of the meat under some stones until the two

younger men could return for it, as both willingly agreed to do the
next day. Taymak had already promised his cousin he would hunt
with him once more the following day. However, he suggested
they go in a new direction—downstream along the small river that
flowed through larger trees out of the little valley below the camp.
It would give him an opportunity to search along its edges for the
special stones he needed now more than ever to begin thinking
about the larger project that was coming to dominate much of his
thinking. His cousin agreed somewhat reluctantly, and Taymak
decided to take his son this time. It would be easier to keep an
eye on him, and he knew the type of small animal hunting the
men would probably be doing along the river would be less intense, and less hazardous, than the more difficult day they had
just completed.

When the four hunters got back to the camp with their loaded
drags of bison meat, there were many good words for their success,
and questions about where they had been from men who had already returned with less good fortune. There was also much talk
in the camp about all the strangers from the destroyed band who
had decided to come back with the two young men that morning,
once again after most of the hunters were gone. Everyone who saw
the refugees was shocked at the condition the other four were in,
and any fear or suspicions a few might still have held about taking
these people into their midst quickly disappeared when they saw
the state of the two women, the small boy, and the old man. Fresh
meat was in the camp by then, and soon there were many offers
to share with the unfortunate survivors of the disaster, the details
of which everyone had heard by then and repeated to anyone who
was not in the camp when the two young strangers first appeared.

Mawra was excited at Taymak's first day's hunting success and
rewarded him for those efforts later after they crawled under their
sleeping fur in a way they had not shared for many days on the
long trail—and after they were certain both children were sleeping

soundly close by with full bellies for the first time in many days. Taymak had also informed Duhann earlier he would be going out with his father the next morning. The excited boy spent much of the evening, while the family was at the fire enjoying their first feast of fresh meat in many days, hardening the sharpened point of his newly made "boy's spear" in the glowing embers of the fire. Mawra expressed her concerns about her husband's sudden decision to take him along on a man's hunt. However, Taymak assured her he believed the next day's hunt would be more about walking and exploring than hunting, unless some small beast looking for water at the stream edge they would follow was too slow—or too old, he joked—to avoid their spears.

This prediction turned out to be exactly the way the next day had gone. The three "men" followed the stream until the sun was high overhead and saw many good places a skilled hunter, even if alone, might find success in the days to come, at least until the beast herds appeared and all the men hunted as a unit. Taymak stayed closest to the water's edge looking for the heavy, dark brown stones he could grind into the fine, red powder he would require to make paint of that color to use in the cave he had found. He knew these heavy stones would have washed down the streams from mountains far beyond any place he had ever been himself. But an old hunter once showed him how and where to look for these special stones and Taymak had never forgotten that lesson. He also knew he would soon have to combine a hunting day with a walk back past the cliff wall to where Hiluk and the others had earlier found the sharp-edged stones. Some of the men were already carrying these back into camp to begin making the new butchering and other tools they would be needing for the days of intense hunting and for the countless other tasks the people would face in the cold season to come.

Duhann was excited that day when his father showed him the fresh tracks of a dark-furred, digging beast near the water's edge.

They followed these to the animal's burrow not far up a sloping bank. The excited boy was shown how to thrust his spear into the hole until it struck flesh and he saw the blood on it when he withdrew the shaft. Then Taymak helped him dig open the hole until the eager young hunter could complete his first kill in the presence of men who had already achieved the important status to which the youth aspired for himself. It was a proud moment for both father and son until Duhann was informed it was now his duty to get his kill back to his mother's fire on his own. The lesson, his father informed him at the obvious request for help in his son's eyes, was no hunter should ever take the spirit of any beast, unless his only purpose was to make meat to feed himself or others. Nor should he kill so far from his camp he would have to waste much of the meat he could not carry, unless there was no other thing he could do. To do otherwise, Taymak told him, would show disrespect for the life of the animal, and would risk the future success of that hunter with the other beasts of the kind he had just killed for no good purpose, other than his selfish desire to do so.

The three hunters made the long walk back to the camp, stopping only to spear a large fish they saw floundering in a shallow pool behind some rocks. Duhann was exhausted from his first full day on the hunting trail and was thinking, perhaps, he should show less eagerness to become a true hunter, at least until his legs got a little longer. Taymak spent much of the walk thinking about his plans for the cave under the rock wall and hoping in the next days he would be able to find the opportunity to take the old man, and possibly Duhann as well, back to that special place to show them what he intended to do there. In the meantime, he would ask about the camp for the proper freshly butchered bones with which to make three oil lamps and also begin to search for or make the other items he knew he would need to complete his ambitious task. But till then, it was only a matter of how much opportunity he would have before the busy days when the great herds appeared, and then how long the old man planned to stay in this camp afterward, which would determine his ability to complete the great idea which continued to dominate so much of his waking, and even his dreaming, mind.

⚊⊰⊹⊱⚊

Several days had gone by since Taymak last found himself kneeling at the narrow gash in the low rock wall and peering inside as the cool air from within brushed across his face and through his red hair. This time, however, as he prepared to crawl inside once more he would not be going alone. The old man would be trailing close on his heels as they made their way down the short but narrow passage to where it soon opened up enough to allow a man to duck low, until he made the last few steps. At that point they would finally enter the high-ceilinged open space, which had so excited Taymak on his first, anxious visit here.

He had also brought Duhann with him once more. However, to the boy's obvious displeasure, the youth was again given the task of "watcher" at the mouth of the opening, just in the event something went wrong while the two older men were inside. Taymak also brought the oil lamps he had finally found the time to complete. It had taken those few days to melt enough of the family's precious animal fat he recovered from various animals he had taken in his recent hunting to fill them. Then he made a tallow-covered wick he felt would allow the mostly hardened, rendered fat to burn long enough for him to do a more complete exploration of the darkened space beneath the rock this time.

Finally, Taymak felt ready and ignited two of the three oil lamps. He handed one to his uncle and kept the third one with him as an emergency light in case the wind in the narrow tunnel blew out one of the others. He turned to his uncle, saw a combination of eagerness and uncertainty in the old man's eyes, and told

63

him to stay close to his feet and keep his head low. There would be two or three sharp stones to squeeze past Taymak warned him, but the slow crawl to where they could stand up more comfortably was not very far. Then he glanced at Duhann, who was waiting to follow them to the entrance, and told his son he would take him into the cave the next time as soon as he could refill the dried fat in the lamps. With that he turned once more to face the cold darkness of the cave, which was again beckoning him into the yawning maw of its total darkness.

Taymak felt the old man touching his feet several times on the short crawl into the larger chamber of the cave. He also heard one or two groans when his uncle bumped his head or scraped an arm on a protruding rock before they reached the point where they could stand in a low crouch to continue. The light given off from the extra oil lamp increased the eerie shadows bouncing off the damp walls around them, until both men finally came to the place Taymak had been thinking about for virtually every moment he had lain awake into the night since his first visit to the cave. As he stood up at last to wait for his uncle to come up behind him, he raised his lamp to reflect as much of its shadow-casting light as he could into the suddenly expanded space before them. Then, he turned to the old man and said in a voice that shook with both the coolness of the surrounding air and the emotion he could feel once again welling up inside him and spoke in a low voice.

"You see, uncle, it is just as I have said. This is the space that reminds me of the cave you and the other men took me into as a boy to gaze upon the pictures of the beasts painted there. Look! See that wall over there. If I were to scrape the soft clay from its surface, it would be flat enough to paint several large beasts. And over there where that round rock juts away from the wall just below where the pointed stone hangs down from the ceiling, a man could easily see a great hump-backed bull moving as if to head right for this opening we have just passed through. Here, uncle, look here!

There is a place just above this corner where I could paint the heads of two or three of the galloping beasts with no horns, who will soon pass by this very place to which you have brought us and give us meat for the cold moons. Is it not as I have spoken, and is this not a place where the spirits of the beasts can be made to appear as one with our own?"

An excited Taymak kept moving from spot to spot along the different rock faces and outcroppings in the small room that made up the main chamber of the short cave. His uncle could see the clear excitement in the younger hunter's actions and hear it in his shaking voice. As he glanced about and followed his nephew's movements in the dim light of the two flickering oil lamps, he also became more excited about the prospects for what he was seeing and for what Taymak was revealing about his plans for this unique space—even if his excitement was for different reasons than those of his eager nephew. The old man knew from the distant days of his youth such places as this had always held a special significance for the people, from seasons since beyond memories had been kept. However, over those seasons his people had gradually left the lands where these ancient places were once known by many bands, who would visit them to restore their link and hunting power with the great beasts they depended upon so much for their very existence.

Over those many seasons, much of that critical link had been allowed to slip away from bands like his own as they moved farther beyond these spirit places, which he and others like him had known and held so close in their youth. Here at last, he suddenly thought, was a place where a new link with that distant past might possibly be reestablished—and at a time of great need for such a link in the life of the people. The uncertainties of the passing seasons and the recent unpredictability of the large beasts' movements were placing his people in a position of risk, the meaning of and reasons for which many of them, except for a few men such as himself, had not yet fully grasped. Perhaps, he was thinking as he followed the excited movements of Taymak around the walls of the small cave, his nephew could somehow become the means to achieve and reconnect with their ancient past in a way the old man had begun to think might have been lost to the people forever. At that moment, however, further speculation was interrupted by the voice of his nephew addressing him once again in an almost breathless fashion.

"Well, uncle. What are your thoughts about what I would try to do in this place? Do you believe it would be a good thing for the people? Think of the young hunters and men-to-be, like Duhann out there, to see such a place as we once did; and feel as I have the spirits of the great beasts entering into our own. Then we may know better the ways to follow and hunt them, as our ancestors did before us?"

"Yes, Taymak. It is as you say, and I do believe it would be a good thing for the people to have such a place to come and know these memories of which you speak. You must tell me more about how you would do this and show me in the smooth dirt or on an old piece of hide the pictures you would make here. Perhaps, I could offer my own ideas and memories to help you do this important thing.

"But while we are here alone and before these lamps burn low and we must return to the light of the living once more, there are words I would speak for your ears only in this place—to tell you it would be good if you did not speak of them to others until I have been able to prepare them for the decisions we must all make soon. To see this place and hear the words of what Taymak would do here have made me feel what I have been thinking is truly a gift from those same ancestor voices. These voices seemed to blow upon the very wind as it struck my face when we crawled together through the darkness to enter here."

Taymak stopped his inspections of the wall to step closer to where his uncle stood still just inside the low passageway they had passed through into the larger chamber. The last words of the old man took him by surprise and forced him to realize, for the first time perhaps, that by revealing the existence of the cave to another he was losing the sole ownership of it and what might later happen here. This was a new and somewhat disturbing thought for the brief instant before he replied to his uncle he would hold close in his thoughts the words which were about to be given. The old man glanced about the space once more as if he was recalling some distant memory and began to speak.

"When a man passes the long season as I have, many things become clear in his eyes and head that other men do not always see or think upon. This is why the people turn to men such as I have become to lead them to the places and in the ways of their lost ones, who now look down from the darkness upon them. A band with no elders is one with no direction, and is one that will not continue to live long. I have seen this bad thing happen to others in seasons not long forgotten. My days of leading the people upon new paths will soon come to an end. It has become my great hope that you, Taymak, a man of my close blood, will one day become someone others will follow in the ways our ancestors have always tried to show us. This is why, nephew, I believe you must complete this idea you have brought me here to learn of, and to do so is even more important than you may have thought before now.

"There are hard days and seasons to come for the people, I fear. My cousin and the other older men have spoken together with me of these things before this long walking began. This is why I have brought you all to this far place. The ways of the beasts are changing and the hunters must change with them, or the people will disappear as others have in the seasons not long past. We need think only of these poor people who have come into our camp and whose land this was before we chose to come here to know the truth of this fear. The shaking earth days may come again and force more bands to move beyond their hunting lands as we have done. I have seen this thing before, as have others. Taymak, I believe now these strangers coming into our camp to seek our help, and this place in the earth you have found and brought me to, are both important signs the people must stay in this new land and not return again to those we have called our own for so long. We must find new places to move our camps as the seasons change and learn the ways of the beasts we share those new lands with, and even those of the other men, perhaps, who make their fires in these strange lands also.

"Nephew, you must paint your pictures upon these walls, and you must do it as soon as you can. There is already growing talk around our fires how the beasts have not come as they should have by this moon. I have heard whispers among the young hunters, and even some of the women, that perhaps I should not have brought the people so far south into such strange lands, where all feel the connection with their ancestors and the camps they knew well from their youth has been broken. Taymak, you must help them find this missing connection once more. Together, we can bring the people here to know their past has not been lost to them. They must see with their own eyes the beast spirits have been summoned here in the same way our fathers and those before them once did to again make strong the bodies and spirits of the people. You are the one our ancestor spirits have chosen to bring their voices back to the people and show them this is the place they must remain, if they are to go forward into the unknown seasons they must now face."

With that, the old man fell silent. The dancing light from the low-burning lamp made from the hollowed bone he held seemed to cast a moving shadow across his face and almost gave the spellbound Taymak the impression his uncle had already become one of the distant ancestor voices himself of whom he had just spoken. There was a moment of silence, broken only by the heavy breathing of the two men, while the younger one tried to sort through the words he had just heard to put them into his new memories of this special place, where both men remained quietly standing as if transfixed in time. Finally, Taymak found the words to answer his uncle in the only way he felt possible.

"I do not know if the words you give me are truly spoken, uncle. But I also believe this cave must be a place that I, alone, have been brought to by the ancestor spirits of both men and beasts to create once more such a place as the other, long forgotten ones you have told of. I will begin the preparations to do as you have asked. I will make the images I would place here on a piece of hide, and when I am satisfied with them I will bring them to you to see if you believe they are the proper ones to make on these walls. If, as you have feared, the beast herds do not soon find their way to us here, then I will have the time to do this thing. It will also mean the need to make the pictures on these hidden walls is even greater for the people to know and feel the power of their images in their own spirits—if they are to remain here in the new seasons, as you have said they must. But we must leave the cave now. The light from our lamps burns low, and I can see the one in your hand has almost gone out. Come, we will crawl back into the world of living men before the darkness surrounds us—and before Duhann runs off to bring others here to find us, as I have told him he must do, if no light or sound comes from within the passageway soon."

Taymak laughed a little at his joking remark, and partly to ease the growing tension and chill in his voice as his uncle stood listening to what he had just said. Indeed, the old man's lamp went out before they could see light from the narrow opening toward which they were still crawling a short time later. Duhann was waiting anxiously by the narrow entrance when his father's dark, red hair emerged. Taymak smiled as he greeted his son warmly, just before he blew out the last flickering flame of his lamp. They had not needed to use the third lamp as it turned out. However, Taymak had been thinking and calculating in his mind on the crawl back about how many such lamps he would need for the time he would have to spend in the cave on each future visit to make the drawings, which he was now more eager than ever to begin in the darkened space behind him. It would require new lamps and more of the precious fat to fill them than he could probably beg from Mawra's equally critical need for it. Perhaps, the old man could find a way to help him with this new problem, he thought, given his uncle's obvious interest and concern over getting started on the paintings as soon as possible.

The three generations of hunters walked mostly in silence back down the slope and along the now familiar little stream running back to the new camp—which was apparently to become a more used one than he had anticipated, or so Taymak thought as he continued to sort through the words his uncle had given him in the darkness of the cave. He could not say to himself those words came as much of a surprise, however, since he was already beginning to suspect they would not be heading back toward their old camping places, once the cold season hunts were finished in this new location. Taymak only mentioned to Duhann how they must take the first opportunity to come back this way to journey up to where the men earlier found the washed-out place where the blocks of sharp-edged stone could be found. Like the others, he would soon be in need of many new tools for the bigger hunts to come.

Unlike the others, however, he would need some special, long blades to scrape the main wall of the cave smooth to remove the loose, damp clay down to the harder surface he could paint on. At other places in the cave, he had already seen on this visit that leaving the clay in place where it had dried would give him a smoother and better, more lifelike appearance for those detailed images he envisioned painting upon them. There would also be new lamp bowls to carve out of larger bones or soft stones from the stream below the camp, better torches to make, paints to grind, and many other requirements for the coming work. All these ideas were swirling about in his head as the three of them walked back to camp. By the time they arrived, Taymak was almost giddy at the thought of what he was about to attempt. He was also strangely at peace after this visit to the cave; for he soon came to realize the old man's words were also relieving him of a burden he had felt himself struggling to carry upon his spirit since before he could recall the time when such strange ideas were not somehow a part of him.

Before he parted from his uncle, he sent Duhann ahead to tell his mother of their return to the camp. Then, he took the old man aside and told him of his coming need for the fat to make the lamps required to do the work in the cave. The elder told him he could certainly see the need for this and he would do what he could to help. However, he informed his nephew unless the men started taking some larger beasts soon, the women's needs for this precious substance in the camp would make it difficult for either of them to acquire what was necessary. Then he surprised Taymak by telling him about a type of tree he knew of which would burn without making much smoke, even in such a small place as the cave they were just in, and he would search the nearby places where trees were growing to see if he could find it.

In the meantime, Taymak was to begin to draw the practice images as he told his uncle he would. Then, the two of them could sit down together to discuss what would be the best way to bring the young painter's ideas to life for the people on the walls of the special cave. The old man sensed, with its narrow passage through the darkness to the chamber beyond, he had just visited one of those unique spaces which formed one of the rare, but critical, links with the world of the living and the world of the dead. These were the special locations men had come to hold as the only ones where the spirits of those who were once alive, but were now on the other side of the light, could be joined with those of their living descendants—both the men and the animals with whom they had once shared that living world more closely. Only in such a dark place in the earth could they receive the wisdom these ancestors once possessed but which they had since taken with them to the far land beyond where they now dwelled in the darkness, those same places through which all men must one day pass on their last journey to join them.

⊷ ⊶

Not many days had passed since Taymak and his uncle visited the hidden cave where together they developed the plan to cover its walls with lifelike images for the people to see as an important part of their fading connection with their past. The hunters continued to go out with only modest success; and the women continued to dry any left-over meat from their kills, and then to stitch together hide bags to hold it or make the larger shelter covers as their individual family's needs dictated. Still, however, the large beast herds were not appearing, and scouts were regularly sent back through the gap along the trail the people had followed earlier to search for them. These hunters went as far as a man could walk and return in one full light, but still saw nothing of the signs they were desperately seeking to confirm they were waiting in a proper place to receive the migrating herds.

There was a growing unease in the camp, which was being expressed mainly at individual family fires only; in the dark of the night between husband and wife; or secretly along hunting trails by pairs of hunters, who continued to grow uneasy at the absence of the larger prey they had come so far to find. By this time, many in the camp had begun quietly to express the idea to each other there would soon be no option for them but to stay in these unknown lands to face the coming cold—and the hunger it would surely bring—in a place which was still strange to them all.

However, there were those among them now for whom these lands were not so strange. The refugees from the lost band, who had been absorbed into the two smaller groups that had come south, were already proving their worth to those who were willingly to accept the strangers into their midst. Except for the one old man, who seemed to have a coughing sickness that limited his ability to interact very much with anyone, the five younger survivors of the tragedy soon began to learn the new manner of speech of their more numerous hosts. They set up two shelters close to the edge of the camp—one for the two hunters and the old man and another for the two younger women and the boy, who had been orphaned by the disaster at the rock cliff of their former camp.

The two young hunters showed themselves more than willing to share their knowledge of the local area with the same men whom they might under far different circumstances have treated as unwanted intruders into their band's hunting territory. However, both those two were also eager to hunt, since it was now their responsibility alone to feed the other four helpless survivors of their people, even if the strangers from the north willingly showed their generosity on more than one occasion when food was needed. But these two young men had also noted the mysterious absence of the large herds and commented on this as being something strange and unexpected when the old man asked them privately about it. Still, the two young hunters first proved their worth when they took a party of the ablest hunters out with them to show them the best places to hunt the larger beasts that also called these small valleys and flowing waters their home in this season.

Taymak went out with this small party of men to see what beasts might be found in the area, where he now fully believed the people would be making their home for the foreseeable days to come. He also wanted to look for a certain type of stone to make the black pigments he would need to paint with in the cave, ones which he had not yet found along the stream edges, or near the place of the sharp-edged stones when he made the journey there with Duhann the day after he showed his cave to his uncle. On that walk he noticed a very promising camping place near the small stream and closer to the source of those important stones. He could not help but wonder if he should not suggest this place to his uncle, when the day came the larger band inevitably split apart, as a more sheltered site their original band should relocate to for the cold moons. If the large herds did not come close to the new camp soon, such discussions might become even more necessary; since the people would have to risk dividing into even smaller groups than usual to keep from exhausting the available remaining game animals in any such confined hunting territory as they would find themselves in over a longer period.

However, on the hunt with the two new men they all went to a place beyond the far side of the river below the camp where none of them had yet ventured. The young hunters showed them a more open valley where tall trees grew in greater abundance than the men from the north were used to seeing. There they hunted the large, often solitary bulls with the curved horns, which preferred those wooded places. It was a beast the men from the north rarely hunted. But it was one they also knew well enough as being an animal that did not move in large herds and was very difficult to hunt. These aurochs were dangerous beasts, which could take a hunter's power—and even his life—if they were hunted in the closed, forested places in which they were usually found. However, their spirits gave new strength to the power of the hunter who could kill such a beast, as well as providing large amounts of excellent meat to repay the risk—if a hunt was successful.

That day's hunt proved both things to be true. One of the large beasts was taken by the six men who had gone to that strange place of many trees to hunt them. The divided meat would feed their families for several days. However, one of the careless, younger hunters received a bad gash in his thigh from the pointed horn of the downed aurochs, when that man closed in too quickly ahead of the others. The young hunter wrongly assumed the several spear strikes on the fatally wounded beast made it helpless to react. But a quick jerk of the animal's head painfully revealed to the surprised young hunter there was still power in the beast's will to live, as soon as he came in too close to finish the kill ahead of the more experienced men who were with him.

Taymak helped to bind the injured young man's wound until they could make their way back to the camp and one of the older men there, who was skilled at such things, could attend to the wound in a proper fashion. At best, it would still mean this unfortunate young man would not hunt again for several days—a hardship for the entire band if the herds came. At worst, it might mean a more permanent injury which might never heal in a way to allow this man to function again as a solitary or more useful hunter in the band. With the injured man, along with the load of meat and hide from the large beast, it had been as much as the hunters could manage, until Hiluk ran ahead to bring others back to help with the loads. They all arrived in the camp by the light of the evening fires, but only after a cold crossing of the small river, which separated the tired men from the warmth with which those fires had beckoned them in the early darkness.

As Taymak lay awake from his fatigue that night, the warmth of Mawra as she squeezed herself tight in against his chilled body when they pressed themselves together under the old furs slowly began to bring his thoughts back to other things. His family now had enough meat that he would not have to hunt for at least three more days, and he knew it was time he fulfilled his promise to his uncle and showed him the pictures on the old scrap of hide he had made in the last days. These were done with a pointed, fire hardened and blackened stick he had shaped especially for that purpose. There might also be some extra fat from the cooked meat from his portion of this kill, which he deliberately selected for this reason, to fill one, or even two new lamps. Earlier that morning, he also managed to pick up two small stones he thought might be the ones that could give him the right powder to mix with water and fat to make the black paint he would need in the cave. If they were, he would return with Duhann in the next day or so to where he found them on the other side of the river to search for more.

Taymak was sorting through these thoughts, when Mawra grabbed him in a way that was certain to focus his immediate attention elsewhere. After a few moments of this, she leaned in close to his ear and whispered quietly.

"I see Taymak is not as tired as he told me he was when he found his way under the furs before I even came into the shelter. If he is not so tired, there is something I would speak to him of before he is lost to sleep. The hunt this day was a good one, and when the men came into camp with so much meat from the large, horned beast many were heard speaking the praises for the two young hunters from the band your uncle has asked to stay with us in this place. The brother of the injured man who was with you said it was those two young men who led you to that beast place and showed the best way to take them. Was this truly spoken?" When Taymak replied, indeed, it was the two new men who were responsible for the hunt having been a successful one, Mawra paused for a moment and continued.

"That is a good thing. There is something I must tell you about one of these new men—the oldest one, the one they call Birsec. In the days past, when you have not been in the camp, I have seen him walk out of his way, I believe, to come close by our fire when Setha was sitting there. I have seen him look her way at those moments. But he is a young man, newly made a hunter it seems, and such behavior is not unexpected. Still, I am also certain Setha has looked back at him in a way a mother can see and know the meaning of. It is a look which gives thoughts to a man she is not made unhappy to be looked upon in such a way. I also believe Setha has gone out of her way, when I did not watch her closely, to go to the stream or to some other place where this man Birsec could see and approach her. I have asked another woman if she has seen this, and she has told me it is so. What does Taymak say to this?"

His wife's words caught him by surprise, and it took Taymak a few moments to reflect upon them as she continued to touch him in a most distracting manner. Finally, he turned his head to be closer to hers and whispered his thoughts to her.

"This is a season we have long known must one day come for Setha. There are not many young hunters in the new band the old man has brought here with us who are looking to find a woman, or who are not of blood too close to our family for us to consider them. I think it is a thing we must watch closely in the days to come. But I will say this from what I have seen of this young man, Birsec: our family should not be made unhappy if the day comes when he approaches me with an offer to make Setha his wife. It is true he is young; but he is a good hunter and a good man, or so I have come to believe from watching him. The others who came into camp from their old band all look to him, I think.

"There is something I will tell you for your ears alone and is not to be spoken of to others. My uncle has said he believes the people must stay in these new lands, now that we have come so far to find them. If this is so, and I believe he speaks truly, then we would not have to worry about Setha being taken from us to live in some distant camp. I believe these new people we have taken in will stay close with us for some seasons to come. For this reason, and if our daughter tells us this is a thing she wishes to do in some moon to come, then I believe it would not be a bad thing to think upon."

Her husband's words were not exactly the ones Mawra had expected to hear. She thought he would be unhappy, and even angry their daughter was behaving in a way that was sure to lead any eager young man on to where they both might do something foolish. However, his words about their people continuing to live in these new lands well beyond the immediate cold season caused her to consider perhaps it was indeed not such a bad thing their daughter might choose to go with a man who would continue to live very close to where they might be, or even choose to join this band. This was a thing that did not generally happen, since daughters were usually separated by long distances from their mothers. These mothers would often not be there for the birth or infant seasons of their grandchildren, which they may then never see, except on those limited occasions when two or more related bands temporarily came together. As a result, daughters married out of a more isolated band might never even be seen again; or they could be lost to difficult childbirth or some other such tragedy, thus leaving parents to grieve alone when they found out about such a loss long after it had happened—if they ever heard any later news of her at all.

Mawra let her husband's words sink into her thoughts as she began to see the wisdom in what he had whispered to her. If he was satisfied this young man Birsec was a worthy prospect as a husband for Setha, then she would do her best to see their daughter was immediately made aware of the proper behavior she must show in the camp to demonstrate she was ready to accept such a responsibility. Before she could think more upon such things, however, Taymak turned his body to face hers. She had unconsciously ceased the movements of her hand upon him as she was thinking about what he had just told her, until his hands began to search out the warmth of her bare skin close to his. A few moments later her thoughts were venturing in another direction entirely, as memories of her own first days as a new wife, and all it had involved at that difficult time for her as a stranger in a new band with a young and eager hunter beside her, came flooding warmly back into her mind and body.

Late the next morning, Taymak sought out his uncle, who was preparing to go off for a short walk down to the river when the younger man approached him. It was a good opportunity for the two men to be alone, and Taymak quickly suggested he, too, would like to go in that direction to search for more of the heavy red stones he was still seeking for his paints. They had walked along the bank for a short distance when the old man pointed out a particular, small tree that grew scattered along the stream edges. He informed his nephew a man could make small torches from the dried pieces of this tree, if he could find them, which would make no smoke in the close spaces of the cave when burned there.

It was an important thing to know, Taymak replied, and it also gave him the opportunity to inform his uncle that in his carrying bag were scraps of soft hide with the pictures of the images he wanted to paint in the cave scratched in charcoal upon them. They soon found a private place away from the noise of the rushing melt-water sweeping by and sat down in a spot where several boulders had once been deposited from the on-rushing little river. Taymak took out the first hide scrap and showed it to his uncle. The old man followed the lines drawn upon it with great interest, as his nephew peered at him awaiting his response. At last, the old man turned to him and spoke.

"This is truly a wondrous thing I hold in my hand, nephew. I never expected to see a season come again when I might gaze upon such things once more before my days in the light are ended. A man can easily recognize the faces of the running and hornless long-faced ones in these three you have shown here; and the pictures of the many-horns we depend upon for our meat and furs in this season seem to want to jump from this hide into my hand. If the larger ones you say you would place on the walls of the cave are done in this same way, the people will believe the beasts you show them must have been made from the spirits of living creatures."

When his uncle returned the hide with the three horse heads and the group of running and jumping reindeer on it, Taymak reached out for it with a smile on his face. Then, he removed another, smaller scrap of hide from his carrying bag and extended it to the old man. Upon it was drawn the image of a single mammoth, with its trunk raised high between two long, curved tusks, as if it were bellowing or sniffing the wind in some fashion. The old man took it, stared at it in open-mouthed amazement for a few moments, and then spoke with a shaking voice.

"Taymak did not speak of such a beast when he showed me the places on the cave walls where he would paint the pictures I saw on the other hide you gave me. Tell me, nephew, where would such a spirit thing as I see before me be made, that others might easily look upon it in wonder as I have just done. How large would it be in your cave?"

"This image has come into my head only since two nights past, when I was awake long into the darkness thinking about a long, thin piece of the wall that sticks out from the surface that surrounds it. It was just behind us where we first stood up near the entrance to the large space we crawled to find. This image of the great one's long nose pointing to the winds came into my head, almost as if it had been sent there by the spirit of one of these great beast ancestors itself. The hunters have not taken one of these important beasts for two cold seasons past. If, uncle, as you have said, our people are to stay in these new lands for as far as you can see into the seasons to come, then would it not be a good thing to try to summon the spirits of these ancient ones to follow us into these lands? Then, our children and their children's children might know the power a man can find in the taking of such an important beast spirit?"

"Indeed, Taymak, it is as you say, and is a thing I have not thought upon myself. It would truly be good If the young men could gaze upon an image such as this, and keep it in their memories as the last thing they see in the cave before they crawl back into the light to be reborn there themselves. Tell me, nephew, when do you believe you can start this work in the cave. There is still no sure sign of when the great herds will pass this way, and I know you must hunt to feed your family. I would ask others to offer meat to you; but I am certain you understand this thing you will do must be kept from the eyes and ears of others until it is ready. Not until you have finished and the people can know why it is so important to them will we take them there together to look upon it and listen to the words I will give them in this new place of power. Does Taymak see why this must be so?"

"Yes, uncle, these are my thoughts as well. There are those in the camp from both bands who will wish to try to return to the old lands as soon as they have made meat and can see a way. Your words in this new place of the beast spirits will speak to their hearts as well as their heads on that day. But it is as you say, and I must hunt again in two days before I can begin to spend enough of each day to complete the work on the cave walls. I must go in the new light across the river below us to search for a special stone with which to make the black paints I will need. We must also hope there will be enough fat to fill as many lamps as a man has fingers on one hand to last long enough each time I go into the darkness to make the light I will need there to do the work. I can also have Duhann keep a fire at the front of the cave to light torches to bring to me of this tree you have shown me this day."

"How many days does Taymak believe it will take him to make these drawings in the manner you have shown me here, and what if the herds come before you are finished, nephew?"

Taymak smiled at his uncle's question and replied if the herds came there would be no great need to complete the work quickly, since the main reason to do so was to summon the spirts of the living animals to this place through the images of their dead ancestors painted upon the walls to guide them into this land. As to how long he believed it would take him, Taymak could give no direct answer, since he had never done such a thing before, nor had he ever known or spoken with anyone who had. The old man

81

laughed a little at this response, but said it was best then he get started painting as soon as possible. Taymak agreed, and they both decided it would soon be time to return to the camp.

In the meantime, he suggested to his uncle they search about for where the old man could show him the best pieces of the dry wood he said could be used to make the smokeless torches Taymak planned to use. He would need the additional lighting in the cave until he was ready to paint the lasting images of the beasts he planned over the first charcoal outlines he would put down on the surfaces. He would not need the oil lamps so much until he was satisfied enough with the first drawings to cover them over with the more permanent pigments he would begin to make in the next days. Taymak also knew when the final painting came he would need his son's assistance to hold the oil lamps close to the surfaces he was painting upon to insure the finished images he placed there would match as closely as possible the clear vision of them he had already created in his head.

The afternoon was growing late by the time the two men returned up the open slope to the sprawling circle of variously sized, hide-covered shelters and smoking fires. Taymak carried a small bundle of the dried branches his uncle had helped him select to make slow burning torches that would produce little or no smoke. When he got to his family's fire, he instructed Mawra this wood was in no circumstance to be burned in her fire. She looked at him questioningly at his remark. However, she knew enough of her husband's sometimes strange ways to silently accept his request and then pass it on to their daughter to make certain the now frequently distracted girl understood her father's orders. As soon as she saw that Taymak would say nothing else about where he had been or what he had done that day, Mawra pulled him aside and spoke to him.

"Setha went down to the river to fill the water bladders and has been gone much longer than is needed for such a simple task.

Did you see her when you came up from there just now? I fear she has gone off to wait near where some young hunters who left to go to the far side of the river earlier have gone. I am certain this 'boy' Birsec was one of them. Perhaps, husband, you should go back that way to see what our daughter is doing so long alone by the river."

"I am tired from the walk from down there carrying the wood, Mawra. I do not think it is a good thing to be seen stalking my daughter as if she was some small beast a hunter was trying to get close to without being seen. I am certain if what you say is true, then there will be others to keep a watchful eye on Setha, if she should do something foolish. I will keep watch here to see if these young men you spoke of return soon. If Birsec is not among them, then that will be the moment for a careful father to make his way down there to see what is happening beyond our eyes. Until then, let us enjoy the quiet of our little fire alone together while there is still good light above. I saw Duhann off with my cousin's younger son on my way back from the river. They were practicing spear casts at stones they have piled together in the shape of some unknown, dangerous looking beast when I saw them," Taymak laughed.

"Come wife, let us warm our tired feet close to your fire while our children are away. Is there a piece of meat with even a little fat left on it I can chew on until they have returned to us? I can see from your meat bag I will be hunting again in one more day. Perhaps, I should ask this young man Birsec to take me across the river and show me the places I would like to see over there?"

Taymak laughed again at his last remark. However, he could see Mawra was not at all amused by it—or by his careless attitude concerning their daughter's extended absence. She searched her meat bag for a scrap of something she could give Taymak to satisfy his request for food. Then she handed it to him with the deliberate comment it appeared there was nothing left in her meat bag with any fat on it which he had not already removed to use in one of his mysterious little lamps.

⊷⊶

Taymak left early the next morning with the young hunter Birsec with whom he had managed to communicate the evening before when the latter came into the camp— along with the other younger hunters and not alone as Mawra feared—about his desire to hunt the following day on the far side of the river. Not surprisingly, given the young man's possible interest in their daughter, Birsec seemed eager to accompany the older man as he requested. It was plain for Taymak to see the young man was quickly picking up the differences in the spoken words of the new people with whom he and the other survivors of his band had recently joined, and his earlier stated opinion to Mawra that Birsec seemed a promising young hunter was readily confirmed, to his satisfaction at least.

Much to his son's delight, Taymak also informed Duhann he would be going out with his father the next day to cross the river, which was a place the boy had not yet seen. He was instructed to sharpen his spear with the piece of chipped stone his father showed him how to use and to harden the point in the fire that evening. It would still be at least a full season before Taymak would show his son how to shape and attach the sharpened, stone tips for his spears, with which the youth would not be permitted to hunt until he had demonstrated his ability to make his own points and was called out to the people as a true hunter. Still, Duhann's excitement was obvious; for he was up and dressed for the trail before his father crawled from his warm furs as soon as the full sun ball appeared to warm the cold morning air; and even before his mother stirred to rekindle the small family fire, which had burned low during the night.

The cold stream water chilled their lower legs when it splashed upon them at the crossing place, where some of the younger men had previously thrown large stones into a shallow spot to make the crossings as easy and as dry as possible. Duhann got wet well above his knees, but he spoke no words of complaint in his excitement at being treated as a young hunter by his father, at least in his own eyes. Birsec wanted to lead them back to the place of tall trees where they had earlier hunted the large, horned bull, but Taymak stopped him before they went very far in that direction. He took two whitish-grey stones from his carrying bag and asked the young man if he knew where more of these might be found.

The young hunter examined them, shrugged, and simply motioned for the other two to follow him. He took them farther downriver than Taymak had yet been, on either side of that stream, to a slope descending to it from a low ridge line off to the west. It was not long before Taymak spotted an eroded gully where he soon began to find a sufficient quantity of the stones he would need for his black paints. Then it was time to hunt, and he told Birsec to take them to the best place he knew close by where they might find some larger meat.

Birsec was leading them back toward the place of the trees when he stopped and signaled he had heard a noise in some low bushes up ahead. Taymak told Duhann to follow quietly while the two experienced hunters crept low to see what was causing the noise. They did not go far before they spotted a yearling, short-faced bear feeding in the small stand of bushes up ahead. The animal was turning over dried or rotting wood and stones as it searched for any nourishment which it could add to the fat it was packing on in preparation for its coming long hibernation. The two men silently separated to bring their thrown spears to the target from different directions. The kill was a surprisingly quick and easy one, and Taymak allowed Duhann to rush in once the bear was down to cast his pointed shaft into the mortally wounded beast and claim a full hunter's share of the heart of the important animal. Taymak knew two hunters would have been hard-pressed—or desperate—to take on an adult bear in such a place. However, a solitary young male of this size, and one new to life on its own, proved an easy victim for their experienced eyes, and the deadly shafts accurately hurled from their spear throwers.

Afterward, they hastily constructed a drag to get the heavy carcass back to the river. That took the three hunters most of the rest of the day's light. The crossing was more difficult, but there was no need to worry about staying dry with the fires of the camp already within view. It had been a very good hunt for such a short day, Taymak thought as he felt the weight of the stones in his carrying bag and noted the soreness in his shoulders from pulling the heavy drag of meat. At the river, Duhann ran up the slope to get his mother and sister to help pull the butchered carcass the last short distance. Many came to note the excellent fortune of the hunters as they brought their kill into camp. Still others requested a particular bone, tooth, or other small piece of this hard to find beast they might have a special need for. If the hunter could supply such a need, it was considered important to do so, since the day would no doubt come when he might also have a request for something the good fortune of another could satisfy. Taymak also knew his share of the meat would be greater, since Duhann had been allowed to participate in the kill, and he had already decided to take as many parts of the bear as he could which contained most of the excellent fat the young animal's body would contain in this moon.

Truly, it had been a special day, one which could not have gone better, Taymak thought while he sat by his fire that evening savoring the juicy meat of the young bear as he watched each bit of dripping fat collecting into one of the soft-stone lamps he had made earlier and placed beneath the meat as they roasted it at the edge of their fire. Mawra was also overjoyed at the success of their hunt, even after each retelling of it by Duhann that evening. She was no longer surprised at her husband's simple statement he would take as much of the rich, fatty oil as she could spare to fill as many of his strange little lamps as possible. She still had no idea why he spent so much time making them and now filling them. But she assumed he would tell her what he wanted her to know when the time came. Until then, she was happy to get all the fat and extra meat she could.

When the hunters pulled their drag to her fire to divide the kill, Mawra noticed the excitement in Setha's eyes at Birsec's first, formal appearance at their fire. She also sensed the young man's nervousness and awkwardness when at one point he cut himself when slicing through a back leg while wrapping his portion of the meat in his share of the hide. Taymak was tempted to offer him extra meat to feed the others of his little band who waited for him. However, the young man was obviously trying to impress the older hunter—and father—with his generosity in this particular instance.

Still, Taymak decided on a more equal division than he had originally thought to make when he considered the hungry mouths of the helpless ones who depended on the two solitary young hunters they came into camp with. Perhaps, Taymak thought, it was time someone said something to the old man about a better way for these newcomers to be brought into the band in a more permanent arrangement, one that would put less stress on the two young men to support them. Then, too, that would also be an important consideration if, truly, this Birsec might be thinking of a formal pursuit of Setha, which he could not undertake as long as his main responsibilities as a hunter lay elsewhere. Later that night, while under their furs with Mawra, Taymak quietly praised the young man when he spoke these things and then mentioned perhaps they should both determine soon just what their daughter's expectations were. Mawra agreed, and that had been the end of it, as Taymak's last waking thoughts quickly turned to other, equally important matters he must now begin to plan.

The following morning, he took the stones he had gathered and went off alone up the slope to the edge of the trees below the long rock wall. He also begged from his wife two small scraps of old hide which he would need to make bags within which to put the powders he intended to spend most of the rest of the day grinding from the two types of stones he had gathered and which by now virtually filled his carrying bag. He took a piece of the fresh bear meat to eat and told Mawra where he would be so she could send Duhann for him if anything important happened in the camp.

Once alone up below the cliffs, Taymak searched for a large, flat rock to use as a mortar and then went to the small stream where he found a rounded stone he could use as a hammer against the harder pieces he intended to grind. For the rest of that morning and well into the afternoon he first rubbed and ground the heavy hematite pieces with their iron-rich content he had recovered from the large stream into the dark red powders he would need. Then he took the newly found whitish stones, cracked them open, and began to reduce the manganese ore within into the powders that would later yield the blacks he would require for his painting.

The sun was dipping low when Taymak was satisfied he had made enough of the pigments he could later mix with water and a little melted fat to bind the two together to do the work he planned in the cave. The next day, if there was time, he would try to make a brush for each color from some long hair fibers from an old sleeping robe, or possibly from the shredded end of a fresh bough from a small tree he would select and experiment with. His initial drawings in the cave would be done with a charcoal stick, just as he had earlier made the small images to show his uncle. But the larger ones would require wood that burned just the proper way. He had already decided when he began his work he would keep a small fire going just outside the entrance to the cave—to make fresh drawing sticks, to ignite lamps or torches, or to warm his hands when needed. The maintaining of that fire would be a perfect task for Duhann, although Taymak did not want to tell the boy his plans just yet.

However, first he would keep his earlier promise to take his son inside the cave with him the following day, when he would also try out the torches he would make from the wood he and his uncle gathered down by the river earlier. Later that evening at the family's fire, he was satisfied his first important preparations were complete. He informed his son he would be accompanying him the next day on a "special hunt" for stones, up the far slope where they had been before. He smiled and winked at the boy's open-mouthed reaction to this sudden announcement to make sure Duhann did not blurt out some inconvenient question while in the presence of his mother and sister. That night Taymak enjoyed his most restful sleep since the first day in the camp, not long after he made his discovery of the wondrous cave beneath the rock wall.

Next morning, he and Duhann gathered what they would need for the day and took some meat and the smallest of the water bladders, more of which would soon be needed from the first bigger animals taken when the large herds appeared, as Mawra reminded her husband when she gave it to him. Taymak and Duhann then quickly disappeared from her sight toward the tiny stream that broke out of the trees above the camp. Once there, Taymak informed his son they were indeed headed for the cave entrance again; that they should gather some dry wood along the way for a fire; and, *yes*, Duhann would be joining his father this time on the crawl through the blackness for his first view of the "special" place. For the first time, Taymak began to speak to his son of the reasons for the things they would be doing in the days to come, and reemphasizing to the awestruck youth how he was not to reveal to anyone, including his mother or sister, anything they would do inside the cave. His father had not yet told him just why he was doing this, when all the other men were consumed by either hunting or scouting for the fresh meat they all needed. He would only say that what they would be working on together was of great importance to the people and all would be made clear to him before their work in the cave was finished.

When they arrived at the sheltered entrance behind the rocks, which blocked their view of the expanding valley below, Taymak quickly built a small fire. Then he prepared two of the new torches he would use to enter the passageway. He had also packed into his carrying bag one of the oil lamps, just in case the torches failed. But if they did not, he would leave this lamp and the others he would bring with him the next time in the main chamber of the cave for future use. When his preparations were complete, he handed one of the torches to Duhann and told the wide-eyed boy to stay close to his heels, and to watch his head on the crawl through the darkness. He swallowed hard, but said nothing as he waited for his father to disappear through the narrow opening, before he proceeded in after him.

Once inside the large chamber, Taymak again explained what he would be doing as he showed Duhann the various surfaces and outcrops upon which he would paint the images he was describing. He told his son the story of his own youthful experiences in a place where this had been done and why he thought it would be such an important and powerful thing for the people to behold in this far land in which they had come to live. The beast spirits would be strong in such a place, he said, and they would beckon to others of their kind to come to the people to sustain them in the far seasons ahead for them.

The new torches worked even better than he hoped and, while there was some light left on this visit, Taymak decided to begin. He handed his torch to Duhann and told him to stand close behind and hold both the torches high. Then, he removed a long, very thin flint blade he had made earlier from his bag and began to scrape and smooth the soft, clay surface of the main wall he would paint upon. The work went surprisingly well, and by the time he noticed the dimming light of the torches he was able to step back in satisfaction at what had been accomplished. He turned to his son, took the one torch, and told him he was to lead them out of the cave this time. Taymak wanted to be sure Duhann would have the confidence to make the crawl through the darkness on his own when a need for the boy to do so might arise in the days ahead.

Back in the light of the early afternoon, father and son rested and ate their small meal of bear meat, warmed over the hot coals of their little fire. Then Taymak made sure the fire would burn safely out on its own before the two decided to go back down the slope and find as much wood as they could bring back up the hill to use for future fires, while there was still light and before they returned to camp. They were just about to begin their second trip back with the bundled wood when Taymak suddenly felt himself losing his balance. He looked at Duhann and noticed the boy also had a questioning, somewhat frightened look on his face. Moments later there was no doubt the earth was shaking noticeably beneath their feet. Duhann had already lost his balance and fallen to the ground when Taymak decided to go to his knees before he pitched forward and risked rolling down the small slope they were upon. He hardly dared to breathe for the next few moments, until the shaking stopped at last. Finally, he looked at where an open-mouthed Duhann was staring back at him and shaking as well in uncertainty at that instant, much like the very land had just done. Taymak said nothing for a while until he was certain no more movement of the ground was coming—at least for the moment—and then stood up.

"Come, Duhann. Leave the wood. We must return to the camp at once. This is a fearful thing, one I have felt before. There may be need of us there. Your mother will be looking for you."

They both began the trip back as fast as they could walk. Taymak thought of how such a thing as had just happened must have been what came in the night and caught the people of Birsec and the others under the rock ledge, which had destroyed so many of their small band. As soon as they broke out of the trees Taymak saw there was great confusion below in the camp. One shelter on the other side of the main fire from his was burning and people were scurrying about trying to pull it down to save the hides. Women's shouts could be heard and Taymak could finally make out the figure of his uncle standing at the central fire shouting orders to the men still in the camp. By the time father and son made it to their shelter, Mawra had run to greet them. She shouted that Setha was down by the river and had not returned yet. Taymak dropped his spear, throwing stick, and carrying bag and immediately began to head in that direction. He did not go far before he saw his daughter and another girl hastening up from the river. No words were spoken when she ran to him to receive the fatherly embrace Taymak quickly offered. Then, he wrapped his arm around her shoulder to still the shaking he felt there when he held her close and they returned to the shelter together.

That evening there was much discussion at the main fire, where even the women and children gathered to hear what the old man and others might speak about what they had all experienced that day. Every hunter who came in told the same story from every direction they had been that day. The old man explained how he had seen this fearful thing at different times in the past, and this was one reason he always made his camps in the open when he could. Many could see the fear in the eyes of the survivors from the destroyed band, and there was a new understanding and sympathy in the camp for their plight after the horrible night of loss and destruction they must have experienced earlier.

Finally, the old man convinced everyone they must go forward in the new light as all had planned to do. There was, he said, no way to say when such a thing would happen, nor how long it would last—only that these shakings often came close together and then would not happen again for many, many seasons. There was still much talk around the main fire after he spoke, until most of the people left in the darkness to find what meager shelter from such a fearful thing their flimsy brush and hide structures might provide.

Most of the hunters did decide to go out again the next day as planned. Taymak's cousin and another man they both knew well asked him to go on a longer hunt on the far side of the river the next day. Somewhat reluctantly, he agreed. He knew full well it would cost him a day in the cave, but he also understood his family would be growing desperate for fresh meat in another day in any event. He did, however, suggest they ask the young man Birsec to go with them into that mostly unknown region of many hidden valleys and trees. The eager youth willingly agreed when Taymak approached him with the invitation. The other young man from the refugee band was standing nearby when Taymak approached Birsec. The older hunter took one look at the second man's eager face and decided to ask him to join them as well. With five they would have a large enough party possibly to seek out a place where another aurochs or some other larger beast might be taken—one that would yield meat, and fat thought Taymak, for several days.

The next day they hunted farther beyond the river than any of the hunters from the newly arrived bands had gone before. Birsec led them to another forested area, but they found none of the solitary aurochs they hoped to locate. However, their diligence was rewarded when a fat female bison and her yearling calf were found wandering alone at the edge of the trees. The hunters managed to easily take them both. There was far more meat than could be carried, and they decided to make a cold cache under some stones until the men could return with help to get the rest. Taymak was pleased with this plan. Now he would have enough meat to allow him to work in the cave for several days, plus he would have the fat he needed for several more lamps. Birsec agreed to return with the others and help to recover Taymak's portion in the days ahead in exchange for Taymak's share of the hides—something he would have to find a way to explain to a questioning Mawra when Taymak told her of his decision.

Later that evening, after his family made a feast of the tender bison ribs at their fire, Taymak told her of his deal with Birsec to retrieve the rest of their share of the meat. In answer to her disappointment and remark they needed such hide pieces badly for new foot coverings, he replied only that he must do something else starting the next day, something his uncle had asked of him. Then he added he had also made this arrangement because he knew the others for whom young Birsec and his friend were responsible were all in much greater need of the hides than they were. It was a response Mawra could not argue with, especially when Taymak nodded over at where Setha was cutting up some meat and said softly for his wife's ear only it was, perhaps, a good thing to show some respect to the young Birsec, just in case he had "larger" expectations in their family.

The next morning Taymak and Duhann once again headed for the cave. This time they brought all the lamps Taymak had made and filled earlier. He decided with the newly acquired fat he would burn these first and bring them back empty that day to refill what he could with the fat he had cut off the kill from the day before and what he expected Birsec would show up with later that day. He would try to make as many of the charcoal outlines on the main wall he had previously scraped smooth and anywhere else there was light enough to do before this day was done. The images he would draw were by now firmly embedded in his mind, and he hoped the initial work would be done in two such days. Then, he would mix his paints and begin the process toward which he had come to feel his entire life to this point had been directing him. It was an unknown feeling of exhilaration in his spirit he could hardly explain—and was one he could barely contain by this point.

For the next three days Taymak and Duhann labored in the cold and near darkness of the cave for as long each time as their other basic duties and the lamps would allow. Taymak did not want to arouse any more undue suspicions in his wife, or any others of the closely knit family groups that made up the larger band, with too many extended absences. By the third day he was ready to prepare the first of his paints to begin the actual work of permanently laying down the images he had long envisioned. He would mix the paints outside the cave to save valuable light and time inside. Taymak knew he would have to be careful not to spill the precious, thickened liquids on the crawl through the narrow passageway into the main chamber. He asked Mawra for the old water bladder he had replaced with the fresh one from the bison kill he had claimed several days earlier, and she had agreed with a silent question upon her face at her sometimes strange husband's often even stranger requests.

Taymak decided to make the group of horses' heads first in black on the smaller space where they would be painted. He had already used a blackened stick to outline the size of the heads to make sure his vision would fit into the space he had allotted for them. When he was done, he decided there was room for a fourth, smaller head and he could extend the neck of the most forward of the four animals to include the front legs moving in a galloping manner ahead of the other three, which he was drawing only down to the base of their necks where their heavy, black mane ended. He was quite pleased with this new idea when he saw how he was able to use the stone jutting out from the wall for the running legs, a thing he had not imagined doing before. He completed the drawing and then began to apply the black pigment. Later, he decided, he would come back to this drawing to brush some red dots along the horses' necks and outline the heads to add a more realistic depth to the whole effect of the image.

By the end of the third almost full day in the cave, he was ready to begin the major group of a small herd of reindeer on the main surface he had earlier smoothed with his scraper. But he also knew before that could happen he would probably have to hunt for at least two days to satisfy the needs of his family long enough to allow him to complete these many-horned beasts. He decided on an earlier visit he would do the long-tusked mammoth by the entrance into the main chamber last, when all else was completed to his satisfaction. That image was the final one he would leave in the eyes and minds of the cave's visitors as they left to return to the light, and Taymak wanted it to be the best drawing he had ever done. He also decided to bring the old man back to the cave as soon as he completed the reindeer herd to see if there were other ideas his uncle might have come up with since his first visit which could be important to the completion and larger meaning of the entire project.

Taymak hunted for the next two days with several other men with only modest success. It was quite apparent the easiest to take beasts within walking distance of the large camp had all been brought in by the many desperate hunters looking for them; or they were moving on to safer grazing grounds in another direc-tion. Were it not for the knowledge of the area provided by Birsec and the other young man from the refugee band, many in the camp would have started to grow hungry even sooner than some were beginning to complain of by then. That the large herds must come soon was mentioned daily now and there was imminent dan-ger of widespread unrest in the enlarged band around their aging leader's decision to bring them so far from their old hunting terri-tory into an unknown place.

Finally, Taymak and Duhann were able to return to the cave. He mixed his reds and blacks and refilled what lamps he could from the meager supply of fat still available. The old man quietly procured enough somehow to fill two more lamps. Taymak hoped these would be sufficient to provide the close-up light he would need for the final panorama of the reindeer herd, which would emphasize several pregnant females as the main images in the foreground of the painting. He would continue to use the torches Duhann held near when necessary. However, he did not like to work with these close to the walls because their light was not constant and the unseen smoke and smell of the burning sap made his head ache for the fresh air when he stood too close to their flame for an extended session of painting.

After one full day on the herd image one of the scouts came in from the direction where the sharp-edged stones were found east of the camp to report a small group of bison was moving south there and could be hunted the next day only, if all the hunters left before the light to arrive at their location. Taymak joined the others, but reluctantly informed his son he was not yet ready to participate in such a group hunt with experienced men. He directed the disappointed youth to go down to the river in his absence to try to find more of the special wood to make the torches they would need to finish their work, or to keep by the cave entrance for others to use when that work was finally completed. The day's hunt turned out to be a fairly successful one and there was enough meat to last the entire camp for several days, although it would take two more full days to retrieve all the butchered beasts, which amounted to the number of fingers on a man's hand. This time, Taymak was able to claim an entire hide to satisfy Mawra's demands, for a modest exchange with his cousin of some extra meat for his share of the hide from the animal they had taken together.

Again, Birsec readily volunteered to return to bring Taymak's remaining share of the kill back to camp, which would be another two day's effort. Taymak also got Mawra to somewhat reluctantly agree that Setha should also be allowed to go back with two or three other women, including those from the refugee band, to help retrieve the additional meat. Mawra was still worried this would mean their daughter would be out of her sight for at least a full day with the stranger, whom both parents were agreed was clearly showing signs of interest in being in the presence of the girl whenever he could. However, Taymak had few worries about the young hunter by this time and reminded his wife there would be many eyes upon them anyway with so many others returning to drag the extra meat back to camp in the following days.

Taymak also refilled two more lamps with fat and felt he had enough to complete the herd image and even to begin the long-tusked beast he would finish with. With so many others out of the camp he thought it was a good time to ask his uncle to return with him to the cave to see what he had accomplished there already. Duhann had also found wood for several more torches, and Taymak felt it was time to let someone else assess his work. The old man readily agreed to the return visit. On the second morning when the camp was nearly emptied of all but the young and old by those going after the butchered bison, or other hunters going out on their own to scout for the herds, the two men returned alone to the cave. Duhann, much to his displeasure, was ordered by his mother to go with his sister on the second trip for the bison meat. Taymak decided not to interfere with his wife's decision, even though his son's silent plea to return to the cave was clearly on the boy's face when he was informed of his mother's orders. Taymak merely took his son aside and told him they would not be painting that day anyway, mainly because of their uncle's visit.

When the old man stood in the open space of the cave once more and beheld the images that seemed to leap off the walls before the dancing light of his slowly moving torch as he illuminated each of them in turn, he could barely contain the praise he began to heap upon a silent Taymak. When he had seen them all and asked when the long-tusked one by the entrance would be completed, he softly began to mouth the words to an old chant—one his quiet nephew had never heard before. Finally, when he was finished, Taymak asked his uncle if there was anything else he thought should be done on the spaces that were still available and could be painted upon. The old man hesitated for a few moments, as if recalling a long-neglected memory from his forgotten past, and then replied.

"I had not thought to give words to this memory until your question just now, nephew. But in the days long past there was a cave I was taken to, even before you were brought into the light and when our people made their camps even farther to the north than in the past seasons of memory. On those walls beside the images were strange lines that crossed each other with dots in a line as I recall. I was told then these were the marks of our people from long seasons before. Some said they were to speak to strangers who might come into that dark place and know this land was the hunting territory of others. It might be good if you could place something like them here or over here on this small space across from the great beast you will paint on the other side of the entrance. I will show you in the dirt outside the shape of these marks as I remember them when we return to the light. There were also red hands on the wall there, which many believe were the mark of the man, or men, who painted in that cave. Will Taymak leave such a sign of his own work in this place when he has finished?"

Taymak had already resolved that question in his own mind. He, too, had seen the marks of the red hands in the cave of the galloping beasts he visited as a boy, when others that day placed their hands upon them to join their spirits, or so it was said then, with the spirits of those who had left their mark in the darkness of the earth in such a clear manner. The young Taymak was one of those who had done so; and afterward he always felt it had been the power of that hand, perhaps, which flowed into him that day and passed its marvelous gift into the youthful hand, which had once reached out into the darkness for that spirit to grasp. However, he simply replied to his uncle, indeed, he would place the mark of his hand close by each of his main images. He would also like to see and learn of these unknown marks his uncle could show him. If, truly, they were an ancient sign of their people, then Taymak would be happy to leave them in this place for all the people to know and see, even into the unknown seasons still to come.

At that, they crawled back out of the cave, where once in the light the old man drew in a smooth space of dirt the crossed lines and dots as he recalled them. Taymak quickly committed them to memory and told his uncle he would be sure to place them on the wall the old man had indicated, before he decided it was time to reveal the existence of the cave and its new contents to the rest of the people. Then he explained the final painting would be more difficult than he had first thought, but perhaps in three more days he would be ready for the others to be told of the cave.

The next day in the cave Taymak was able to complete the reindeer herd. He had previously calculated from the position of the cave opening that these beasts would be facing the entrance to the valley where the camp was made below the great rock, which marked the entrance out of the narrow gorge from where any beast herds moving south would approach. It was a comforting thought to think the spirits of his images might lead others of their kind into this valley to sustain the people in the far seasons to come. He stepped back to admire his finished work and held his lamp high to move it across each of the red, many-horned animals in turn. When he got to the last one he happened to notice a small, flattened surface just beyond the last figure. A sudden idea flashed through his head and he quickly searched about for the remains of one of the fire-blackened sticks he had used earlier to outline his initial drawings. He told Duhann to hold the lamp high while he quickly traced the outline of another, smaller beast than the several he had already completed.

This time, however, he drew the beast facing in the other direction, toward the back, narrower portion of the cave, which sloped downward to the low wall that headed in the opposite direction from the entrance—the one leading into the darkness of the earth, if another passage leading from the large chamber had been underneath. This last reindeer, he decided, would be added to mark the path of the lost spirits of those beasts from the living ones he had completed, which would be taken by the hunters to sustain the people once they were summoned to this valley. It was the path their spirits would set off on to begin their final journey, which all living things took through the darkness of the earth on the way to the unseen part of the sky on the other side of the darkness in each new season, once their days in the light were ended. He would also paint this beast in black when he mixed that color to begin the long-tusked mammoth he was going to start the next day.

Later that night as he lay awake in the same, inevitable darkness he must also some day journey through to pass from his final resting place in the earth, Taymak remembered from what he had seen before such a beast image describing that final journey must be shown without the eyes of the living creatures he had already painted in the cave. The dead had no use for their eyes on the great journey into darkness they would undertake. Nor, would their spirits need those eyes to see back into the living world from that darkness, which was already lit by the moon and the countless stars, which were now the true spirits of the ancestors of living men and beasts who once walked upon the land. He also decided he would not tell the old man of this last image, until the cave was completed and he was taken there with the other people to gaze upon its wonders. The next day, Taymak decided, he would also paint the signs his uncle showed him earlier in the dirt. Finally, along with the excitement and anticipation over the approaching completion of his work continually swirling in his head, the hunter turned artist found the comfort of sleep.

The painting of the long-tusked one indeed took longer than Taymak anticipated, mainly because he had not worked on such a rounded surface before. However, early on the third day after he began the last part of the painting Taymak was finally satisfied his work had the power to speak to the others who must soon come to behold it. True to what he told his uncle he would do, his last act in the cave was to cover his right hand in red paint repeatedly and impress that image onto the wall close by each of the major beast scenes painted there. Then, he took Duhann to the darkest corner of the cave, a place they had not ventured together before.

But this time instead of painting their hands red he took the last of the red paint into his mouth, pressed first his hand and then his son's against the wall, and then blew the red pigment in a fine spray against their two spread hands. When they pulled these back, a perfect reverse image of each hand outlined by the splattered red paint was clearly visible. They had pressed their hands beside each other's, and Taymak told his son in the far seasons to come it would now be his right also to bring others to this place to show them what he had once helped his father to create. Having shared this moving and important moment, father and son quietly left the cave together for the final time when it would be a place of their knowledge alone. Soon, Taymak said, the rest of the people would be led inside to hear and know the important words the old man would reveal to them all in this special place.

The day Taymak had long been anticipating finally arrived. Mawra had noticed his growing excitement and inability in the past two nights to sleep comfortably. However, she refrained from asking any questions to which she felt she might not have liked the answers. No signs of the approaching herds were as yet being reported, and some men were already discussing making a hunt to the north for an extended period of days, if needed, to see if the large beasts were even still moving in this direction. The old man reluctantly agreed to let them go; but he asked them to delay their departure for two more days. He wanted all the people to remain in the camp for something important, he explained to their questions about his decision. However, he would not tell any of them why he felt so strongly about this. Still, there was a growing sense in the band something unusual must be about to happen, perhaps, as some were speculating, even a decision to relocate the camp back in the direction they had come.

The old man was up early that day to make sure no one left the camp. This alone caused some worry and quiet conversation as the people gradually learned they were all to gather as soon as they could by the main fire. When all were assembled, even the refugees from the lost band, Taymak was summoned forward to stand beside his uncle. At last, the old man took a step forward, a clear signal for all to fall silent, and he began to speak.

"My friends and those whom I look upon as my children, even those of you who have followed me here from other bands and those who have agreed to join us here in this new camp. When we leave this fire we will all walk together to a special place, which is even within sight of where we now stand. My nephew, Taymak, a man you all know and believe to be a person to whom our ancestors have shown a path no one else among us has the skill to follow, discovered this place below the great rock wall over there that shelters our camp. In this dark opening in the earth Taymak has used his gift to make a place like ones some among you have seen in the days and lands where our people and your own ancestors dwelled far from these unknown ones I have brought you to.

"Many are saying the great beasts have chosen not to follow us to this new land. I say to those who speak these words you must first see this thing that will be revealed to you in this new light before you decide coming here was the wrong thing to do. Return to your shelters. Bring an oil lamp if you have one. There will also be torches at the place of the rock wall to use. Wear your head coverings or other furs if you feel the need. Then, we will all go together to this place and return before this light is at its highest."

With that he fell silent. The people looked questioningly at each other and then quietly began to drift off to do as they were instructed. Taymak had said nothing, having merely stood expressionless behind his uncle. When the old man was finished, Taymak saw Mawra standing between their children and smiling at him. He nodded back at them, and then grinned at Duhann as if to say it was now alright if he answered any of his mother's questions before they returned with the others to proceed up the slope to the hidden cave entrance. His uncle soon left to make sure the old woman who could speak with the refugee band gave them all his instructions and they would follow the others when the time came. Taymak had already prepared himself that morning for his own special day and remained close by the main fire to wait for the people to return.

When the band made it up the slope and through the trees to the secluded spot, many of them noted the remains of the several fires, the old and new torches, and the remaining lamps that could still be used near the hidden entrance to the cave. As the old man explained, all the people could not go into the cave at one time. First to go in would be the hunters, the old men who had been hunters, and the young men who were to be named as hunters. In his pride at that moment, Taymak beckoned Duhann to him and told his son he would be granted the right to lead the first group of men into the cave, crawling in front of his father. The torches and lamps were lit, and the men began to squeeze through the narrow opening and onto their knees to make the passage to the main chamber. The old man came last and told the women and others remaining behind they would soon make the short journey.

It took only two trips for Taymak and his uncle to show everyone all the wonders the hunter turned artist had painted upon the walls at the end of the dark passageway. When Mawra and Setha went in behind Taymak, who led the second group, she stood beside her husband as he explained what everyone gaped at in openmouthed wonder and squeezed herself to his arm in pride and admiration for what he had done. Even the sickly old man from the refugees, who had spoken few words since the survivors joined the band, was seen to have tears in his eyes when he left the cave. He was not the only one to express such emotion, Taymak noticed after the last group of women and children were led out of the "cave of the silent beasts" as some were already calling the place. When all had returned to the midday light, and the last torch or lamp was extinguished, the old man called all the people near and spoke once more.

"We will build our camps in this place to which our ancestors have led us and where they have shown us this cave of wonder to mark our first fire in this new land. The beasts will come. I tell you this is truly said. The gift of this cave and the hand of our brother Taymak, who has shown the beasts the way to follow us here, must be honored by those who still walk in the light that we may show respect for those who have come before us. Our band may break apart into others in the seasons to come; but we will remain one true people in blood and friendship as long as the spirit of this place is kept strong in our hearts and memories. We will return to the camp now and begin each new day from this season forward knowing we have marked this land as our own, and our children, and their children's children, will look to us in the far seasons, just as we have looked to those who have led us to this land."

As they were returning together to their family fires, a great sense of excitement and renewal with their past swept through the entire band. Many came to speak to Taymak to offer thanks for what he had done, and some even expressed their gratitude with small gifts. Others were speaking together privately about how Taymak must someday soon be the one they would look to when his uncle no longer walked among them. All praised and marveled at his skill in painting the beasts in a way they seemed to leap off the cave walls, almost as if they were alive. Taymak had not shown his uncle the solitary, black reindeer heading in the opposite direction until Duhann was leading the first group of men from the cave and the two stayed behind to be the last to leave. The old man understood the significance of this drawing immediately, but thought it best not to explain it to the others, at least until after a successful hunt of these same horned beasts could be completed.

To the surprise of no one at this point, that successful hunt finally occurred only three days after the band's visit to the cave. The first evening after the visit a young man who had hunted and scouted as far to the north as he could in a day returned with the exciting news a large herd of the many-horned beasts was moving through the narrow valley and toward the gap that would bring them past the camp in two more days. These exciting words would give the hunters time to prepare, and a fever pitch of anticipation instantly swept through the people. Indeed, the beasts appeared as predicted and for two days the pent-up energy of the hunters enabled them to take them in great numbers. Then, the large herd moved beyond where several men could separate and surround small groups, or single out individual beasts to take with their deadly, stone-tipped spears. Afterward, individuals or pairs of hunters could pursue the herd and take single animals as they desired and cache their meat some distance from the camp, if they could not carry it back with them.

There had been a feeling of great well-being in the camp after the last of the large herd passed through the valley. Others would follow, no doubt, or so the men were now convinced. The prospects of full bellies and warm clothing and shelters for the coming moons lifted the spirits of everyone in the camp. Even Mawra chose not to complain to Taymak when she saw their daughter accepting a small gift of fur from the hunter Birsec, when Setha did not know her mother was watching from a distance. Taymak continued to receive the good wishes of the band when he walked about the camp. However, the smaller group who had come south with his larger band was already speaking of finding a suitable camping place of their own, but one which would remain very close to the larger band and still in the new lands with them. Everyone had taken the old man's words to heart, and the desire to remain near the obvious spirit power of Taymak's paintings continued to grow strong in all the people.

It was nearly midday of the third sun after the last of the first large reindeer herd passed through the valley. The camp was still busy processing meat and preparing hides and furs for the coming cold season—which unbeknownst to the people would not be nearly as severe as they had expected—when the shaking of the earth came once more to remind them all they still lived in a land and a season of much uncertainty. This time the shaking was more powerful and lasted longer than the previous one, which was almost forgotten by then. Just as the shaking stopped, a great rumbling was heard above the camp and many looked in that direction just in time to see a large portion of the rock face break off near the end at the highest point where the valley began to open up. It slid down the slope amidst a cloud of dust and the crashing of trees being felled in its path. Once again there was terror among many in the camp. But then the shaking of the ground ended and everyone was looking about to assess the state of their own family and shelters, several of which had toppled over.

As soon as the dust began to settle and he saw his family was not among those few who had suffered some minor injury or other little disaster, Taymak was suddenly gripped by another sickening feeling in his insides. Without a word to Mawra, he signaled to Duhann to follow him. Together they set off at their quickest pace to head for the cave entrance. There were downed trees to climb over where the earth holding their roots in place on the slope had slid away. Even some large boulders had tumbled down from above, which father and son were forced to avoid. When they got to the base of the wall, Taymak saw immediately the large rock that jutted out and hid the narrow gash in the low rock face was no longer there. It must have been the big one they had just climbed passed, he thought as they moved quickly to get to the cave entrance as fast as possible.

A great deal of dust was still in the air, but Taymak could see instantly the land above the narrow gulley leading to the entrance had flowed down into it from above. The large amount of dirt and stone which that flow of moving earth carried with it had completely filled the little indentation in the low rock face to where it was almost level now with the side walls. The entrance to his cave, and his important work there, was now sealed, perhaps forever. The painter could only stand there with his heart racing, gaping helplessly at the disaster that had befallen him. Then Duhann, who must have already said something his father did not respond to, tugged at his arm and said.

"Father, is the cave also filled with the earth now? Are your pictures destroyed? What will the people do? They will have no place to come to summon the beast spirts, as uncle has said they will in the seasons to come."

Taymak was shocked into the present by his son's simple questions—the same ones he knew would be on others' lips when he brought the words of what happened here back to the camp. He thought for a few moments about these things, and more. Then, he turned, smiled briefly at his son, and replied.

"No, Duhann. I am certain the cave and the beasts we painted within are still as they should be. See there above. If the cave were filled with earth, there would be a great dip in the land on top, but it is as it was. Only the entrance and part of the passageway perhaps has been blocked. The true spirits of the cave will still have their power to call the beasts to us in this land. The people will soon understand this. As long as we remember the meaning of the cave, its power will not be lost to us. This land is ours now. Your children, Setha's children, all the people's children will make their fires here for as long as there are those among them who keep and honor the spirit of this cave—and the spirits we summoned forth inside who brought us here. No, I am no longer saddened at the thought we will never again stand in its darkness and stare upon what you and I together created there. We will remember it always.

"Come, Duhann" Taymak said as he smiled again and reached out his hand to affectionately rub his son's red hair, "we must go back down the slope and speak with the others now. There will be much to do to restore both the camp and the people's belief in all the old man promised us over there in the hidden darkness about the seasons that have come before—and all those beyond our sight yet to be born."

THE POTTER

AD 193

"You look tired, young man. Have you walked far today? Where are you headed?"

The young man paused a moment to take in the first words he had heard in two days. He brushed some dust from his worn tunic, laid down the heavy bundle he had slung across his shoulder, and replied to his questioner with the hint of a smile.

"I have been on the old road from my village on the other side of the gorge for two days. Yours is the first voice I have heard in that time, and 'yes' I am very tired. I slept alone last night in an abandoned hut near the road, but dared not make a fire for fear there might be robbers about. I am bound for the Tarn and the big Roman pottery nearby. I was told I could find work for my skills at that place by a man who knows someone there. Tell me, friend, will I be able to find shelter before darkness falls, and perhaps something to warm my insides if I continue on this path, or must I sleep with only the stars for a roof this night?"

"If you continue past the great rock cliff you will pass up ahead, you will come to the old Roman camp on top of the hill you will see beyond. There are some families living on top who will some-times take in travelers for a coin or two, and the Romans keep a small lookout post to watch the roads from time to time. But I doubt any soldiers will be there in this moon, and I would not trust to go to that place alone as you are. I have heard some bad things about the men who live up there and the small inn they keep. Listen, young man, you seem like an honest youth. If you will help me drive these swine up that little path over there, I am sure my wife can find enough bread and soft cheese to fill your belly for one night. There is a dry grain crib out of the wind where you are welcome to sleep, if you can stand the smell so close to the sties."

The older man laughed a little as he waved his arm for the weary traveler to follow him. Then he turned to continue with his task of driving the handful of variously sized hogs in the direction he was moving them when he had encountered the solitary young man on the narrow road. After his invitation, he didn't even both-er glancing back to see if the stranger was going to accept his offer of a place to stay the night or not. The young man sighed at the dubious prospect and picked up his bundle, which was wrapped in the worn and faded cloak his mother had given him to wrap his few possessions in when he left his family nearly three days before. The old cloak had been his only blanket for the past two nights and would have to serve him again he feared. Then he caught the first full whiff of the hogs he was beginning to catch up to just ahead of where his prospective host for the night was already yell-ing at and poking individual animals along with the long staff he carried.

It had not taken long to drive the swine up the winding road that led to the dilapidated farmstead which stood in the muddy field at the end of it. At one point the tired young man was forced to chase after a wayward pig's attempt to break away from the small herd when the older man pointed him after the fleeing animal and signaled for him to chase it back. The farmer laughed at the youth's obvious inexperience in performing such a routine task, until he was finally forced to yell at the young man to instruct him in the proper way to drive the adventurous pig back to the others. Still, it would be a small price to pay for a dry bed and something to eat the youth thought, as he at last managed to push the dirty animal in the direction he wanted it to go.

The farmer's wife seemed none too pleased at the prospect of feeding this unexpected guest when her husband instructed her to offer the stranger something to eat. Little was said as the three sat around the smoky fire in the corner of the stone and thatched hut, which seemed to the young man who was accustomed to much neater surroundings, to be not much cleaner than the pig sties he had passed on the way in. The woman, who seemed somewhat older than her husband and well past her child-bearing years, reluctantly gave him the end of a piece of bread, undoubtedly left over from the day before he thought, and a piece of hard cheese already beginning to mold on one end.

The young man accepted it graciously, however, despite the look in the woman's eye that made it clear this was all he would receive. He noticed the couple shared a loaf of that day's bread with some soft cheese for their meal. There was also a wonderful aroma emanating from something simmering in an iron cooking pot at the edge of the fire. His nose told him it most certainly contained at least a little pork, but he realized whatever it was would not be consumed until after he had left for the thatched, wattle and daub grain crib the farmer had pointed out to him when they first arrived.

The next morning, he was up before first light to make his way back to the main road that would lead him down to the River Tarn, sometime by the end of the day he hoped. He had asked the farmer the night before and been told a hard day's walking should bring him to the river, where he could then get directions for the place he sought. He was also eager to get back on the road early because the smell and the noise of the swine in their two pens close behind where he slept had been more than enough to awaken him at several points during the night. At least he had been dry and out of the wind, he thought when he wrapped and tied the old cloak around his bundle of the few possessions he had brought with him. When he did so, he found the last two of the apples his mother packed for him earlier and decided to eat one as soon as he set out and to save the other for a midday break, if nothing else turned up in the meantime. He sighed at that unhappy prospect as he shouldered the heavy bag once more and began to walk without looking back at the silent residence where his two strange hosts still slept. After only a few steps, his tired body told him he must find something more substantial to eat before this day was over or he would probably become too weak to continue his journey.

It did not take him long to reach and pass through the narrow opening leading out into the broader valley, which opened up from the tiny stream that led him out of the area of the deep gorge and surrounding hills forming the confines of the small world in which he had grown up. As he passed below the steep hill he had been warned to avoid by the swineherd the day before, he was glad he had heeded that warning when he saw the steep path he would have needed to climb to get to the small collection of structures on top. He could barely make out most of these from the distance. However, the Roman watchtower, which could be used to keep an eye on the intersecting narrow roads below, could still be seen clearly from any distance around.

He had traveled a short way to the north and east before as a boy; but this was his first journey so far south and toward the larger Tarn valley, where so many others he knew from childhood had migrated in the past to be nearer the various trading centers the Romans first began to set up there over a hundred years earlier. It was not an easy choice for him to leave his family behind, for how long he could not even guess. He only knew from what he had been told by a friend, who had seen the large pottery works the Romans kept at several locations along the river they called Tarnis, this must be his best chance to find an outlet for his pottery-making skills. He had steadily developed these since the first time he had sat at the wheel and held the finished product an old man helped him make many years before. Since that day he had not only learned to cast the wet clay into a pleasing shape but to carve it before it was fired; or to paint it after it was finished ways which seemed to give satisfaction both to him and to those who looked at his pots and desired to acquire them for their own use. His growing skills were even starting to help the rest of his family acquire the occasional necessity or even a rare small luxury, which might otherwise have been beyond their means.

There were other reasons for his difficult decision to leave the only home he knew to venture so far on his own. His family's once prosperous small farm had been all but reduced to a mere subsistence level after his father died leaving only his mother, older brother, a sister who had already left home, and himself. His father had been well-known locally for the horses he had bred and raised and from which the family once prospered when compared with most of their neighbors. However, one day when the young man was still a boy, Roman soldiers came and took all the family's horses. It seemed to him afterward his father never recovered from that unfortunate event in the family's fortunes, nor did he live long afterward. His own recent decision to head south to seek his future amongst those same Romans while his older brother maintained what was left of the small farm had seemed like an easy choice once his mother reluctantly gave her blessing to his venture. By this third day alone on the road, however, the inevitable feelings of homesickness, loneliness, and regret at his momentous decision were beginning to creep into the young man's thoughts as he plodded along, not knowing what awaited him at the end of his solitary journey.

Early in the afternoon he came upon a man and his wife leading a tired looking, broken down old horse, which was struggling to pull a small cart with two heavy and crudely made, wooden wheels. The rickety cart seemed to be loaded with baskets of freshly pulled carrots. The desire to speak with someone suddenly overwhelmed him and he asked the couple where they were headed with the hope he might get some information about a possible destination himself. The man replied they were also headed for a small settlement along the Tarn where there was a fair-sized market. They hoped to spend two days trading their produce before returning to their farm, which they had left only that morning.

When the youth asked the man also told him the large pottery he sought was upriver a short distance from the market village, but he would still not be able to walk there until the following day. There was no need for him to go past their own destination, the man said, and he was welcome to walk along with them. When the woman offered him two nice carrots from one of the baskets, it was an easy decision for him to make. He would find a place to sleep over until the following day and perhaps barter the smallest of the three pots he had in his pack when he got to this market for something more substantial to eat than stale bread and moldy cheese. Then, he would trust to the gods for a place to shelter for the night and hope the new day would bring him to his long-anticipated destination.

The next morning for the first time in four days he did not get up until well after the sun. It had been confirmed by more than one source the evening before that a walk of no more than half a day would bring him to the destination he had been imagining for nearly a month. Still, he was excited to finally get there, and he left the small market town on the banks of the Tarn as soon as he had prepared himself for the last walk he hoped to make for some time. His pack was lightened by the removal of the smallest of the pots he had brought with him to help prove his credentials and ability for the work he hoped to find. He had reluctantly traded the rather plain bowl more easily than he would have expected the evening before for an entire loaf of fresh bread, some newly made soft cheese, and half a smoked fish. It had been the first time he had gone to bed with a full stomach since his mother had filled it the night before he began his journey. He would chew on the remains of his bread as he walked up the well-worn path that followed the south bank of the river, which he was told would take him to his destination by the time the sun was high.

The young man's heart was beginning to pound noticeably by the time he saw the fires, the wide clearing, and the various structures in and around it, which must be the large pottery works he had heard so much about. Just beyond along the same path he was following he could also detect the presence of a small settlement similar to two he had passed through already that morning on his walk along the road beside the river. On a rise above the pottery and at a distance back from the river on an elevated terrace sat the well-shaded structure of what must be the villa of the Roman owner of the sprawling manufactory. It was by far the grandest structure he had ever seen, and the youth's mouth dropped open in amazement at the thought of what kind of person must live in such a place.

However, the path he was on led him away from that appealing sight and directly toward the cluster of buildings surrounding two large kilns down the slope below it. These were obviously the source of the smoke he had been seeing for some time curling into the bright blue morning sky above the fast-moving river flowing not far below the entire complex, which seemed to keep expanding as he came nearer. Familiar smells and sounds began to assault his senses, and he soon found himself among many very busy people, none of whom paid any notice of him as they passed by and moved in various directions to and from the bustling establishment.

There were no walls or gates to suggest to him where he might find someone responsible for greeting, or challenging, strangers. He began just to stroll about in the hope of finding someone or something that might lead him to discover what he should do next. At last, as he was wandering across the open space between some sort of workshop and a three-sided storage building in which he saw several of the largest clay pots he had ever seen, or even imagined, he was brought to a sudden stop by the sound of his name being called from somewhere off to his left.

"Athon, Athon! Is it really you? I cannot believe you have actually come. I had given up on seeing you again until my next visit home."

The young man turned instantly at the sound of his name to see his boyhood friend, the same person who had told him he should come to this place nearly half a year earlier. His face brightened immediately as he dropped his shoulder load, which he kept tied in a bundle on the end of the short stick he used to balance it as he alternately moved the load from shoulder to shoulder as he walked. Then, he extended both arms to grasp those of his friend, Peliot, who had just reached out to grab them.

"Yes, I have come at last. I had to wait to help my brother get in the first harvests, but my mother finally gave me her blessing to leave. It was a long walk, I must say. I have never been this far south before. This place is truly as wondrous as you said it was. Do you really think I will still be able to find work here, as you told me before?"

"Ha! Once they see your work, they will not let you get away. Do you have anything in that bundle of rags to convince them, as I told you to do when we talked last summer?"

"Yes, I have two pieces of my best work, I think. I had another nice, small bowl, but I traded it last night for some food. I ran out a day ago and there was little to be found on the way here."

"True, True. There are not many places a careful man would want to stay once you get beyond the gorge of our home valley.

But the people here along the Tarn seem to be more generous and used to dealing with strangers always passing through. Now then, pick up your bundle and come with me. There is someone you must meet before anything else is settled. We just call him 'The Greek', but he is the man who assigns the work and keeps an eye on everyone and everything that goes on here—and determines your payments! His real name is Aristides, but you must not address him by his name—only by *major domo*, which I think is the Roman talk for *the man who tells everyone else what to do.*"

Peliot laughed and grabbed Athon by the arm before he barely had time to pick up his bundle and stuff it under his other one. Then he led him off toward the longest building at the edge of the field where the large kilns sat in the middle of the surrounding structures. It was a low roofed, well-ventilated shed which Athon saw contained almost as many potters working at their wheels as he could count on the fingers of both hands. Everyone seemed busy, and his immediate thought was the question of how he could possibly fit into such a large operation as this place seemed to be. His friend looked about until he spotted a short man standing by a table of finished, wet clay pots, making marks on some sort of tablet he carried around his neck. Peliot put out his hand and told Athon to stand just inside the door and then walked over to the man, who Athon noticed was not covered by spattered clay as was nearly everyone else he had encountered since entering the pottery works' grounds. He watched as they exchanged a few words. Then the man known as "The Greek" stared over his way, laid down the tablet, and walked with Peliot back to where a suddenly very nervous Athon was standing and feeling conspicuously alone. The middle-aged man stopped, looked him over carefully for what seemed a long moment to Athon, and then spoke.

"So, you are this bowl painter Peliot has assaulted my ears about ever since I have put him in charge of the second kiln. He tells me you are not just another pot thrower who can sit at a wheel, but that I must see your skills for myself. Well, boy, Peliot says you have some of your work in that bundle under your arm. Are you going to show them to me or just stand there? I have important things to do and no time to waste on every farmer's son who walks in here looking for work."

Athon listened hard to understand the man's heavy accent of the words he was rapidly speaking. The young man was not accustomed to hearing his language spoken by those who had learned it later in life and used a different rhythm in speaking it. He said nothing but stooped down to untie his bundle wrapped in the old cloak. Inside were his spare shirt, an old pair of sandals, a small bag of his tools, and his lighter, newer tunic. Besides these, he had wrapped inside his extra leggings each of the two better pots he had brought with him. He slid the first one out and held it up for the man Aristides to grasp. It was a finely polished bowl of a deep red color. Around it Athon had carved an intricate pattern of intersecting straight lines and triangles. Some were deeper and wider than others and the overall appearance was one of regularity and symmetry that even the inexperienced eye could see were done both with great care and skill before the pot had been fired and finished with a high polish. The eye of Aristides, however, was hardly inexperienced, and he examined the bowl closely as he ran his fingers over the intricate outer surface and then into the smooth inside. He said nothing as he did so, and when he finished, he merely nodded and pointed toward the other legging as Athon slowly removed the second bowl from it. Aristides did not return the first pot, however, but laid it carefully on the ground beside him as he reached for the other one, which Athon was extending toward him.

The older man's eyes widened noticeably as he grasped the new offering in both hands as soon as he saw it. It was a larger bowl, but more shallow—something between a good-sized dish and a serving bowl. The highly polished outer surface had been

fired and buffed an even darker red than the first pot. The inside, however, had been painted the color of fresh cream, although not buffed to the same glossy surface as the outside of the vessel. Upon this softer, inside surface were painted in black the very realistic and finely detailed pictures of four running horses, which seemed to be chasing each other in some perpetual race around the middle of the bowl. At the center on the flattened bottom a geometrically perfect star or sun sign had been executed in the same fine, black brush strokes. Even the talented eye of Aristides was instantly impressed with what he was seeing. However, no one could have guessed at such thoughts from the fairly expressionless look he was able to maintain. Only his lips seemed to purse and move somewhat in the silent conversation that was going on in his head. Finally he looked up, and the first hint of a smile crept into the corners of his mouth as he spoke.

"Well, Peliot, I see there was some small justification for your enthusiasm when you spoke to me before. Athon, is it? If I may, I will keep these pots for a short time. There is someone else who must look at them before I can speak with you further. You will remain here as our guest, of course, until you are sent for. The day grows short soon and the hour for the end of our work day grows near. Your friend here will take care of you until you are summoned and will tell you what you must do next. Until then, get this young man something to eat, Peliot, and for the love of Jupiter, clean him up. Take him to the bath house first. Then young man, you must put on that clean shirt and tunic, and those fresh leggings in which these wonderful bowls we have here were hidden."

With that, The Greek carefully picked up the first bowl and with one in each hand strode through the door and disappeared. Athon merely stood there in shocked disbelief at what he had just heard. Peliot saw his blank expression and laughed at him once more. Then he helped Athon put the remains of his bundle back together. As they stood up, he took his younger friend by the arm and said.

"You see, Athon, I told you, and you should have come here sooner. I have never seen the *major domo* with so few words to say about anything or anyone, and he speaks in our words quite well. Wait until the first time he swears at you in that strange Greek tongue he uses when he gets really mad. But come on. Let's get something to eat before I take you down to the bathhouse. These Romans have the awful custom of bathing for no reason. But by the great goddess Epona, you do smell like one of her horses, I must say; or is that the odor of swine upon you? We have to get you cleaned up, and then I will show you how things work around here. Something tells me you are going to be staying with us for a while, my friend."

Dusk was just falling when Athon was finally summoned by a boy who was sent to find him in the barracks-like building Peliot took him to after his wonderful experience at the baths. He felt clean in a way he had not experienced since the previous summer, when he would occasionally bathe in the small stream that ran below the family farm. After he put on his spare shirt and tunic with his other pair of leggings, Athon felt almost like a new man and ready to face whatever wonder might occur next. When he asked about washing his old clothes, Peliot merely laughed and told him he knew a woman in the nearby village who would clean and mend them for him for the cost of what he would soon earn on one good pot. His friend winked at him at the mention of this woman, a young widow with a child he said, who also cooked for boatmen when they passed through on their way downriver to earn her way "until a new husband came along", Peliot laughed and winked again.

Peliot also told Athon this building would be his home while he worked here. The long structure was divided into small stalls down each side, much like the horse shed Athon could remember as a boy, where his father used to keep his best mares in the winter months. He was shown the empty one he could use, not far from where his friend kept one for himself. Inside each space was a straw-stuffed mattress made of old sail cloth, a crude three-legged stool, and a fair sized wooden box for his few personal possessions. On the low dividing walls were pegs to hang his clothes. Beyond these meager furnishings there was barely room to walk about.

When Athon asked if all the men who worked here stayed in such a small place, Peliot laughed again and replied only the "poor ones" like themselves lived here. Others, he said, were married and kept houses nearby in the village, or somewhere close on either side of the river. Peliot then told him he only stayed here part of the time himself. He had an "arrangement", as he called it, with the same young widow he had mentioned. He often spent his free time there when he brought her food, or other work, such as Athon's dirty clothes, to help her earn a coin or two. For this she was always "grateful" in a most acceptable manner, and Peliot again winked in a way even the inexperienced Athon could well understand.

When the boy arrived with the message for him, Athon asked his friend about the leather collar the youth wore. Peliot told him that it meant the boy was a slave, which was a class of human Athon had never personally encountered, even though he knew well the Roman reputation for such a practice. He also knew his own people, the Rutheni, had often kept slaves in the past. But now only wealthier ones who were close in some way with the Romans did so, and Athon had never known anyone who possessed such a servant. Peliot could not say where the light-skinned boy's tribe was from, and simply shrugged at Athon's question and answered he was probably from north or east and beyond the Rhenus River, where the Romans had been at war with the Allemani and other tribes for generations.

He also said there were other slaves, both male and female, about the pottery and especially in the villa's main house. That was where he had just been summoned apparently to meet with the master of the pottery works who lived there and whose family in Rome had built this complex years before and still owned it. To his surprise, Athon also learned that as large as this pottery appeared to be, it was not the only one in the Tarnis Valley—as the Romans named it—or in the larger, more populated area upriver closer to the Aveyron, which was the stream that flowed through the narrow gorges of his home valley. As he knew well enough, the clay deposits in these steep valleys were the best to be found in the entire great province of southern Gaul the Romans called Narbonnensis, and even beyond.

After Peliot carefully instructed him in how he was to behave and what he was to say when addressed by the master of the pottery, he was led to the short path that would take him up the slope and through the tall linden trees to the sprawling stone villa situated amidst them. Peliot left him there and told Athon he would see him when he returned and was eager to learn what kind of "offer" would be made to him. Then, Athon once more found himself alone as he cautiously approached the main entrance to the villa. There, the same boy who had delivered his summons earlier appeared to be sitting as if waiting for him to arrive. The youth stood up at his approach and simply motioned for Athon to follow him through a narrow entrance and then across a well-kept courtyard with a stone fountain in its center to the doorway of another section of the surrounding structure on the opposite side. At that point, he was halted in a high-ceilinged, unfurnished waiting area of some sort where the boy then left him standing alone again.

It took a nervous Athon a few moments to look about before he realized he was standing in the middle of one of the most remarkable things he had ever seen. As he stared down in amazement he saw the spectacular outlines of the mosaic he stood upon. Even in the dimming light he could make out the clear scene depicted in the variously colored, tiny stones that seemed to jump off the flat surface beneath his feet to engulf him into it—almost as if he was himself a part of the action pictured below. There was a hunter with a bow and several dogs pursuing a great stag, with trees, birds, and even small plants. For the eye of an artist trained to see every detail of the natural world around him, as Athon had taught himself to be, the entire effect was almost beyond belief. He wanted to stoop to run his hands over the minute stone pieces making up the picture, but all he could do was stand and gape at it in open-mouth bewilderment at the skill and patience of the artist who must first have first conceived and then created such a wonderful thing.

Just then, however, he heard the sound of approaching feet coming from inside the open doorway he was facing and forced his eyes and his thoughts back into the present. A moment later the now familiar form and face of Aristides appeared, looked him over from head to toe, nodded in apparent satisfaction, and then beckoned Athon to follow him into the spacious room beyond. There were other wonders for the young man to behold when he crossed the smooth, stone floor as they headed for a dark-curtained area. These red curtains surrounded on three sides a well-carved table and beautifully made chairs, two long sofas with furs upon them, and two remarkable iron tripods upon which were set bronze braziers, which were glowing with the light of two steady flames, which illuminated that entire side of the large room. Athon noticed immediately his two bowls standing on the far side of the long table, which were surrounded by parchment scrolls, two carved wooden boxes, a small oil lamp, and one or two other items he did not recognize.

A moment later a tall, well-proportioned man entered from behind the scarlet curtain and walked immediately to the far side of the long table opposite where Athon had come to a halt, with Aristides a few steps off to his left. The beardless man appeared to Athon to be in his middle years. He was wearing a single piece, white tunic embroidered in dark green lines, the intricate pattern of which Athon could not make out. However, the cloth was of the lightest and finest he had ever seen and seemed to move with the same effortless grace as the man who wore it when he walked. Athon swallowed hard to clear his thoughts just as the man stopped, picked up first one of the two bowls in front of him to look it over briefly, set it back down carefully, and then did the same for the other one. Then he looked up and spoke in Athon's language, but with an accent that was even thicker and less practiced than the one Aristides had used. It was obvious to his young listener this man must have picked up the more unusual speech of the local Rutheni people at a much later point in his life.

"You must be Athon, who I am told has come far to seek to join us. I must say, Aristides, I expected to see a man fuller in his years when you first brought me these two bowls. I am Marcus Petronnius, young man, and it is my family who owns this pottery and all the land you see about it. Tell me, did you make these bowls as well as place these wonderful figures on them? I am told you walked far to get here. From what distant place do you come to us?"

"Yes, *Dominus*," Athon responded, with the proper form of address he had been instructed to use when speaking to the master of the villa. "The bowls were cast by own hands. I have walked four days from the valley of the Aveyron to the north. My family has a farm there just beyond the deep-walled end of the gorge, above where the river starts to widen."

"Ah, yes. We have heard there may be good clays to be had in that direction, have we not, Aristides?" The Greek responded with a simple affirmative nod. "I can also see you have a remarkable eye for horses, young man. Tell me, how did you come by such a skill?"

125

"My father raised fine horses while he lived, *Dominus*. I grew up around them as a boy and spent my youth caring for and studying them every day. They are the noblest of animals, and I often portray them on the bowls I paint."

"Indeed, Athon, they are noble beasts, and you draw and paint them quite well. We have not much need for another pot maker at this time. But a painter of fine bowls is a skill we can always use. I believe we can make a place for you here, if it is your desire to remain with us."

Athon's mouth had gone dry, but he managed to bow his head slightly and respond it was his wish to work here for as long as he was welcome. Marcus Pretonnius smiled subtly and then looked over at Aristides who also was revealing the beginnings of a knowing smile.

"Good, then it is agreed. Aristides will instruct you shortly in your duties and the other arrangements to be agreed upon. I look forward to following your work in the coming days and months, young man."

Then, he turned away from Athon to address Aristides more directly for the first time. However, when he spoke it was in the language of the Romans and not the local language, and a nervous Athon could only stand there in mute ignorance, since he understood nothing of what was being spoken—only that it must surely have something to do with him or with what had just been said.

"Treat the boy well, Aristides. I believe he is going to make us a lot of money. If the horses on that bowl there were turned into centaurs, the fine shops of Rome and Athens, and even our buyers in Hispania and beyond, will go mad for all we can supply. Be fair with your offer, but not overly generous. I doubt if this young man has ever had as much as two silver coins in his hand at the same time. Your problem will be how to introduce him to Arcturus. I do not want him to drive this one off like he did the last young apprentice painter we gave him. Besides, this boy may be far more gifted than even Arcturus ever was, and I believe his skills will develop beyond what we can imagine—if he is treated properly. But we must still handle the old man carefully, even though it seems he grows more obstinate with every new gray hair that appears upon his head."

Aristides merely nodded in agreement at Marcus Petronnius's words. He had already been pondering how he could best introduce Athon to the pottery works' master painter, who would undoubtedly resent both the youth's obvious talent and the fact his own brush hand was again being called into question by the introduction of another "boy" to train in his workshop. Then, the *Dominus* motioned for Athon to come forward to the edge of the table. He opened the small box just beyond the two bowls, removed a pair of shiny brass coins, and extended them to Athon with a nod he should accept them. Marcus smiled and said these were payment for the two bowls—which he would keep—and he hoped these were but the first of many such coins Athon would earn in his time here. At that, he nodded to Aristides and departed in the same abrupt manner as he had entered only moments before.

Aristides came over to stand beside Athon, who was still fixed in place with the two brass sestertii clutched tightly in his hand. The Greek looked at his fist and smiled knowingly. He had seen the effect on more than one occasion of even a single coin on these local people who came to them from the poorer country villages. He placed his hand softly on the boy's upper arm to get his attention and spoke in an almost fatherly manner.

"The *Dominus* can be a most generous man. Those two sestertii are as much as he would pay a master painter for those two bowls of yours. But if you are to work here, there are things you must agree to before we can assign you a position. You will not be shaping your own bowls here. In truth, we only make so many original bowls or other vessels. Much of our production is done by the use of molds, a thing I am certain you have not seen before. But it is of no consequence. We have other painters for those. You will be assigned to our master painter, Arcturus. He will instruct you in what you must do when you see him tomorrow. I will speak to him first; but I will say this to you now, Athon, you must do your best not to anger this man. He can be difficult to work for. However, if you have a problem you cannot resolve, or a strong idea you wish to put forward, you must come to me first. Do you understand this clearly?" Athon merely nodded in reply, and Aristides continued.

"Good, then. You will be paid one copper or brass dupondius for each bowl you complete. That is one half the value of each of those coins the Master just gave you. Anything that is different, or of your own design as were those two, you will receive the same one sestertius for those. If you break or damage beyond use any piece you are working on through your own error, your pay will be reduced by two times the value of the bowl, since you will also have destroyed some other man's work. You will receive payment on the first day of the new month, less a small charge of one quadrium per day for the cost of bread. Your other food will be provided at the end of each day with the other workers from the main kitchen. You will be shown how this is done by Peliot or someone else. Anything in addition to that, or wine beyond your one cup a day allowance, you can purchase in the village or from one of the traders who are always setting up just outside the pottery. Everything else you must provide for yourself—except the place to sleep which you have already been shown, of course. Other rules about your behavior here or what Arcturus may tell you will be given to you later by him. Do you understand these conditions and accept them, or do you have any questions?"

Athon could think of nothing else to ask, even though he had no idea what value a quadrium or even a dupondius carried, but replied quickly he agreed. His head was still spinning at the thought of the coins in his hand and how many more he could earn in the months ahead. He warmed inside at the thought of how much these would mean to his mother and brother, once he figured out a way to get them back to his home. Perhaps he thought, Peliot could help him figure that out. But for now, he turned to follow Aristides, who had signaled he should follow him out of the villa. Outside, full darkness had almost set in and the older man walked with him a short way before wishing him a good night and saying he would see him first thing in the morning. Athon recalled Peliot had told him the Greek had a wife and family at the far edge of the nearby village, and he assumed the man who would soon become important in his life in this place of strangers was eager to return to those with whom he frequently spent far too little of his always busy days.

By the time Athon returned to what was to be his new home, he found Peliot waiting anxiously to interrogate him on every detail of what had happened to him in the great house on the terrace, which looked down over the lives of all those below whom it controlled in so many ways. When he showed his friend the two coins the Master paid for his bowls and told him he would receive that same amount for others of equal quality in the future, Peliot informed him this was as much or more than even the older potters made for throwing a special vessel. Athon had to ask him what the real value of the different amounts he had been promised were, and when he was told what each would purchase in the village the young man was not quite as excited as he had been earlier about his prospects for accumulating a large amount for later use. Still, it was real Roman money and not the old, now nearly worthless copper coins his people had once produced and which were still mostly found in some remote places, such as in the far valley from which he came. Athon could see he must be wary of acquiring too many of the desirable things he had already seen in the small markets along the river he noticed in the past two days, if he was to have enough left over to fulfill his dream of restoring his family farm—and his family's life—to its once more prosperous condition.

The young man finally went to sleep that night with great difficulty. So many new thoughts were racing around in his head. They were much like the painted horses on his bowl—which he would probably never see again, but couldn't help but imagine what use it might be put to in so wondrous a place as he had just visited. He also felt concern about this man Arcturus, for whom he would apparently be assigned to work the next day. The Greek's words of caution concerning the older man certainly gave him pause; but he knew there was nothing he could do about any of that until he found out just what his duties would be. This part, at least, fully excited Athon as he was already beginning to imagine and lay out in his mind the many designs and scenes—such as the beautiful mosaic he had stood upon—he, also, would soon be in a position to create and have others marvel upon as well.

The half-moon was nearly full high before an excited Athon eventually found the sleep his tired body finally, and forcefully, reminded him it needed. It came not long after he heard Peliot creep as silently as he could back into his little "room" from where he was returning from a visit to the widow in the village, as he had explained when he left earlier. Peliot's and Athon's sleeping spaces were separated only by the one of an older man, whose loud snoring Athon was already starting to fear was going to become a regular part of his new life as well from this day forward.

The next morning Athon waited for Aristides to appear near the two great kilns in the open center of the complex of structures. He had gone there with Peliot, whose position it was to supervise the loading, firing, and unloading of the larger of the two mounded pits. That kiln was used mainly for the mass production bowls, jars, and other vessels the great manufactory produced in large quantities. The nearby smaller kiln, as Peliot explained, was reserved for finer wares, or those needing to be fired at a higher temperature. For the first time, Athon noticed the tall stacks of wood at more than one location around the wide field, which comprised the fuel for the demanding kilns and many other fires.

By the end of that first day he would have taken notice of the various carts of different sizes that made daily deliveries of wood or clay. Some of these would leave immediately, while others would remain until they were reloaded with various pots to be taken to destinations, which Athon could not yet visualize. Indeed, as he would learn later, it was not just the excellent local clays that had made this valley and the surrounding area an important source for finished pottery used throughout the vast Roman Empire. It was also the great forests which bordered the fast-flowing rivers which allowed both the pottery manufacturing and the many equally important ironworks in the region to thrive. The Romans had come to conquer over two centuries earlier. However, they stayed and settled because the land and the people supplied all the things they needed to produce the kind of massive wealth that continually flowed into Rome and the other great cities of the empire from many lands and from the hands of many different, conquered peoples.

Those vast forests also supplied the wood for the many boats that were built along the smaller rivers, like the Tarnis, which flowed down to the great river Garumna, which would later be known as the Garonne. It led west to the major port city of Burdigala, or Bordeaux as it would be called one day. That important town was situated on the broad estuary the river created not far below the narrow channel separating the far-flung interior of southern Gaul from the important province of Britannia. From Burdigala, waiting ships carried the pottery Athon was to help produce to and around Hispania; back through the Pillars of Hercules, and on to

Rome; or even as far as Greece, Byzantium, and the eastern provinces. The great families of Rome, like the Petronnii who owned this pottery, dominated these far lands with huge estates. These were created from their past wars of conquest and run in absentia or directly by lesser members of the family—men like Marcus Petronnius. Altogether, it formed a vast, interlocking system that would eventually spread Roman culture into many lands, which would forever change the people of those lands in countless ways, long after the Romans left, became absorbed into the local populations, or were driven away.

Athon was about to become one of those people whose life would never be the same, once he came into close contact with all that was Rome—and what it meant to be the subject of such a power. Aristides, whose own great culture had long ago been absorbed by the Roman expansion machine, found the young man that morning standing close to the kilns and watching the products of the previous day's firing being carefully unloaded. There were hundreds of smaller vessels being removed from the stone platforms surrounding the yawning maw of the giant cone, once the top level of bricks had been removed. The young potter was fascinated by the scale of the operation, even though it was merely a vastly larger version of the same type of kiln he often built for his own use. Aristides surprised him by appearing unannounced as he was watching the process, which would take all morning before the kiln could again be reloaded and new fires built underneath. Athon suddenly felt as if he had been caught doing something or standing somewhere he was not supposed to, until the *major domo* greeted him enthusiastically.

"Well, I see you are already about and learning something of what we do here. Not the kind of kiln you are used to seeing, I would guess. But come with me, Athon, I have been to the painting shed and Arcturus is expecting you. He was not as unhappy at the prospect of a new apprentice as I thought he would be. But you must still be careful to use your eyes and ears and not your tongue in this place, at least until the two of you have come to know each other a little."

Aristides then led Athon to a smaller, open-sided shed on the far side of the complex back in the direction of the villa and just at the bottom of the slope, where a couple of tall trees stood nearby and cast their shade over the edge of the elongated, thatched shed. Here, there was little danger of a spark from the kilns carrying so far, and it was the first thatched roof made in the local style Athon had seen. Inside were two long tables and some small stands of shelving. There was also a wood cabinet, which he would quickly learn contained the better paint pigments and the scrolls or parchments upon which the many master designs were kept. The one table was covered with vessels of many shapes, and Athon could quickly see as soon as they entered these pieces were more finished and much different than the ordinary ones he had just witnessed Peliot and others removing from the large kiln. At the other table, there were fewer vessels and several scrolls spread out and held down by stones at the corners. Paint bowls and brushes of different sizes were strewn about. In the center of it all sat an older man with a short beard and unkempt hair, both of which were streaked with grey well mixed through the once jet-black strands.

"Arcturus, this is the young man of whom we just spoke. His name is Athon, and he has come from a valley not far to the north of here. I will leave the both of you to get to know one another. I have had no time to instruct Athon in the rules we expect all of those who work here to follow. Perhaps, this morning would be a good opportunity for you to do so. I must go now to attend to the matter of which we were speaking before. May the gods continue to favor you in your work."

With that, Aristides left Athon standing at the entrance to the painter's shed—once again waiting for another new person to tell him what he must do next. Athon resigned himself to the fact he was going to have to get used to this very situation, at least for the next several days if not longer. Meanwhile, Arcturus forced himself slowly to his feet and walked toward this new arrival, who was waiting expectantly for whatever would happen next. The shorter Arcturus looked Athon over, staring particularly at his hands as they hung loosely at his sides, and then spoke in a manner that gave no indication of anything he might be feeling about this unexpected intrusion into his private, little world.

"The Greek tells me, boy, you fancy yourself a painter of pots. He also says I have instructions directly from the Master, Marcus Petronnius himself, to instruct you personally, as if you were someone I myself had chosen from those many down below in the pot shops over there—those who would seek to move up and one day gain the crown of 'Master Painter' to wear upon their own heads here in my place. We shall see. We shall see. But come along, Athon, is it? It will not take long to learn if you are worth any more of my time than was that last clumsy, dirt clod of a boy they sent me."

Athon swallowed heard at this somewhat unpleasant greeting, even though he had been prepared for something of the sort. He was also surprised at the older man's excellent use of the local dialect. It contained little of the heavy accent the *Dominus* had used the night before, or even of the more practiced Aristides. Athon wondered how long Arcturus had been here and where his original home might have been, since it was immediately obvious he was neither Rutheni, nor Roman. Arcturus quickly led him to the space between the tables and began to explain the things he was pointing out and where other items he could not see might be found. Athon said nothing, however, although he was already happy he would be doing his work in the natural light of the open shed, and not by some artificial lamp or inside a darkened space as he had feared when he first saw inside the other buildings.

When Arcturus asked if he had any questions, Athon merely shook his head to say *No.* He was suddenly unsure about just how he should address this man, who was now to rule much of his daily life. He wanted to ask how a finished piece would be determined in order to receive his pay, but he could think of no good way to do this. Finally, Arcturus informed him at the end of each day he and he alone would judge a piece as finished or not and set it aside, where the Greek would then come by and record it on one of his many wax tablets. That daily count would decide his pay at the end of each lunar month, less any charges against him. He was also warned once again about the charge for breaking or damaging a piece—or a paint pot, or for losing a good brush, or any other necessary implement, the importance of which Arcturus seemed especially eager to stress.

Arcturus then went on to discuss other rules he considered important, mostly about places Athon could or could not go, how to behave toward any of the women who also worked in certain parts of the facility, and how to act with the many, sometimes important, visitors who frequently stopped by or were brought to the "painting house" as he would soon learn to call his new workplace. Arcturus was about to speak of his personal rules about no eating in the shed, where the water jar was to be kept, and such routine things when a sudden commotion in the main area near the kilns caught their attention. Arcturus stopped instantly, nodded in that direction, and calmly said.

"Come, boy. I was going to talk about punishments for those who do not follow the rules or do as they are told here. But we will go down near the kilns so you may see for yourself how "Roman Justice" is meted out in this place."

A curious Athon followed Arcturus down the sloping path that led between two storage buildings into the open space around the kilns. There, a growing crowd was spilling out of the various structures to gather near a post sunk into the ground, which he had paid no notice of when he passed it earlier. He immediately saw a man being tied facing the post while two other men dressed as soldiers stood by. Their leather armor was badly worn and the swords they carried at their sides appeared to be of a sort that had not been in use for a long time. One of them stood close by the man tied to the post, while the other produced a short whip and approached the back of the tied man. By then Athon and Arcturus had arrived not far away, where they stopped together to witness what was about to happen. Just then, Aristides walked forward from the direction of the villa and the buzzing of the crowd of on-lookers immediately ceased. When he reached the post, the Greek stopped and spoke in a voice that was far more forceful than any Athon had heard come from his lips earlier.

"This man, Bithias the woodcutter, has been judged and found guilty by our Master, Marcus Petronnius, of the offense of the theft of six sestertii from the house of Lucius Barcanum, the candle maker in the village. He has confessed his guilt before witnesses and will now be punished. He will receive lashes upon his back in the number of three for each sestertius stolen. Then, he will be made to work in the clay pits without pay for one full annum. May all of you present and the gods above witness the shame of one who has betrayed the trust the great house of Petronnius has falsely placed in this man. Let the punishment now be given."

After those words, the surrounding silence was broken only by the cracking of the lash upon the man's bare back and the gradually increasing moans with which he received each new one, until the eighteenth blow had fallen upon his bleeding flesh. At that point, he was untied and his slumping body was virtually dragged away to a waiting four-wheel cart, which Athon suddenly remembered had been standing near the same entrance to the pottery when he passed through only the day before. Except for a seat for the driver, the cart was enclosed in heavy wood with flattened iron bars to cover the open spaces. Inside, he could just make out three or four shadowy figures, which were soon joined by the unfortunate man who had just been scourged. As soon as Arcturus saw the man was in the wagon, he motioned for Athon to follow him back up the slope to the "painting house" while the rest of the assembled crowd also began to drift back to their work places. When they arrived, he turned, pointed back to where the heavy wagon was just then pulling away, and spoke.

"Ahh, it was a just punishment for a small crime. Our Master Marcus Petronnius is indeed a merciful man, as many have noted before. It is the good fortune of that miserable woodcutter he was not found guilty of such a crime in Rome, or in one of the towns nearer the coast. Had he been so judged in Rome, he would no doubt have been sent to the arena as fodder for the gladiators and the amusement of our Emperor, the 'Divine' Commodus. Or he might just as well have been sent to the galleys to row away the last few months of his hapless life, before his worn-out body was cast into the sea to feed the fishes.

"But the lesson here, young Athon, is the rules are to be heeded by all in this place. You will find most of our Roman masters have little care for those who break them. This woodcutter will likely survive his year in the clay pits, even though it is a hard life. The others in that wagon you saw pulling away must have been judged by the *Legatus* down in Tolosa. They will be heading for the clay pits upriver as well. But I suspect the length of their punishments will be much harder for them to endure. But come, the sun is nearly high and the best time for painting without shadows is upon us. Let us see what you can do with a brush in your hand. The Greek tells me you like to paint horses."

Arcturus motioned Athon back into the painting house and removed a thick, well-used scroll from the wooden cabinet. He spread it onto the long table, weighted it down, and then began to point out several figures drawn upon it. Athon quickly learned these were various star configurations and their Roman names, some of which mirrored the stories from his own people's beliefs. There was the archer, the bull, the fish, the twins, and others. But there were also strange shapes and creatures with which he was not familiar. Finally, Arcturus pointed out the half man, half horse form of the Centaur, looked Athon in the eye, smiled, and said.

"So then, let us begin with this one. Here is a useless bowl with a crack no one made the effort to find before they sent it up here to be painted. Take that brush there and show me the paints you would use to make this figure inside the bowl. There is another stool in the back, or you may sit on the ground if you prefer. Bring me the vessel when you have finished."

"In what manner shall I paint these figures, Master Arcturus?"

"Why, in any manner you choose, boy. Show me what you see in them and let your brush reveal what your mind's eye tells you. And do not call me 'Master'. There is only one Master in this place, and he lives in that villa up there. I am Arcturus, and that is the way you will address me. We are all of us who carry no Roman blood in our veins equal here. You are of the many Ruthenii tribes in these valleys and must surely know the ways of our Roman 'masters' by this point in your life."

Indeed, he did, and for the first time Athon began to get a glimpse into the true feelings of Arcturus for those he had come so far to serve. He had assumed Arcturus, who bore a Roman sounding name, must come from the land of Italia to the south; but it would be some days before Arcturus's story was revealed to him. In the meantime, he went off to the far edge of the shed where the afternoon light was beginning to stream in; spread out the old piece of paint-splattered sail cloth he found in a corner; and then went to the table to retrieve the items he would need. Finally, he took up the bowl, saw the slight crack down the side that would obviously make it useless, and examined the drawing of the centaur one more time to commit its details to his practiced memory.

Then he returned to the spot he had picked out, sat down on the ground as he always preferred when painting or carving a pot, and began to work. The sunlight was beginning to fade when he was finally satisfied he had accomplished what he wanted with the bowl. He stood up, took a final look at it, and then walked over to the table where Arcturus had been working all afternoon on several similar bowls spread out before him. Athon had noticed earlier he was painting the identical pattern on each one, as he worked the same parts of his design on each bowl in succession, before he switched brushes or colors to again paint on each in turn. It was something Athon had never seen before, but it immediately made good sense to him. He waited for Arcturus to look up at him, and then he laid his completed bowl down on the table for the older man to see. The master painter picked it up, examined it carefully, and then looked up at Athon with a strange look on his face.

"I have not imagined two centaurs painted in this fashion or in this position before. I see the horse in the figure as much as I do the man. Perhaps, the Roman wives in the shops of Italia will like it, perhaps not; but it will be something they are not used to seeing, for certain. You have a good command of the small brush and an eye for detail, I must say, young man. It is just possible we can find a place for you here, if you are willing to learn to be a little less free with your imagination. Now then, there is just enough light for you to take one of these wet bowls that have just come up from the potter's shed over there and show me what you can do with a carving knife, before we cover that lot up with wet cloth until I can get to them in the new day. Use the pattern you see on that third bowl on the second shelf behind you, and let us hope you can help me with the larger cuts while I do the fine lines tomorrow, before they dry out in the afternoon's light."

Athon picked up the two bowls and took both to where he had been painting. However, he did not take the two knives on the end of the table Arcturus had indicated for him to use. When he sat back down, he reached into the small pouch he wore on his waist band and removed three, thin blades of the gray flint from near his home, which he used for carving the wet clay of his own pots before firing them. Athon much preferred the thinness of these sharp-edged stone knives, especially for trimming rims and incising extra fine lines on his pots. The pattern on the bowl Arcturus told him to copy was not a difficult or especially intricate one, and Athon seemed to work with amazing speed as he quickly turned the small bowl in his hand. As slow as he was with his detailed painting while he visualized the complex scenes he often created, Athon was just the opposite with the geometric patterns he had a sure gift for carving. When he was finished, he once again stood and took his bowl over to where Arcturus had been watching him out of the corner of his eye, as he finished up his own work for the day. When Athon set the bowl in front of him, the painter did not need to pick it up to see the exact pattern he had wanted executed already completed around the small bowl.

"I saw you using your flints on this," he smiled. "You truly are a Rutheni. My first wife's father used such blades from time to time for many small tasks in his leather and harness shop. Perhaps, The Greek has spoken truly when he advised me of your skills. I can see I may not have to take time from my own work to clean up your messes, as I had to do with those last two they sent me to train. Even that skilled Dacian slave they gave me for a time before he ran off and disappeared was not this good."

At that, Arcturus carefully picked up the damp clay bowl Athon had just set down, turned it over, and used a small, pointed stick to make some sort of mark on the bottom of the bowl. Then, he turned it back over and held it up for Athon to take a look at it. A slight smile was almost visible on the older man's face when Athon reached out to take it from him. As he let go, Arcturus nodded toward the end of the table where his finished work sat.

"Set this one over there with the others. I have placed a mark on the bottom that will let the Greek know it is one of your pots and not mine. Tomorrow, I will show you this mark; but only I can place it on your finished work, understand? The mark of Arcturus is esteemed in many lands, I am told, and so shall yours be—if you desire it and continue to grow in your skills. So then, young Athon, you have earned your first coin here. Let us hope there will be many more to come. But the shadows grow long, and my hands are tired. We must always leave time at the end our day for cleaning our brushes, and putting away the paints and the scrolls before we leave. Then, I will walk you to the kitchen on my way out and we will see what the cook has made for us today. I doubt it will be anything new, but it will be hot and perhaps fill our bellies. If nothing else the cup of wine is always a good ending for the day."

After about ten days, Athon had fallen into the routine that would mark much of his life in the months to come—or so he thought. Although most of the work was repetitive and Arcturus could be a demanding "master", Athon caught on quickly and was already finding certain familiar patterns more interesting or challenging to do when he was called upon to paint or carve on the various vessels set before him. Nevertheless, he was beginning to long for the opportunity to express some new manner of executing these patterns, or even one of his own ideas, which would often jump into his fertile imagination as he was painting. However, to this point any such opportunity was denied him. Then one morning Aristides appeared at the painting house and held a brief conversation with Arcturus. When the *major domo* left, Arcturus called him over and simply stated to Athon from this day forward he would be allowed to create one painted bowl of his own design every third day. If it was accepted when the pot counts were made, he would be paid one extra sestertius for that pot only.

Athon soon discovered from comments his mentor often let slip that the older man held no great affection for the Romans for whom he toiled. Late one afternoon as they were cleaning up, he managed to ask Arcturus from what land he came and how he had come to speak the local language as fluently and with as little accent as he now did. The older man's reply surprised him in more than one way when he willingly answered the questions the young man would not have dared to ask him earlier.

"I come from a land in far Italia known as Etruria. It was once a great and ancient power, and known, I must say, far and wide for its fine pottery. But then, in the distant past, the warlike Romans rose and conquered my people, as they did all the many tribes of that land. I was born into a good family that lived on a great estate, even larger than this one, which was also owned by the powerful family of the Petronnii. When I was a young man, not much older than you, Athon, I was recognized as having some skill at the pottery in which I worked. I was sent here, when this estate was acquired by that family in a manner I do not know. Perhaps, they gained this land in one of the many wars fought in those days, or perhaps one of your many Rutheni leaders sold it for his own gain, as sometimes happened back then I have been told. I do not know or really care, only that I had to come here.

"I was here only a year or so when I met and married a Rutheni woman from upriver near the town of Albium. I brought her here to live and we were happy for many years. But then she caught a fever from some soldiers passing through, as I was told, and she died. So did the daughter she had borne me, who was only a child then. We also had a son. He was killed only three years past now, while serving as an archer with the legions in a battle with the Allemani tribes somewhere on the other side of the Rhenus River.   Sadly, he is buried there in an unknown grave I shall never see. Not long after my first wife died I married another Rutheni woman. But that time I did not choose as wisely. She was too young, I think, and ran off downriver with a boatman only two years later. I have not seen or heard of her since. So you see, Athon, there is good reason why I speak your language so well; because it has become so close to my head, and my heart, much more now even than the one I was born to.

"As for my love for the Romans, I should think I am not alone in my feelings for how they treat many of those whose lands they have taken for their own. But do not get me wrong, Athon, there are some among them—like our Master, Marcus Petronnius—who are good and fair men. He has always treated me well here, even if my memories of his family from the days of my youth are not as pleasant. The noble and truly divine Emperor, the great Marcus Aurelius, ruled us wisely then for many years and forbade many of the bad practices of those who had come before him. But since his death, his reign of peace in these lands is threatened by the actions of his unpredictable son, this Commodus, who now rules in Rome with an iron fist—or so I have learned from those who pass through here on their way north and when they feel free to speak of such things.

"Look here," Arcturus said as he reached into his belt purse and pulled out a silver coin larger than any Athon had yet seen. "I traded a matched pair of fine, decorated drinking cups to a wine merchant up from Rome not long ago for this." Then he looked about to be certain no one was close, lowered his voice, and passed the coin over to a silent Athon.

"Here, my young friend, gaze upon the face of a madman. It is the likeness of this Emperor Commodus, whom I have been told has already caused the death of many of the people from my old home lands. Let us hope his reach does not soon extend here."

Athon looked at the face on the coin for an instant, and then handed it back to Arcturus. He was not sure what he was supposed

to have seen in it, or why the older man had made a point of showing it to him. But in that moment, he felt that the two of them had
achieved a sort of closeness beyond their past working relationship.
Perhaps, the young man thought for an instant, it was the sadness
he saw earlier in the old painter's eyes at the mention of his son's
death and burial in a far land, and Athon's realization he must be
about the same age that son would have been at the time. In any
event, the very next day he began to experience a softening in the
older man's attitude toward him and a new eagerness, almost, to
help his young student with things he had not shown him before.

The following morning Athon noticed Marcus Petronnius riding down the slope from the villa on his fine, gray stallion, accompanied by the same two soldiers he had seen before. This was
not the first time he had noticed the Master leaving. Athon knew
the *Dominus* had many duties beyond the pottery works, since the
great estate he oversaw conducted many other important activities
close by. In fact, it was self-sustaining in most every respect. There
was an ironworks upriver he soon learned, as well as boat-building
sites, and the clay quarries. There were farms that produced the
foods they ate, and vineyards for the wines they drank and also ex-
ported in some of the long jars made here at the pottery. Almost
all their needs were produced locally on the farms, forests, or in
the villages; and many of these products were also sent to far off
lands as well. Only the wheat for their bread, which was not grown
so much locally, had to be brought here in great quantities from
the broader plains to the south near the Middle Sea, or across the
mountains from Hispania.

The morning was cloudy and Athon moved his old canvas outside the shed to gain more light for the fine lines he was incising
on a set of matching, unfired bowls. It was something he had started doing in the mornings, before the light was high enough not to
cast too many shadows across his hands. It was also closer to the
small fire Arcturus would usually build nearby on the increasingly

cold mornings of the advancing season. Out of the corner of his eye, Athon happened to notice Arcturus get up from his table and walk over to where he was sitting on the ground. He nodded back toward the slope leading up to the villa and spoke in a low tone.

"It seems we are about to get a visit from the young mistress of the villa. Be alert and watch your tongue. If the past is any path to the present, I fear she will ask you many questions."

Arcturus then returned quickly to his work inside the shed, and Athon looked in the direction he had indicated. A tall girl dressed in what appeared to be riding clothes was striding confidently down the slope directly toward where he was sitting. Athon suddenly felt a new kind of nervousness as he glanced toward Arcturus, who had already sat back down—too late to ask the older man how he should address this girl. He set the bowl in his hand down and picked up another one he had not yet started to carve. He did not want to run the risk of ruining the delicate lines he was incising with his flint blade in case this girl intended to interrupt him in some way. As soon as she came near, she stopped to stand directly above him, looked at the bowls he was working on, and without any introduction whatsoever began to speak directly to him.

"You are the new painter, the one called Athon, are you not? I see you are dressed as a Rutheni. I have some Rutheni blood, myself. Does that shock you? You are the one who painted the fine bowl with the running horses on it father keeps on his desk. I thought you would be much older. Will your man's beard, when you get it, be as dark red as the hair on your head, Athon, the bowl painter?" She grinned openly as she nodded toward the first hairs of manhood Athon had begun to sprout on his chin. She did not wait for an answer, but quickly continued.

"My father said he would take me riding when he returned, but he is late, so I have come to watch for him. Will it disturb you if I wait for him here and watch you work?"

"No, you will not disturb me while you wait, and what would you know of a man's beard?"

He responded without heeding Arcturus's warning, and when he saw a slight blush appear on the girl's cheek, he instantly regretted his reply. But she had been so forward herself, and he found the remark about his hair somewhat offensive as she stood there looking down on him. He spoke up quickly to get himself out of the potential predicament his thoughtless tongue might have just created.

"And *yes*, I am the one who painted the bowl with the running horses upon it the *Dominus* was generous enough to purchase from me." The information that Marcus Petronnius still kept his bowl on his working table sent a wave of gratification through Athon at the thought of the girl's words. However, she rapidly changed the direction of the conversation once more before he could speak again.

"I have my own horse, you know. Her name is *Medea*. Father gave her to me on my last birthing day. I was seventeen years that month. Do you have a horse, Athon? Is it that one I see on the necklace that has slipped out of your shirt, or are you a follower of the goddess Epona and wish to call her eyes upon you to guide your hands?"

These were strange, and very personal, questions Athon thought, as he unconsciously reached up to touch the necklace that had, indeed and unbeknownst to him, slipped out of his shirt. It was a ceramic horse head he had made and painted himself some seasons earlier, and he always wore it now to keep fresh in his thoughts the many pleasant memories of his youth the simple image always recalled. This time his reply was less abrupt and more measured, but the sound of the words still fell upon surprised ears when he heard himself uttering them.

"No, I am not a follower of the great goddess of horses. My father once raised them and the necklace is an image I made and painted myself. It is of a horse I knew well as a boy. I wear it to remind me of the man, and the horse, who are both now gone from my life."

"Oh, I see," she paused to reflect and changed again to a new subject. "My mother used to tell me many wonderful stories about the goddess, who she says is now also held close by many Romans in this land and beyond. But now mother is a follower of the one god, the new one from the East. Those stories are not as much fun when she takes me with her to hear them; but I am learning to listen and understand more of what I hear. What happened to your horse? Did it have a name?"

"My horse was called *Taranis*, 'the Thunderer', after our god of that name. His hooves always reminded me of that sound when I sat upon his back and rode him as a boy. But he was taken away with all my father's horses back when I was younger by some soldiers moving past our valley on their way north. I always like to think *Taranis* was treated with kindness and served his new master well."

"That was a terrible thing. They were Roman soldiers, I suppose. Father says many of those men would be common criminals, if they were not in the legions. But I have heard of this god of thunder, also. My mother knows many stories of the old gods she learned from her mother, before she married father. Tell me, Athon, painter of pots, would you paint my horse on a bowl, something like the one you did my father has, if I asked you—and paid you for it, of course? Would you need to see my *Medea* to do this?"

"I will be happy to paint your horse on a bowl, and I will not need to see her, if you tell me the way she is colored and marked."

"Oh, that would be so wonderful. She is the color of that thatch on your shed roof there, only not quite so dark I think. Her right foreleg up to her knee is black, and her mane and tail are darker, of course. When can you do this?"

The girl's sudden excitement was obvious, and Athon was almost caught up in it himself. He asked her what type of bowl she wanted. She glanced over at the shelf in the shed where Arcturus kept sample sizes of all the usual vessels they worked on. Then she pointed at the first one on the second shelf—which was not quite as large as the one her father now possessed, and said: "That one." He smiled and told her to come back for it in three days and it would be finished. He was about to explain how he would first have to get one made in the potter's shed and then fired, when she interrupted him once more, but this time for a different reason.

"Ahh, there is father coming up the pathway from below now. But that is strange. He is walking and leading *Hannibal* by the reins, and look, the soldier with him is riding ahead to the villa. I must go and see what is going on. I will be back for my bowl in three days, as you have promised, Athon. And my name is Petra."

Athon watched her as she started to walk in the direction her father was heading. He also noticed the big gray stallion the *Dominus* was leading was walking slowly with an obvious limp and was favoring his left foreleg. As he watched, Petra came close to her father just as a young groom came hurrying down from the villa to take the reins from his master's hand. However, the groom must have pulled overly hard to get the horse to follow, which had put new pressure on the stallion's foreleg where he limped. The animal made a noise as in pain and jerked his head hard, which pulled the reins from the hand of the surprised groom. Then, he reared up, twisted his body and began to run wildly back and forth along the slope right in the direction of the painting shed. The boy chased after him, yelling all the way for the horse to stop, followed closely by Marcus Petronnius, and then his daughter.

Athon knew immediately the great horse, as he thrashed about madly with no thought of direction, was in danger of falling and severely injuring or possibly breaking his damaged leg. The horse needed only to come down on the leg in a way where the pain it was causing might result in the leg giving way at the wrong moment. Without thinking about what he was doing, Athon laid down the bowl he was about to start carving and jumped up to run toward the fast approaching horse. He began to wave his arms as he moved directly toward the stallion to keep its attention focused on him, until he came close enough to make a lunge and grab the loose rein that trailed from the horse's neck. Just as he managed a firm grip on it and pulled the head toward him in the way he had often seen his father do with a startled animal, the horse jerked around, lost his balance and went easily to the ground on his good leg with a gentle push from Athon. He immediately threw himself across the beast's neck to force its head down to the ground—a position that would keep him from trying to regain his feet and possibly cause the injured leg to collapse and splinter the delicate bone in the process. With that done, Athon took the mane in one hand and with his other he reached out and wrapped it around the horse's ear and gently pulled it toward where he began to whisper soothing words to the frightened animal.

By this time, the others had slowed their approach to where horse and man lay together, and Athon let go of the mane for an instant to motion them to stay back. Even the *Dominus,* a man who knew horses well, quickly heeded this warning and put out his hand to stop his daughter as well. In a few moments, the young man sensed the horse's rapid breathing and uncontrolled snorting had begun to subside. He removed his hand from the ear to grasp the rein close by the head and with his other hand began to pat the animal's withers above the hurt leg, while he continued to speak softly. Then, he gradually slid off the neck he had kept pinned to the ground, reached his right arm underneath, and slowly pulled the horse up to its feet as he rose himself to stand with the rein still pulling the head firmly down to keep the stallion from possibly deciding to bolt and run once more.

As soon as Athon saw there was no more danger of this, he was about to offer the reins to the frightened groom when Marcus Petronnius quickly stepped forward to take control of his animal himself. Athon handed him the reins and then stooped down to carefully lift the horse's left foreleg to see what the problem that had caused all this might be. It took him only a moment to see what was wrong and assess how it must have happened. He turned to face the *Dominus* and spoke.

"Look, *Dominus,* see here. The strap that holds the leather hoof cup has come loose, or has been poorly attached. The brass plate underneath the hoof has moved and caused the whole boot to slip. See, the metal clip that attaches the leather to the hoof on this side has been forced out, and the sharp point has moved up and is piercing the flesh almost to the bone here where it is now stuck in the hide above. The leather boot is nearly full of blood by now. Your fine horse must have been in much pain to walk with the weight of a man with each new step. *Dominus,* you were wise to dismount and walk him when you noticed his limp and before he took a fall with you on his back."

"Yes, I can see it clearly now," he said as Athon slowly let the animal's injured foot slip softly from his hand to the ground. The horse whinnied as Marcus Petronnius then began to stroke its muzzle and said some soothing words to it Athon could not understand. Then he turned to Athon, who stood up and began to brush the dirt he had been laying in from his tunic, and spoke.

"Young man, you have my gratitude for what you have just done. I feared he must surely fall with a broken leg, and it would have broken my heart as well to have been forced to see him destroyed. If I find someone's carelessness has caused this," he said as he stared at the nervous groom standing nearby, "that man will feel the lash of my anger upon his back. You certainly know your horses, Athon, is it? I have not seen that trick of lying upon the neck to prevent an injured horse from rising, and I can see your knowledge of the *hippo sandal* is also obvious."

"Yes, *Dominus,* I learned these things from my father, who was said by many who knew him to have known more about horses than any man. Our people have used this way of placing metal shoes upon horses, since long before your people came to this land," he said with the hint of a smile. "It would perhaps be best, *Dominus,* if you led him yourself to his stall. It would be good for him both to feel and see a firm but familiar hand on his rein leading him. With your permission, I can remove the metal clip from where it is sticking in his foot, before he is forced to walk upon it once more."

When Marcus Petronnius simply nodded to give his permission, Athon quickly walked to the painting shed and picked up one of the small knives from the table of Arcturus, who was standing just inside the shed watching the entire scene as it had just unfolded. He gave Athon a wink and a smile, when he walked past to retrieve the knife. Athon then returned to where master and horse still stood quietly, picked up the foreleg once more, and deftly pried the offending brass clip from the animal's flesh. That done, he spit into his hand and spread the saliva onto the open wound to help close it and stem the trickle of blood that still oozed from the puncture.

When the *Dominus* saw Athon was finished, he was about to turn and lead his horse away when he suddenly stopped, reached into the purse tied to his belt, and withdrew a silver coin very much like the one Arcturus had shown him earlier. He reached it out for Athon to take. Marcus Petronnius clasped it into the young man's hand and squeezed it warmly when he accepted the gift.

"This is but a small payment with my gratitude for saving the life of one I hold dear. You are a most unusual young man, I think, Athon of the Ruthenii. I shall watch your progress here closely in the months to come and pray to the gods they continue to show you their favor."

With that he turned to lead his horse up toward the back of the villa, where Athon knew the horse stable must be. The chastened groom silently fell in behind, and Petra joined her father as soon as he came to where she was standing, still frozen to the spot where she had watched everything that had just happened. Athon glanced quickly at the coin in his hand and saw there was a different face upon it than the one Arcturus had been so unhappy with before. Then, he also turned away to head back to the shed and resume his work. Petra joined her father, and when they had gone only a few steps she could contain herself no longer.

"Oh father, wasn't he wonderful. The way he pushed *Hannibal* to the ground and threw himself across his neck to calm him— and then how he found the trouble with the leather shoe and used his knife to remove the metal point. It was just like the story of the man who pulled the thorn from the great lion's paw, which Aristides sometimes told me when I was little."

"Yes, Petra, it seems our young bowl painter is a man of many "talents", as they say."

Marcus Petronnius looked at his daughter and smiled as he said this. However, he noticed a look in her eyes that immediately disturbed him in a way he had not felt before. It was not just the look, but the unspoken thoughts behind it that gave him a strange, undefinable feeling—his first, perhaps, as the helpless father of a girl of marriageable age about a man he knew he could not approve of for her. Just then, as he was about to sort out that troublesome thought, Petra interrupted it as she spoke again.

"And father, Athon has promised to paint me a bowl like yours, but with a painting of *Medea* upon it. I will have to pay him for it, but I have no money, as always. Will you give me the proper coin when I need it in three days' time, when I am to return for the bowl?"

"Of course I will daughter. Do I not always give you everything you ask for, even when I know it is probably the wrong thing for me to do—as your mother often tells me afterward?"

He laughed and extended his free arm to wrap it around her shoulder and pull her close as they walked slowly up the slope together. Meanwhile, Athon had made his way back to the paint shed and returned the knife he had taken without asking to where Arcturus was once again sitting back down at his table. He looked up at Athon when he laid the knife down and spoke.

"That was quite an entertainment you just provided for us, Athon. It seems you have a special gift for calling our Master's attention—and now his daughter's as well—to your many skills. But you must tread very carefully there, my young friend. These high-born Romans, I have observed, will turn on each other for little reason and upon those like ourselves, whom they see as beneath them, often for no reason at all. Take care in your dealings with this girl, Petra that you do not give her father one of those reasons to call down his attention on you in some way you would not like. Now return to your work. There is still good light, and I will still need those six bowls finished before the end of the day."

Athon barely managed to finish the bowl he had promised Petra before she returned for it late in the afternoon of the third day after the incident with her father's horse. His actions that day had become the talk of the entire complex, as Athon learned much to his embarrassment when he returned to his sleeping room that evening and Peliot and others pressed him closely for the details. When he showed them the silver coin that had been his reward, even his friend was impressed and stopped teasing him how he had acted only to impress their Master's daughter. Somehow, Athon managed to find the extra time in those three days to buff the surface of the bowl he was to paint to a higher luster than anything he had done before, and then paint the two bay horses as he envisioned them facing each other on the inside surface.

When Petra saw the bowl and looked inside, she clapped her hands together in glee at the sight. She praised him for his work and said he must surely have seen the horse to have portrayed it so. He laughed and replied simply that once she had described the animal's markings so well, all horses were pretty much the same. Petra gave him the two sestertii for the bowl and then asked if she could come back again and watch him work. He said she could, of course, and that had been the end of it, or so he thought. When he showed the bright, new coin—which also had the new, young emperor's face on it—to Arcturus, the older man simply grunted and told Athon if he kept destroying pots, like the one he had clumsily chipped so badly the day before, then he would need all his money to pay for his carelessness. But Athon knew he had made that mistake the previous before only in his haste to finish his work in order to have the opportunity to complete the painting of Petra's bowl on time. Besides, he realized Arcturus was simply reminding him of his earlier warning not to get too involved with the girl.

Petra did not return for several days. However, once she did, her unannounced appearances soon became a regular feature of Athon's days—but, as he soon began to notice, only when the weather was good and he was working alone outside the paint shed. They soon began to speak of many things, as she sat opposite him and asked random, often surprising, questions about his work and about his life before he had come here. Some of her questions made him uncomfortable, and he would occasionally recall Arcturus's warning—now increasingly distant--not to become overly captivated with this strange girl. But Petra was also beginning to reveal details of her own past and of a lifestyle which was all so alien to an intelligent and curious youth like Athon. She would then sometimes teach him the Latin words for things he would ask of her, and to anyone watching them closely it would soon not have been clear who was teaching whom the most.

He learned much about her past, as well as having revealed many things about his own in their conversations. Her mother, Lucia, was the daughter of a Rutheni woman, who had married

Petra's grandfather, a former Roman soldier who, when his service ended, had stayed and taken land in this province. He had started a small ironworks somewhere upriver when he married and then became modestly successful. When Marcus Petronnius, who was newly arrived from Rome back then, came to purchase the ironworks to add to his family's growing properties along the river, he had met Lucia, fallen in love, and brought her to the new villa he was building. Petra was their only child, because her mother had some problem during her birthing, which prevented her from bearing more children. Athon quickly came to understand Petra was part of a very close-knit family with loving parents, a situation he had not ever thought much about in respect to Romans before meeting her.

The year was waning fast by then and they were sitting close by the fire one afternoon with Petra watching him paint a well-known scene from Roman myth upon a nearly flat bowl. She quite abruptly asked Athon what gods he personally held close or in whose names he made offerings or sacrifices. Her unexpected question forced him to think in a way he had not done very often since becoming a man, and he paused to reflect for a few moments before making his reply.

"My father was a man who held our many gods close in his heart and in his words. He would make offerings and sacrifices on the biggest feast days, or any other occasion he thought important enough. But he would also curse them to all who could hear him when he was angry. My mother says it was the anger of the gods for such behavior which brought him and our family all the trouble that later fell upon us. I suppose, when I was younger and he was alive, I also did what was expected of me. I made offerings to the earth mother and prayed to her to receive my father into her bosom when he died. But as I have grown older, I suppose I do not ask for the help of the gods in the ways other men do. It seems to me they are a fickle lot, who care little for a man's real troubles and will only come to his aid if he offers them a 'gift' or something in return. Still, there are days when I ask the old god Lugus to aid me in my work, usually to remove the cloud from my mind's eye when there is something I wish to paint, or a bowl I wish to shape I cannot seem to see clearly."

"Mother has spoken of this god, Lugus. Is he not the high sun god of the peoples of Gaul?"

"Yes, that is true. But he is also the one who watches over craftsmen and guides their hands while they work—or so it is said."

"Ahh, like our Roman god, Vulcan, "the lame one." Aristides, who seems to know everything about such things, has told me all the gods must be the same and equal in their power, or none of them can be real." Petra smiled as she almost seemed to be making light of this entire discussion—one which she had started—leaving Athon feeling completely confused as he sat watching her.

"Athon, have you not heard of the one true god, or of his divine son, the one they call *The Christ*? His power is supreme, and there are no other gods below him—only men, who are all equal in his eyes. He requires no blood sacrifices in his name, nor does he reward those who set themselves above others only because they have more wealth and can offer greater gifts in his name. Even the slave is loved by the one god, it is said, and will be taken to be judged equally with his master before the one god and his son on the day of each person's passing from this world to the next."

"I have heard something of this new god from the East, but only since I have come here. There is an old man and a potter who sleep in the same building as I do who often sit together and speak about such things and offer prayers to this god. How do you come to know so much about him, and do you believe he has this all-seeing and all-knowing power you and the others I have heard speak about?"

"My mother has become a true follower of this god. She takes me with her when she goes to hear the one they call *The Teacher*, when he speaks down in the village. I think he moves from place to place along the river and comes here one or sometimes two times in each month to read letters from others like him in far way places, and even, they say, from Rome. Men ask him questions about *The Christ* at these meetings, and he tells us what others have said about him. I have started to listen to his words more closely than I did at first. Mother asks me questions about what *The Teacher* says afterward, and then explains what the true answers might be, or other things about what was said she wants me to know, or I did not understand. I have seen the effect of this man's words on those who come to listen to him, and many are changed when they leave. But some others are not, and do not ever come back again."

"What of this son, *the Christ,* of whom you speak. Is he a god, or is he a man? How can he be both? It is hard for me to understand the things you speak of, Petra."

"His followers believe he was a living man but one born of the one god and an earthly mother and that he now lives in the heavens beside his father. I am not sure I always understand what mother tells me or how everything happened either before or after he died as a man."

"How did he die? If he was truly a son of this one god, then why did the god not save him from the death an ordinary man might have to endure? I do not understand this part either, Petra."

"He was condemned and executed by the Romans in a faraway province at the eastern end of the great inland sea. When I asked Aristides, he told me this place is called Judea, and that it is now a part of the great Province of Syria. He says some of the pottery made here, Athon, has surely found its way to this place. *The Teacher* says the Romans condemned him, because they feared his message of peace and love was for all men and the one god wanted to embrace them all, no matter whether they be slave or master, or in what language they might call to him. It was only after his earthly death when men discovered he had been taken up by his father, the one god, to sit beside him in the heavens. That is all I know except for this."

Petra glanced around for an instant and then pulled out from her tunic a small, wooden cross. She showed it to Athon, and then quickly returned it to where she obviously wished it to be hidden from sight.

"It is a cross of wood, like the one *The Christ* was nailed and cru- cified upon by the soldiers a long time ago in that faraway place. Those who truly believe he now sits with God and heed the words he spoke when he walked among living men carry this sign upon them always. Mother gave me this one, which is just like hers. They say in the past, and even in these troubled seasons, many have died because they refused to renounce this symbol, or his name. But his message has spread into many lands, and even important men in Rome and other places Rome controls are now believers in his words of peace and hope for a new life for all men. Perhaps, Athon, you should come to see *The Teacher* when he speaks to us here next time. I will tell you how you can do this when the day comes, if you like."

Athon was not exactly sure how he should respond to her in- vitation, and replied only that he would think upon her words, which contained much that was new to him. But, he also told her, he might, indeed, like to hear this man, *The Teacher,* in his own words when he spoke again. They left their discussion of gods at that point, and for a while their brief, occasional conversations slipped back to the more mundane subjects Petra usually managed to spring upon him in her unpredictable manner.

Some days after their conversation about the new god from the east, she reappeared to ask him if he was planning to attend the big feast of the old god Saturn, which was to take place in the village in three days. Athon had heard much of it, since many in the pottery works were speaking of it with excitement and expecta- tion. However, he had made no plans himself, since he assumed it was a Roman festival, even though it came only short days before the winter solstice festival, which his own people always celebrated with great merriment. Still, it would be an important break from their seemingly never ending daily routines, and in the last few days he was also finding himself being caught up in some of the growing anticipation. When Petra asked him about it, he replied he did not know what he should, or would do, when the day came. She laughed at his ignorance of such things as she did at other times, although never in a way that was insulting, but only for his usual lack of knowledge of things Roman.

"It will be great fun and is my favorite day of the year. The village will be decorated with all sorts of greenery from the forests, and the candle maker will have worked very hard to satisfy all the demands put on him. Long tables of boards from the boatyard will be set up in the square, if the skies are clear. There will be many fine foods, fresh fish from the river, and fowls of all types. A whole swine will even be roasted at the big fire for all to see. Father will give an entire barrel of wine for everyone to enjoy. The most fun thing is the Roman tradition where our family dresses as servants for the feast, and we must then serve those who have done so for us during the past year. Everyone will sit at the long table and we will bring them food and drink. Even Aristides, who I believe does not like this idea much, will join us in this. Mother always does such wonderful things for the people. I think she loves it so, because it reminds her of her mother's stories about her own past. I help her pass out the gifts to the workers at the end of the feast, and father usually stands at the end of the table as they pass by and gives them a coin or two, as Aristides whispers in his ear how much each one has deserved for his past year's efforts. You must come, Athon, you simply must."

He quickly agreed, since she insisted, he would certainly come with the others—a thing he had already decided upon anyway. When the day came, everyone at the pottery works and in the village was allowed to finish his work early to prepare for the *Saturnalia,* as Arcturus called it. Even he was caught up for once in the excitement, Athon noticed. That evening Athon walked to the village with Peliot and others just as dusk was setting in, and was amazed at the appearance of the houses and shops decked with boughs and candles. He had been there on numerous occasions for various things in the recent past, but had never seen so many people about, nor had there been the several long tables and the great fire in the center of the small square before. Peliot quickly abandoned him to go find the young widow with whom he spent increasing amounts of his time and whom Athon had met some time back.

The evening unfolded very much as Petra had described it. The food truly was the best he could remember, and Athon even indulged in a second cup of wine, something he rarely did. Others, he noticed, showed no such restraint, however. By the time darkness was coming on and the main table was cleared—this time by the real servants and not their Roman masters dressed as such—everyone soon began to press toward it to see what gifts would be offered this year. Aristides made a fine speech about the grand plans for the coming New Year and how everyone would be expected to continue in their efforts on behalf of those who had already done so much for them. When Aristides was finished, Marcus Petronnius, stepped forward to the cheers of all those present, and gave a much shorter address also thanking everyone for their past and continuing efforts on behalf of his family. Then, he told everyone to fall into a line to receive their "rewards for his appreciation of their work" as he waved his hand to the far end of the table to the sound of one final, loud cheer.

When Athon finally passed through the line to where he could see the two stacks of gifts Petra and her mother were giving out to the eager hands of each worker who stopped before them, he saw he would have to make a choice. There was a new tunic, made in the local fashion, or an excellent pair of leather sandals, which others in the line were saying must have been brought all the way across the mountains from Hispania. When he saw Petra smile at him as he came near, the choice for Athon was instantly made. However, instead of offering him one of the tunics from the stack in front of her, when she saw him Petra reached behind her and produced one that appeared to be of much finer quality than the others being offered. He accepted it with a questioning smile in response to her own wide grin as she extended it across the table for him to receive.

When he got to the end of the table where Marcus Petronnius was standing in front of stacks of various sized coins on the table behind him and where Aristides was reading off the name and the amount to offer to each person who passed by, Athon noticed the *Dominus* said something to the *major domo*, who simply nodded and smiled in response. Then Marcus reached into the purse at his belt for a coin instead of picking up one or more from those on the table. He extended it with a smile and the usual word of gratitude Athon had heard him offer to each of those ahead of him. Athon responded as he had heard others before him answer and accepted the coin with his own smile and lowered eyes. He was surprised at the small size of the object he felt in his hand, especially when he noticed the much larger coin the man ahead of him had received.

Had he done something to displease the Dominus he suddenly wondered— or was he showing his displeasure at the attention his daughter was giving him? Or was it merely that he had been here a much shorter length of time than all those who had passed ahead of him? Athon was wondering about these things as he approached Peliot and a couple of others from his dormitory who were standing together near the fire and comparing what each had received in gifts and money. He clutched the wonderful tunic tightly under one arm and cupped the small coin close in his other hand. When he came near, Peliot motioned him over and said in a voice the other two men could also hear.

"Come here, Athon, and let me see that tunic. I happened to see the Master's daughter give it to you. It was certainly not from the same pile as the one I chose." He laughed and looked at the other two as if in confirmation of some private joke they had just shared at his expense. "What coin did the Master offer you? I will wager the four sestertii he gave me against whatever is in your hand your coin is larger. Come on, let us see it!"

When Athon opened his palm to reveal the tiny coin to them, and to himself for the first time also, he heard Peliot gasp as he blurted out for the other two to hear as well when the light of the nearby fire illuminated the even brighter coin in his hand.

"By the great god Lugus, would you look at that! It must be a golden *aureus*. That is ten denari, at least. I have never seen one before. Athon, my friend, the Master must place a great value on your skills—or on that gray stallion of his you saved. You must buy us wine for the next month to keep our mouths closed on this."

The other three all laughed when Peliot clapped Athon on the shoulder and they congratulated him on his good fortune. A stunned, and even confused, Athon then put the coin in his belt pouch, and followed the others to where the barrel of wine standing close by had not been fully drained quite yet by the many revelers. Peliot offered him another cup full, and for once Athon accepted without any further argument from the distant warning voice of his mother echoing somewhere in his head how he must not do such foolish things the same way as his father. Then he looked at his friend and asked.

"Peliot, how many painted bowls do you think this golden coin is worth?"

His friend laughed even harder than he had before—and they both took another long drink.

The first day of the New Year came not long after Athon's evening of good fortune at the feast of the Saturnalia. That celebration was followed a few nights later on the eve of the winter solstice by an immense bonfire and gathering marking the birth of the New Year by the local Rutheni people and others who came from various Gaelic tribes farther north to work at the pottery. However, none of the Romans from the villa attended this rowdy ceremony conducted by a local priest of some sort. Afterward, everything seemed to have fallen quickly back to normal routines. Nevertheless, because of events in far off Rome begun on the very first day of the arriving year, this New Year was to have profound effects for many—not the least of whom would be the young potter and bowl painter himself.

Athon soon grew tired of Peliot asking to see the golden coin every time his friend stayed in the workers' sleeping building, which he was doing less frequently since he spent more and more of his nights in the village. He finally decided to ask Arcturus what he should do with it and the rest of the coins he had accumulated in the last two months. His mentor smiled and was also impressed when Athon showed him the gold coin for the first time. Then he gave Athon a small chipped bowl that was about to be discarded and led him over to the cabinet where the paints and tools were kept. With a little difficulty, they moved the cabinet forward slightly and the older man said to his young assistant.

"See that flat stone just inside where the back leg was. I have dug a small hole under it where I keep a small pot with my own coins. I do not trust these boatmen who pass through the village so close by my house. You should dig a hole yourself where the other leg is. I will find you something to cover it with while you work. Make it deep enough for the bowl. Then we will move the cabinet back where it was to cover both our 'riches'." He laughed and left Athon to do as he had suggested.

As the days grew colder and shorter, Petra came to talk and watch Athon work much less often. Arcturus soon sent for heavy sail cloth walls that could be tied to the sides of the painting shed on the colder days, when he would leave only the back end open where his fire was kept to warm their hands and the paints they used. Some days were too cold even to work there and on these they moved to a small space attached to the warmer potters' shed, mostly to carve designs on the many fresh clay bowls continually being produced at the wheels or in the molds there, no matter what the weather outside. Peliot complained to Athon daily of the cold and the amounts of wood he had to stack for the firing kiln; but the work continued unabated as long as the clay continued to arrive from upriver, or unless a hard storm fell upon them.

On one of her infrequent visits Petra was excited to tell Athon her mother had told her the man she called *The Teacher* would be in the village in two days. There would be a gathering of those who identified themselves as *Christians*—and anyone else who wished to come—to hear what new words of empowerment the old man would offer them. Athon somewhat reluctantly agreed to attend, but quickly forgot his hesitation when he saw Petra's happy reaction to his acceptance of her invitation. She told him where he must go and when, but nothing of how he should behave, or anything else about this strange idea of a one god. He had not thought much more about any of this since she first told him all about this one true god from the east that seemed to be causing such excitement in those who had chosen to accept him over the many lesser deities and spirits they had always held close before.

When the evening came for Athon to go to the gathering he followed her instructions, which led him to a large boat-building shed just upriver from the village. He waited outside for a short time in the vain hope of seeing Petra and her mother arrive before he entered the building, which was lit by many candles. He soon decided they must already be inside, where he went himself and saw as many people as he could count on both his hands two times and a few more perhaps. They were seated on the ground or on benches hastily made from the wood drying in the shed, or just standing around. All the women, who seemed to be slightly more numerous than the men, were on one side of the room and the men were on the other.

Athon was immediately greeted warmly by one of the two men he shared rooms with, who welcomed him to their "*Ekklesias*", as the man called it. He would learn later by questioning Petra this was a Greek word used to identify different groups of the one god's followers at various locations in the valley and beyond. Athon noted where Petra was seated with her mother, when she turned around once to smile at him. He quickly decided to sit on the dirt floor near the rear of the other men in order not to call any undue attention to himself.

A short time later a simply dressed, elderly man appeared and walked to the front. He had a flowing beard and an intense look in his eyes. However, when he welcomed all those present in the name of the one god, he spoke in a warm tone that was far different from the cult leaders Athon could remember hearing in the religious ceremonies and sacrifices he had attended as a boy. The man spoke for what seemed a long time to Athon. He read to them from a parchment he said was a letter from a man in a distant land whose name the others seemed to recognize. He told some stories about the life of *The Christ* and of miracles he was said to have performed when he lived in the days of a Roman emperor Athon had never heard of before. Athon listened carefully to his words and found them interesting, but not easy to accept as truth. At last, the old man began to hold dialogues with one or two men in the front and answered their many questions. Athon noticed, however, that no questions or comments came from the side where the women and girls sat in almost complete silence.

Finally, the elder summoned forward by name two of the women and a man. Another man produced a bowl of water, into which the elder dipped his hands. He then placed some of the water on the heads of the three who came forward and said a few words, which seemed to make all the others in attendance shout praises. Then, he saw the man with the bowl give the three "initiates" small crosses of wood—much like the one Petra had shown him—followed by more words of appreciation from all who were watching the simple ceremony. Athon would learn later this act had bound those who now accepted the teachings of *The Christ* to him in some way. Those initiates were swearing to follow his teaching all the days of their lives. At the end of which he would draw them to him in this heavenly place of the one god, where they would all dwell together in the peace and love he had promised—and which so few of them had ever known in their earthly existence. As he listened, Athon could not help but wonder if Petra had also made this same vow when she had received her cross.

When the ceremony and the old man's teaching ended, the people began to leave quickly to return in the darkness to the various and different lives they had temporarily put aside to join as one in this new idea. Athon waited to see if Petra would say anything to him on her way out; but her mother led her from the old shed not long after *The Teacher* was finished. Before they left, however, Athon saw Petra's mother go to the old man and discreetly place some coins in his hand and clasp it warmly, as she said a few words for his ears only before turning and leaving quickly with her daughter.

Immediately after, Athon left as well. What he had just witnessed and heard gave him much to ponder, as he began to do on the cold walk back to where he would sleep far less comfortably that night than in recent days. Some of what the old man said sounded reasonable and even hopeful to his youthful ideas. But there were other things that still seemed far less believable, even challenging, to his skeptical mind, which was so unused to such ways of total acceptance of another man's words.

Two days later he was back at the painting shed tending the fire outside when Petra came down the slope, apparently on her way to the village, and swung by when she saw him to ask what he thought of the things he had seen and heard. She was obviously eager to hear his answers so he tried to frame them in a way he thought would most please her. She left him with a smile after only a brief stay and a few words encouraging him to go to the next gathering, when its time was passed by word of mouth from those in the village who arranged such things. He promised her he would like to go once more.

During the second month of the New Year, *The Teacher* appeared twice more and Athon kept his promise and went to hear him each time. Others received the water blessing of the elder and took up their tiny crosses at the end of each meeting. The second time this happened Athon noticed Petra turned to where he was sitting, as if to encourage him to stand and move forward with the others when the old man called for "his sheep to come forward to be received by their shepherd." It was a strange summons, Athon thought, until he recalled one of the elder's earlier stories about the life of *The Christ*, when he had walked among men as one of them. Still, however, the young listener had not yet come close to committing himself to the many things which seemed too far beyond his reason to understand. But the idea of the one, supreme god, who oversaw all things and directed every man's life, was an easier and more appealing idea for him to grasp and replace his old, pagan beliefs; and that part of it, at least, was already beginning to implant itself firmly in Athon's thoughts.

By the end of that second month, the harsher weather of the winter moons was starting to subside and the promise of an early spring was already in the air. Arcturus soon began to roll up first one side, and then the opposite, of his shed on good mornings to take advantage of the sunlight as it moved to the afternoon. On those occasions Athon would move his old canvas out closer to the fire to paint again by the direct sunlight he felt he needed for his more delicate brushstrokes. He was also finally able to take advantage of his opportunity every third day to produce a design or a bowl of his own choosing once more. He soon began to create some remarkable scenes, which even caught the eye and approval of his mentor, Arcturus. He was earning extra coins again for these pieces, and the young artist was starting to wonder how, and when, he might ask to return to his home to get this badly needed money to his family in the little valley to the north.

The warmer days also brought Petra to resume her occasional visits, when she would watch him work and speak of many things that never ceased to amaze and fascinate her eager listener. She had a way of introducing strange topics in surprising ways. She even began to make suggestions for his bowl designs, and on one occasion he found himself indulging her by agreeing to do a painting of her story about a Greek named Androcles and a lion, a beast he had never seen until Arcturus showed him a drawing of the animal from one of his many picture scrolls. Mostly, however, she wanted to hear his thoughts about the last meeting of *The Teacher* they had attended. On that subject, he was beginning to detect some impatience on her part, due mainly to his usually vague replies and reluctance to commit to accepting his little cross of wood at one of the meetings.

Then one day just into the new month, Petra came by and seemed to be greatly distracted and strangely silent, as she simply sat and watched him work for a long time before she said anything after her initial greeting. When she finally spoke, her words sent a chill into Athon that went deep into his soul—the soul *The Teacher* and Petra had said he possessed and which he had only of late begun to search for in himself because of her.

"Athon, father has received a letter from his uncle Sextus Petronnius in Rome. He is an important man, a senator, and the head of our family there. He is also the man who asked my father to come here for the family before I was born. Mother told me of the letter and how excited father was when he read it to her. She says that on the first day of this New Year, the young emperor, the one father called 'mad Commodus,' was murdered and a man named Pertinax has been given the Crown of Caesar. Father says this man is an important senator and nobleman, and a friend to our uncle and our family. Father also says this new emperor has already begun to restore the old rules of law and of the senate which Marcus Aurelius gave to the people when he was Emperor. Father and Aristides told me many stories of Marcus Aurelius when I was a girl, and I think he must have been very important to them both. I know mother has said many times father would never go to Rome as long as that man's terrible son was Emperor there.

"But now father seems very excited, because Uncle has told him it is a good time for him to return, and there is much that needs to be settled about our family's affairs he should be witness to. He tells mother since his father died some years ago these things can only be done in Rome. Father has also told her as soon as the weather breaks for certain, we will travel by road down to Tolosa, and then on to the coast to Narbo, where we will take one of our family's trading ships and sail on to Rome straight away."

"You do not seem to be very happy about all this, Petra. From what you have told me in the past, I would think you would be eager to make this trip and see the many wonders you have described there, things that are scarcely believable, I must say. Are you not excited to see these things, that you may convince me of their truth when you return—just as you have managed to do about the knowledge of the one god and his son you have brought me to know?"

"There was one thing more in this letter, Athon, which father has discussed with mother. He also said that, indeed, it was time we all went to Rome, so he could find a proper husband for me there. He must have sent a letter to his uncle sometime in the past, because in this new letter Uncle Sextus has said to father he has already begun to pursue some possible *useful arrangements*— concerning me which would be most beneficial to our family."

"I see," a suddenly thoughtful Athon managed to reply—barely able not to choke on the words he was forced to restrain from passing through his lips, and for fear of the quivering in them he was beginning to feel. Instead, he merely avoided her eyes and muttered.

"You know I shall miss our conversations, and all the things you have taught me. Will I see you again before you leave?"

It was a stupid thing to say, he knew, and he regretted his foolish words as soon as he uttered them. But Petra did not seem to have heard them, as she stared into his eyes as if she could hear the real words his head, and his heart, had been forming in his mind. But she said nothing and then stood up slowly, looked down at him, and spoke in her usual direct fashion.

"And I shall miss them also, Athon. It is my fondest hope you will continue to go to hear the words of *The Teacher* when he is here, and the day will soon come when he places his hands upon your head and you take up the cross of *The Christ* he offers you then. I shall take with me the bowl with the painting of *Medea,* who mother says must also be left behind, as a remembrance of her. I will think of you with great affection every day when I look into it and see your face there as well, Athon of the Rutheni. May the blessings of the one god continue to fall upon you."

With that she turned to leave without looking back. Athon sensed she was about to say more, but like his own parting words, they had been too difficult for her to speak in that moment. He stared after her until she disappeared through the trees and then passed beyond them to the great villa, which would soon be empty of those who had changed the young potter's life in so many ways he could never have imagined before he came here. Then, he looked toward Arcturus, who had stopped his painting and obviously understood much of what had just transpired. The older man flashed a sympathetic smile in Athon's direction and then shrugged with a simple gesture, which was all he could think to do to remind his helpless, young pupil of his previous warning not to allow himself to get too close to this Roman girl. Now, it appeared to a dumbstruck Athon that very warning had suddenly become a reality for him.

It was some days later, and Athon had received no more visits from Petra, when he noticed there was unusual activity around the villa, with much coming and going of servants and others from the pottery works and the town outside. Even Aristides, whom Arcturus told him would not be leaving, but would stay behind to run things in the Master's absence—much as he did even when Marcus Petronnius was here, Arcturus joked—seemed unusually frantic in his actions this morning. It was not yet mid-morning when a large, four-wheeled wagon Athon had never seen before appeared from somewhere behind the villa and then began to move down the slope toward the river road, which would take it to the big town of Tolosa, and then on to the coast city of Narbo. The wagon was completely enclosed by wooden walls, except for a small window on each side; covered by a strong, rounded canvas top; and drawn by a matched pair of dark brown horses. Marcus Petronnius was out in front, riding a big black horse Athon had not noticed him upon before, along with two soldiers in front with him and two more riding behind the wagon.

Athon stared as it passed down the slope, not far from where he sat by a little fire with what suddenly felt like a totally useless bowl in his hand. He peered at the narrow, opened window in the hope he might catch a last glimpse of a certain face he could recognize, who would be riding inside with her mother and a servant or two, perhaps. However, no face he could distinguish appeared, and much too soon, the wagon reached the bottom of the slope, passed between the last two buildings on either side of the entrance to the pottery works, and disappeared beyond his sight and onto the road heading downriver. He continued to gaze in that direction until long after the wagon disappeared—for what reason he could not clearly define. He then reluctantly turned his eyes back toward the bowl he was about to begin outlining his first design upon. Athon had felt hunger in his insides many times as a boy after the hard seasons his family had experienced when his father died. But in that moment, the emptiness gnawing at his gut was like no feeling he had yet endured to this point in his young life.

The early spring had come and gone and the month of the summer solstice with its warmth and flowering fields was upon them. By this time Athon had finally managed to return to a somewhat normal routine, at least in his work. However, any time he sat outside the painting shed to work he would frequently catch himself involuntarily glancing back up the slope toward the empty villa in the hope of seeing a familiar form striding toward him. Arcturus did not fail to notice the changes in Athon: a lessening of his normal eagerness to learn or try new patterns, or to suggest some usually improbable, painted scene. These he would then have to explain to his young student why they would not be good for the markets to the south, for which they mostly toiled. Then, when Athon began regularly to mention his desire to return to his home and family to the north for a short visit, and to take them some of his accumulated earnings, the older man finally gave in and told him how he could do so.

Arcturus explained in the month of the solstice, when others who worked at the pottery or other places on the estate desired to make short visits to their more distant homes, such requests were more routinely granted. Then, Aristides could more easily plan for all the absences at the same time. Athon easily recalled it was a year ago in this same month when Peliot returned home and first encouraged Athon to seek his own future here. Athon had once hoped he would be able to send money home by Peliot when the latter returned to his home again. However, Peliot had finally taken the young widow in the village as his wife and moved in with her. She was already expecting a child, no doubt from one of his friend's earlier visits, as Athon surmised when Peliot informed him of his not so unexpected, if somewhat rather sudden, marriage.

Therefore, by early in the month Athon was finally convinced his true obligations lay with helping his mother and brother by sharing the fruits of his labor with them, just as he had always planned. Besides, his earlier homesickness was returning with the warm days. He increasingly wished just to spend some time in the open air remembering the quiet of his boyhood, instead of being forever in the continuously smoky bustle of the pottery works with its never-ending painting and incising of pots, a thing he did not find nearly as exciting as he had when he first arrived. But Athon also suspected there was perhaps another reason for this longing to be with his family again.

After Petra and her mother left for Rome, Athon ceased attending the gatherings of the local Christians which occurred whenever the old man they called *The Teacher* appeared in the village. For two months he had simply not felt like going. However, when the young Christian from their sleeping rooms told him the elder would soon be paying another visit and it was being said he would have important news from Rome to share with them, Athon felt drawn to attend once more. In his growing loneliness, he had started to ponder more deeply the basic messages of the one god which he had heard the old man deliver in every one of the earlier meetings he attended. These words finally began to find a place in his head, and in his heart, where he realized they were able to soothe some of his longing for things he could—and could not— identify in either place within him.

At this meeting, the old man read to his followers, as he often did, a letter from other followers of *The Christ* in a far land who reported on the growing power of their belief—or the setbacks—those believers in this rapidly spreading Faith were experiencing. This time, however, the letter came from one of their important leaders in Rome, who described new problems threatening the growing church's followers there. Another new emperor, it seemed, had already been named—the second since the brutal Commodus had been killed on the first day of the New Year. There was great unrest in the city, and rumors of invasion from beyond Italia by powerful generals seeking the crown for themselves, amid growing fears of new persecution of the Christians, which they all knew from earlier read letters had frequently occurred in the past when the Empire, and Rome in particular, was in some larger turmoil.

Athon listened to every word *The Teacher* conveyed to them that night, and he was not alone among those who heard them with his thoughts and concerns for Marcus Petronnius and his family—upon whom so many of them depended in one way or another—as well as for their fellow believers who perhaps faced serious new threats. When the old man called upon them all to pray for the safety of their fellow believers and former friends now in Rome, Athon had found himself quietly uttering the words the old man led them in offering to their god with the same deep intensity and sincerity as the others around him. To his amazement, as the gathering was ending and the old man called for all those who sought redemption and the eternal love of the one god and his son to come forward to receive His blessing and their own cross to bear in His name, Athon found himself on his feet together with three others who went forward to answer that call.

Afterward, he experienced both relief and guilt for several days at what he had done that evening. He felt a heavy burden of some sort had been lifted from his troubled spirit; but he also felt guilty for not having taken those few steps earlier, when it would have meant so much to Petra. Nor could he keep from wondering what course her life might have taken since she left for Rome. Had she been given into a marriage at her father's insistence and found a new happiness; or as a true believer in the one god was she now threatened as were the other Christians in that troubled city? That disturbing uncertainty was one of the main reasons Athon finally decided he needed to visit his home as soon as possible where he hoped he might restore some order to his life, which suddenly felt terribly out of balance in so many ways.

Then one morning near the middle of the month of the solstice when Athon was planning to ask Arcturus what day and for how long he could plan his journey home, the morning was unexpectedly disturbed by what appeared to be a burst of activity in the pottery—and up at the villa as well. Arcturus finally saw Aristides and signaled to The Greek to ask him what was going on. A very excited Aristides walked over to where both painters were watching all the comings and goings and replied.

"A messenger has only just arrived this morning from Tolosa. He has apparently ridden all night. Marcus Petronnius arrived two days past in Narbo. In two more days the *Dominus*—and his family—will be returning. I must go now; that is all I know and there is much to do to get the villa and the pottery ready to receive them. Arcturus, old friend, try to get things cleaned up a little more around here. I will send a boy to take away that pile of broken and damaged pots and other debris you have allowed to grow far too large over there."

With that Aristides raced off toward the villa. Soon, house servants and slaves began to leave, and a steady stream of comings and goings to the village or elsewhere to procure fresh foods, flowers, or other necessities to restore the mostly deserted villa to its normal condition and appearance for the arrival of its former occupants was underway. Athon's heart had raced up the slope with Aristides that morning, and only with great difficulty could he contain his many conflicting emotions the rest of the day and the busy one that followed.

Late the following afternoon, the wagon Athon never expected to see again appeared at the entrance to the pottery works and made its way back up toward the villa. Marcus Petronnius was riding in front once more, but this time on a different horse and with only the two old soldiers who always accompanied him around the villa. However, just as before, Athon saw no familiar face looking his way from the small window, which he could see was open on the side of the wagon, before it disappeared through the trees in front of the sprawling villa. Because of his growing anticipation, Athon experienced an extremely long night, one with little sleep and many thoughts fighting in his head for attention.

However, when the next day came and despite the fact he had very visibly set his painting mat outside the shed, his very frequent glances back up the slope revealed no one approaching his way from the villa. Perhaps, they were too tired from their long journey his mind told his heart; but his disappointment continued into the next day as well when he saw only Marcus Petronnius leaving the confines of his home to ride somewhere beyond the pottery. Even Aristides was not to be seen making his usual rounds that first day, nor did he appear at all until after the Master left the villa. Athon's disappointment was becoming palpable, until late in the morning of the third day after the family's return when he looked up once more and saw the figure of Petra walking down the slope toward the painting shed. There he sat working, looking exactly the same as when she had last seen him nearly four months before. At that instant, all his well-developed plans to visit his home vanished from the young painter's thoughts, as if they were a puff of smoke from the nearby kilns.

Their first conversation proved awkward and difficult. Each must have had many questions for the other, but neither could seem to find the right way to ask them. She asked if he had painted anything he thought she might like to see, and he replied the weather had been bad and when it was good, there were always more demands on him to do the usual designs. He asked her if she had enjoyed Rome, and she replied it was truly spectacular, but not at all what she had expected.

He wanted to know why they had left so soon to come home; but he knew such a thing was beyond him to ask. Most of all, he wanted to know about her father's promise to find her a "proper" husband; but of course that question could not be asked either. Finally, they were running out of such small talk as they could devise and Petra was obviously about to leave when she looked at him more intently and asked in an almost off-hand manner if he had continued to go to the gatherings when *The Teacher* had come to the village. In reply, Athon simply smiled and removed the tiny wooden cross, which was nearly identical to the one he knew she always carried, from his small, leather belt pouch.

Her instant reaction seemed to break the unexpected barrier that had grown between them in their long separation. She congratulated him warmly, and he felt she might have reached out and grabbed his arms—at the very least—if they had only been alone. But instead, after a few words of praise and encouragement, she simply said she must go and give the good news to her mother, who would also be very proud and happy for him. Their reconnection ended so much better than it had begun, Athon thought. He watched her wave at a watchful Arcturus and then head back toward the villa, while he tried unsuccessfully to avoid staring after her until she disappeared completely.

In the following days their visits resumed as before and Petra gradually revealed most of the troubling things that happened to them after they arrived in Rome. She also told him of the many wonders she saw there and described sights and people, which he could only barely accept as the truth when he heard them from her excited lips. Many of the events and names she spoke of were beyond his understanding. Still, she thrilled him with her tale of when her father took her to the great *Hippodrome*, where they watched magnificent horses and chariot races, and of how she had thought of him and her own *Medea* at that time. However, he soon quickly realized many of the very unfavorable reports about Roman behavior and customs he had often heard from the lips of his own people were apparently equally true as well. This was despite his own experiences of the Romans whom he had come to know here, and who had managed to convince him all Romans were not the horrible beasts his father and others from his childhood always spoke of them as being.

Finally, she told him why they were forced to leave Rome so soon after arriving, most of which she said her father explained on the unexpected voyage home. At the very time they arrived in Rome, the new Emperor Pertinax was slain by his guards. Her father said they and others who had profited from the excesses and corruption of Commodus were apparently angered by Pertinax's orders of strict discipline for soldiers and his many reforms aimed at restoring the power of the Senate and the health of the depleted treasury. After the untimely death of Pertinax the Praetorian Guards who murdered him announced an auction of the Emperorship to whoever paid them the highest bounty.

Didius Julianus, a wealthy man not well liked by the Petronnii, had offered the most and was made Emperor. When this news reached other leaders in the Provinces some of whom were generals were angered because they had not had the opportunity to compete for the crown themselves. One or two threatened to bring their legions to Rome and seize the Crown of Caesar for himself. Other powerful men in Rome wrote letters to one or the other of these generals promising their support if they would hasten to Rome to overthrow the new Emperor. One such general, a man named Lucius Septimius Severus, came quickly from across the Danube and had already landed with his soldiers somewhere in Italia. At that point, Petra said, her father had consulted with his uncle and decided he should return to look after the family's interests in the north as quickly as he could. By then, all of Rome was in complete turmoil as powerful houses and senators began to align themselves with one faction or another. Some were threatening to take over the city or to march out with an army to oppose anyone threatening to break the old law against a general entering the city with his army.

All this information seemed quite alien to an amazed and confused Athon. He was not terribly disturbed if the far away Romans were fighting and killing each other. He was only happy whatever was happening there had forced Marcus Petronnius to return so quickly with his family before he could find a husband for his daughter. Finally, one morning when Petra was telling him of the wonders of Rome's many markets her mother took her to when they first arrived and before the troubles began, Athon jokingly asked if she had not also shopped for the new husband she had mentioned before she left for Rome. Petra replied in her usual mock serious, teasing manner, which she used with him when she wanted to remind him he was not so very much older than she.

"You may joke, Athon, but when we first arrived our Uncle Sextus had already arranged two visits for me with men I heard him tell father were 'acceptable and safe' directions for the family to look. When the first man came to Uncle's villa, mother had me made up to look much older when he arrived. But he was too old, surely close to thirty years. His first wife had died childless and he wanted a new wife quickly. But he was also fat and smelled too much of garlic. The next day I was taken to the most magnificent villa and made to sit still while some men and old women paraded by and inspected me as if they were looking to buy a new horse. Then I was introduced to this awful boy, who was definitely much younger than I. He took me to walk with him in their beautiful gardens; but all he wanted to do was talk about how wealthy his family was, and he kept trying to touch my breast whenever he thought no one was watching. Right after that the big troubles started, and I heard no more talk about a husband from father, or uncle. I told Mother later I would have had neither one of them, in any event. Besides," Petra said as she stood up to leave and winked at Athon with a smile, "neither one of them had red hair. I now think I like red hair in a man."

Petra laughed and left him with his mouth open. She did come again for a few days, and their routine once again settled into a familiar, if somewhat unpredictable pattern. Nearly a month passed when one morning Athon noticed once again there seemed to be a great amount of activity and some disturbance coming from the villa, which soon filtered its way down the slope to the pottery sheds. Arcturus could not find Aristides to see what was going on, but at last the Greek appeared and the old painter managed to get his attention to find out what was happening. Athon stood close enough to hear the *major domo's* words, which had the effect of throwing Athon's entire world into uncertainty.

"*Dominus* has received a letter by fast ship and rider from Rome. It is from a man who serves the Master's family there much as I do here. The Master has read it to me to help him decide what he must do next. The letter says another new emperor has seized power, some general from beyond the Danube, and a man who was not born in Rome. It was his army that first responded to the calls from men like Sextus Petronnius to come to Rome to restore power to the Senate. But the Petronnii lent their support to another man, who said he would bring his soldiers, but did not arrive in time. A general with an army from the city supported by the Petronii and others was sent out to battle this Septimius Severus, who, instead of fighting them, promised the general who was supposed to defend the city and his men a great deal of money to join him. The two then joined forces and marched back into Rome together. All those who had opposed him either fled or were killed—even powerful senators—and their lands and estates were confiscated. Sextus Petronnius and his entire family have been murdered, including his son with his wife and small child, it appears.

"This man has told our Master it is only a matter of time before his recent visit to Rome and the men he met with there will be known, when his uncle's papers are examined and his many estates reclaimed by this new emperor to pay his supporters. The letter says our Master should look to his own safety now; for the knowledge of the profitable Petronnii lands in this Province will soon come to the attention of these brutal men, who now rule Rome with a bloody and unforgiving hand. The *Dominus* has just instructed me to find trustworthy men who can be sent to the south to watch the roads and warn of the approach of any unknown soldiers from that direction. I must also send a man to Narbo to watch the ships arriving there from Rome. That is all I can say for now, except the *Dominus* has made it clear to me the work here and everywhere else on the estate must continue as before."

Aristides left immediately after delivering his sobering message to a stunned Arcturus, and to an equally upset Athon. *How can I continue to work like this?"* Athon asked himself, as it occurred to him that, perhaps, he should have returned home when he had wanted to earlier. *If only she had returned just two days later, I would not have been here to be put through this agony again.* That was his thought as he mindlessly returned to his work—work which had once been the most important thing in his life but for which he was now losing all energy and enthusiasm.

⟫+⟪

Petra did not appear again for several days, and when she did, there were none of the easy, pleasant exchanges which had begun to return to their recent conversations. This time, she reported there would be no visit from *The Teacher* this month. Apparently, leaders of their *Ekklesias* in the village had heard rumors all large gatherings of Christian followers here and close by would be temporarily suspended, mainly because the elder and others had been summoned to some unknown location. This troubling information brought further worry to them both.

During this same visit, Petra also revealed a disturbing conversation she had overheard between her parents shortly after the warning letter from Rome arrived. Her mother was telling her father they must make plans to leave again as soon as they could. However, he had become angry at those words, something Petra said she had never heard him do with her mother before. He had replied forcefully to her he would not be driven from their home, if he did not have to be; and besides, he told her, there was no place anywhere they could run to now where powerful men like this Septimius Severus and his supporters could not find them, if they were determined to do so.

However, despite Athon's concern, the next month saw a semblance of normalcy return to the pottery works, at least—if not to the villa and his relationship with Petra. Nevertheless, an undercurrent of fear and uncertainty coming from those who had contact with servants or slaves from within the villa's walls permeated the atmosphere of all who lived and worked nearby. Athon had not spoken with Petra for several days, even though the warm weather drove him outside the old shed to do his finer detailed work. On one such sunny afternoon, a fast riding messenger arrived and went straight to the villa. Within a short time, a troubled Athon and Arcturus could plainly hear shouts and other noises coming from that direction. Not long afterward, they noticed some men from the pottery sheds and elsewhere below were leaving their work and the pottery altogether. Arcturus told Athon to remain at the shed while he went to see what was happening to cause so much excitement. When he returned, he immediately confirmed the young man's worst fears.

"A woman who is a servant in the villa has sneaked away and told her husband all is now fear and confusion up there. A messenger who was sent to watch the roads from the south has ridden all night and brought word that two days past a body of strange soldiers left Carcasso, crossed the mountain on horses, and arrived at the old soldier camp in the hill city of Castrum. If they left there this morning and moved quickly, they could be here sometime tomorrow, if this is their destination. There is great fear in the villa among everyone, and now that fear has spread to the pottery sheds and will soon grip the villages along the river. Many have already walked away from their work and have gone to look to their own and their family's safety."

When Arcturus was finished, a frightened Athon looked up the slope toward the villa but could see no one coming from that direction. He had to fight the nearly overwhelming urge to head up there to offer his assistance in whatever manner he could. But he knew full well such was not his place, and for him to do so would only add to the confusion which must be holding sway up there at that very moment. Still, he had rarely felt as helpless as he did just then. Finally, he looked at Arcturus and asked what the painter thought they should do. The older man merely shrugged and then replied.

"I think, my young friend, perhaps now would be a good time for you to make that visit back to your home and family you were so eager to make until the Master's family returned. As for me, I think I will find a boat across the river and spend this night with an old friend who lives on the far bank upstream a short ways. But first, lend me your strong arms and we will move the paint cabinet to retrieve what we have buried there. I do not believe we should come back here until things are settled one way or another up at the villa, and we may surely need what is hidden beneath the paint cabinet in the days to come."

Athon helped Arcturus move the cabinet, and each of them recovered his pot with the coins they had stashed there in the last months. There were more than Athon recalled when he dumped them into his leather pouch and retied it to his belt, while Arcturus did the same. In a few moments, they were finished and quickly put the paints and their tools from the table back into the cabinet and secured it, perhaps for the last time until who might know when. By then Athon could see Arcturus was getting anxious to leave. He picked up a couple of his personal tools he had kept out to take with him, looked at the older man, and said.

"Arcturus, you have been like a second father to me these last months. You have taught me much, and I hope the day comes soon when I can return and sit by your side and learn from you once more. You have also been a friend and a man whose words of good sense I will always cherish."

"No, my young friend, it is I who has learned from you. You have a rare gift, Athon, one I could never possess, and I should not have held it against you in my arrogance when you came to me. I, too, have come to look at you, Athon, as the son I shall never see again. I will be waiting here for your return when the day you have spoken of comes; for no matter who occupies the villa there behind us, the pottery will go forward. Of this, I am certain. But you must go now and prepare for your journey. If I were you, I would wait for darkness before leaving. There are those who certainly know you may carry money, and they would seek to earn it easily by taking it from you. They may have their eyes set for you when you depart. Be careful, and may the gods—all of them—look after you until we see each other once more."

With that, Arcturus turned away and headed down the hill toward the entrance without looking back. Several others were also headed in that direction by then. Athon, however, thought of the journey he must soon make and decided to head back up the slope and off to the left where the kitchen was. Perhaps, he secretly hoped, he might even catch a better view of what was happening at the villa. He sensed there would be no summons for the evening meal at the end of the work day, and no one would have appeared if it had been given. But Athon managed to find a large loaf of the morning's bread and a sizable piece of hard cheese and some figs amidst the scurrying of the two women still left there. He took these without a reproachful look from either of them, before he headed back down the slope to pack for his long journey.

When he got to his dormitory, everyone who still slept there had apparently already collected their belongings and left—except for the one-eyed old man, who said he had nowhere else to go and no more fear of Roman soldiers in his life. Athon decided he would heed Arcturus's advice and wait for nightfall to leave. In the meantime, he laid down on his pallet to rest for his long walk and thought about all that had suddenly gone so terribly wrong. All too soon, he saw the last long shadows of dusk creeping through the open doorway and decided to get up and make his travel bundle. Memories of better times and smiling faces flashed through his mind when he placed the fine tunic, which he had only worn twice, into the center of his bundle of the few things he would take with him. He was just about to tie it when he heard the sound of running feet entering the long room. He looked up to see a man he recognized as the groom—the one who had once made the mistake of losing control of the *Dominus's* fine stallion and thereby altered Athon's life. The young man caught his breath and said.

"Praise swift-footed Mercury I have found you! *The Dominus* sent me to search you out and told me not to return otherwise. I feared you would be gone with the others and I would have to go into the village. You must come with me straight away to the villa. Leave that bundle and come."

Athon dropped his bundle but picked up his purse of coins and retied it to his belt as they walked as fast as they could back up the road to the front of the villa. They arrived as early darkness was setting in and entered the front, just as Athon had done his first day here. The groom pointed him to the same room as before and then scurried away. This time, Athon did not stop to admire the grand mosaic. The same young slave he had first encountered at that very spot on that distant first day was passing by with a bewildered look on his face. He carried a rolled up scroll with a ribbon around it in one hand, and was staring blankly at two silver coins in his other when he went by. Athon looked beyond him and saw Marcus Petronnius sitting alone at his long desk. He was writing rapidly with a quill and there were stacks off different coins and some purses before him, as well as several more of the scrolls like the one the slave boy had been carrying. *The Dominus* looked up at the sound of Athon's approach, smiled quickly, and motioned him to come forward without delay. When he came to a stop at the opposite edge of the desk, the older man laid down his quill, fixed Athon's eye, and spoke immediately.

"Praise Jupiter you have been found. I feared you might have fled with the others. Athon, you must listen carefully and take to heart every word I am about to tell you. When you leave here, you will pass out the back way over there through that doorway. You will follow the passage to the outside and across the back to the stables. There you will find two horses tied and equipped for a journey. One of these you will recognize, I am sure, as my own stallion, *Hannibal.* The other is a mare you may also know. Waiting with them will be my wife and daughter.

"You will lead Petra from this place and down the family's private path to the river road. Once there, you will head downriver until you come to the old Roman wagon bridge. You will cross it and head north. Take my daughter to this hidden valley of yours, but under no conditions from this day forth are you ever to reveal her true name or identity. Do you understand all this? Good then. Petra has been given these same instructions; but Athon you will have to watch her closely and be firm, even if she wants you to return here. Stop for no one. You must be certain not to let the new sun find you on this side of the river. Do you understand what I am telling you to do?"

"Yes, *Dominus,* but your own fine horse. There is no way I can . . . ."

"Athon, you must consider the horses as a partial payment for those which were taken from your family by my people. Ahh, do not act so surprised, my boy. Petra has told me of how they were stolen from your father, and how your family was ruined by it. What she does not know, however, is my father served as commander of the cavalry cohorts with the legions serving here in those days. That was why he chose to acquire these lands before he left. But it is of no matter now. Petra, and her mother also, have told me other things I should have listened to about you after we left Rome to return here. Still, a watchful father can see and know certain things, if he chooses to. I had thought to find her a proper husband by taking her to Rome. However, I was blind to think my daughter could be forced to do something I had not even done myself. I have come to see it was a mistake for me to believe otherwise. But it now appears this new one god you have all taken to so much has chosen to give a foolish father a last opportunity to correct his mistake.

"Here, you will need this," Marcus Petronnius said as he picked up the largest of the bags of coins just in front of him and tossed it across the table for Athon to catch. "I wish it could be more; but as you can see, I have many other obligations to take care of this night, and there has been little time to prepare."

Then, he stood up and thrust his hand across toward Athon where the light caught the large signet ring Marcus wore on his right hand, which he had been using as a seal for some of the papers piled up beside him. When he was certain Athon could see it closely, he spoke with a new tone of desperation in his voice the young man had not noticed before.

"Look closely at this ring, Athon. Do not ever respond to any messenger who might come to you and tell you to return with Petra, unless he can deliver this ring into your hand. Be absolutely clear on this. If, after two months have passed and you have received no such summons from me, and me alone, you will take Petra for your wife—with my full blessings and my hope for your future together. If you are as smart as I believe you to be, Athon, you will use some of those coins to start your own pottery somewhere up there in this Aveyron Valley you have apparently talked to her so much about."

Then, Marcus took from his belt a gilt-handled dagger in an engraved silver sheath and walked around the desk to stand in front of Athon. Marcus placed the dagger firmly into Athon's belt beside his old purse and said in a calmer voice this time.

"You may have more need for this in the coming day than I; but let us hope it does not come to that for either one of us. The dagger comes from the East, where this strange, new god is from. It was once a gift to me from my father who travelled there. I had hoped to offer it one day to my own son."

Athon still had the purse of coins in his hand, but when he reached to adjust the dagger in his belt, he noticed the red jewel in the pommel. He looked up just as Marcus grabbed his wrist there, and then the other one and pulled him to where he could look him in the eye directly as he spoke.

"Athon of Rutheni, I believe you are a man any father would be proud to call his son. From this day forward you must honor me with the thought you might have come to know me in this same way. You must also promise me, in the name of this new god of yours and Petra's, you will take care of her, and you will see that my blood—if not my name—passes into the seasons to come. That is all any man can ask at such a time as this. But now you must go quickly. I hear feet approaching in the courtyard outside. That will be Aristides with the others I have asked him to find and bring to me. I do not want anyone to see the way you are leaving."

A stunned Athon could only nod his acceptance of everything he had just been told and mutter his solemn promise for all that was being asked of him. He was turning to leave when Marcus Petronnius spoke one final time.

"You must keep a firm hand on *Hannibal's* reins. If he feels too light a touch, he will want to bolt and gallop on his own. Follow that same advice with Petra, my boy," he seemed to smile. "Keep a good pace this night, but take care not to wear out your horses. You may have need of their strength in the days ahead. May the gods— both yours and mine—watch over and protect you both. Now go."

Athon left and moved quickly. When he came out of the villa at the back, he looked across an open space and saw two horses tied to a post with iron rings and two women talking quietly as they stood beside them. When Petra's mother saw him coming near, she reached out and hugged her daughter close. He noticed both horses were well saddled, and there were bags and cloaks in front and behind the leather saddles. He could see Petra was strangely dressed as any common Rutheni girl might be. As soon as Athon came to them, Lucia gently pushed Petra away, came over and em- braced Athon warmly, and whispered to him.

"Praise God and our *Christ* you have finally come, Athon. We were about to give up hope. Surely, He looks after us on our day of trouble. You must help Petra mount her horse. She has refused to do so and would not leave on her own until she saw you."

Athon had already tied the larger purse of coins to the other side of his belt, and he used both hands to help Petra mount. It was the first time his hands had ever touched her; but she said nothing as she quickly adjusted herself in the saddle. She was obvi- ously fighting back new tears when she looked down at her mother and spoke.

"Why will you not come with us, mother? Athon can quickly prepare another horse, I am sure."

"I have told you, Petra just as I told your father at his same demand. My place is here at his side, just as it always has been. Now, go and remember everything you have been told. Athon will take you where you will be safe, until you can be sent for. God go with you and protect you both."

With that, she untied both horses' reins and reached them up to Athon. He pulled both animals' heads around and headed for the gravel path leading down the back way to the river road. It had been many years since Athon last sat upon any horse, much less one as fine as this stallion. But all his memories and reflexes came rushing back in an instant, and by the time they made it down the slope he was fully in command of the animal, if not of his own uncertainties. He stopped then, handed Petra the reins to *Medea,* and told her they would follow the road by the light of the newly risen moon reflecting off the nearby river's glossy surface.

They moved downriver for most of the night, skirting any small villages that showed signs of activity or lights beyond the small houses they contained. It was still full dark when they finally came to the old, Roman bridge across the Tarn, the same one Athon had crossed from the other direction, what seemed like half a lifetime instead of much less than a year ago. He decided to walk the horses across to rest them and reduce any unnecessary noise their crossing might make. Once on the other side, they quickly remounted and rode easily until the full dawn found them on the same road north Athon knew would lead him to his home in two days of good riding. They were both tired of the saddle by then and so rode less and walked the horses more than the night before, but only when Athon could see both directions were clear of any other travelers.

By late morning, he could see the old watchtower on the solitary hill looming ahead that marked the passageway past the great stone buttress, which would then lead him to his home valley. He decided to seek a safer path below the road which passed too close by the hill. He found one through some trees marking the course of an ancient streambed, which no longer carried water except when there were storms. When they had gone beyond sight of any watchers on the hill, he halted and told Petra they would eat and allow the horses to graze near a pool of clear water he found nearby. He removed the cloak from behind his saddle and used the leather ties that held it to make hasty hobbles for the horses' forelegs to keep them close, as both fed on the lush, midsummer vegetation. Petra found a food bag on her horse, and they sat down together on the cloak to see what had been packed for them. Inside they found bread, some dried figs and cheese, and meat from a large fowl of some sort, which must have just been prepared the day before.

Petra had spoken little during the long night they passed riding side by side, but Athon had heard her sobbing quietly in the darkness on more than one occasion. As they ate, she asked him how long it would take to get to their destination and how much longer they would ride this day. He could see she was obviously very tired—as was he—but Athon wanted to heed her father's words and put as much distance as he could between themselves and the river behind them while there was light. Still, he could look into her eyes and see she was wondering what must be happening back at the villa, just as he was. Finally, he saw *Hannibal* was getting restless. He told Petra they must leave soon and they would ride until they came to an abandoned hut he knew of off the main road where he had once stayed the night.

That afternoon the rested horses picked up their pace and they covered good ground. At one point Athon noted the path leading to the old swineherd's farm, where he had spent such a miserable night on his journey down to the river. He even wondered if that strange man and his stingy wife still lived there. The light was still good when they finally came to a clearing where he saw the partially collapsed hut he had been searching for in some trees just beyond the main road. They had seen no one all afternoon, and he felt safe enough to stop before darkness overtook them to spend the night in this familiar spot. When they got there, they unpacked their gear and Athon removed the large sack of grain tied to his saddle in front and divided it between the two horses. Then, he told Petra he was going to take the animals to a small water pool he had found once before to let them drink, before he tied them up for the night. He had already decided he would not remove the saddles in case some emergency came on them. However, he loosened the cinches to give the deserving beasts what little comfort for the night he felt he could.

After he tied them to a corner post at the end of the old hut, which was only knee-high where the low remains of the wall on that end had allowed half of the structure's roof to collapse, he stepped inside and saw Petra huddled against the full wall on the other end which was still covered. Their belongings were beside her and she was wrapped in her cloak with her knees pulled to her chest and her head resting upon them. She looked up at his approach, and he saw she had been sobbing once again. He said nothing but sat down close by with his back to the other wall where it made the corner they shared in the dimming light. Finally, he broke the long silence that was oppressive to both of them.

"We will rest here until the sun finds us, or the horses awaken us first. Perhaps we should eat something, if there is enough for tomorrow? We should get to my home by late in the day, if nothing delays us. We will cross the river below the gorge, and once we are up the far side the riding will be easier. My mother will surely have a fire and a hot kettle on. She will open her arms to welcome you as she would my returning sister who, as I told you once, left two years past to move to the coast with the tin trader, and we have heard nothing from her since."

He tried to offer a smile for her as he spoke these last words of encouragement. However, Petra looked up from reaching for the food bag and stared at him for a moment, almost as if she were somehow angry with him. Then she replied with the most words she had spoken to him since they left the evening before.

"Athon of Rutheni, must you always act as if you can hide your true feeling from my eyes? It is not as your sister I would wish to be greeted when I meet your family for the first time on the morrow."

"Nor is it as my sister I would have them know you from this day forth, Petra of Rutheni." He replied quickly, with a sudden smile of relief at having finally expressed what had been in his heart for so long.

They both grinned then at his remark as she dropped the food bag and eased her way over to force her body in close against him. He extended the cloak over her he had wrapped around his back when he sat down, as soon as he felt the shiver in her body from the cooling air. He was certain she also shook from the sobs he noticed still lingering on her cheek, when he pulled her against his chest and held her there with his arm. Moments of silence passed, and then she sighed deeply, pulled herself away slightly, looked up at him, and whispered.

"Athon, I believe mother and father must soon stand before our one, true God and face His judgement, as *The Teacher* has said all men must do on their final day."

"Yes, Petra, I also fear it could be so."

"I know mother will be received by *The Christ* and shown the path to the eternal land of light and hope her love for Him has promised her. But father has not taken the cross of the true believer, and I fear God may deny him entrance into the land of eternal happiness and life."

"Your father is a good man with a generous heart, and I am certain our God will look into it and see he is worthy to receive the love and peace He has promised to all men. If He is the one, true

God, as we both believe in our hearts, then your father will not be denied the reward his good life has earned him in the heavens."

"Oh Athon, I pray it is so. I truly do."

She pressed her head back against him, and he reached over with his free hand and wiped away the last tear that still glistened upon her cheek. She was silent for a few moments and then looked up at him, smiled for an instant, and then said one of those amazing and surprising things she always seemed to throw at him when he was least expecting it.

"Athon, I have thought much about it and have decided I would not be *too* unhappy if our first child should be born with red hair."

He laughed out loud for the first time in many days, disturbing *Hannibal* where he stood tethered a short distant away. The stallion responded with an angry snort, causing them both to laugh a little this time. At that, he pulled her back to him, stroked her dark hair affectionately in his hand as he laughed softly once more, and then wrapped both cloaks more tightly around them both. She sighed deeply and nestled even more closely in against his chest. They soon drifted off to sleep for the first time together—just as the rising moonlight illuminated them for an instant and cast their mingled shadows as one against the far wall of the old stone hut.

THE CARVER

AD 1295

"Will we carve again tomorrow, *Papa?*
"Of course, Phillippe, we carve every day that is not the Sabbath or the feast day for an important saint. Why would you ask such a foolish thing?"

Having replied, the father looked at his son's face and immediately sensed, as well as saw, the disappointment reflected in it. He thought for only a moment before returning his eyes to his hands which had temporarily ceased their movements at his son's query. He knew almost certainly there was more to this unexpected question than he yet knew. However, he waited patiently for the usually reticent Phillippe to get his true reasons into words and present them to his father. After an elongated silence in which he could hear only the boy's irregular breathing, he laid down his wooden mallet and small chisel, turned to his son, and stared at him as if to say: *Well, out with it!*

"I was just wondering, *Papa.* Raymond and Jean told me last evening they plan to go down to the river tomorrow early. Jean says the trout are running already this season, and they plan to fish all morning and catch enough to trade in the village. Jean knows a place where we can catch them easily before others learn of them running. He knows some women in the village who will offer fresh pies or eggs for the trout. There is also the butcher, old man Benet, who may even pay in coin—if the fish are fresh caught that day, Jean says. Of course, I could keep some of what I catch for us to have for our own supper, if you say I can go. It will just be for the one day, and then I will work extra hard to catch up with you for what I have missed—if you say I can go, *Papa*."

"I see. I might have known Jean Maury and that brother of his were involved in this somehow. Those two have little enough to do on their own but get into trouble around here. Now, they want you to join in it with them." He looked at his son and saw the look of utter disappointment in the boy's eyes before he smiled briefly, waved the hand with the chisel in it in disdain, and then replied.

"So, at least this time those two have come up with an idea that might have a grain of real thought and worth behind it. The trout are already running, they say? I have not heard this; but then we have been busy here till late most days. I suppose I can get by without you for one day. There are new planks outside to shave before I can start the next bench anyway. I do not need you for that work. But you will have to catch up on the polishing of this one I am about to finish. You are already behind on it, and there will be staining for you to do on the new one, which I will need you to help me set in next day. I could tell your head and your hands have been on something else all day, Phillippe. I just could not see it was a fishing pole and a sack full of fresh trout. Just be careful at the river. I have no trust in Jean Maury and that lazy brother of his—or anyone else in that family, now that I think about it."

"Oh, thank you, *Papa*. I will be careful, I promise, and we will have trout, and maybe a meat or fruit pie, for supper tomorrow. But you really should not speak so badly of Jean all the time. He gets the blame for every bad thing that happens around here, even when people know it was Raymond and not Jean who did it. He's my friend, and I think people should not blame him so much because there were some bad people in his family a long time ago."

"Perhaps you speak truly, Phillippe, and I should not think such bad thoughts of others, especially here in the church. Father Guillaume would certainly take me to task for my words if he had been here and heard them, no doubt. No man should suffer for the past deeds of his family, or else all of us would spend our days doing penance and little else would be accomplished in this world. "

He grinned broadly, reached out and rubbed his son's head, and then both of them went back to work with renewed purpose. They worked together mostly in silence for the remainder of the afternoon, and the father could see his son's concentration on his work and his desire to complete what he had been told earlier would be his goal for the day had been renewed. Finally, the shadows being cast by the light coming through the open church door indicated it was close to the hour they usually laid down their tools for the day. Still, there would be things to put away and sweeping up to do in order to leave the church as they had found it that morning before they could begin the long walk back to their farm. This time, however, the father judged he had finally finished the scrolls he had been carving on the end of the new pew they had set in that morning and there was no more he would do on it, at least before the final finishing work when the entire row of new benches would be completed. He put his chisel into his wooden tool box and fingered through its contents until he found the short, iron rod with the wood handle he had been searching for and handed it to his son.

"Phillippe, we are done with this one, I think. Take this out to the fire the smith will still have going. You know where his workshop is around the corner. Make sure you get the end to where it is turning from red to white and then hurry back here. I will clean up and put things away while you are gone. I want to leave and get home well before dark this evening."

The boy smiled as he took the short poker and hurried away as he had been instructed. It was a task he had done before when he worked alone with his father, although the older man usually did this himself, if he was not in the hurry he appeared to be today. When Phillippe got to the blacksmith's shed, the man laughed when the boy asked him if he could heat the iron rod in his fire. The soot-covered man in the blackened leather apron merely motioned him toward the fire nearby and went on about his business. He knew well enough what the boy carried in his hand, since he had seen the father come here with it himself several times recently. Besides, he was the one who had made the poker for the boy's father some years earlier and knew it well. A few minutes later he saw the boy scurry off with only a quick wave of his hand in thanks and the glowing, white hot iron clutched tightly in the other.

When Phillippe came back through the church door he saw his father kneeling in the dimming light next to the end piece of the new bench they had been working on all day. At first, the son thought his father was there in prayer; but then he saw he was running his hand softly over the curved scrolls and flowers he had carved into the wood that day. He looked up at his son's approach, smiled when he saw the brightly glowing poker in the boy's hand, and quickly waved him over to where he was kneeling at the front end of the pew. As Phillippe extended the poker to him, he carefully took it, spit on the end to test the power of the heat still there, and then firmly pressed the flattened end of the iron onto a place he had already selected, which was near the stone floor and nearly out of sight.

Smoke rose immediately from the scorching wood, and Phillippe could smell the distinct odor of the burning walnut as the hot iron burned into it. An instant later his father withdrew the poker. He looked up at his son and smiled in satisfaction when he handed the now rapidly cooling instrument back to him. Then, he bent low to examine what he had just done, grunted his approval, and slowly eased himself to his feet using the end of the pew to raise his tired legs and knees up from the cold stones. He looked about him in the fading light at all the work they had already done here—and all that still remained for the days to come—and spoke.

"It is a good mark. The iron was still hot. You did well, Phillippe. Sometimes, I fear, my feet are getting too slow to get back before the heat is lost. I think I will use yours for this from now on. I do wish Father Guillaume would let us keep a fire close outside, but he insists it will blacken his stones too much. Here, give me the iron and I will put it back in the box for another day. Do you want to look at the mark?"

The boy smiled and stooped to find where the last bit of smoke emanating from the fresh impression made the otherwise nearly hidden mark just visible. Phillippe also knew the staining and polishing of the wood he would do himself in the days to come would further conceal it from any eyes not looking for it. It was the mark of the maker of the bench, and the one, final thing his father always did. He had told his son it was to make sure his work would be known by others who came long after he was gone and before the long life of the hardwoods he had learned to carve and shape in ways that would please others for generations to come had ended, or so he hoped. The boy could see the familiar mark, which was no more than half the length of his small finger now embedded in the wood, just as he had seen it so many times before. It was in the shape of a small dagger, with the initials *PG* at the end of the dagger's hilt. The letters stood for *Pierre Gambolet*, the maker of any finished piece that carried that mark.

"Yes, father, it is a good mark. I can see it clearly—if I know where to look."

"True, we hide them just enough that only those who would seriously want to know the maker of such a work will think to look for and appreciate them. To burn them where all could see would distract their eyes from the beauty of our work—and make them easier to find and remove perhaps, ehh Phillippe. Someday, if you continue to learn and wish it to be so, this mark will also be yours to own. You know, that is one reason I fought so hard at your naming to convince your mother Phillippe was a much better name for you than Bertrand. I suppose I did not want to have to add another letter to the old mark later. But come, it grows late and we must still stop at the well and wash before the walk home. The geese and the hog will need to be fed before dark, and I will have to fix us a quick supper. Perhaps tomorrow we can have fresh trout and something from another's hand to feed us, ehh; but only if you are as fortunate as Jean Maury says you will be. And that I will believe when I see it."

They both laughed a little at his father's little jest. It was a re-mark the son had heard from his father's lips on more than one occasion before, but was one he still enjoyed. They stashed their tools in a corner away from the main aisle of the small church and headed for the village well, which was not far away. In a short while they were headed down the road that would take them to their home in about an hour of brisk walking in the cool air of the clear, early spring evening. They had not gone far when Phillippe asked the question that had been on his mind since his father had once again mentioned his naming. It was a question he knew his father had answered before; but he had been younger then and did not pay as much attention to it as he could have. Now that his father had told him the symbol on the iron poker might one day become his mark, too, Phillippe was more curious about why his father would choose this strange symbol to be his maker's mark.

"Father, can you tell me again how you came to use the sign of the dagger as the mark you place with your naming letters to show others who made the carvings they admire? I know you spoke of it before, but there are parts of the story I do not remember as well as I should."

"Ahh, it has been some time since I have thought about that old tale. But it is a good story to tell and hear, I suppose, even if it is just an old legend passed down across the years, with many mouths and many ears no doubt adding their own words to it. I first heard it from my grandfather, Armand, a man who could tell a good story like none other I can recall. It is the story of how our family came to own such a fine piece of land in this valley. The last part of it where our house and fields stand is all that remains of what was once a much larger farm. The legend goes that in the long forgotten past there was an ancestor of our family, one whose name was lost many generations ago, who had somehow come by a silver dagger of great value. No one could remember how this had happened or for how long it had been possessed by the men of our family; but for many, many generations it was passed from father to oldest son as the family's most treasured possession. If a man had no son, it became the dowry of the oldest daughter to ensure she could attract a proper husband.

"Finally, one of our ancestors had twin sons and could think of no fair way to divide the dagger and the family's farm, which had grown very small by that time, when they came of age. Both twins were eager to receive the dagger. Those were days when great lords managed to take and own so much of the land that had belonged to others in better days, before their debts to these lords reduced them to being peasants working only as tenants on the land they had once owned. The story says at that time there was a lord, a count perhaps, who heard of this silver and jeweled dagger and wished to possess it himself. Our ancestor decided to strike a bargain with this nobleman, who owned much land in the valley at that time, since he was afraid this man would soon find a way to get the dagger from him anyway.

"This nobleman, who lived in the old castle on the high rock down near Bruniquel it is told, had four daughters but no sons. He was rich in land, but had no silver or gold to attract good husbands from the nobles of Toulouse, none of whom wanted land in the valley, for his older daughters. Therefore, he offered his two youngest daughters in marriage to the twin sons, since our family still had an old and good name along the lower Aveyron, in exchange for the silver dagger. To complete the bargain, he also offered as dowry the piece of land the father of the two brothers wanted so that each son would have a proper farm when it was divided between them. The deal was struck, and that was how we came by our land. The one brother wished to raise horses and took the parcel that is now owned by the Girards, who sold some of their land away to others many years before I was born. The other brother wanted to grow grapes and make wines, so he took the piece of land where our house still stands. The father was deeply saddened at having to trade the dagger away, but his sons wanted and needed land and he could see no other way. Well, that is how it all happened, at least in the story as it has been passed down for so many generations it is impossible to know if there is still any truth in it.

"So then, Phillippe, such is the legend of the great silver dagger of the Gambolets and how it was lost by a father who could not decide to which son he would give it. But a man cannot grow food on a silver dagger, I suppose, and the land we have is good, although no one has grown grapes on it since before your grandfather's time. When I became a wood carver and others wished to hire me, I decided to leave a mark on the wood somewhere when I was finished. I thought the sign of the ancient dagger would be as good as any beside which to place my initials and honor the name of our family and its long history in our valley. Well then, Phillippe, what do you think? Do you believe the story, and will you remember it better now to pass on to your own sons one day?"

"If you say it is true father, then I shall believe it just as you have told it with no changes. But what happened to the two brothers, and why did the land beside ours pass to another family?"

"Ahh, as the story goes one of the brothers and his wife and children were traveling down to Bordeaux sometime after they were married to sell horses or other animals when some very fierce Norsemen raiding up the Garonne caught them. They killed the man and took captive the wife and children, who were never seen again. The nobleman who was the father of the wife had already died and there was no one to reclaim the land. The other brother did not want it and sold it out of the family, and that was the end of it. To our good fortune, his descendants have kept a firm hold on our farm through many troubled times since, and it will be your responsibility one day, Phillippe, to do the same. So, you must work hard and learn as much as you can; for the future of the good name of *Gambolet* will rest upon your shoulders alone one day."

The boy fell silent for a while as he thought about the weighty words his father had just laid upon him. The last part of the story he could not remember having heard before and somewhere in his mind he was wondering if his father had not perhaps embellished it a little to add to the importance of his final words. However, the story of the silver dagger was a wonderful thing to reflect upon, and he could not help but speculate about how it would have felt if one day he had received such an impressive gift from his father, as had those many ancestors before him.

"Father, what became of the silver dagger after our ancestor traded it for the land?"

"And for his wife, Phillippe; do not forget her. That woman's blood as well as his still flows in us, you know. The story does not tell what became of the dagger afterward. A thing of such beauty and value must have passed through many hands once it became known beyond our family. Who can say? But we have the iron to mark our work, do we not? Through that, we will always possess its image and memory—although I must say the silver and one of the many jewels supposedly encased in the handle would have been a good thing to have on more than one occasion. Maybe it was lost during the great troubles in the last hundred years. Still, I believe it is out there somewhere, and I like to think about all the fathers and sons of our family who once passed it from generation to generation. It is always good, Phillippe, to hold on to such memories. In the end the thoughts of family are what truly sustain us for the certain ordeals to come."

At that Pierre fell silent as the tiring day of sitting or kneeling upon the stones of the church floor and the long walk along the river until they turned away to head for their small house began to catch up with him. Phillippe remained silent as well. As he gazed at the river, his thoughts were already on the next day and all the fun and potential rewards he might reap from his day of fishing with his two friends. His father's story of the twin brothers, and his thoughts of the two Maurys he would meet at the secret place they had arranged for the next morning made him think about what his own life might have been like if he had a brother.

But Phillippe was an only child, the son of a mother who had disappeared from his life when he was very young. Her face was already fading from his scant memories of her and he knew his father had been unwilling to speak of her for as long as Phillippe could remember. Truly, there were many things about his family he did not know or understand. He could only hope his father, whom he held close in every way possible, might someday reveal to him things much closer to them than long held legends, like the one of the amazing silver dagger.

⚔ ⚔

Two days had passed since Phillippe enjoyed his day of adventure and fun with the Maury brothers at the river and later in the village.

They caught some trout, but not nearly as many as they had hoped. By the time they traded some to the housewives to whom Jean made promises earlier there were precious few to divide among themselves and none at all to sell to the butcher. When Jean suggested they return the next day to catch more, Phillippe was forced to decline, knowing full well his father would never approve a request for a second day away from their work. Still, he managed to bring home two fat trout and half a small, goose pie, which was his final share of the day's efforts—after the three had eaten all the fresh currant bread they obtained from one of Jean's "customers", as he called the women. His father had still seemed happy at the results of his day, however, when they enjoyed their fine supper together that evening.

But now they were back at work together in the old church, replacing two short rows of benches with the new ones they had been working on all winter. Phillippe was pushing hard both days to catch up on polishing the ones that were already finished, while his father began shaping the end pieces of the wood he had previously shaved smooth for the next long pew. Once these were set in place, he would begin his carvings outside before the final nails or pegs attaching each end to the new bench was done inside, where he would finish any small carving he still needed to do out of the cool and damp weather of that season. Phillippe would then stain the wood and apply the wax he would buff and polish before the final oil was rubbed in. It was a process father and son shared for many weeks, but was one which kept them mostly indoors during the worst of the winter months, unlike so many of their neighbors.

Most of those neighbors were small farmers, who possessed few skills they could use to add to the often meager supplies of food they raised on their tiny plots along the river. Some also kept small shops in the village. However, there was little money flowing through such an isolated valley even in the best of times, and barter was the mainstay of the local economy. Even the small shop keepers who lived in the village usually maintained garden plots somewhere close by with which to sustain their families. Pierre and Phillippe raised much of their own food as well, but also managed to obtain better supplies than many others from Pierre's skills. These were usually in demand by one of the many churches, or coffin makers, in the small villages along the river—both of which could usually afford to pay for his services in kind, if not coin, even when no one else could.

As Pierre often told his son, they may be as poor as their neighbors, but they were never hungry, even if the food was as basic as most everyone else's. A fat hog could be butchered, cured, and smoked once a year, and there were geese and chickens to roast on special occasions and for eggs, or to trade when needed. Beyond that, they had their fruit trees, the vegetables they grew, and the wild things they collected in the summer and fall months to add to their diet. As long as they had their land Pierre was certain they would somehow manage to survive the harsh times, which seemed to descend regularly upon their little valley, or so it always seemed to the wood carver as he got older.

This day, however, Pierre was working alone outside beside the stone church while Phillippe continued to catch up from his missed day inside. He was carefully shaving the next bench when he happened to glance up and see the brown robed Farther Guillaume approaching. The priest was from a local family himself, a not uncommon occurrence in the more isolated villages, which somehow still managed to maintain a church of their own. He was also a man Pierre had known nearly all his adult life. Pierre had not seen the older man for two or three days and was used to having him come by often to examine his work and to ask one more time when the carver thought he might finish the two new rows of dark, walnut pews for his church. Pierre's answer would always be the same: *As soon as I have finished and am satisfied they will last as long as the church stands, Father.* On this visit, however, the priest simply watched for a few moments and then rather abruptly asked.

"Is Phillippe with you today? I did not see him two days ago when I passed through the church. I hope he is not ill. I have heard there is a winter sickness still going through the village, as is usual in this month."

"He is inside, working hard to catch up from when I let him go fishing two days ago when you were here last. I am always glad we live away from the village when I hear of the sickness there."

"Ahh, yes, the bad air from the river mists is good for no one in this month. But I must tell you, Pierre, only yesterday the widow Rives from the village came to me to say that a certain fresh baked loaf she had cooling in her kitchen widow was stolen. She said it was just after three boys came to her door to offer to trade her some fish they said they had just caught. She turned them away, but when she went to retrieve her currant bread later, it was gone. She told me she recognized the Maury brothers as two of the boys, and thought Phillippe may have been the third. Do you know anything of this?"

"No, Father, I do not. But I will certainly try to find out from Phillippe. We could question him right now, if you wish. Otherwise, I will speak with him later, and if I am not satisfied with his answers, I will send him to you and you may offer whatever punishment you think is fair, with my blessing."

"No then, we will let him stay at his work. I will trust your judgement in this. I can certainly believe Jean or Raymond may have gone back to take the bread; but I cannot see Phillippe allowing himself to be dragged into such behavior. He is a good boy, Pierre, and you should be very proud of what you have done, you know, raising him alone without a mother. Still, he is at an age when a woman's hand to guide him would not be a bad thing for either of you. There are women in this village and others I know who would make a fine wife for a man like you, and be a good mother to your son. I have told you before there are good reasons the impediment of your first marriage could be easily removed by the Church, so you could take another wife. You should think about such things and not continue to dwell upon the bad ones from your past. I worry and pray often about your future, Pierre, and I don't just mean in this life, but in the next one as well, my friend."

"Truly Father, I know I should give heed to your good words. It is just such a difficult thing to think upon after so many years alone with just the two of us and our work. But you are right, I know. Phillippe needs more guidance than I alone can give him. It's just the women I see here all have a look in their eye that tells me they are thinking about what happened to me before. Perhaps, I should look elsewhere—if ever I can find work beyond the valley."

"It is indeed strange you should say this just now, Pierre. There is another reason besides your son I have sought you out this day. It is a most important matter and one to which I hope you will give serious thought. A man came to see me two days ago and your name came up in our conversation. I am sure you have heard of the great cathedral that is being raised over in Albi by our new Bishop. He has already completed the wondrous new palace for his residence next to the old church of the Holy Martyr Sainte Cecile above the river there, and the construction of the first walls of the grand new cathedral in her name is well begun."

"Who has not heard of this, Father? It is being said every brick maker and layer from the Tarn to the Lot Valley has been brought to Albi to work on it. Is it true this Bishop plans the whole structure to be of brick? If so, no one will ever have seen such a church before, or so people are saying. And I have heard also this grand new *Palais* of his is more fortress than Bishop's residence, with towers and walls which are even stronger than the old walls near here at Castlenau and Puycelci, which withstood even the assaults of de Montfort and his Crusaders in my grandfather's time."

"Yes, but such a strong residence was seen as necessary, what with all the past trouble in Albi over the heresies in these valleys; and, as you say, the entire cathedral is also to be of brick. His Grace, this Bishop Bernard de Castanet, wishes only local materials to be used where possible; and, as you know, our stones are not of the same quality as those available to the north, where so many grand, new cathedrals are sprouting from the earth like spring flowers. I think he also wants the Archbishop in Toulouse, and even the Pope himself, to see how he is committed to stamping out once and for all the last heresies of the Cathari in these valleys, as every priest in the Archdiocese knows well enough this Bishop has sworn to do.

"But let us speak of this other matter I mentioned, Pierre. The Friar who came here is an agent for the Bishop—one of these new Dominican Brothers he surrounds himself with, who I fear he also uses to spy on local priests like me. This Brother Gerard who came to see me, however, is a man who travels throughout the entire Languedoc lands looking for men with a skill the Bishop needs for the raising of his grand cathedral. It seems the Bishop himself sent him to make inquiries, and he was then sent to find me. Two months ago the Bishop was returning from a trip in the north, where I was told he went to visit new cathedrals being built as far in that direction as Orleans in order to get ideas for his own in Albi. On his return he happened to stop for the night over at Puycelci and, of course, visited the old church while he was there. Apparently, he was quite struck with its new decorated wooden altar and asked the name of the carver who had done it. Father Michel, whom you know well of course, gave him your name and the location of your home church. Sometime later, the Bishop must have had this man Brother Gerard place your name on a list of people he was to find and try to arrange to come to Albi to work on the new cathedral. Anyway, Pierre, I was asked to approach you and encourage you to take up this offer to go to Albi and work for the Bishop. What do you say to that, my friend?"

Pierre had listened in rapt silence as soon as he began to sense where Father Guillaume's conversation was heading. A knot also started to form in his stomach, and his mind started swirling in a thousand directions at once. Every great possibility and opportunity that had just been laid before him was wrapped equally in one reason or another which immediately worked against it, almost as soon as it jumped into his head. Finally, he managed a sober response.

"I can hardly believe such a thing as you are saying, Father, can truly be possible. What of my work here? We are a good month still from being finished. I have never walked away from a job half done. It is not my way, even for an opportunity such as this. I would also have to find someone to tenant the farm while we are away, and who could say for how long that might be. Still, to leave my work for future eyes to gaze upon in such a place as this fine church would be is something beyond my greatest dreams, and I know I must give serious thought to what you are asking."

"I am glad you are willing to consider it, Pierre. I could, of course, help you find someone to look after the farm. I know a young couple new to the village who would be eager for the opportunity if it was offered. They would be trustworthy, I am certain, since I know both their families well. As to your work here, you would most certainly be allowed to complete it before you left, of that I made certain in my conversations with this Brother Gerard. Speaking of which, there is another matter that must, unfortunately, be discussed since you have shown your willingness to consider his request. He did quite naturally ask about your family, what I knew of your past, and if there was any contact with or heretics in your background. You must understand, Pierre, due to my own circumstances here and things that went on in these valleys in the past, I was forced to be totally honest and direct with this man."

"I see, Father. Certainly I am not surprised such a question should arise, what with this new Bishop's known position and the

Inquisition he has begun over in Albi. What did you tell him about us?"

"I told him many years ago you lost your wife to a notorious *Parfait,* one of the Perfects as they called themselves, who were leaders of those many believers the Church calls Cathari or Albigensi. I said as a result of this man's influence your wife took up the Cross of Occitan, as had others in our village and throughout the Aveyron and Vere Valleys back then. This was even after this Perfect—a man whose name I cannot ever bring myself to utter for the trouble he caused us—was later condemned and burned by the Inquisition in Toulouse, as you must know. Then, I told this Brother Gerard I believed you to be a faithful son of the true Cross, and a man I would personally vouchsafe for before I would allow you into my own church. And then I said your wife had not been from this valley, but came here after her marriage from a village to the south, and she had made few friends here and I believed no others were tainted by her actions when the Great Heresy came upon her, or after she ran off and disappeared.

"Anyway, this Dominican seemed to be convinced by my words, although I fear because of so many others from hereabouts who joined one or the other of the past heresies my own reputation with the Bishop may not be the best one to offer such a recommendation. Still, I hope my faith in your loyalty to our Church has not been misplaced, Pierre. There have been times when I am not so certain what I see in your face on those rare occasions I notice it at Mass might lead me to think you may not truly believe the words your lips are repeating."

"I know, Father, we do not always make the long walk to Mass as often as we should, and my confession has not been as dutiful and perhaps as complete as it should have been at times. It has been hard to get the bitterness of Grunelle's memory from my heart, even if my head has removed her image from its thoughts long ago. But in no way would I ever abandon our Church and take up those beliefs that drove her from our marriage bed long before they drove her from our home. It is Phillippe whom I worry about the most, especially when I know he hears others who say once the Great Heresy finds its way through the door of a house, it will infect all those who live there until it is burned out."

"You must not listen to the words of careless tongues, Pierre. I have preached against such ideas many times. Was it not the false accusations of the grandfather of these same unhappy Maury brothers who caused such great harm to our neighbors not so many years past? Those old wounds have still not healed, and there are some who continue to blame that family for the loss of loved ones back in those dark years. Your Grunelle was not the only victim of the Devil's charms then, and even now still, I fear. I once protected those whose beliefs seemed harmless and were sincerely held. But now I am sworn to bring these same misguided souls to the attention of the Bishop's many watchers, even if I only suspect their beliefs may not be exactly what the Church requires. These are still difficult days, my friend, and if you choose to take your skills to serve the Bishop in Albi, you must be very careful of your words, Pierre. I have heard others speak things I knew to be false about you in the past because of what happened to you back then, and I told them so. But this does not mean these same people might not one day believe they have reason to want to harm you or your family, if they still can.

"With this new Inquisition in Albi, and the zealotry of these Dominicans, who have of late gained so much influence in a very short time throughout the Languedoc, a man cannot be too careful about who he is seen with and what he is heard—or even suspected—of saying. Be advised, Pierre, you must watch your every action once you have gone beyond what little protection a poor village priest of not such a good reputation himself it seems can provide. There will be many eyes and ears upon any stranger in a place now growing as fast as is Albi, and since this powerful Bishop has made it his home. If you decide to leave and go there when you have finished the new pews here, I will give you the letter of introduction which Brother Gerard left with me. It contains instructions for you to present yourself at the Bishop's Palace when you get to Albi. I can read it for you when you leave if you like."

With those words, Father Guillaume placed his hand on Pierre's shoulder and whispered a short prayer of blessing. He then turned and walked away, leaving the carver to think about all he had just heard. It was a few minutes before Pierre recovered enough to pick his draw knife up again and continue shaving the edge of the walnut plank he was about to finish when Father Guillaume first interrupted him. He had heard many things that excited him and about the possibility of working on something which would be as enduring as the grand new cathedral under construction in Albi. But there were also many troubling aspects to the not so subtle warnings the friendly priest had spoken. His words about the circumstances of his wife's abandoning him those many years ago to follow her strange beliefs also dredged up old memories—dark ones which Pierre still continually fought to keep buried deep in his unconscious thoughts.

Nor had Pierre ever been aware of the Priest's past efforts on his behalf to suppress the whispered suspicions about him in the village, which he knew were still held by those who had never liked his wife from the day he had brought her here as a stranger not long after he married her. He was also well aware that for her part she had never made much of an effort to become close to them either. Pierre had long ago come to the conclusion this marriage was the worst mistake of his life. However, every time he looked at Phillippe, he also knew but for what was once a shared passion, which had too soon flamed out between him and Grunelle, his fine son would never have been brought into his life.

He quickly began to think about what the opportunity Father Guillaume had just presented might mean not only for his future, but even more for Phillippe's. Rather surprisingly, the usually careful Pierre quickly decided he would only think about it for one night. If in the new day he could see no reason to change his mind, he would tell his son of his decision to go. They would then make every effort to speed up the work of finishing the last row of pews for the Father's church; say a temporary farewell to their home; and then head to Albi, where the greatest opportunity any artist could hope for in his life was sitting and awaiting his skill to be revealed to generations yet to come.

He also made a vow until the day of their departure, he would attend Mass on a more regular basis to thank the good Father for all his efforts on their behalf and offer a prayer or two in thanks to God for this opportunity. By the end of the day, Pierre's excitement was growing to the point it was increasingly difficult to contain it and keep his mind on his work. At last, he decided to tell Phillippe they would leave the church early that evening. He wanted to get home in time to kill and butcher a fat chicken for their supper. When his surprised son asked his father why they would be having such an unexpected extravagance, especially so soon after their special meal only two nights earlier, Pierre simply rubbed Phillippe's red hair and laughed.

Moreover, on their walk home he did not even bring up the matter of a certain sweet currant loaf that went missing from the kitchen window of the widow Rives in the village two days earlier—and what knowledge Phillippe might have of it. At this point, Pierre was inclined not to hold his son too accountable for the actions of one or the other of the Maury brothers, even if he had possibly shared in the ill-gotten bread. Besides, he was certain this same Rives woman was one of those whom he knew to have spread the rumors in the village about his failed marriage over the years. In truth, Pierre's only thought about it as they walked along in silence that evening was some regret he hadn't received a piece of the purloined, warm currant bread himself.

Spring was giving way to summer before Pierre was fully satisfied his work for Father Guillaume was complete and he and Phillippe could think about leaving to begin what he was starting to anticipate as the great adventure of their lives—or at least of his own so far. Phillippe had gradually become excited at the prospects as well, although he remained somewhat reluctant to abandon his few friends in and around the village to set off on what his father kept describing as a "Heaven sent opportunity for 'men' such as we." Unfortunately, the completion of their work at the church had been slowed first by bad weather and then by the many Easter Season services and events which kept them from their work inside. However, when the new pews were at last finished, Father Guillaume and many others in the village praised their work highly and expressed their desire to see them return soon. Others, though, showed little or no interest in the imminent departure, or return, of either father or son from their tightknit little community along the river.

True to his word, the aging priest found a young couple more than willing to move to the Gambolet family farm to look after it for an as yet undetermined length of time. Pierre liked them both immediately and set forth generous conditions for their occupancy, which Father Guillaume witnessed and approved. It was obvious the young woman was with child and husband and wife, who were both from nearby farms, were genuinely excited at the prospects of being able to raise their child—along with Pierre's animals—in the quiet setting they could now enjoy. Once this final obstacle to their leaving was satisfactorily arranged, Pierre managed to raise a few coins with Father Guillaume's assistance to sustain them until their situation in Albi was finalized. The priest also gave Pierre the name of a tile maker he knew from downriver, a man who had previously relocated to Albi to work on the cathedral and who was someone he felt certain would be willing to take Pierre and Phillippe into his home, at least until they could get themselves established.

At long last the day came to leave. Pierre had told Phillippe countless times he expected it would take them nearly a week of good walking to reach Albi, if no other means of transportation presented itself along the way. He hoped once they reached the Tarn the well-worn river road along its banks might offer an opportunity to catch a ride on a wagon or even a small boat, if the downstream current was not still too strong to row or pole against it in these dryer months. Finally, they bundled their scant clothing and a minimum of provisions into packs they could carry on their backs. The biggest problem had been what to do with the many tools Pierre wanted to take. Finally, he decided to have Philippe pack most of the clothing and their extra shoes, while he would carry the two canvas bags he had made for his tools slung across his shoulders and under his arm. In the end, he was still forced to take only his prized small chisels and curved carving blades, leaving most of his favorite large wooden and leather-headed mallets behind in the hope he could more easily replace them at his destination. At one point, he had even decided to leave behind the monogrammed poker, until the obviously disappointed Phillippe succeeded in convincing him he be allowed to carry it in his pack rather than leave it behind.

They said their few goodbyes the day before and left the farm one clear morning in late May to begin the long trek down to the Tarn Valley. The hillsides were in bloom and the many wildflowers painting the cleared meadows and pastures they trudged past gave a new meaning to "spring" in their walk and conversation. It would be Phillippe's first trip of any distance beyond the Aveyron Gorge area, as well as the first for Pierre since he had brought his wife home to his valley over fifteen years earlier. Those difficult memories for him soon began to fade, however, by the second day after they passed the fortified hilltop of Puycelci, where shortly thereafter they left the main road for a more direct route to the river by narrower, back country tracks. By the afternoon of the third day they reached the river and the small village of Lisle sur Tarn where they spent the first night of the three or four more it would take to make their way along the winding waterway to Albi.

The next day, they came early to the old river town of Gaillac and Pierre decided to stay there and rest until the following day. It was the first real town Phillippe had ever visited, and Pierre allowed his son to wander about and marvel at the contents of the many small food, wine, pottery, and other shops, which displayed a variety of wares the boy had never seen before. Pierre soon found a smith who had a fine-grained stone wheel for sharpening blades, which was better than any he had used for several years. He spent some time working on the edges of all his chisels and small knives, after a short conversation with the smith about his destination and what he would be using his tools for. Everyone he talked with seemed to know something about the new cathedral under construction up river, or they knew someone who had already gone there to work on it or provide some service for those who were.

It was in Gaillac where Phillippe first noticed a woman who passed them on the street with a yellow cross about the length of a hand sewn onto the front of her dress. She had lowered her eyes as if in some embarrassment at his look when she shuffled past. He wondered about this but did not ask his father why this woman was so marked or what the symbol meant until a short time later when he saw a man with a similar yellow cross on his tunic. When his son asked for an explanation, Pierre thought for a moment, stepped closer to him, and looked around to be certain they were alone before he replied.

"This yellow cross is the mark of the repentant heretic, Phillippe. The people you have seen have been brought before the Inquisition or their Church and have confessed to having strayed from the path of the true Cross, or to having followed one or more of the beliefs of the Heretics of Cathar. Those wearing it have been made to do a term of penance and to once again take the *Eucharist,* which their heresy forbade them to do, before they are accepted back into the true Church. They are also forbidden to speak in public or associate with true believers until they have ended this penance. Others, however, are not so fortunate. Some receive terms of imprisonment. And, of course, there are those who refuse either to give up their false beliefs or to swear an oath asking the Church for forgiveness and are condemned to be burned at the stake as unredeemed heretics. This has gone on here for a hundred years and there were those who believed the bad times were mostly past. But now this bishop we go to find has begun his new Inquisitions, and it is but one of many the Pope himself has ordered to be used to root out the last of the old heresies here in the King's new lands. Father Guillaume has told me of other Inquisitions down in Carcassonne and Toulouse being brought against the people in the mountains to the south as well. I fear the old days of burnings; the splitting apart of families; and the confiscations of property may be returning once more.

"But it is not for people like us to judge such things, Phillippe. You will see many things in the days and months ahead which may, I fear, trouble your thoughts. You must remember why we have come so far and that what we will be doing is for the good of the true Church and not concern yourself with these people who have taken another path. Still, we must be careful of what we say and do. Many things will be much different here than in our own village and the Aveyron Valley. Remember also every person you meet is a stranger, and there will be many you cannot trust with your words, or with anything else. You must always be careful of our belongings, especially our tools. There will be thieves about in a city like Albi—and I don't mean those who just play at it, like your friends Jean and Raymond."

They both laughed at this reference to Philippe's friends and Philippe almost immediately changed the direction of the conversation, before his father brought up any of his own past behavior.

"Yes, father, I will be careful as you say. Will we stay in the city and have our own house? It will seem strange not to be at our farm with the animals. I wish we could have brought *Jacques* with us. But I know he was too old for the long walk, and he would miss chasing and barking at the geese. Do you think we could perhaps find another dog in the city, or even a cat, if there is room for one? This man we must look for, what if he has no room for us? Where will we stay?"

"You ask too many questions for which I do not have answers, Phillippe. We will worry about these things when we get there. We must first concern ourselves with where we can sleep and eat tonight. I don't want to stay in the open as we have been doing in such a place as this with so many people about, and I feel certain the inns I have seen are going to ask for more money than I wish to pay. The blacksmith told me if we go to the big Abbey that is close by and tell them we are headed for Albi to work on the cathedral, the friars there will usually take such travelers in for the night and offer them a meal. When I told the smith I had a letter asking us to come, he laughed and said that was sure to get us a dry bed and full bellies. The Brothers, he said, are noted hereabouts for the wine they make and serve at their table—if not so much for their generosity with it, or their bread. I think we should try to find this Abbey before it gets too late and their generosity has been given to other poor travelers."

Pierre laughed and wrapped his arm for a moment affectionately around Phillippe's shoulder, pulling his son to him. Phillippe smiled at his father and the two of them set off for the Abbey, which they soon located after asking a man who was unloading a cartload of carrots nearby for directions. When Pierre asked at the Abbey door if there was a place for them to stay and showed the letter, which he could not read but which must have carried an important seal, the young Friar who answered their knock seemed very impressed and immediately invited them in for the night. They were taken to a kitchen, where they were given food and drink with several other men, who must also have been guests for the night. The cheese and bread were fresh and filling, but there was no meat, nor any butter or oil to soften the bread—and only one half-filled cup of the good wine for each.

Then, they were given a candle, led to a small room with two straw pallets on the floor, and told it was theirs to use if they needed it for more than the one night. They slept past daylight for the first time in several days and awakened well rested to begin the last leg of their journey. Pierre found out that morning the others with whom they had eaten the night before had all been forced to sleep together in a single crowded space with only scattered straw to pile up for their bedding. For the first time, he began to realize the letter Father Guillaume gave and read to him before they left for Albi must carry some authority or power he had not suspected until now.

After a breakfast of hot barley porridge with goat's milk, they thanked the young Friar who still attended the door, accepted his blessing, and set off. He told them they should make it to Albi by the middle of the following day and even gave them the name of someone who might take them in for this night, if they wanted to walk that far. Pierre thanked him warmly and they headed back to the main river road. It was soon obvious there were now many more people moving in the same direction as they were, and the crowded and dusty road as it followed the twisting river would slow their progress.

Whenever the road ran directly close to the Tarn they could see the river traffic was very heavy with many vessels of different shapes and sizes, most of which were loaded with exotic products heading down river to the broad Garonne, and then perhaps on as far as Bordeaux and the coast. Phillippe had many questions about the things they were seeing, and Pierre answered them as best he could. However, some of those things he had not seen before either, since it had been many years earlier when he last left their valley himself.

By the middle of the next day they saw the smoke and first large buildings of Albi looming ahead on a bluff above the river. There were roads from other directions joining the main road by then and ever greater numbers of people moving along with them. There were two and four wheel carts loaded with produce from the countryside, mules burdened with fire wood, thatching, and any number of other loads of all descriptions, and people pulling loaded handcarts. Occasionally, they would pass a well-dressed man on horseback and Phillippe would stare at clothes he had never seen before, or the polished and decorated leather of the horse's tack. Finally, they began to descend toward the main town just above the river when the towers of what must be the Bishop's new palace came clearly into view for the first time. The bright, red bricks caught the descending light from behind their backs and seemed to bounce back at them, almost as if four giant candles were looming and beckoning to them in the near distance.

The road with its many travelers soon approached the highest and most magnificent bridge Pierre had ever seen, before they finally turned away to head for the brick towers of the new palace, or fortress as it appeared from a distance. It didn't take long for the two of them to see the activity going on just next to it, where two long walls were being raised. It could only be the site of the vast, new cathedral, Pierre thought as they headed for it. Suddenly, however, he realized he had no real plan as to what he should do next; nor any idea of how to go about finding the man Father Guillaume had told him to seek in such a place of swirling humanity as the "City" seemed to him to be. They simply continued to allow themselves to be drawn along with the others heading in the same direction, much as if they were so many moths moving to a flame, the blinding light of which they were helpless to avoid.

Finally, however, they came to an area of many food stands and various other stalls, which seemed to turn the streets around the construction site into one large, permanent market day, or so it seemed to the father and son who had never encountered anything like this before. The appealing smells emanating from the cook pots of several of the stalls led Pierre to decide they should first find something to eat from the many choices presented. This would also give him the opportunity to ask questions about how to go about finding a person he knew so little about in such a big place. They were soon enjoying a fine, hot sausage and a half loaf of bread—but for twice the money Pierre would have expected to pay. He then began to ask the questions he hoped would lead him to someone who might help them. After what seemed like a dozen false leads, he finally found a man who, when he learned the individual they were seeking was a tile maker, informed Pierre he should go back, cross the bridge to the part of town on the other side of the Tarn, and look there for the shops of the clay workers. He knew there was a tile-making factory over there, which served the roofing needs of the many new structures constantly going up in the city. Perhaps, he said, Pierre could find a guild master there who might know this man he sought and where to find him.

It was late in the afternoon by the time the two weary travelers made it to the place for which they were searching. Phillippe had been dazzled by the walk across the high bridge and the view of the river flowing below with the many vessels tied up along the banks on either side. They soon learned it was a toll bridge, but only wagons or other conveyances paid the fee for passing over. At last, Pierre found the tile merchant with the workshops in the rear and asked about the man they sought. Someone from the shops was summoned and was able to tell him where he thought they could find the house of this man. Fortunately, it was not a long walk and Pierre soon realized many of those who worked in the main town must be living on this side of the river.

Dusk was just beginning to fall when Pierre came to the single floor cottage, surrounded by the remains of an old, wattle fence with no gate. There was a small, dusty garden in the narrow space between it and the similar house on one side, with an empty space on the other. They walked slowly to the pieced together wooden door, and when Pierre saw candle light through a narrow opening in front of his face, he knocked. Moments later a man's face appeared at the opening and Pierre spoke.

"Is this the home of Pons Belot?"

"Yes, it is. Who are you, and what do you want?"

"My name is Pierre Gambolet. This is my son Phillippe. Father Guillaume de Montricoux has told us you might offer us shelter. We have just come from the Aveyron to work on the new cathedral at the Bishop's request. I have a letter that … ."

"Ahh, Father Guillaume has sent you, you say." The man's face disappeared, and a moment later the creaking door swung open and a man about Pierre's age stood before them in the dim light coming from within. He hesitantly looked outside past where his unexpected visitors stood for an instant and then said.

"Come in. Come in. You have travelled far, I can see. You must excuse me for my hesitation. A man can never be too careful in these times whenever a stranger knocks at his door. Leave your packs on the floor there, and I will tell my wife Alissa we have visitors. Unfortunately, our meal this evening is quite a simple one, but you are welcome to share it."

Pierre and Phillippe dropped their packs and Pierre told his host they had eaten in the market place by the main square earlier. Pons Belot seemed relieved and soon summoned his wife to introduce her to their guests. He told her they were from the Aveyron Valley and Father Guillaume had sent them, which seemed to relieve her initial look of concern. They were led to the kitchen, but accepted only some hard cheese and warm, dark bread, which appeared to have been baked earlier that day. After their two hosts had eaten and the wife was cleaning up, Pons produced a good-sized jug of wine and two cups. He filled them, handed one to Pierre, kept the other himself, and spoke.

"How is the good Father Guillaume these days? Still trying to convert everyone in the valley who keeps a Cross of Occitan hidden somewhere, I suppose. Oh well, I should not complain of such things. Alissa and I both owe him more than we can ever repay for helping us out of our own little difficulty not so many years past. But there is no need for either of us to speak more of such things here. I trust he will have had his reasons for sending you to us, and it is best that here of all places the less one knows of these things the better for everyone, ehh. You mentioned before the Bishop himself has summoned you here to work on his grand monument to his victory over the Heretics. Tell me, Pierre, what skill is it you possess to draw his Lordship's attentions from such a distance?"

"I am a wood carver. I suppose I have shown some skill in the work I did for the old church at Puycelci, which the Bishop saw when he visited there. Afterward, I was asked to come here to work. That is all I know except I was told by Father Guilllaume to present the letter I carry at the Bishop's Palace when I arrived in Albi."

"I see, but you must have undervalued your talents considerably to have drawn such attention. I am surprised the good Bishop would even have visited the church in that old nest of heretics up there at Puycelci. Even the great Cathar slayer himself, Simon de Montfort, could not force those people to open their gates to his Crusaders when they besieged that fortress of a town, or so my grandfather once told me. Ahh, but that was many years ago, when our land still belonged to the noble and more reasonable Count of Toulouse and others like him, and not this far away King in Paris. It seems now the old days of leading our own simple lives here in the Languedoc are gone forever, since we have all become a part of this king's France. But enough of such talk, ehh Pierre.

I suppose your son is with you as your apprentice. You must watch out for him here. There are many unholy men in this city who are not filled with the same religious zeal of our great Bishop, Bernard de Castanet."

"Yes, Phillippe has been warned to speak and tread carefully and to be watchful for thieves. But I am surprised to see so many men, and even women, wandering the streets here who wear the yellow cross. I would have thought the Church would not want so many of these people to be seen so close to where this new cathedral that will bear the name of the Holy Sainte Cecile will rise."

"Ah yes, but you will find our good Bishop seems to keep a steady stream of new penitents issuing forth from his far-reaching Inquisition—if they do not find their way to the dungeons of his new palace. He seems to have discovered he can use those reformed heretics who have skills needed for his grand building by paying them nothing and feeding them little while they work out their penance to God for him. And there is still the occasional burning of some poor soul in the church square, which also has the effect of keeping all the others in line, although I must say these have diminished to almost nothing in the last year or so. These new Dominicans, however, whom we are starting to see everywhere these days, do not show the same easy forgiveness in their hearts for the people here that men such as our good Father Guillaume and others—even the Bishop himself sometimes—have shown in the past. Men say it is the King up in Paris, as much as this new Pope, who has brought these Inquisitions upon us to enforce his rule, now that all the Languedoc lands have come fully into his power.

"Still, who can speak with true wisdom about such matters? You and I are only poor men, trying to feed ourselves and our family and do some good for each other when we can, ehh? In the morning, you will walk to the Bishop's fortress, or palace, or whatever it is, and begin to learn these things for yourself. I will go back to making tiles for the roofs of the grand houses of wealthy men, who seem to be everywhere in this town these days. And you, my friend, will begin carving for the greater glory of God—and Bishop Bernard.

"But for tonight, and until you can find a place of your own, you are welcome here. Alissa has just nodded at us, which means she has the little room in back against the kitchen wall ready for you both. Sadly, it is not large, but it will be clean and warm against the house wall. I will help the boy with your packs while you finish your wine. Now that's the one thing here that is always easy to find—and cheap to buy. Everything else, I'm afraid, is not. So then, Pierre, you must be sure to strike a good bargain for your skills with the Bishop; or you will soon find yourself an even poorer man here than you may ever have been in the Aveyron Valley."

Two full days had passed since Pierre first presented himself, and his letter, at the entrance gate of the Bishop's residence, which stood in grand splendor directly adjacent to where the construction of the new Cathedral of Sainte Cecile was well under way. However, even though work at the site had been going on for more than five years already, Pierre was more than a little surprised when he beheld how little seemed to have been accomplished, despite the constant work by the many hands that seemed to be going on everywhere he looked. When he and Phillippe were stopped by a soldier at the outer entrance gate, he presented his letter to one of the guards. This man, who obviously could not read the letter himself, took it into an inner courtyard, which was overshadowed by the great towers and walls surrounding it. Not long after, the guard returned with a young friar or monk, who introduced himself to Pierre, asked a couple of questions, and then informed him he must return in two days' time at this same hour, when the

Bishop would be in attendance and conducting interviews in his residence with those who had business with him.

Pierre took back his letter and left, disappointed at the additional wait they faced after having come so far. However, those two days gave both father and son the opportunity to look about the bustling town and learn many things about what was to be their new home for a period of time Pierre could not yet define. Before going back to the house of Pons Belot that evening, Pierre used a good portion of his remaining money to purchase some sausages, a sack of radishes and one of onions, and another good-sized jug of wine to offer his hosts to help repay their hospitality, which was obviously going to be important to Philippe and himself for a while longer, at least until his situation with the Bishop became clearer.

When they left the Bishop's Palace that first day, Phillippe wanted to go down to the river to look at the many boats tied up and passing by. They sat together on the bank and watched the continuous stream of barge and boat traffic come and go and marveled at the many goods as they arrived and were quickly unloaded. Pierre was amazed at the seemingly endless line of barges carrying bricks from factories somewhere upriver, which new ones seemed to appear as if by magic as quickly as one was unloaded. Some boats carried produce of all kinds from farms and forests, while others brought finished goods, including wood tables, chairs, and other furnishings of every description. It was quickly apparent Albi was a fast-growing city with an insatiable appetite for products and foods of every kind. It was also apparent the driving force of it all must be the grand building being raised not far back upon the hill above where Pierre and Phillippe sat watching it all. Finally, hunger drove them both back there toward the bustling market square to join the many others drawn to its ever-changing array of beckoning aromas and unusual sights.

That same evening as Pierre and Pons sat sipping some of the wine Pierre had bought, he asked his host many questions about what he and Philippe had seen their first full day in the city. So much of what they observed was either alien or new to his experience he wanted to know more about some of it. One of the more surprising things had been the many boats loaded with bags of plants he did not always recognize. There were also barges being loaded with large barrels setting off downriver, whose contents he had wondered about as well. Pons laughed and told him he had been looking at the true wealth of the city, and not the false wealth the Church and its Bishop created mostly for their own benefit.

"You see, Pierre, the real money here is made by the *pastel* merchants. We are on the edge of the region here and to the south where the great *Woad* industry has begun to thrive. Since we have come under the wings of the King of France, the demand for the colors the leaves of this plant produce has exploded like so many spring flowers themselves. The fine blue dyes produced here and to the south make their way down to Toulouse and then to Narbonne for shipment to Rome or Venice and even, it is said, Constantinople. Or they float down the Garonne to Bordeaux and then to England or up to the Flemish cloth makers. That is what you undoubtedly saw in those barrels, although a good deal of wine also finds its way down the Tarn from the many vineyards all around us. Grapes and Woad, Pierre—purple and blue—a man can become rich, if he has enough of the right kind of land in these times. Those who do, build their fine houses here to remain close under the Bishop's protection. Some of them, though, move down to Toulouse to be nearer the coast at Narbonne. That way they can count their sacks of gold even faster when their ships return with the fine things from Italy or Barcelona their *woad* profits there have brought back, which make them even more money when they sell them here.

"Ahh, to be a *pastel* man, my friend. They should all paint themselves blue to honor the humble plant that has made them rich men. But I will tell you this, Pierre, you will never see any of those men with a yellow cross upon his fine, embroidered tunic, even if more than one, I have heard it whispered, should be made to wear it. It seems our Bishop is a judge whose head can be turned away from some men with a known heretic sitting on an easy to see branch of their family tree—if a proper 'donation' has been made to his grand project. I can tell you many of those red bricks in his fine palace would be better painted blue from the *woad*, if the truth of who has paid for them were to be known."

Pons laughed at his last comments, and Pierre could easily see his host was a man who would say things when he was enjoying a couple cups of strong wine he might not otherwise have uttered. Still, in the two nights before his appointment at the Bishop's residence came around, he learned a great deal from Pons Belot that was either strange, troubling—or both—about certain things or persons he might encounter in the days ahead. It gave him much to think about that last night, before he and Phillippe arose early to prepare themselves as best they could for their long-anticipated appointment. Alissa Belot had cleaned their best clothes for them the day before, and they left early to be sure to arrive at the same gate where they had been before in plenty of time.

They arrived early for their opportunity to present themselves to the Bishop. Nevertheless, there were still many ahead of them by the time Pierre presented his letter at the main entrance and was shown into the inner courtyard to wait with the others already there. The same young monk as before took his letter of introduction when they arrived and quickly disappeared, leaving Pierre and Phillippe to mingle with the growing number of persons who had come on some business or other in the hope of seeing the Bishop or one of his representatives in person. They waited most of the morning as others came and went around them. Pierre noticed many of those reemerging from the door into which they had disappeared earlier wore looks of disappointment upon their faces. Finally, the young monk reappeared and summoned Pierre by name. When they got to the door, he politely informed Pierre that Phillippe would not be admitted and must wait outside for his return. Pierre informed his son and pointed to a shaded corner not far away and told him to wait there for him.

The monk led him up some stairs and then through a short passageway, which soon opened into a large, sparsely furnished room. It was well lit from several high windows on one side. At the far end a handful of robed and well-dressed men stood around a middle-aged man who sat in an ornately carved chair. Pierre admired the chair even before he more closely inspected the man seated in it. The Bishop, who was not as finely dressed as Pierre would have anticipated, stopped talking to the dark-robed Brother standing beside him, turned, and eyed Pierre's humble clothing and appearance as if he were bored. Then he began to read the letter which the monk handed him. As soon as he was finished, the Bishop looked closely at Pierre as if he were recalling something and then spoke not to his petitioner, but to the man standing beside him.

"Yes, Brother Gerard, I believe I recall the matter now. We were at the old church at Puycelci where I very much admired the new altar I was told had just been installed there. So, this is the man you have managed to find for me who claims to have carved those wonderful images I beheld that day."

The Bishop then turned to where Pierre stood most uncomfortably, looked him over from head to toe once more, and addressed him directly this time.

"Tell me, Pierre Gambolet, are you the man who carved the altar I just spoke of? I do recall now the Priest there, Father Michel as I remember, spoke most highly of your skills. Why has it taken you so long to appear before us, since Brother Gerard says he wrote this letter more than two months past?"

"Yes, Your Grace, it was I who carved the altar you spoke of. When I was told of the letter by my Priest, he thought it best when

I asked him what to do I be allowed to finish the work I was doing for our small church, before I made the long journey here. I did not wish to leave my work unfinished, although I was most eager to answer Your Grace's most generous summons."

"Indeed. It speaks well that you are one who takes enough pride in his work to see it through. You will find there is much to be accomplished here for a man who believes God does not place a time limit on how men use their talents in His name. I remember quite well this altar you carved, now that I think about it. I was struck by your choice of woods and the unusual dark coloring and high polish you achieved in your work. Tell me, master carver, for as a boy I had some experience in a wood worker's shop myself, why did you choose the wood of the walnut tree? Is it not difficult to carve, and one most woodworkers will avoid when other woods are available to them? "

"Yes, Your Grace, it is so. The wood is difficult; but my grandfather taught me the skills of using small blades and how a careful man can use the grain, once he has learned to see it. He also taught me a carving in walnut that is well cared for will last far beyond anyone's memory of the one whose hands shaped it."

Pierre smiled and lowered his eyes as a sign he was finished speaking. The Bishop smiled in return at these last words. Just then the man at his side leaned in and whispered something into the Bishop's ear. The Bishop seemed a little irritated by what he was hearing and his smile quickly disappeared. Almost immediately, he waved the Brother off with a quick motion of his hand and then once more addressed his petitioner.

"Your words are truly spoken, master carver. That wood will long outlive the man who has the skill to shape it. I am told also your house was once tainted by the Devil, who carried off your spouse and turned her against the true Church. Brother Gerard tells me this priest of yours, this Guillaume de Montricoux, has assured us of your personal loyalty to our Mother Church and the true Cross. I suppose we must take him at his word, although I believe he is one of many local priests from those valleys about whom we have had our own doubts. But then we cannot get rid of every one of our parish priests in this *prefecture* who has the smell of some past heretic still lingering on his cassock because he once stood too close to their heresy. If we did, I doubt we would have many village priests left above the age of twenty anywhere in the entire Archdiocese from here to Spain, ehh Brother Gerard.

"Now tell me, master carver, if I accept you into the service of the Holy Martyr Sainte Cecile to work upon this grand cathedral we will raise in her name to the greater glory of God, will you commit yourself as loyally to our service as you have to this Father Guillaume what's his name? Consider your answer well before you give it; for we shall not look with kindness upon those who abandon a work not finished."

"I have considered it much already, Your Grace. It has never been my way to place my mark upon even a simple bench that has not been completed to the satisfaction of the eye of him who asked the thing of me—or of my own—until we were both satisfied I have done the best I could."

"Truly, that is a very proper answer. But we will not be making benches here, master carver. If your skills are truly what we have been told, you will be asked before your days here are finished to do things with them you have never before attempted. If you wish to join us in our efforts, I will look for you on the morrow after the bells for the first *Matins* have sounded. I will be beside the east wall, where the Master Architect keeps his tent. Look for me there. The artist's drawings I would have you see will be there as well, and we will decide together if there is some portion of those images your skills can bring to life. I will look forward to following your work, Pierre Gambolet. Perhaps, we can even speak more of your knowledge of different woods. This is a subject that remains close to my heart from the days of my boyhood and memories of those often happier times I still hold dear."

With that the Bishop smiled at Pierre one final time and then motioned for the young monk, who had ushered him into the palace, to step forward. At his signal, the monk approached Pierre, touched his arm, and led him back out from the Bishop's presence the same way they had come in what seemed like only a few seconds earlier. Pierre's feet seemed hardly to touch the smooth stone of the floor as he followed the young man out. The exhilaration he was experiencing, along with the anticipation of what he was committing himself to, was nearly overwhelming him just then. Bishop Bernard de Castanet was not at all the kind of man he was expecting from the things he had heard from Pons Belot and others in the last days. Pierre had felt dazzled by the man's sheer presence, and his power to control everything, and everyone, around him. Now, however, these impressions of the Bishop were quickly dispelled by new and evermore exciting thoughts, which seemed to jump into his spinning head with each new step he took.

As he came back into the courtyard, he was nearly blinded by the sunlight, which was almost directly overhead and shooting its brilliant shafts of light straight down between the high walls surrounding the narrow open space and keeping it darkened most of the rest of the day. His thoughts were brought back to the present and he immediately turned to the corner where he had told Phillippe to wait for him. The boy was still seated on the ground against the cool wall, but he jumped to his feet as soon as he saw his father emerge from the narrow doorway he had entered only a short time earlier. Father and son were quickly reunited, and Pierre grinned, wrapped his arm around the boy's shoulder, and led Phillippe back out past the guarded gate and into the bustling city, which quickly enveloped them—for the first time since their arrival, perhaps, as two of its own. When they were outside once more, the smells of the many market stalls immediately assaulted their senses. Pierre rubbed Phillippe's hair, as was his habit, laughed as he had not done in many days, and said to his son's surprise.

"Let's find something to eat, and not just a hard sausage and cold bread this time. I think we have enough money for a half a fat hen, or even a small shank of mutton. What would you say to that, Phillippe?"

The boy glanced up at his father with a quizzical look, saw the broad grin there, and quickly mirrored it back to him with one of his own. Then, they both laughed and headed off at a brisk pace together in search of one of the various food stalls, whose many delightful aromas they had always passed without stopping to buy in their earlier trips through the town's sprawling markets.

Pierre and Phillippe got up early again the next morning and returned to the cathedral construction site to find out just what they had been summoned from so far away to work upon. This time, Pierre brought all his tools and neither father nor son wore his best clothes in eager anticipation their work might commence immediately. Pons Belot was most curious the evening before to hear the details of his guests' encounter with the famous Bishop, a man he had never even seen himself, except twice at a distance. However, Pierre was fully aware of his host's ambivalent feelings about the Bishop and his Church. Thus, he had chosen his words very carefully while withholding some of his more favorable impressions, which he knew ran counter to what Pons had told him concerning his own feelings toward the famous man.

When he and Philippe arrived at the bustling work site on the east wall of the cathedral, Pierre had no trouble finding the tent where the Bishop told him he would be. Workmen seemed to be everywhere. New scaffolds were being raised or existing ones used to haul up the endless loads of bricks and mortar being sorted and produced below. Each new level to which the walls, with their hidden buttresses built inside, were raised required the wooden scaffolding also to rise to accommodate the many bricklayers. Pierre would soon learn more than one of these men had fallen to his death or been seriously injured in past accidents, and these accidents would only increase as the outer walls grew ever higher. Nevertheless, nothing but a shortage of bricks or some other essential material would ever slow the progress of raising the outer shell of the great building, which was rising nearly as high as the fortress-like towers of the Bishop's palace directly adjacent to the growing cathedral.

This morning there were many men milling about the largest tent in the center of several others like it and various similar temporary structures on the east side, where they could face the light from the morning sun. The tent of the Master Architect had its wall on that side raised when Pierre and Phillippe arrived. They could see from the many differently dressed men including monks, and even a couple of soldiers, the Bishop must, indeed, be visiting that morning. Pierre would soon learn Bishop Bernard kept a close eye on the progress of his grand project and had immersed himself in countless details of the ongoing work. He was also about to learn the Bishop somehow knew and was interested in much more than the average churchman about many things, not the least of which was wood working. The two new arrivals, however, were instructed to remain outside the tent as other, more important visitors came and went. Pierre was becoming frustrated, until finally the Bishop happened to catch sight of him and quickly ended his conversation with the workman he was talking to and waved for Pierre to come into the tent. This time the carver pulled his son in with him before anyone could tell him to leave the boy behind.

"Ahh, come close, master carver. This is the man I was speaking of earlier this morning, Maubrey," he said as he turned to another man standing at a table close by. "Come here, Gambolet, is it not? There is something I wish you to see. Brother Jean, hand me those drawings I asked you to bring out earlier. This is the carver I am hoping can give life to them." The Bishop reached his hand toward the older monk standing behind him without even looking in that direction.

"Is this boy your son? But of course, he must be. That hair is too like your own. In this light it is much the same color as the bricks we are piling up here," he laughed. "A sign from Heaven, a sure sign, I think." Others standing around the table also laughed at the Bishop's joke, and Pierre blushed a different shade of red, as Phillippe pressed even more tightly in against him. Still, he found the words to answer as he bowed low to address the Bishop.

"Yes, Your Grace, this is my son Phillippe, who is my apprentice, and who is also most eager to lend his humble hands to such important work. "

"Ahh, excellent, we will have work for the hands of all God's children before these walls are raised to the height we would see them, ehh Master Maubrey. But come close here, wood carver. I would set out your first task, and then we shall see if your skill— and your ambition—can match your eagerness to set your hands to the Lord's work we do here."

Pierre handed Phillippe his shoulder bag of tools as a sign he should remain where he was and then stepped forward to look at the many drawings and plans already spread out on the long table in front of him. Those who were standing next to the Bishop moved away slightly and Pierre suddenly found himself the sole object of the great man's attention. The first thing that struck his eye in the center of the table was a drawing of what appeared to be the master plan of the final shape and size of the great cathedral as it would look when it was finished. His jaw fairly dropped open in wonder at what he was seeing. However, before his eyes could wander to the many other drawings catching their focus, the Bishop laid down a rolled parchment in front of the two of them and began to speak.

"We will not concern ourselves today with these other plans, master carver. You are here to work on the vision of our artists for what the grand interior will one day look like. Some of these things we or others like yourself may bring to life, and others perhaps not. But it is for God to judge which; for it is in His good time much of this work will be completed, and not ours. Here," he said as he unrolled the long parchment. "I wish you to look at these figures of the twelve apostles of our Lord and Savior and tell me if you can give life to them in wood in the way the artist has envisioned them."

Pierre's heart nearly jumped into his throat at his first glimpse of the drawings the Bishop unfolded before him on the table. Twelve figures of Christ's apostles had been depicted in various poses and clothing by an artist, who obviously possessed great skill. Pierre was not accustomed to carving human figures in the round, but he had done so with animals and birds many times. Still, he could sense immediately it would be the greatest challenge of his life to undertake such a project and his heart was fairly racing with the prospects. Finally, without looking at the Bishop for fear his uncertainties would be clearly evident in his eyes, he took a deep breath to clear his throat and spoke.

"These are truly wonderful images, Your Grace. The artist is without a doubt a man of great skill. I have never seen their equal. What size would these statues be, and how close would they be placed to the eyes of those who will look upon them?"

"Why, we would expect them to be as close to life-size as they can be made from a single piece of wood. The plan is to have them on the last columns leading to the altar on either side and on pedestals where men might kneel before them and speak their prayers directly to these saints. Tell me, Pierre Gambolet, are you the man to bring these figures to life, and can you carve them in walnut, as you did the altar at Puycelci?"

Bishop Bernard's question had not caught Pierre by surprise, but apparently it did some of the other men standing close by, and one or two low murmurs were soon exchanged. Pierre thought for a moment as a thousand questions and more than a few doubts raced through his thoughts. Then, he tried to pull himself to his full height, turned to face the Bishop, and spoke."

"Yes, Your Grace, I believe what you ask can be done. But I fear it will be difficult to get walnut wood in the size and quality needed for such large figures. There cannot be many trees of the needed size and without defects in the wood, which sometimes reveal themselves to my hands only after the carving is well underway. Surely, the best trees for this must come from the north. But I must tell Your Grace that even then, to finish but two such figures in a year would be all that I or anyone could do."

The Bishop laughed out loud at Pierre's last remark, and several of those standing around the table chuckled as well when they heard the Bishop's sudden outburst. When he quickly regained his composure, Bishop Bernard smiled warmly at a blushing Pierre and said for all to hear.

"My dear, foolish, carver, none of us here will ever live to see the day these statues are put in place, as the Master Architect and we have envisioned them. Nor will even your son's children gaze upon the finished interior of what these walls we are raising will contain. Many other hands work each day to fill this great cathedral; for it is not, my friend, just a monument to the glory of God. This church is to be a testament to the faith and loyalty of those in this troubled land who once turned their eyes from His True Church, but have since returned to His welcoming arms to renew the bond of Faith with Him once more. It is that great and final victory over ignorance and evil we celebrate here in this city, and in this land of so much past trouble.

"No, master carver, you must not worry about such things as Time. Nor must you concern yourself with the supply of wood. I will see you have sufficient pieces of good quality with which to begin your work. When each statue is completed to our satisfaction, it will be placed with the fine works of other artists in the lower chambers of my residence. There, each piece will await the day it can properly be installed inside Our Lady Sainte Cecile's church, if not by me then by one of my successors. This you must understand and accept before you begin. But tell me; for I have been curious to know this since I first saw your work, how is it you achieve the dark coloring of the fresh walnut and are still able to reveal the beautiful grain in the wood? My memories of the carver I knew from my boyhood do not contain such knowledge."

Pierre was somewhat embarrassed at having so totally revealed his ignorance of what everyone else involved in the planning and design of the cathedral so clearly understood and took for granted. Others standing nearby had crossed themselves or uttered quiet *Amens* at the Bishop's words, causing Pierre to blush once more when he heard them. But now the Bishop was asking him something about his work, and this Pierre could answer with confidence. He quickly glanced at his son and smiled, because he knew Philippe would recognize and appreciate what he was about to say, before he answered the Bishop.

"Phillippe and I prepare our own stains from the rotting outer husks of the walnuts after they have fallen from the trees. These stains give the wood its dark color without hiding the grain, when they are absorbed into the wood as no oils from any other source would be. Then we apply beeswax as a polish, which makes the wood glisten and will not dull its gloss over time. Thus, your Grace, the beautiful grain of the wood is preserved for all to see, and the life of the carving will endure many times that of him who carved it. It is a fine wood to work in—for the carver who can unlock its secrets."

"You see, Maubrey! I told you this was the man to bring those drawings to life. Who here would think to use this dark wood? The oaks and softer woods you have mentioned would surely rot in my cellars and yellow with age long before these statues find their way to the columns in your great Nave. Brother Jean, you must take our carver here, and his fine-looking son, over to the woodworkers' sheds and introduce them to the Guild Master. Tell him this man has my full authority to begin work there as soon as proper woods can be found. In the meantime, he can employ his skills as they are needed. You must also have that talented young monk you found for us begin making larger copies of each of these individual drawings of the saints. Tell me, woodcarver, who of the Lord's Apostles would you choose to carve first, and we will get that drawing to you as soon as we can?"

Pierre looked at the scroll with the twelve figures spread out before him. Each of the drawings was no bigger than the length of his hand, but he could already see the detail and how he might attack and begin each one. He thought for a moment, looked at the Bishop, and smiled.

"I believe I would like to start with the figure of Saint Peter, Your Grace."

"Of course, of course," the Bishop laughed aloud once more, as did the others standing nearby. "Brother Jean will get you a larger copy of the figure in the days to come. Jean, you must see to acquiring the wood and tell me when it arrives, so I may come to see how he will begin his work on it. Explain to him the necessary conditions and payments for his work while you are taking him to the woodshops. Be sure to include the boy there on your lists as a half-share in the daily food allotments. I am certain he will earn it. Now then, where were we, Master Maubrey? I believe you were about to explain some changes you are thinking of making above the main entrance."

With that the Bishop turned from Pierre and resumed his business with the Master Architect, almost as if everything that had happened in the last few minutes never occurred. Pierre took his tools from Phillippe and both of them followed the older Brother Jean out of the tent and headed north along the edge of the river to a place Pierre had noticed earlier, which contained many workshops and activities of various kinds of craftsmen. On the way, the older monk asked if they had a place to stay and Pierre replied they were rooming with someone they knew from near their home. Brother Jean nodded and explained the Church provided temporary quarters for workmen from outside the city who needed them. Then looking at Phillippe he whispered to Pierre he believed it best for the boy if they continued to avoid those usually crowded accommodations.

He also informed them at the end of each day they would receive a daily food and drink allowance from the Bishop's kitchens and told them where and when to present themselves. He promised to place their names that very day on the list of those who received rations in this way. For everything else, they must provide for themselves. He also explained since Pierre was apparently not a member of any artisan's guild, the Guild Master they were about to meet would have to determine at what level of payment—from helper to master—Pierre would be entered on the ledgers in order to receive his monthly wages from the coffers of the Bishop's construction funds. This was all nearly overwhelming to Pierre, who was trying to take it in as he also kept visualizing the image of Saint Peter he had seen on the drawing, which was already becoming fixed in his thoughts in spite of the fact he had studied it only once.

By the time they arrived at the place above the river where the various busy shops and working sheds were kept for the artisans at work on the cathedral, Pierre began to worry about the man he would soon meet who would determine his level of competence as a wood worker. Suddenly, his confidence in his skill was a little less strong, and he hoped his abilities would be judged by this stranger on something other than his age and appearance. He and Phillippe would need money soon, and he readily recalled Pons Belot's warnings about the high cost of everything here, something he had already encountered and begun to worry about. However, he knew they were now committed for better or worse and he should cease spending so much time thinking about things he could not control. That had always been his way once a project was set before him and begun, and he was already beginning to latch onto this one with every fiber of his being.

The guildsman at the collection of wood workers' shops and storage sheds was soon introduced as Master Reynaud. He was an older man apparently in charge of all the wood work being done in this place. He quickly determined Pierre had never passed any guild administered tests of his ability and began to set him to specific tasks, such as identifying certain tools, how to use them, and then demonstrating his competency with each. It had all been very basic and even boring to Pierre, but he easily progressed through each test as quickly as he could. Near the end of the day when Reynaud gave him a small block of soft wood and told him he had one hour to carve a complete figure of his choice, Pierre carved an excellent figure of a horse and returned it to the Guild Master with a little time to spare. The older man smiled at the quality of the likeness, and only then interviewed Pierre more extensively about some of his past larger works and where they might be found. At the end of the day he finally called Pierre and Phillippe over to where he was speaking with another man.

"Well, Gambolet, I am satisfied you have the kind of experience we can use here, even if you did not already have the confidence of the Bishop himself. I have given instructions for you to be entered on the pay lists as "Master Carver with Apprentice". It is our second highest rank. We would also like to invite you to join our Guild as a provisional member, if you will consider it. If you accept, your obligations will be explained later. But I believe you will find the advantages of becoming one of us are considerable, especially in a city like this with all the work a skilled man can find, if he has others to help find it for him. You do not have to make your decision just now. There will be time later. There is always time when working for the Bishop, it seems. If you are fortunate, you may find opportunities here that will be more profitable for a man of your skill in addition to those of the Church. We will look for you in the morning at the hour that was mentioned. You two should leave now, or you will find only stale loaves and dregs of wine left at the Bishop's kitchens when you get there."

Pierre and Phillippe returned to the Belot home that evening and shared the simple food they had received from the Church kitchens with their hosts; a loaf and a half of bread, a small cheese, and two sausages. Unfortunately, Pierre learned he would have to bring his own container to receive a portion of wine or of small beer. Pons laughed at that and quickly provided father and son each with a stoppered jar they could use in the future. They also talked about the possibility of Pierre and Phillippe finding a more permanent lodging arrangement as soon as they could, now that they had guaranteed employment and the promise of a decent wage.

Pons also explained to him from his own experience how if he became a guild member the days he did not work for the Church would be kept separate. On those days, the Guild Master would assign him work and, for a small fee, would add him to his own payment lists for that day. It was a good arrangement, Pons explained, one that allowed anyone who wanted to make extra money to do so and still fulfill his obligations to the Church. In the days to come, after Phillippe told him how he had traded the small horse his father had carved for a little food in the market place, Pierre began using his spare time and evenings to make small figures of many kinds, which a couple merchants in the market places were more than willing to buy or trade for to sell in their stalls. This soon allowed them to supplement their food allotments from time to time, as well as obtain a few extra coins for other needs.

It took more than a week, and the considerable help of Alissa Belot, for Pierre and Philippe to find lodging closer to their work. She finally directed them to an older woman, a Madam Dugué, who lived alone in an old house with two floors on a narrow side alley off the main street which ran parallel with the river on this side and not far down from the high, stone bridge below the cathedral. The widow looked them over and decided to take them in and rent the two small rooms upstairs. Her son, a boatman she told them, had only recently left to go to Narbonne to work on ships carrying *pastel* to its many destinations in the Mediterranean. She did not know when he would return, except that it would be at least a year. The old woman agreed to prepare their meals as well, if they shared their food allotments with her, which they readily agreed to do. Phillippe was also very happy when he discovered the three cats the woman kept in the small house. They said their grateful goodbyes to the helpful Belots and moved in as soon as they were able.

Pierre also informed Master Reynaud he did indeed desire to become a guild member, and they both soon settled into a daily routine. Pierre had already been informed it would be some time before the wood he required to begin work on the grand statues could arrive. But, in the meantime, it seemed the Bishop usually had one monk or another arriving at the shops with a task for the men there to turn their attentions upon. Pierre soon discovered most of the other men who worked there were carpenters of one kind or another. There were only two other carvers, neither of whom was ranked as high as he was by the Guild Master. Phillippe soon found Master Reynaud had an eye for idle hands, and once Pierre agreed to become a provisional guild inductee, his apprentice also fell under the supervision of the Master. As a result, any time his father did not need his help, Phillippe found himself doing some less than desirable tasks around the wood shops and sheds. It did not take him long to figure out the best ways to avoid the watchful eyes of the ever-present Master Reynaud whenever his father did not require his help.

It took nearly a month for the first boat load of walnut logs of the proper length and thickness to arrive from upriver. In the meantime, Pierre worked on smaller carving projects, including the great doors that would someday in the not too distant future hang on the main entrance to the cathedral. During one week just before the wood arrived, he also found himself in the Bishop's residence doing some decorative carvings on the ends of some exposed beams in one of the smaller rooms. He even saw Bishop Bernard on one of those days when he stopped by to admire Pierre's work, speak of his boyhood memories of the wood carver he had known, and even make some suggestions. Most of all he was eager to know if the first shipment of walnut logs had arrived and how long it would take Pierre to determine if they were of the proper quality to begin the carvings, which the Bishop seemed most eager to see started.

Finally, the first shipment of twenty logs arrived and was unloaded. Pierre, Master Reynaud, and Brother Jean examined them together. Much to his disappointment, as well as the other men's surprise, Pierre quickly determined fewer than half of these should be dragged up the hill directly to the wood shops. The others had too many knots or other problems with the grain he could easily see, even before all the bark had been removed. However, all three men knew the remaining pieces would surely be put to good use for other purposes. Pierre had already remarked—and Brother Jean quickly agreed—the Bishop would undoubtedly soon come up with new ideas to add to his grand schemes.

At long last after the weeks of waiting, Pierre was able to identify the single piece upon which he would begin his first carving of St. Peter. Brother Jean also showed up the next day with the enlarged drawing of the original one Pierre had earlier imprinted in his mind. The details were not as artistic as he remembered in the first artist's drawing; but he knew much of what would emerge from the wood could only come from his own skill and imagination anyway. At long last, the day had come for him to begin his life's work, he sensed—and his anticipation could no longer be contained.

Pierre had been working on the statue of Saint Peter for nearly a month, and the work was progressing about as he expected. Bishop Bernard had come to the shop where Pierre was working on two occasions since he started, and on the second visit Pierre realized the Bishop seemed somewhat disappointed at the speed of his work. However, after he watched "his carver", as he was heard to call Pierre, using his finest-edged tools and listened to his explanation for what he hoped to achieve beyond the outlines of the artist's sketch, which as Pierre pointed out did not include the back of the figure, the Bishop seemed pleased and said only that he would return again soon to see the work.

Pierre was already beginning to feel the burden of the difficult task—and the hardness of the wood—he had taken on. There were soon days when his hands and arms simply needed to be rested. On those days, he was assigned to other jobs the Guild Master always seemed ready to offer him from those he contracted for with the many wealthy home owners and merchants who increasingly populated the growing city. This work was often less tiring but, in many ways, less rewarding, as Pierre began to suspect. When he received his first wages, he noticed his calculations for the days he had worked for the Church met his expectations; but for those days when he had been assigned work through the Guild Master the pay did not seem to be the correct amount. It was not a large sum, but all his earnings were significant to his growing needs. When the second month came around and the same thing happened, Pierre began to suspect he was being cheated in some way he could not as yet determine—or accuse Master Reynaud of directly. Also, Phillippe began to complain he was being asked to do more and more work away from his work bench than the other, even younger, apprentices in the two wood shops were asked to do— more unpleasant jobs such as sweeping out the sheds, or trying to trap the large rats that always seemed to come up from the river and the many boats tied there.

Therefore, by the end of the second month when the reduction work on the statue was less tiring, Pierre was happy when on those fewer occasions he might need a break from his work, he was often requested at the Bishop's residence to do finishing work on earlier pieces brought there, which Bishop Bernard apparently used to decorate his many rooms and which he had accumulated from various sources to help fill his grand residence. Those requests seemed to cause his relationship with Master Reynaud to sour somewhat, especially when Pierre always insisted Phillippe accompany him whenever he was away from the shops.

When they were working on the statue, Pierre usually took his midday break for a small meal of sausage, cheese, or fruit down among some shade trees close to the river below the craftsmen's buildings. This was a popular spot for many when the late summer days brought cooling breezes from the river. He knew the workers who occupied the larger area of sheds above where he worked were the weavers and dye makers. He observed many of those who worked there were women, and that a few of them were wearing the yellow cross on their work tunics. He was not surprised the weavers and dyers were mainly women, because most of the weavers he had seen in his life were females.

However, he was somewhat surprised these penitents he observed were permitted to work in such close contact with others, considering what he had heard earlier about the requirements of their penance. But then he remembered Pons Belot telling him the Bishop frequently took skilled workers from among these unfortunates and employed them for the Church on his great project, and at a considerable savings of wages. Pierre wondered what these weavers were doing for Bishop Bernard as he watched them when they came to the river to get water to boil their dyes, or simply to relax just as he did in the cool air that usually swept along the river's shores in early fall.

One of the women who wore the yellow cross began to attract his attention each time she showed up with one or another of her fellow penitents to enjoy the shade by the river at midday. She appeared to be nearly Pierre's age, and he soon started to wonder how she had come here and under what circumstances she had been made to accept the yellow cross for a period he knew would be at least two years. She was fair skinned with light hair, and Pierre found himself often thinking and wondering about her in a way he had not done for a very long time, nor even expected to do perhaps ever again. Her hands bore the blue stains of the dyes she worked with, and he wondered what other skills she possessed to have brought her to work in the shops of the weavers employed close to where he was working. He soon noticed the penitent women usually sat some distance away from the others and seldom had much to eat at midday, usually only a piece of fruit, a carrot or two, or perhaps a crust of bread. He quickly surmised they obviously did not receive the same food allotments from the Bishop's kitchens as did the other workers.

As the summer wore on into early fall and the statue of St. Peter grew ever nearer to completion, Pierre began to anticipate seeing the woman. He even noticed her glance occasionally his way and how she no longer instantly averted her gaze if their eyes met. One day, when he was certain she was aware of his presence and none of her usual companions were with her, he observed she had not taken anything to eat from her small canvas bag as she and the other workers usually did. Acting on a sudden impulse, he found himself walking toward her and then sitting an arm's length away. She lowered her eyes and he could see she had been caught off guard by his sudden approach and seemed very confused. He was silent for a few moments before he found the words he needed to address her.

"I have noticed you here before. You must work with the weavers and dyers, since I see the blue stains on your hands and clothing. My name is Pierre and I work in the wood shops above. I see you have nothing to eat with you today, so I thought you might like to have this last bit of sausage. It was really more than I needed, since I prefer not to eat very much at midday when I am working. I would be happy to share it with you."

At that, the woman stared intently at him. There were many questions in her eyes as she looked at the half sausage Pierre was holding out to her. She was about to shake her head in silence as she had been told she must do when meeting a stranger who was not a penitent. However, instead she glanced about quickly to see if anyone was watching and then reached for the sausage. She took one bite of the delicious meat and then, having devoured it in a few mouthfuls, responded.

"I am most grateful for the meat. It is a rare indulgence for me. You must surely know I am forbidden to engage in conversation with someone like you while I wear the yellow cross upon my chest. But I believe there are no watchers here, as there are on the streets and in the marketplaces. I too have seen you sitting here before. This is a good time of the day to get away from the boiling vats and looms to enjoy the river's cooling air. My name is Fabrisse, Fabrisse Blanchet. Still, we must be careful. You are kind, and I would not wish you to suffer for being seen speaking with me."

"I care little for such things, Fabrisse Blanchet. Besides, it seems I have the good will of Bishop Bernard himself looking over me." He smiled as he silently pronounced her name once more in his thoughts. "My name is Pierre Gambolet. I am a wood carver from near the lower gorge of the Aveyron Valley. Are you from Albi, or were you brought here by the Inquisition?"

"I was brought here from my village of Lautrec. It is a small place to the south a short distance below the hill where the old Roman walled camp was and where the town of Castres is now. I have noticed there is a boy who sits with you some days. Is he your son?"

"Yes, that is my son and apprentice, Phillippe. He is soon to be fourteen. We are here alone." Pierre added this last little bit of information without thinking, until he heard himself speaking the words. Even then, he could not guess why he had decided to add such a remark at just that moment.

"I see. He seems a fine boy. I have a daughter near his age who was brought here with me. But she was taken away when I was forced to stand before the Inquisition to receive my penance. She was sent to the Sisters who keep the nunnery by the old church of Saint Salvus, back up in the old town. Her name is Marie, and I have not been allowed to see her since that awful day more than a year ago."

Pierre could find no words to respond to the sadness he saw in her eyes at that instant. However, the look on her face was from that moment on imprinted upon his mind as clearly as had been the image of the statue of St. Peter the first time he had stared in wonder at it. He was searching his thoughts for something else to say when Fabrisse began to rise to her feet.

"I should leave now. The Master of Weavers will send someone to look for me if I do not return soon. Thank you for sharing your food with me. It was a great kindness. Perhaps, we shall see each other again, Pierre Gambolet."

The next two days found Pierre working at the main cathedral site under the instruction of Master Reynaud. Since the statue was nearing completion, Pierre's skills could be employed elsewhere until the stain and beeswax Phillippe needed to begin the finishing process could be prepared. There had been a delay in acquiring the walnut husks from which to make his stain for the wood. It was still too early in the season for the nut husks to find their way to the market and to the man with whom Pierre had arranged to supply them as soon as possible. This was his first autumn here and he decided they should make and store enough stain for the future. But that had not prevented the delays with this first statue. Bishop Bernard had already seen the nearly finished carving, however, praised his work highly, and even sent others to admire it. He had also asked many questions about the finishing process and hinted he might decide to keep the sculpture on display in his residence, instead of placing it into storage as he had first indicated he would. He was already speaking of which saint would be Pierre's next subject. When Pierre simply smiled in reply to the question and said the choice must be His Grace's, the Bishop quickly decided on St. Luke who had, he said, always been his personal favorite.

After the two days at the main work site, Pierre resumed his work back at the wood shops. The previous day he made certain to acquire a little extra food to take with him for his midday break at the river. But Fabrisse Blanchet did not show up that first day. Neither did she appear the next day. Pierre began to think he must have somehow frightened her away, or that she had been seen talking to him and been warned to stay away from strangers. On the third day, however, when he went down to the river, he found her sitting alone in the same place where they had talked before. This time he did not hesitate, but walked directly to her and asked if she would like to share some food he had brought. She simply nodded in agreement, and he sat down a little closer this time.

"I have been working on the big doors up at the new cathedral the last two days. I was hoping to see you again. I hope our last conversation did not cause you any trouble."

"No, nothing was said. But I was not certain it was wise. Others have been punished harshly for such behavior. A man I know who works behind the wood drying sheds told me you are the carver who is making the grand statues of the apostles for the new cathedral. He says you are a man of great skill, and the Bishop himself often comes to see your work."

"Yes, I am the carver, but I believe the Bishop thinks I am much too slow."

Pierre spoke as he began to remove the bread, cheese, and sausage from the cloth sack they were in and offered some to Fabrisse. She took the food politely but also eagerly and they ate together in silence for several minutes before Pierre asked the question that had been in his thoughts since the first day he had spoken to her.

"This village you came from, Lautrec. I do not know it. Was there heresy there that caused you to be sent before the Inquisition? You do not seem to me to be the kind of person to take up the Occitan Cross and renounce the true Church. I have seen this type of person in my own life, and they are, I must say, well, more open about it than many I have seen here who wear the mark of the penitent on them. I suppose it must be a fearful thing to stand before the men of the Inquisition and know full well that one false step can send a person to the stake."

"Truly, it is a most awful thing, even for those who know they are innocent of any false beliefs in their thoughts or actions. I was accused by a jealous woman, who denounced me and another neighbor because she believed we were trying to steal her husband from her. I was a widow and younger than she. In truth, her husband—a wicked man himself—had made advances toward me and the other woman, but we both rejected him. This must have made him angry when his wife found out. He then accused us both of casting a Satan's spell upon him and we were denounced before the local priest, who told his superior and we were both taken away and brought here. Both of us proclaimed our innocence before the Bishop's court and were made to answer many questions and swear many oaths. Still, we have to wear the penitent's yellow cross for two years. My daughter was taken away and I have been forced to work in the dye shops and sometimes as a weaver, since I told them I had some skill in that craft. I have not seen the other woman since the day we stood before the judges, nor my dear, sweet Marie."

"It is truly an awful thing to have others speak ill of you, when they know nothing but lies and suspicions others have cast over you in their ignorance. The valley I come from still suffers greatly from the sins committed there against the true Church in the past. But tell me, if you will, Fabrisse, how do you live here? I am told you and the others who wear the cross receive no pay for your work. Are there many of you in the craft guilds' shops, and where do you shelter?"

"I live with the other women like me back beyond the shops in the old quarter. The Church owns all the houses on one small street there. The women live in some and the men, who are not as many, live in two of the others. The houses are crowded and sometimes when it is cold there is not enough wood for the one fire in the kitchen. There are deliveries of bread and other scraps from the Bishop's kitchens every day or two, but they are mostly old or uneaten leavings. We do the best we can by making soups or stews, but there is never enough for so many hungry mouths. The work is hard and the days are long. Still, in less than one year, when my penance is finished, I will be free to leave. But I see no way I can ever again go back to my village, and, of course, I must try to get Marie returned to me. I have been told this may be very difficult, once the Sisters have kept her for so long. Thinking of her is almost more than I can bear. She must feel as if I have abandoned her, and so soon after her father also was taken away from her. It is a cruel life to be alone in such a place as we now find ourselves."

Pierre had been able to say little in response to the sadness he felt as he listened to her story. He could see in her eyes the hunger both from lack of food and from longing for her daughter. He could only imagine what his own feelings would be if Phillippe were suddenly taken from him and given into the care of strangers—with the prospect he might never see him again. Indeed, he finally agreed, life could be unrelentingly cruel and harsh. But somehow, he reminded her, she must find the hope to go forward, if only for her daughter's sake. In that moment, Pierre felt a bond being forged between himself and this stranger with whom he already shared so much, as well as feelings of longing for an undefined something arising deep within him he had not felt, or even desired to feel, for many years.

In the days and weeks that followed they continued to meet either in the same place whenever they felt it was safe, or in a more secluded spot Pierre soon found farther downriver a short distance into a small grove of trees. They would share the food he brought and speak together of many things. He finally unburdened himself of the memories that lay buried in his feelings of the trouble his wife once caused him, both before and after she abandoned them to pursue her own form of heresy. Fabrisse also revealed to him how her husband, a wood cutter, had died. One day he had lost control of his axe and gashed his leg so badly it could not heal. The injury had finally poisoned his blood, or so she was told, and he died of a fever after a painful month for them both. Afterward, she used her weaving skills to barely support herself and her daughter, until the false accusations against her turned their world upside down and she was brought here to Albi to face the Bishop's Inquisitors.

By this time, the carving of St. Luke was starting to take shape. The first statue had been removed to the Bishop's residence once the staining and polishing were completed. Phillippe had spent nearly a month crushing walnut husks and soaking them to make enough stain to last at least another year. He had also been present just before the statue was removed to witness the praise and admiration of all who saw it. Just before the removal of the statue, when they knew they were alone, Pierre heated the old poker once more and secretly imprinted their mark on the bottom of one of St. Peter's feet. Even Master Reynaud was effusive in his praise when the statue was loaded onto a wagon and hauled to the Bishop's Palace, although Pierre was still certain the man was somehow cheating him in his monthly wage, even if not as much as before, perhaps.

As fall progressed into early winter and the weather began to cool and the days shorten, Phillippe was not so eager to spend as much of his free time wandering the river banks or the market places as he did in the warmer weather with the other boys he had met near their home or elsewhere. Pierre finally told him about Fabrisse when Philippe asked why his father did not seem to mind so much when he did not want to eat with him at midday by the river as often as before. Pierre also told him they had been here long enough that he felt more confident Phillippe could look after himself and avoid the trouble he could spot on his own by then. Phillippe smiled and replied he had learned to be careful and, besides, he knew his way around the many streets of the town far better than his father. Pierre laughed and agreed he was surely right on that account.

As the months passed, both father and son also grew much closer to the old woman from whom they rented their two small rooms and who prepared their meals. Phillippe in particular seemed to have been warmly taken in by Madame Dugué, who lived downstairs. Often when Pierre came home late from working at his carving bench, or in the great Residence when he wanted to take advantage of each day's declining light, he would usually find his son in the old woman's kitchen playing with one of her cats or listening to one of her many stories about her two sons. It quickly became apparent the younger one must have died when he was about Phillippe's age, and as a result the woman had become increasingly fond of her young tenant. Phillippe had also turned fourteen at the end of August, which they soon learned entitled him to a full food portion at the Church kitchens each day. Those days when he wanted to work late, Pierre would send his son to collect both their food allotments and then take them to Madame Dugué to share with her when she prepared their suppers and the food they took with them the next day. He also knew Phillippe enjoyed the extra time in the evenings before dark to spend with his new friends near the river.

Pierre also continued to share food with Fabrisse whenever they could meet, sometimes with even a little extra for her to take with her for later. Once he even secretly went to the street where her house was and saw the crowded conditions where the many penitents bound to the Church in some fashion or another managed to live on the barest edge of any normal existence. However, with so many obligations of his own Pierre was increasingly forced to spend more time doing his small carvings in the evenings to trade in the markets. He even taught Phillippe a couple of basic figures he could also make and trade for his own needs, such as warmer clothing. This little side business soon proved to be a boon when the busy Christmas and New Year's seasons came with more demands from the merchants for his popular carvings for children's gifts.

Pierre was finally able from time to time to put away a few coins in the expectation at some as yet undetermined date they would need and want to return to their home to check up on their farm and animals, if nothing else. Phillippe, it seemed, was lonely for them and kept asking when they could do this. Pierre's agreement with the Bishop had no specific time limits as he well knew.

However, for many reasons by then, he was finding it increasingly difficult to continue to put off answering Phillippe's questions about when they might make even a short visit back to the Aveyron Valley.

Both also found the time to maintain their friendship with Pons and Alissa Belot, who occasionally invited them to dinner. Sometimes Pierre would drop by in the evening on his own, whenever he managed to acquire a small jug of wine in the markets. He finally got around to telling them about Fabrisse and the troubling situation she was in concerning her daughter. This seemed to loosen up Pons, and especially his wife, a little to speak more than they had been willing to do before of their own past. Apparently, like so many others, they had once faced accusations that could cause them potentially serious difficulty with their Church. It was only the intercession of Father Guillaume, Pons told him, which saved them from more serious problems. This was why they still felt so much in the Priest's debt and had taken in the strangers who knocked on their door those many months earlier.

As Pierre listened to his friends' story and remembered some of their earlier comments about the Church, he wondered if, perhaps, there might possibly have been more of a grain of truth than either was willing to admit concerning the suspicions about them in those days. Still, he liked them both and could easily see from his own experience, and now from that of Fabrisse and others, how there were many people who had reason to be less than enthusiastic in their attitude toward the Church, even if they had never been the more serious heretics so many others, including his long missing wife, had proven themselves to be.

Pierre also learned from Fabrisse more about the work she did. In addition to making dyes she worked on small weavings which were used for many decorative and functional things in the Bishop's residence. Other, more accomplished guild weavers were engaged in creating a great wall hanging that would one day grace the new cathedral. When that work would be finished she could not say, but the artists had already been told the completed work would be put into storage in the Palace by the new cathedral with the many other fine works the Bishop was commissioning. There, much like Pierre's statues, it would await the distant day when all would come to marvel at the fulfillment of Bernard de Castanet's great vision—and to sing his praises for his great victory over the Cathari and the many other troublesome heretics of the old lands of Languedoc.

The winter months turned out to be not as harsh as many were anticipating and by the beginning of March hopes for an early spring permeated the City at large and the workshops in particular. Nevertheless, during the last two months of winter Pierre found ever fewer opportunities to meet and talk with Fabrisse, even though he had come to look forward to his meetings with her far more than he could ever have imagined earlier. Not many workers went to the river banks for their midday breaks in those months, and to have met in a more conspicuous place would have presented difficulties for them both. Pierre sensed Fabrisse had come to depend on their conversations as well, both to keep up her spirits and for the additional food Pierre somehow always managed to have to share on those few occasions when they did manage to meet. They soon agreed on any day that would not arouse suspicions they would go to their private place by the river at the same time to enjoy some rare moments of solitude together. He could not be certain if she was developing feelings for him in the same way he was coming to believe he felt for her, but he was still willing to take the risks to use every opportunity to help her in any way he could.

After seeing the generosity of others at Christmas, Pierre decided he would share with Fabrisse and her companions in the over-crowded house when he could find a way. It all began when he took a small commission from Master Reynaud to carve a pair of griffins in his spare time to frame the doorway of a wealthy merchant who came to the guild shops early in the New Year. Pierre had never carved such mythical figures before, but he managed to find one to study on another building he was directed to. It had taken him more than a week in his extra time, but the demands for his smaller carvings in the open markets were diminishing somewhat as the weather grew colder and some of the merchants closed their stalls for the winter. When he finally finished the pair to his satisfaction, the Guild Master told him to take them to where the man lived and mount them himself.

The man's house turned out to be one of the very lavish ones Pierre had seen along the river upstream where many such houses were being built. When the man saw the carvings on either side of his front door, he was overjoyed and heaped praises upon their carver. Among this merchant's businesses was the operation of several small fishing boats up and down the river. It was late in the day when Pierre finished, and one of those boats had just come in with an exceptionally fine catch to unload not far from the man's house. Out of gratitude, he told Pierre to fill a large sack with as many of the small, but fresh fish as he could carry. Although it was not far to the bridge and Mme. Dugué's home, Pierre nevertheless struggled back under the weight of the fish he had been given.

The widow was delighted but said, regrettably, this was far more fish than she could use, since she did not have the proper salt she would need to preserve the rest. She suggested he share some with his friends so Pierre decided to wait for dark, walk back to the town and find the street of the penitents where Fabrisse lived. He took the sack of fish, laid them in front of the door, knocked, and then hastened away to watch from a shadow created by a second-floor overhang of a house on the corner. When the door opened, a woman appeared, looked about, picked up the sack of fish, and immediately disappeared back inside. This simple act filled Pierre with a gratifying warmth and a new determination to help these poor penitents, who had been condemned to suffer for no good reason he could see except mostly for the lies or faults of others.

In the days and weeks ahead he continued to make every effort when an opportunity arose to help Fabrisse and her friends. It might have been a sack of barley on one occasion; a leg of mutton that his friend the sausage maker mentioned was about to go bad and he could not sell on another; one of two large cheeses he bargained for with another merchant he knew; or some other item of food he or Phillippe could obtain without putting their own needs at risk. When he could provide no food, he would enlist Phillippe to help him find and carry a bundle of wood for at least one good fire on a cold night. When he told Mme. Dugué what he had done with the fish that first evening, she laughed and said it must surely have been the hand of St. Peter which was laid upon him from the statue he had taken so long to carve. Pierre laughed also, but her comment still gave him a moment's pause and a strange feeling at the time.

Finally, one day Fabrisse confronted him and asked if he knew anything about the unexpected knocks in the dark on their door and the helpful deliveries they found outside with each visit of their mysterious benefactor. Pierre simply shrugged and said nothing in reply, but she still grabbed his hand and quickly kissed him on the cheek. It was the first time they had touched in any way, and in that very special moment a wave of new and strange feelings raced through the head, and the heart, of the wood carver. She told him how grateful all the women of her house were, and how they often speculated about whom their "angel of mercy" could be. Fabrisse told him his secret was safe with her; that is, if he just happened to know anything about their unknown night visitor, whom she told him had already saved them from many hungry nights and cold mornings.

It was around the first of March when Master Reynaud sent two carpenters from the guild shops for a "special task" requested by a Dominican brother who appeared there one morning. When they returned near the end of the day, it was whispered about and then confirmed they had spent their day erecting a small scaffold upon which two upright posts were mounted. This was a definite sign there was to be a public burning in the main square adjacent to where the last remains of the old church of Ste. Cecile still stood and where the new cathedral was being raised in her name. This would be the first such public execution delivered by the Inquisition since Pierre had arrived in Albi nearly eight months earlier. A sickening feeling enveloped him when he and Phillippe walked together back to their lodging, directly past the new scaffold and its two stakes. Pierre's thoughts kept turning to Fabrisse and what she and the others like her, who were still under the watchful eyes of the Bishop's many spies, must be feeling as word of the event rapidly spread through the entire town.

That evening, Pierre decided to pay a visit to Pons Belot to see what he might have heard about all this. He knew both Pons and his wife kept their ears to the ground for any rumors of actions against real or imagined heresies coming to the attention of the Inquisition and the Dominicans, who now seemed to be the main instigators of its court. He did not know how his two friends learned about these things, but he suspected they would know something. After he talked with them for a short while and enjoyed only a single cup of wine with Pons, a rare thing in itself, he learned a great deal about what would be happening soon. Apparently, a well-known *Perfect* and his wife, who had been hiding in the small villages of the mountains to the east of the city, were recently found and taken into the Church's custody. They had already been tried and condemned as heretics with their own words by the Inquisitors under the Bishop's direction, and their public burning would take place within a few days.

Pierre learned this same evening that Alissa Belot was close to a woman who worked as a laundress in the Bishop's Palace, and this woman often proved to be a reliable source of information about many of the private things going on there. She had told Alissa there was much talk in the Palace of great pressure being brought to bear on the Bishop of Albi from Toulouse and even as far away as Rome to increase his suppression of past and new heresies in his Diocese. He was under orders to do so in a more public manner with more imprisonments and fewer lighter sentences, even upon those who took new oaths of loyalty to the true Church. It was a disturbing bit of information, and Pierre could not help but fear for Fabrisse and those living with her who were already in the city and at the mercy of the strict interpretation of such instructions as the Dominicans continually showed themselves so willing to carry out.

When the public burnings were announced for two mornings later, Pierre made certain he and Phillippe stayed away from the main square all day. Others, however, seemed to relish the opportunity, and he heard from those returning to the shops afterward that a large and raucous crowd had witnessed the event. The Bishop and many other churchmen were also present, and Pierre could not help but wonder what this man, whom he thought he had come to know somewhat, must have thought as those he had condemned faced their last, terrible moments. Two days later, when he walked across the main square, he saw the blackened paving stones where the scaffold and stakes had been, and he could still almost smell the burning flesh in his nostrils. *Had a fate such as this perhaps befallen his wife in some unknown village square?* Pierre could not help but wonder and shiver at this thought as it raced through his mind in that instant.

Nearly a week had passed since the burnings and most things seemed to be settling back into their normal routine. However, Pierre had not seen Fabrisse since before that unhappy event. He arrived late from his work at Mme. Dugué's one evening and was enjoying a warm supper when there was an unexpected knock at the door. Pierre decided to go himself to see who it might be, and when he opened the door slightly, he was surprised to see Pons Belot standing there. He seemed agitated and looking quickly about he whispered for Pierre's ears only.

"Can you come with me to our house? Alissa has received some news from her friend at the Palace, which I think will be of great interest to you."

Pierre nodded and returned to the kitchen just long enough to tell the widow and Phillippe he was going to the Belots on an important matter and would return as soon as he could. Then, he left to follow Pons home without even thinking to grab his cap against the cool evening air from the river. When they got there, Alissa had a cup of warm wine for each of them. She offered Pierre a seat at their table and the three of them sat down together. She wasted no time in getting to her news.

"There is disturbing talk in the Bishop's Palace that there will be new trials starting in two days to be led by some Dominicans just up from Carcassonne. Some newly accused heretics have also been brought in from the east and south. But more importantly, it is being whispered even those who have already received a light punishment or penance in the past but are still serving their terms here may be recalled to answer old accusations, or even new ones against them. This will include many who still wear the yellow cross. It is said these people will be rounded up by the Bishop's guards in two days and that many will be sent to the dungeons until they can be questioned again by this new Inquisition. I thought you would want to know these things, Pierre, since your friend Fabrisse may be one of those to be taken back into custody. You could even be at some risk of being denounced yourself for being seen with her."

"We have been careful, but I thank you both for your good thoughts and warning. Still, a man can never be certain what others might say or who they might name to lighten their own pun- ishment at such a time. Perhaps, that is why all this is happening so soon after the two burnings last week. I must leave now to think about what I can do. But I thank you both again, and let me know if you hear anything else that might be important or helpful."

Pierre left immediately and returned to Mme. Dugué's with his head spinning from all he had just heard. He finished the rest of his supper without even tasting the food, and then said he would go to bed early because it had been a long and tiring day. However, he was still awake when Phillippe crept quietly into bed later and went right to sleep. It was long into the night before Pierre was finally able to find sleep for himself. He lay awake and thought of a thousand possibilities about what he should, or could, do when the next day came. Most of them were too desperate to even con- sider seriously, but he knew he must do something. At last, he hit upon a sort of plan, which was based more on a blind hope than anything else. But even then it could only work if he could find the opportunity to set it in motion—and only if the man he had come to believe he could put his trust in could be convinced in some way to help him face his awful dilemma.

⊨⊣ ⊢⊨

Pierre and Phillippe left unusually early the next morning to head for the workshops. When they arrived, however, Pierre told his son they would not be working there today. Instead, he told him they would both be returning to the Bishop's Palace to complete a small job he was working on there, but had been in no hurry to fin- ish earlier. More particularly, he wanted to get to the wood shop before Master Reynaud usually came in. Once there, Pierre told Phillippe to look around and make sure they had all their tools, for they would be taking everything of theirs with them to the Bishop's that morning. It seemed a strange request to the boy, but he helped his father gather even the larger chisels, which he knew would not be needed that day, and stuffed them into one of the canvas bags each of them now carried. When the Guild Master finally came in, Pierre told him he would be leaving to complete the work at the Palace he had suspended a few days ago and he would need Phillippe's help with mounting the two heavy carvings to the wall. Master Reynaud merely grumbled some complaint about needing Phillippe for something else but quickly acquiesced when he saw they were already carrying their tools to leave.

When they arrived at the Bishop's, Phillippe was greatly surprised by their slow progress on the already nearly finished work during the morning, as well as by the longer midday break they took. He could not see why his father had been so insistent on packing all their tools, or on bringing him along. They finally finished the polishing and started to hang the two carved, walnut wall sconces to be set on either side of a well-framed doorway in a narrow passageway, which Pierre said led to the Bishop's private office and living rooms beyond. By late afternoon, they were nearly finished putting the second of the two carved angelic faces in place, when his father surprised Phillippe once more. He told him to leave early and take the rare opportunity to go to the nearby kitchens and get the first of the fresh food to be set out for the workers who received their allotments there. Next, Philippe was to go straight back to Mme. Dugué's and wait for him; nor was he to leave her house once he was there under any circumstances. When his father looked him in the eye, placed his hand on his shoulder and told him he would answer his questions later, Phillippe simply shrugged and did what he was being instructed to do.

After Phillippe left, Pierre kept trying to look busy while he waited for what he hoped would be the Bishop's appearance. When he had worked in this spot before while preparing the space for the carvings, he noticed both times Bishop Bernard returned to his office and private quarters at the end of the day just before the first evening bells sounded across the city. Every hope Pierre had entertained after his sleepless night of worrying now depended on the Bishop's regular appearance. But as the late afternoon grew into early evening, the carver became almost frantic with the fear his one opportunity was going to be missed. He was beginning to pack his tools to leave when he finally heard the sound of two pairs of footsteps on the stone floor of the passageway leading to where he stood just outside the finished doorway. The Bishop soon appeared accompanied by an older priest Pierre did not recognize.

"Ahh, Master Carver. I see you have found the time to finish my doorway at last. Look at these faces he has carved, Brother Dominic, are they not truly 'angelic'—and in your beautiful walnut as always, Master Gambolet. Let us hope these heavenly faces will keep the dark demons from my door, ehh Brother."

The Bishop laughed and was about to reach for his door latch when Pierre boldly stepped forward, cleared his throat, and addressed the Bishop in a more direct manner than which either was accustomed in their past encounters.

"I am happy Your Grace has once again honored my humble efforts on his behalf. I was wondering if I might have a word on a more personal matter, if Your Grace is not too busy to take the time at this hour."

The Bishop stopped abruptly and stared intently at Pierre for a moment, as if trying to sort through several thoughts at the same time. Then, he smiled for an instant, turned to the priest beside him, and spoke."

"If you would be so kind as to come back to my office after I have dined, Brother Dominic, we will speak further of that situation we were discussing. It seems I have another matter I must attend to first." Then he turned to Pierre and said in a low voice. "I hope this will not take long, Master Carver. And I do hope it is important. But come, I suppose it is only fitting you be the first to pass between these wonderful angels you have placed here to guard me from the evils of this world."

As soon as they passed through the door, Pierre noticed at once the sumptuous furnishings of the Bishop's office. Near the center was an ornate desk with two freshly lit candles already in place. Apparently, he was not the only one who knew the Bishop's devotion to his daily schedule. The Bishop walked around the desk and began to remove some items from under his robe as Pierre walked over to stand on the side of the desk opposite him. Bishop Bernard finally looked up as if to say his guest should be the first one to speak. Pierre hesitated for a moment to collect his thoughts and began.

"Your Grace, I have heard there will soon be new trials and that those who have already received a penance may be called again to answer old or new charges. Is this true?"

"Hmm, and how would you have come by this information, Master Carver? But I suppose that is of no importance just now, is it? Why should this concern you in any event?"

"Your Grace, there is a woman I have come to know who is still required to wear the penitent's yellow cross for another year. She was once falsely accused of a heresy I am absolutely convinced she was innocent of when she was brought here. It is my hope you might intercede on her behalf, if Your Grace was told the truth of her story."

"I see. You do realize, my friend, you have also placed yourself at some risk by speaking with this woman, as well as adding further to her own jeopardy now. Tell me, who is she, where is she from, and why should I concern myself with one repentant among so many?"

"Her name is Fabrisse Blanchet. She is from the village of Lautrec to the south, and I believe with all my heart she is completely guiltless of the accusations brought by another against her, and that she has always remained a faithful believer in our true Church."

"I know this village of Lautrec. It lies not far beyond the old hill of Castres, and I passed through it on my way across the mountain from Carcassonne a year or so past. But it is hardly a nest of heretics, and I have heard of no serious charges against anyone from there. This woman must have been convicted of some minor offense. But it is easy to see, Master Carver, you are, indeed, convinced of something with your whole heart where this woman is concerned."

Pierre blushed in silence and Bishop Bernard then turned and walked over to peer out the narrow window looking down into the long courtyard surrounded by the high walls of his fortress-like palace. After a couple of moments thought, he turned and addressed Pierre once more.

"There are many who are accused and even condemned who, if the truth were known, are as innocent as this woman who has caught your eye appears to be. Such things are common, even unfortunate, but are also necessary for the good of all and the continued strength of our Holy Church in this troubled land. I have sent those to the stake whom I knew were probably guiltless, but the choice had to be made as an example for others. Do you know how I knew they were innocent, wood carver?"

When Pierre only shook his head in the negative and lowered his eyes at the Bishop's quite astounding remark, the latter stared back out the window once again, and then without looking at Pierre said to him.

"When the guiltless are at the stake, they will always shout out their innocence and beg for mercy as they are tied to it. When the torches are laid upon the wood they soon begin to shout to God and ask Him to save them. Then, when the first flames light their robe and they feel the burning on their flesh, they realize their last hope is gone and their shrieks quickly turn to the pain of their final suffering, until those flames extinguish the air in their lungs and they are consumed in silent agony. But when true heretics, those whom I know to have been guilty of the crimes for which they were brought before me, are faced with the purging fire, they make no pleas for mercy; nor do they call out for God's salvation or forgiveness when the fire is upon them. Only the final, brief screams of pain are heard to escape their dying lips as they face the eternal flames they are being sent to endure in that moment."

With those words the Bishop paused in thought, then turned abruptly, walked to his desk, and sat down. He reached into a drawer and pulled out a piece of paper with some writing on it, took a quill from an inkpot, and rapidly scratched a name on the paper. Then, he picked up a stick of sealing wax which lay next to the candles and began to heat it. He looked up at Pierre with a strange sadness in his eyes, one the carver had never seen there before, and spoke softly and calmly.

"This woman I will give to you has nearly finished her penance you have said. Unfortunately, my friend, I am not so near the end of my own. Mine is to hear those final screams and cries for the mercy I cannot grant to the many I knew to be innocent who were still sent to a fiery death. That penance is upon me every waking moment and in my dreams, and will be so until I stand before God and He in His mercy chooses to remove that burden from me on my day of judgement. It is my great fear now there will soon be more of those screams I must hear and endure until the Judgement Day comes for me. I will allow you to take this woman away, but you should go yourself as well to be safe, and as soon as possible."

The wax was hot by then, and Bishop Bernard moved it over the bottom of the paper which lay before him and allowed a thick glob of the red ooze to drip upon it. Then, he removed the largest ring on his right hand and quickly impressed his seal into the wax. He wiped the ring clean and replaced it on his finger, picked up the paper, and folded it with the writing and seal to the inside. He laid it back down in front of him and stared once more at a wide-eyed and silent Pierre.

"I have enjoyed watching your work and our pleasant conversations, Pierre Gambolet. If I give you this woman, will you swear an oath before God and the image of our Savior on the Holy Crucifix, which hangs on the wall behind me, when her penance is past you will return to finish the carvings you have agreed to do? I would also have you swear for as long as we both shall live you will return here to my cathedral one year in every three until your work is done, or until I—or the final Judgement of God upon either one of us—has released you from this vow?"

Pierre hesitated for an instant at the Bishop's sudden and surprising demand. He knew also it was meant to be a deliberate trap to catch him if his own loyalties had not remained strong. Any person who had accepted the great Cathari Heresy could never take such an oath, there being a firm and complete prohibition in their beliefs against any oath taking—an enduring belief which had sent many of them to the stake in the past hundred years. However, Pierre felt no hesitation in responding as sincerely as he possibly could to the Bishop.

"Yes, Your Grace, I do swear it. And I will also swear that as long as my hand can hold a carving chisel, I will honor my word to complete any task I have agreed to take on for you, or any man."

The Bishop smiled broadly, held out the letter for Pierre to take and stood up. When he took it, however, Pierre cleared his throat nervously and addressed the Bishop once more.

"There is another matter upon which I would ask the guidance of Your Grace. This woman has a daughter who was taken from her when she was brought here. The girl has been given into the care of the Sisters who keep the Nunnery by the old church of St. Salvus in the city. If I could … ."

Before he could finish, Bishop Bernard raised his hand and interrupted.

"I am sorry, wood carver, but I am afraid I can be of little assistance to you on that. Those Sisters are of a Roman Order, and I have little influence over them."

Then, Bishop Bernard reached into his desk drawer, opened a small box and removed two large, silver coins. He laid them on the desk between them and said.

"These will seal your oath, Master Carver. I will look for you no later than one year from this coming Easter. Do not fail me. I hope you will marry this Blanchet woman; for it will be safe for you to bring her back with you by then if you choose. Consider these coins as a small token of my appreciation for the pleasure your work has already brought to my eyes and my memories. I sincerely hope you will both remember me in your future prayers, and ask God to protect us all from Satan's great power."

He turned to leave with his strange request still echoing in Pierre's thoughts. However, just as he was about to get to the door to his private rooms he suddenly faced about and spoke once more.

"When you leave here, Master Carver, you will see an old monk's robe hanging on the wall just up the passageway beyond the door. It has been there for many days, and I do not believe its owner will return for it. A clever man might find a use for such a robe on a night like this."

With that he turned and disappeared, leaving Pierre clutching the sealed paper and staring at the two bright coins on the desk in front of him. He was about to reach out and pick them up when the realization the Bishop had just laid another trap for him flashed through his head. If he took them and failed to return, he could be branded a thief and brought back to face the Bishop's anger. Pierre smiled at how the great man had, indeed, bonded him to his oath. At the thought he reached out and picked up both coins to stuff in his pouch with the folded paper. Then, he quickly left the room, grabbed his bag of tools he had left just outside the door, found the monk's robe up the passageway, and rapidly made his way outside the Palace and into the growing dusk. He walked as fast as he could to the high bridge and on to Mme. Dugué's, his head swirling with the many new prospects, and problems, the Bishop's generosity had surely opened for him. By the time he arrived, an entirely new plan was beginning to take shape in his head—one that caused his heart to race with the possibilities it suddenly presented.

⟛ ⟛

Phillippe was eating and hand-feeding a kitten when Pierre arrived. He sat down and ate his own meal as quickly as he could. Then he took out the Bishop's paper, laid it on the table, looked at Phillippe and nodded in a way to insure the boy's silence, before he spoke to Mme. Dugué.

"I have just received this letter while at the Bishop's residence. I am told it is from Father Guillaume, the priest in our home village. He has advised us there is a problem at our farm and we need to return home immediately to deal with it. That is all I was told it says by the monk who read it to me. I am afraid we must leave tonight. I have found a man with a wagon who will take us down the river road; but he insists we must leave this very evening if we wish to come with him. I am sorry to treat you like this, Madame Dugué. You have been like a mother to us both, and we will miss you. I hope we can return soon, but I cannot say at this moment when it could be."

Then Pierre reached into his pouch and took out a few small coins and laid them on the table. He told the old woman he hoped these would help her until she could find another tenant for her rooms. He could see the tears beginning to form in her eyes as she looked first at him and then at Phillippe, who was too dumbstruck at his father's words to say anything. Finally, the woman slowly got up from the table and told them she would put together a small sack of what she could spare for them to eat on their journey. Pierre then told Phillippe to bring his tool bag and they would go upstairs to pack to leave. When they got to their rooms, he came close to his son and whispered to him the true reasons they were leaving so suddenly. At Phillippe's questioning look, he said he was sorry to have lied to both him and Mme. Dugué, but he wanted to protect her from any questions she might be asked about their sudden departure later. They started to pack as soon as he was finished.

"Take nothing you cannot carry on a long walk, Phillippe. We can make our bundles into packs in the morning. Look in your tool bag and leave anything behind we don't need. I will wrap the chisels in the oil rags so they will make no noise. If only we had a boat to get back across the river, we could avoid the night watchmen on the bridge, who will surely be suspicious at this hour."

"My friend Robert's father has a rowing boat. We have used it to go fishing on the river many times. They live not far around the corner on the main street by the river. Perhaps, he will lend it to us if we ask him, *Papa*."

"Perhaps, perhaps not," Pierre replied with a sudden thought as he remembered the two big silver coins in his pouch. We will go see him when we leave. If you are finished with your bundle, you should go downstairs and say your goodbyes to Madame Dugué. She will miss you very much, I think. I will finish up here with the tools and other things and make a last look around before I come down."

Pierre finished quickly, retrieved their saved coins he kept hidden, and soon took his things downstairs, where Phillippe was just receiving the sack of food the old woman had prepared for them. When she saw Pierre coming down the steps, she grabbed Phillippe and gave him a last, long hug as she fought back her tears. Pierre walked over, kissed her on both cheeks, and thanked her again for everything she had done for them. Then they grabbed their old cloaks and caps from the pegs beside the door and disappeared into the night.

Once they were outside Pierre told his son to lead him to the house of his friend Robert. When they arrived, he knocked on the door and a sour-faced man opened it, stared at Phillippe, who he knew to be a friend of his son's, and asked them what they wanted at this hour. Pierre told the man he knew he had a small boat and asked him if he would be willing to sell it. The man stared at them for an instant and then laughed. He was about to close the door in their faces when Pierre extended the shining silver piece he had already put in his hand toward him and said.

"Would this change your mind, perhaps?"

The man took the coin eagerly, bit at its edge to test the silver's purity, looked both visitors up and down again, and laughed at their apparent foolishness. Then he shrugged and replied that for this much they were welcome to the boat. Phillippe said he already knew where it was tied. They were about to leave when the man said.

"You must be desperate to leave the city at such a time and to be in need of a boat this late. I must tell you from the looks of you, if anyone should come here and ask me later about this I will tell them you stole it. Do you understand what I am saying?"

Indeed, Pierre did understand, and he told the man so. They left and Phillippe led them down a narrow path to the river where they found the boat tied to a stake. Phillippe was struggling with the knot when his father took a knife from his sack and severed the rope in two quick strokes. Then he told a surprised Phillippe to get in the back while he shoved the boat out, jumped into the middle seat, and rowed them across the river in the darkness. The fast current took them a little downstream from where he wanted to land and they quickly pulled the boat a safe distance up the low bank together. Then, Pierre told his son to stay in the shadows, watch the boat, and speak to no one until he returned with Fabrisse.

Pierre found a path up to where the streets began and walked along the mostly abandoned narrow alleyways until he came to the old part of town. The hour was already growing late when he located the deserted street of the penitents' houses where Fabrisse lived. He came to the familiar door he had knocked upon anonymously many times before and knocked once more. However, he did not scurry away this time. The anxious face of a young woman he did not recognize soon appeared at the narrow space created where she slightly opened the door. She just stared at him until he spoke.

"I am a friend of Fabrisse Blanchet. May I speak with her?"

The woman was about to turn and close the door when she smiled and replied.

"You must be Fabrisse's friend from the wood shops. I have not seen you before, but your knock has a familiar sound to it. I will get her for you." She smiled again and softly closed the door.

When Fabrisse appeared a few moments later, she had a very uncertain look on her face when she opened the door halfway. Pierre said nothing. He simply took her arm gently, pulled her outside, and pushed the door closed very quietly. He stared back at her wide eyes for an instant and spoke.

"Have you heard the rumors about the new trials that will be starting soon?"

"Yes, everyone here on the street is very frightened. There are many who think they may have cause to fear the new Inquisition after the burnings last week. I am frightened also, Pierre; but why have you come at this hour."

"I have found a way to take you out of the city with me Fabrisse. But we must leave this very night before the guards come to this street to search out those who must face new trials. I have a paper from the Bishop himself that will offer us some protection, but we must be gone tonight. Will you trust me and come with me? Phillippe and I have a boat waiting at the river."

"Yes, Pierre, I do trust you. But you know I could never leave without my dear Marie, no matter what the risks to my own safety would be. I just cannot. Surely, you must know this."

"I do, Fabrisse; but if you will give me your trust, I have a plan that might work to take her with us." Her face brightened instantly at his words and she almost began to shake, as she merely nodded to his question. "Good. First, you must go upstairs and quickly pack a bundle of what you can carry, any warm clothing for certain. Then you must drop it to me out the window up there, if that is still where you sleep. I will wait for you in the shadows by the house at the end of the street. Tell no one inside you are leaving, and act as if you want to step outside for just a moment. You must hurry."

She nodded again and went back inside immediately. Pierre waited for what seemed like a long time until the shutters above his head opened and Fabrisse dropped a bundle of clothes to him. He left and waited for her in the old spot from whence he used to watch the front door to see who would pick up his food offerings. At last she arrived, and this time she hugged him tightly, but still said nothing. He took her hand and led her back the way he had come, down along many, short winding streets until they came to the river. In a few more minutes they were at the boat greeting Phillippe, who was surprised by their sudden appearance and was playing with the same kitten his father had seen him with in the kitchen earlier.

Phillippe quickly explained that Mme. Dugué had given it to him with some soft cheese it would eat. He promised he would make certain it stayed in his tunic where he had hidden it before and make no noise. Pierre merely shook his head in mock disgust and said nothing. He walked over to the boat, retrieved the monk's heavy robe, and went to where Fabrisse stood shivering in the cold air. He took off his old cloak, draped it around her, and pulled her to him. Then, he whispered he was off to get Marie, if he could, and left them both staring after him, until he quickly disappeared into the darkness.

By the time Pierre got back to the old town, his previous confidence was beginning to wane. What must happen next might surely be the hardest thing he had ever attempted, and he prepared his mind for the many unforeseen problems he might soon encounter. When he got to the old church of St. Salvus, he headed for the garden gate on the far side. He had been here once before to replace the arm of a statue of the Saint, which must have been broken off during the past heresy troubles in the city. He knew where the entrance to the Nunnery was and headed across the small garden for it. He had already stopped and donned the hooded monk's robe and held the Bishop's letter in one hand when he knocked firmly on the door. A short time later, the door's viewing port was opened and a young woman's face appeared in the light from the candle she held. She asked him what his business was at such a late hour.

"I have an order from the Bishop requesting I return to his Residence with the child you have here by the name of Marie Blanchet."

He held out the paper for the woman to see, but did not give it to her. She looked at it, told him to wait outside, and then closed the portal and disappeared. He was hoping, much like himself, no one here would be able to read it either. He waited once more for what seemed like an eternity and began to shiver noticeably, although it was not just from the night air. Finally, the portal was slid open again and a much older woman's face appeared this time in the dim light of the candle she held.

"What is this about a request from the Bishop for this worthless Blanchet girl we have been forced to keep for the past year? We were told today none were to leave here or be admitted this night for any reasons. I do not recognize you, Brother. What is your name?"

"I am Brother Reynaud, and have come to the Bishop's personal service only in the last month. Here is the letter. Surely, you recognize his seal." He held it up close to the light at the open portal. She stared at it for an instant, and he hoped again she could not read it either.

"Yes, I see it is the Bishop's personal seal well enough. But what can His Grace possibly want with this child, and at such an hour and on such a night as this?"

"We have only just learned she can give important testimony before the Inquisition on the morrow, and she must be prepared and made ready to answer the questions they will ask about her relatives. You must tell her to bring her things. I do not believe she will be coming back here when we are finished with her."

"No, I should expect she will not. Well, if that is the case, I will bring her. But I cannot see how you will get anything that can be used against the heretics from her. We have been unable to get her own confession since she was sent here, even with the use of a stiff rod. Wait here, Brother Reynaud."

The portal was slammed shut again and Pierre waited once more until the main door was finally opened and a frightened girl clutching a small bundle was thrust through it by the elderly nun he had spoken with before. Pierre breathed a deep sigh, took her hand, and pulled her through the door. The old woman stared at him intently once more as if to remember his face and said.

"Take her and good riddance to this Devil's spawn. She eats too much anyway." Then she slammed the door and was gone.

Pierre gently grasped the girl's shaking hand and led her through the darkness across the garden. There, he stopped to kneel in front of her, smiled, and spoke softly.

"Are you Marie Blanchet?" She simply nodded in the affirmative. "My name is Pierre. I am a friend of your *Mama's* and I am going to take you to her right now. But you must be very brave, Marie, and stay very quiet. Do you understand what I am saying?"

This time the girl's face brightened and she was about to blurt something out when Pierre gently placed his hand over her mouth, nodded and smiled once more, and then stood up. He took her small bundle in one hand and then grasped hers with his other one and led her from the garden. By the time they reached the streets descending to the river he could sense she was too weak to keep up with his rapid pace. He reached down and picked her up and carried her surprisingly frail body the rest of the way down to the river path. At last, he saw the boat ahead and a moment later Fabrisse was rushing toward them. She took her daughter from his arms and began to weep as he led them to where Phillippe had gone to stand by the boat. When they got there, a tearful Fabrisse set her daughter down, went to Pierre, and hugged him to her as tightly as she could. She had no words for him, only her shaking body and the tears he finally reached over to wipe from her eyes. He looked at her, smiled broadly, and said.

"We should get in the boat now and onto the river. We have far to travel and I want to get as far away from this place as we can before the sun is up full. Phillippe, get everything in the boat. Don't forget your kitten," he laughed. "Fabrisse and Marie will sit on the back seat. I will row while you sit up front and warn of any rocks or floating wood we must avoid. Keep your eyes sharp on the water ahead."

The boat was quickly loaded. Pierre took off the monk's robe that had served him so well and threw it on the rower's seat. He thought of the Bishop's strange choice of words when he told him to take it and wondered if by some remarkable chance this had all been part of a miraculous plan he could not see. Then, he and Phillippe eased the boat out into the water and jumped in to assume their places. Pierre took the oars and rowed out into the steady current of the Tarn as it flowed rapidly west in this month. He quickly learned he would barely need to exert himself to row because of the speed of that current. He needed to use his oars mainly to steer the heavily loaded boat, or to avoid a sudden obstacle when Phillippe quietly called one out to him.

Pierre steered the rowboat as it was swept along by the swift currents till well after midnight and until the land began to flatten out some when the widening river slowed the effects of the more easily moving Tarn. They made good progress past the firelights of many small villages and farmhouses Pierre judged, until his arms began to grow tired and his eyes heavy. He had kept those eyes mostly focused on the back seat, where Fabrisse sat huddled with Marie pulled close in against her. At one point she had softly hummed an old tune, which had seemed to bring some sleep to the tired girl. As the half-moon rose, Pierre saw the mother shivering in the growing cold of the long night. He took the heavy monk's robe upon which he had been sitting and handed it to Fabrisse to wrap around them both. She offered to return his old cloak, but he declined and answered his rowing kept him warm enough. However, he finally noticed Phillippe was becoming less attentive and with two or three hours of darkness still left, he rowed them ashore to a secluded spot, beached the boat, and told everyone they would rest here until daylight. They all needed to stretch their legs and relieve themselves by then anyway, and Phillippe volunteered to remain watchful while his father tried to sleep for even an hour or two after his long and exciting evening and night.

The new sun found them ready to take to the river once more, after they had broken into Mme. Dugué's food bag and eaten nearly everything they found there. Marie ate sparingly, however, although Fabrisse kept telling her it was alright for her to take as much as she wanted. Once they resumed their journey, Pierre looked at Fabrisse soon after and said to her.

"There is a small knife in my tool bag near your feet. Take it out and remove all the yellow crosses from your clothing. You will have no more need for them where we are going."

Fabrisse looked at him with some doubt on her face for a moment, and then did what he had asked. When she was finished she made a wad of the several crosses, smiled at him, and dropped them over the side of the boat. He used his oar to press them under the murky waters of the Tarn, and they continued on their way. Phillippe kept asking if he could row some, and his father finally consented and changed places with him. Soon, Pierre noticed his son seldom took his eyes from where the fair-haired Marie was seated. When his kitten suddenly poked its head out of his tunic and cried out at one point, the girl's mouth flew open in surprise. She looked at him wide-eyed, and Phillippe handed her the tiny animal. She reached for it, clutched the kitten to her, and soon began to mouth the same little song her mother had sung to her earlier. Fabrisse nodded at the children and offered a smile to Pierre when he nodded back with one of his own, which contained the first true relief on his face he had felt that night. She returned his grin with a look clearly expressing her own immense joy at that moment as well.

It was nearly midday when they finally came to a small town not far downstream from where Pierre and Phillippe had crossed the river to begin the final part of their journey to Albi ten months earlier. Pierre pointed out a place and told his son to beach the boat there. It was just above the village, and he wanted to have some privacy in the small grove of trees they saw until he could think about what they would do next. Everything was so busy the night before, he had given little thought to his next move, except it would be to get back to the farm in the Aveyron Valley as quickly as they could.

After a short rest, he told Phillippe to stay with the boat and to watch Marie. He gave Fabrisse a few coins and told her she should buy as much food with them as she could, while he tried to trade the boat for something they could use better. When they came to the village, they separated and Pierre went to the river and finally found a man who was interested in the boat and said he had an old two-wheel cart that needed some repair he would trade, if he liked the boat. Pierre went back and rowed the boat down to where the man quickly agreed to the trade. When Pierre saw the cart, however, he knew he would have to fix one of the wheels and replace some missing side boards before it could make the journey north.

He found a blacksmith who also had some cut wood and purchased a handful of nails and some board scraps. The man also gave him an old hammer. Pierre asked him if he knew of anyone who might have animals for sale, and the smith told him about a man who kept a stable on the other end of the village who might have something. Pierre went there and used his other silver coin to strike a bargain for a horse that appeared to still have a couple of working years left in its legs. He was hoping for a good mule, but the man said he had none. However, he was overjoyed at his good deal for Pierre's silver, a rare thing in that place it seemed, and he also threw into the bargain some hitching harness and a large sack of feed grain as well. Pierre told him he would come back for everything before dark.

He spent the rest of the afternoon repairing the old cart. When he was finished, he returned for the horse and grain, took them to the cart, hitched the horse, and led it back to the trees where he had left Phillipe and Marie earlier. When he got there it was nearly dusk, and they were all eating. Phillippe was very excited when he saw the horse, and Marie was playing with and feeding the kitten this time. Fabrisse offered him some fresh bread while she sliced a large sausage for him. She showed him what she had managed to buy, and he told her she had done well. When he was finished eating, he told Phillippe to look about for some wood for a fire. As soon as he returned they made a small fire close to the cart, after he untied the horse, gave it some of the grain, and tethered it in the nearby trees for the night.

As darkness fell, the fire soon warmed them into drowsiness. Fabrisse finally came to where Pierre sat against the cart wheel he had repaired and pressed her body in close against his. She took his arm in hers and whispered her effusive "thank you" into his ear for all he had done for them. He turned to her and answered back he would continue to look after them both, if she wanted it. She said nothing, but reached up with her hand, turned his face toward hers, and kissed him on the lips for the first time. That night she and Marie—and the kitten—made their bed on the old monk's robe under the cart. Pierre and Phillippe would sleep just beyond close to the fire. He laid awake thinking about what the next days would bring and how he must see Father Guillaume at the first opportunity about his earlier promise to remove the burden of his first marriage from his life, which his wife's heresy and abandonment would make possible. Then, with Fabrisse, Marie, and Phillippe by his side, he would fulfill the first part of his promise to Bishop Bernard and marry "the woman", as he had called her.

He also thought about how he would one day manage to fulfill the rest of his great bargain with the most unusual and extraordinary man he had ever encountered. At last, the overwhelming fatigue of the previous days and the crackling of the nearby fire— along with the warmth of the new contentment within him—finally brought Pierre to the peaceful sleep the rest of his new "family" had already found. Pierre soon went to his own dreams under the trees beside the old river. The ancient stream, as it had done for so many before them, had brought them all one step closer to the home and the new life awaiting them in the little valley, which seemed to him at that moment to be not nearly as impossibly distant as it was only yesterday.

THE DANCER

AD 1935

"Will you show me the music box, *grand-mère*, and help me wind it? I can't turn the key as easily and carefully as you tell me I must."

"Oh, very well, *Béatrice*. But you really must learn to do it for yourself, you know. You're old enough not to break it, and I certainly have other things I need to do. I promised to help your *Mama* with the jam she is making and I would have these strawberries boiled down before she returns from the village with your *Papa* and your sister. Go and get the music box. You know where I keep it in my room."

The girl got up from the kitchen table where she had been watching her grandmother cut up the strawberries which had been washed and spread out on the cloth before her and then place them in a large ceramic bowl. In a few moments, she returned from the smaller of the two bedrooms on the far side of the kitchen. The painted, porcelain music box was carefully secured in both hands. She set it down on the table between her grandmother and the chair in which she had been sitting and eagerly resumed her seat. The older woman laid down her paring knife, wiped her hands on the edge of the towel in front of her, looked at her granddaughter, and smiled.

"Here, Béatrice, watch closely so you can learn to do this for yourself. You know I have told your *Papa* to be certain, when the day comes, you receive this from my things. I want you to have it always. But for now, we will listen to it once more and watch the ballerina do her little dance. I have to admit, *chérie,* just like you I never get tired of watching her spin about."

With that, she picked up the box and turned it in her hand to admire the finely painted figures just as she always did. They were starting to fade with age and use, but she never tired of admiring the skill of the artist who had painted them. She sighed wistfully at some nearly forgotten memory and began to wind the small key inserted into the back of the box. When it was wound tight, she set the music box down in front of her granddaughter just before the lid slowly opened and a tiny ballerina popped up and began to turn to the tinkling sounds of a Viennese waltz coming from beneath her feet. The girl watched the repetitive movements of the miniature dancer intently for a few moments, and then looked at her grandmother, who had been watching her all the while, and grinned broadly when the music ceased. The woman smiled back at her, picked up the music box, and held it toward her granddaughter.

"Now then, let me see you wind it this time. Really, I don't know which of us is worse about this old thing. Every time I hear that little tune, I just have to play it one more time—or maybe two."

She chuckled a bit as her granddaughter began slowly winding the magic key until she was confident, with her grandmother's urging, to make the final turn that would spring the lock to release the lid. She quickly set it back on the table, just as the ballerina appeared once more for her little performance. They both listened intently, as *grand-mère* hummed along with the familiar waltz and then picked up her knife to resume cutting the strawberries as she watched her granddaughter's smiling face focus on the music box until it ran down. Finally, the little girl closed the lid, looked up and asked a question the woman was not certain she wanted to answer.

"Can you tell me again, *grand-mère*, how you got the box and what the drawings on it are? It's been a long time since we talked about it, and sometimes I forget things, you know, just like *Mama* tells me I do when she is mad at me for something."

"Yes, my dear *Béatrice*, I'm afraid we all forget things sometimes, but mostly when we are very young, like you, or very old, like me." She laughed a little as she smiled at her granddaughter. "But your *Mama* loves you very much, even when you think she is a little mad at you.

"I got the music box from my own *Mama* for my birthday once when I was not much older than you are right now. She and father went on a short trip down to Toulouse, and she convinced him to buy it for me because she knew I liked to dance about the house so much. *Papa* was never happy with my dancing but *Mama* would often sing some little song when we were alone in the house or he was away selling his wine, and I would make up a dance to go with it. *Mama* knew lots of songs, and we never got tired of entertaining each other. I would also dance with my little brother, *François*, until he got too old for such things.

"But then, when he was nine and I was fourteen, he got the fever and died. After that, *Mama*, did not want to sing or watch me dance as much. I think it made her unhappy to remember the three of us in the kitchen together and how much fun we had back then. From then on, I mostly played the music box when she was not home, or when I was upstairs in my little room by myself—the same room you and Annette sleep in. But I would still try to dance like the tiny ballerina. If we play it again, why don't you try to dance like she does? I'll help you if you like. It would be fun to see you dance, *chérie*."

They played the box once more. Then they both stood up and the woman held the girl's hand over her head as she attempted to spin first one way and then the other to the waltz rhythm and the movements of the music box figurine. When the music ended, the grandmother laughed, leaned over and affectionately kissed the girl on the head, before she sat back down to resume her work. The girl sat down and watched her grandmother in silence for a few moments before she spoke up once more.

"I don't think I would be a very good dancer, *grand-mère*. It is too hard to get my feet and hands to move together at the same time like they are supposed to. But I like the music. *Mama* says next term in school, if I want to and the music teacher comes back, I can choose an instrument to learn to play from the ones he has. *Papa* says he might even buy one for me to practice with, if the teacher says I am good enough. *Papa* also says you were a very good dancer many years ago and even danced for famous people in Paris before you married grandfather. Is that really true, or was *Papa* just telling me one of his stories, like he does sometimes to make me feel better when I am sick?"

"No, *Béatrice*, your *Papa* was not telling you one of his made-up stories, although he has certainly been guilty of repeating some big ones, ever since he was a little boy. But yes, I was a dancer once a long time ago, and I did live and dance in Paris for a while in those days, before I came back here to live with your grandfather and your *Papa* was born. You know, I even taught others like you, *chérie*, to dance many years ago in the very same school you are going to right here in the Valley. What do you think of that?"

The girl said nothing as her mouth flew open at hearing this surprising and never before heard thing about her grandmother.

"Can you show me how to really dance sometime, *grand-mère?* Maybe not as good as you or the lady in the music box, but just a little bit?"

"Perhaps sometime, *Béatrice*, when you get a little older and the boys from the village start asking you to the dances they have sometimes down at the school. But right now I think you should help me with these strawberries before your mother gets back, or we may both be in trouble. Then I shall have to ask your *Papa* to make up one of his stories to get us out of it, just like he used to do to me when he was your age and needed an excuse for not doing his work."

They both laughed and *Béatrice* was assigned the task of pulling the green, leafy stems from the fresh strawberries as her grand-mother continued to slice them. However, as the grandmother looked at the girl and then the music box still sitting on the table between them, memories began flooding back into her mind. Memories of her days as a dancer in Paris; how it had all started— perhaps with the gift of this very music box when she had been a girl; and also, how it had ended much sooner than she had want-ed. All these recollections of a past she usually kept buried deeply within her flashed through her consciousness in rapid succession. Immediately, her thoughts drifted to places she did not often allow them to go anymore, as she mindlessly continued slicing the ber-ries and watching her granddaughter, who was humming a little tune of her own to accompany their work.

AD 1898

"You are a good dancer, Paulette, but you could become an ex-ceptional one and take a regular place in the cancan line, if you would only set your mind to it. But you are too much like some of these other girls who have come here thinking they will dance for us only until they get 'their big break' and join one of the op-era companies, or some other "proper" dance troupe. Why don't you forget that silly notion and stay here? There is more money to make at the Moulin Rouge and lots of rich men to watch you dance. I can't name all our girls who have already found a wealthy husband here. Why do you think we have to keep hiring new ones like you, ehh? I know, I know, you think Monsieur Zidler—God rest his just departed soul—hired you mostly because he liked your red hair; but he told me at the time he picked you from the others auditioning that day because he thought you had real talent. I think he held hopes in time you could even dance as a stand in for *la Goulue* herself, if you worked hard at it. Now *that* was truly why he liked your red hair," the man laughed.

"So, what do you say, my dear Paulette, will you sign on for another season? Now that our dear friend Charles is gone from us and we are reopening soon, I could really use your help. You are always so much more dependable than some of the other girls. Besides, I do hate the auditions so much when we lose one of our top dancers. I never like to have to tell all those girls who have come so far they do not have the talent someone back home told them they did. They all go away so unhappy at the thought of returning to a boring existence in some little village somewhere; or worse, they decide to stay in Paris with some grain of hope, until they end up in one of the bordellos off the Boulevard de Clichy. It is so sad for them, is it not?"

"So then, Paulette, won't you please sign on for the new season? What if I promise to give you billing on the show bills when you dance in the main *quadrille* line, ehh? If you do, I will see you have no more matinees to dance with the comedians or other short acts, unless it is an emergency, or you still want to, of course. By the way, we are thinking of adding a little comic opera piece to the early evening show. Perhaps, we could include a little serious dance element to it to play off the *Footit and Chocolat* comedy act that is so popular, if that would interest you. With the world coming to Paris now since the Grand Exposition we are expecting exciting things and a big turn in our fortunes. We will need you."

"Well, monsieur, you make a tempting offer, I must admit. But if I sign on again, it must be with the understanding I could still attend a tryout with one of the opera companies, if I should be offered one. Can you agree to that?"

"Of course, Paulette, of course. I have your contract here already prepared. If you would just sign it here, and again here, I will add the dates. You have my gratitude, my dear Paulette. If there is anything else I can do—except more money, unfortunately—please ask. Ahh, but it has been such a difficult and tragic year since our dear Zidler left us. We will miss him terribly."

"Yes, monsieur, he was indeed a fine man, and I will always be grateful to him, and to you as well, for what you have done for me already. But for now, I am content to continue as we were before. I would be interested in looking at this new comic opera piece you just mentioned, if you do consider making it a part of this season's schedule. You will let me know, will you not?"

The man behind the desk agreed quickly as he watched Paulette sign her contract for the upcoming 1898-99 season at the already well-known Moulin Rouge Review. Then he stood and escorted her to the door and thanked her profusely once more as she left. Once outside, Paulette was not at all certain things had just gone exactly the way she was hoping when she first entered Monsieur Oller's office. She was still a little uncertain if she was totally committed to signing on for another year of the difficult work she had been doing now for nearly two years. However, as always or so it seemed, Monsieur Oller was very persuasive. Everyone knew he often used his considerable arts of flattery to get what he wanted from those whom he employed in the unique setting and show, which he had helped create at the foot of the Montmartre Hill by the old windmill that stood in the *jardin de Paris*.

Paulette Gambeau had come to the "City of Light" more than two years earlier seeking work as a dancer. She was just like so many other young women drawn to the great city at the time, hoping to fill one of the many opera or ballet companies, which seemed to be everywhere in a city thriving with both commerce and arts of every kind. In her mind, she had been just like those other country girls M. Oller had mentioned earlier, except Paulette soon came to understand whatever classical dance instruction she had been able to acquire by that point in her young life was going to be far too little to attract the eye of one of the major dance companies. Other eyes, however, had been watching one of her failed auditions back then, and she eventually received an unexpected invitation to try out for the new theater in the famous Montmartre section of Paris, which had suddenly become the rage of the City and beyond. Much to her surprise after that unanticipated tryout, she received an offer to train as a dance company extra at the Moulin Rouge, and finally with some reluctance she accepted.

Paulette was twenty back then, and on some days it seemed to her she had aged ten years in the two that had passed since. She had left home shortly after the death of her mother and something of a bad falling out with her father over the direction in which each wanted her future to head. Her beloved mother's somewhat sudden death after an unexpected illness left the young Paulette devastated and confused about the future she longed for. Her mother had always been there to support Paulette's pursuit of the arts and had, perhaps, even sacrificed her own health somehow to earn a little extra to pay for Paulette's dance lessons.

The young Paulette was never as close to her father, who considered such activities a waste of time, especially for a girl. When her brother died while still a boy, her father was greatly affected by his loss and spent more time in his vineyards and less time with either her or her mother, or so it had always seemed to Paulette. Still, when her mother passed so suddenly, Paulette could not help but sense her father somehow blamed her for the loss of his wife. After the inevitable, angry confrontation with him over her desire to go to Paris—or somewhere—to pursue her dancing, instead of remaining on the farm to take care of him, or marrying the young man who had been pursuing her for some time, Paulette finally left home with more bitterness than regret. Nearly a year went by before she could bring herself to write her father to tell him where she was and what she was doing. Even then, it was not her father but the young man she left behind who answered her first letter.

It seemed to Paulette this young man had been chasing her since the very first day he came to the farm to help her father in their vineyards. His name was Marcel Poincaré and her father met him on a wine-selling trip to Toulouse where Marcel was a student at the university back then studying modern agricultural and wine making techniques. He had been very complimentary of her father's wines, and the older man offered him a summer position working in his vineyards while they experimented with some of the new methods Marcel soon interested the elder Gambeau into trying. After that first summer together, they enjoyed some minor success with their experiments. As a result, when Marcel returned the next year, he decided to accept her father's offer to go into business with him and work full time on the farm. He moved into Paulette's brother's old room, which had become Paulette's by then, and she had been relegated to the small room upstairs to accommodate the new member of their tiny household.

Her room eviction seemed to get their relationship off to a rocky start, although Paulette was more put off at the time by how serious Marcel always seemed to be. She, on the other hand, was more easygoing and adventurous. Marcel was three years older than Paulette, and far more world-wise than she when she turned eighteen that summer. She had finished her public-school education that same year and was beginning to think seriously about a career in dancing. When her mother died so unexpectedly shortly thereafter, Marcel began to place more and more pressure on her to allow their fast developing relationship to become more serious—and more permanent. This had frightened and confused Paulette so soon after the loss of her mother and hastened somewhat her decision to seek her future beyond the confines of the vineyards and the small, stone farm house, which suddenly held so many unpleasant memories of her mother and brother.

In her mind, at least, she had never exactly rejected Marcel's serious advances, once they became accustomed to and respected somewhat each other's individual differences. She knew she had experienced feelings for him which were unlike any she may ever have felt for boys she had enjoyed spending time with while growing up. Indeed, when he began to show serious interest in being alone with her even that first summer, his rugged good looks and maturity proved very attractive to the emerging woman in Paulette. After he moved in, they began meeting in secret and talking about their individual hopes and dreams for the future. Once, in the vineyard among the vines he seemed to love as much as her father, he took her in his arms and kissed her in a way that left her both giddy and certain of his ultimate intentions toward her. Soon thereafter, he professed his love. However, their deeper conversations seemed always to reveal a gulf between their diverging ambitions, a gulf which a confused Paulette was unable or unwilling to reconcile.

Perhaps, Marcel's serious nature frightened her more than she wanted to admit, and possibly she was running away from him as much as from her father. After all, as she often rationalized in the months after she left home, Marcel was far too much like her father in so many ways. She did not want to see her own dreams of an exciting life squashed in the same way she remembered having seen her mother's. She felt this would surely happen if she assumed the ordinary life of a wife and mother on a back-country farm with no town of any size nearby to allow for the possibility of ever seeing operas, ballets, or similar exciting shows. The unfortunate loss of her mother at such a critical point in the development of Paulette's expanding world view left her with an insatiable desire to strike out on her own—and, unfortunately, to strike out at anyone who stood in her way. As a result, the bitterness of her departure from the Aveyron Valley did not begin to subside until she was well established in her new life in Paris, regardless of what that life was turning out to be.

After an extended delay in answering his first letter, Paulette finally began an irregular correspondence with Marcel the second year of her absence. She would describe the exciting sights of Paris and reveal to him some part of her feelings she hoped would make him understand her need to continue the life she had chosen. He would keep her apprised of events on the farm and in the valley, their successes or failures in the vineyards, and mention her father's declining health in a way that never failed to make her feel guilty for being unwilling to say when she might come home, even for a visit. Marcel always ended his letters with either a vague or a direct plea for her to return, as much for himself as for her father, with whom Paulette was still unwilling and unable to reconcile. Perhaps, she concluded, it was her growing guilt about going back at all which had caused her to hesitate to sign on for another year with the Moulin Rouge this time.

Being conflicted was nothing new to Paulette. She had often felt the need to escape from one dilemma or another as she grew to womanhood within the narrow constraints of the small farm surrounded by the many vines, which seemed to her to be reaching out through her father's unbending attitude to strangle her ambition. Had it not been for her mother's encouragement, she knew she could never have come as far as she had already. Early in her life it was her dancing and love for its freedom of expression that sustained Paulette through the loneliness of her life on the farm. As she grew older, however, especially after her brother's death at a young age and the unspoken wedge that sad event seemed to drive between her parents, Paulette soon found a new outlet for her expressive personality as she spent more and more of her time alone.

In her fourteenth year, hard times had come to everyone in the valley, including her family. The only gift she received that Christmas from her parents was a drawing book and some pastel pencils her mother found for her in a village shop. This was to have been the year she began dance lessons with a part time instructor who visited the school two days a week; but suddenly there was no money for the promised lessons. Paulette was at an age when broken promises, regardless of the validity of the reason, were difficult to understand, and she became at first angry but then more disconnected, even from her mother, than she had ever been before. During those long winter evenings alone in her room, when even the music box held little hope for her dreams, she began to take up the pencils and the art pad and discovered a new and exciting aspect of her talents—one which she did not previously know or even suspect existed in her.

Paulette could not say whether it was the vibrant colors of the pastels that first captured her imagination, or merely the loneliness—either real or emotional—she was feeling at the time that first drew her to the blank pages of the sketch book. However, she soon began looking for subjects on which to focus beyond the music and dancing figures, which had also begun to stop dancing in her head that same year. She began with the ballerina and other figures on the porcelain music box and quickly discovered the artist who had painted them in such exquisite detail possessed a skill which was well beyond hers. And yet, to her mind at least, here was a new way she could fulfill her passion and abiding need to express her view of the world, if only she could learn to transfer it from her feet to her hands.

Within a year, she was drawing scenes from the farm: at first the stone buildings; or perhaps a bunch of ripening purple grapes hanging from a vine; and then gradually scenes of movement like a dog running or a goose flapping its wings as it tried to decide whether to run or take flight. The ones Paulette liked she kept in the sketch book. The ones she did not she ripped out and burned in the kitchen fireplace. Still, she worked alone and kept her developing skill from everyone, especially her parents, but even from others such as her teachers at school.

By the next school year her family's fortunes had improved enough for her mother to again arrange for her to begin dance lessons. It did not take long for the instructor who had told her mother he would take her on as a student the year before when he first saw her audition to compliment her on how much freer her movements seemed to have become in the intervening year. He commented it must be because her muscles were simply maturing and she would not suffer from the missed year of lessons. But Paulette suspected her new freedom of expression came from within, and from her new ability to view shape and movement together in a way she could never have imagined before. It was the growing ability within her for hands, feet, and imagination to work in a new and exciting unison, one which would renew her fading hope to seek a life on a stage far grander than any she could ever find in the Aveyron Valley.

Coming to Paris had proven a revelation to Paulette in every way she could have envisioned. Every form of the arts was going at full throttle there in the exciting years at the end of the Nineteenth Century. The City was the center of the international art world in so many ways, and the awestruck young woman from the obscure valley far to the south immediately found herself surrounded by every form of stimulation—both good and bad—a hopeful but inexperienced girl from such a background could possibly imagine. After struggling without success to find a position as a dancer in a "proper" venue and having signed on as a fill-in and back-up at the Moulin Rouge, she began to see her skills improve quickly and dramatically as she watched and practiced daily with other more talented, and famous, dancers of the well-known revue.

After three months of struggling to find a place for herself, a two-week stint in the cancan line—the highlight of each evening's show—as a replacement for one of the regular dancers who had taken a fall in practice and injured her knee, gave Paulette the first real attention she had ever received. That and her red hair, it seemed; for as others kept mentioning, she bore a close resemblance from the distance of the audience to the spectacular *la Goulue*, the most famous performer of the revue and one of the most recognized women in the entire Parisian arts' scene. After that, she began to receive more opportunities to dance in the daily shows or to fill in on the *quadrille* line any time there was a vacancy. When a permanent opening became available early in her second year, she became a regular of the famous dance revue. She soon learned her new situation would present her with many opportunities as well as with unwanted attentions from gentlemen of sometimes questionable intent.

Paulette had earlier found a place to live just outside of the famous Montmartre district where so many members of the local art scene resided and so many other Parisians came to enjoy the night life, being drawn to it like moths to a flame. She shared two rooms just off the *Rue d'Amsterdam* with another young dancer she met shortly after arriving in Paris. They had both tried out for various dance companies together and became friends as well as co-sympathizers with each other's unfulfilled dreams and frequent failures. Finally, her friend Julianne got an offer to dance with a minor touring company about the same time Paulette signed on with the Moulin Rouge. They decided to live together to stretch their meager budgets, which remained extremely tight in a city that could eat up what little pay they received in those days as quickly as it was earned.

Julianne came from the south of France as well, somewhere near Lyons. However, she had received more classical dance instruction than Paulette who, despite her natural talent, had ever been able to find, or afford. Still, they shared a lot in common, and the decision to share a place to live quickly proved to be an easy and beneficial arrangement for both. By the second year, however, Julianne's dance company was beginning to make longer trips to perform in cities both in and out of France, and Paulette was starting to feel pressure from some of the other regular danc-ers to move into one of the larger establishments most of them occupied nearer the theater. She remained reluctant to take the step, mainly because of the additional cost and the many stories she had heard around the dressing rooms about some of the things that went on in these larger boarding houses. However, just before she signed her new contract for the upcoming season, Julianne informed her that her company would soon be leaving on a three-month tour of the Continent. As a result, they both rather reluctantly decided they would have to end their lodging arrangement.

Paulette finally, if somewhat skeptically, decided to take a room in the smaller of the two houses just off the Blvd. de Clichy where most of the girls from the theater lived within easy walking dis-tance of the Moulin Rouge and its distinctive windmill. She had been something of a loner most of her life, and the shock of being thrown into a place of such constant activity and with so many gregarious and ambitious young women would prove quite an ad-justment for Paulette. Julianne remained close, but she was fre-quently away for long periods with her dance company. In the past Paulette had never minded this, since it allowed her occasion-ally to be alone in their tiny sitting room with her sketch pad and pencils—an activity she still enjoyed on a quiet evening after the raucous activity of dancing and music, from which she increasingly sought refuge at the end of her long days.

Now, however, Paulette was about to be cast into the footlights of the notoriety and instant, if fleeting, fame toward which her am-bition was propelling her. For the inexperienced and often con-flicted country girl, who had come to Paris with a vague dream for which her sheltered past could not have prepared her, Paulette was about to be changed in ways she could never have imagined.

"Paulette, there is someone by the stage door who says he would like to meet you. Should I tell him to wait and you will see him when you have finished dressing and are ready to leave?"

The girl watched Paulette, who was trying to rearrange her long hair into the more comfortable and less conspicuous fashion she preferred once the show was over. She glanced back and saw the familiar face of one of the several young women employed by the theater to help out backstage in the dressing rooms, or with costumes and the other countless details such a fast-paced and busy operation required. Paulette looked at the girl whom she knew and liked, shrugged, and responded while ignoring the low whistles and suggestive comments suddenly coming from the three other women with whom she shared the small room. Besides, she knew these were just the usual reactions following any such not uncommon announcement at their dressing room door.

"Oh, which is it this time, Bernice? A well-dressed, middle-aged gentleman with a bunch of flowers in his hand and an inattentive wife somewhere; or is it some fresh-faced boy who absolutely has to tell me I am the greatest dancer he has ever seen and that his life will be complete if only I will have dinner with him just this once? So, which is it?"

"Why mademoiselle, he is neither of those. Well, he is a gentleman of the age you describe but he has no flowers in his hand. I really think you should have me tell him to wait for you. I am certain he is someone you will wish to talk to; for he is a very famous artist and a man quite well known here at the theater."

"Really?" a suddenly attentive Paulette stopped fiddling with her hair and stared at the door, as did the other three dancers. "And just who would this 'famous' artist be who wishes to wait to speak with me."

"It is Monsieur Toulouse-Lautrec, the friend of Monsieur Oller. He often comes to the theater to paint the dancers or make the beautiful posters that hang outside and in the hallways. Shall I tell him you will speak with him as soon as you are finished, or should I tell him to come back here, now that you are dressed? He is often invited to the dressing rooms."

"No, no, Bernice. Do not tell him to come back here. Tell him to wait. I will see him as soon as I have finished my hair. Wait, no. Tell him to wait by the side entrance past the curtains. It is more private there."

Paulette suddenly became very flustered at the mention of the well-known artist's name. The other three dancers were giggling and whispering back and forth, until one of them laughed and spoke up as soon as Bernice left to deliver her message.

"My, my, Paulette. It seems you are about to be honored by our most famous customer and patron. That red hair of yours must have caught his wandering eye finally; but be more careful of his wandering hands, if he invites you to his studio to sit as a model. Even you must have heard the stories of our famous Henri and his many artistic "gifts"."

The young woman laughed aloud once more, drawing forth the knowing giggles of the other two and causing a suddenly embarrassed Paulette to blush nearly the color of her hair. Indeed, she had heard the stories of the well-known artist and his notorious escapades with other members of their dance troupe, including the rumors of his on-going liaison with the most famous star of the revue, *la Goulue,* herself. No one who worked at the Moulin Rouge could have escaped the whispers about the sexual prowess of the diminutive Lautrec, and the unseen physical attribute that had brought him such a reputation. However, as her companions continued to tease her, a suddenly reflective Paulette was not thinking of their stories at all but of the fact she had so unexpectedly drawn the attention of one of the most famous artists in Paris.

She quickly finished her hair, grabbed her light evening cape, and headed for the side entrance where she had told Bernice to have her "gentlemen caller" wait. As she approached, she recognized the unmistakable figure in the dim lights by the door. She had seen Toulouse-Lautrec speaking with other girls, or in the lobby holding court with his admirers, and occasionally in the nearby cafés she sometimes visited. However, she had never been introduced and was suddenly apprehensive about what he might say or ask her. He was as always well-dressed, with his short, neatly trimmed beard, as he leaned on his cane with one hand and held his bowler hat in the other. Paulette was well aware as she approached she was going to be nearly a full head taller than the famous man, whose childhood deformity had left both legs childlike in length, while his torso was that of a man of normal height. She told herself not to stare at the sight of his most unusual figure. But she was still uncomfortable as she stopped an arm's length away, just as he came to his full height and tapped his cane twice in the habit he had when preparing to address a taller person.

"Ahh, Mademoiselle Gambeau. I cannot tell you what a pleasure it is to meet you at last. I have enjoyed watching you dance for the past year and have often remarked to my companions, and even to my dear friend Monsieur Oller, that you must surely one day take your place as a headline performer in the Grand Revue."

"You do me a great honor, Monsieur. Indeed, it is I who has admired your work on many occasions. Your spectacular poster of our beloved *la Goulue* inspires us all, and I have seen it in so many shop windows around the city. The way you deepen your colors without losing any of their brightness or intensity is truly a wonderful gift."

"So, Mademoiselle Paulette—if I may call you that, and you must certainly call me Henri—I see I was not mistaken in seeking you as the artist of that little pastel of Mademoiselle Avril, our well known *la môme fromage*, that someone, you perhaps, posted on the little announcement board outside of Monsieur Oller's offices. When I saw it, I was most curious about the initials *P G* at the bottom, and I was forced to ask around until your name came to my attention. I detected a certain skill and uniqueness of form in your little drawing, and I could not help but wish to meet the artist of such a fine sketch of one of my favorite dancers."

"Really, Monsieur, I mean Henri, you flatter me far too much with your generous praise. It was a simple sketch, which one of the other girls saw me working on it and asked for. I was most surprised myself when it turned up where you saw it."

"Nevertheless, any good eye can see there is real talent there. Do you draw often, Paulette? If so, I would be most interested in seeing some of your work. A suggestion here or there, perhaps, or even some private instruction might bring out more of your talent. I must say, I was quite happy to learn after my inquiries the artist of that sketch was not only one of my favorite dancers, but Monsieur Oller also mentioned you are from somewhere in the Aveyron Valley. You know I was born and raised in Albi, and my parents still make their home there. If you would do me the honor, perhaps, of dining with me this evening, I know a nice little café a short distance from here. It is not so crowded and we can have a more private conversation about such things as art and home—and anything else you would like to speak of. Please say you will join me, Paulette. I will be so disappointed if you refuse me, mademoiselle. I cannot imagine what I should do in that unhappy event."

At these last words he smiled subtly and bowed, and even though Paulette knew they were spoken mainly in jest, she also sensed his invitation was sincere and genuine. She needed only a moment to think, as all the scandalous things she had heard about the little man standing in front of her flashed through her head, before she smiled as he looked up at her with a hopeful grin on his face. She bowed politely back toward him herself, and replied to his request.

"I would be honored to accept your generous invitation, Monsieur Henri. It will be most pleasant to speak about our mutual homes with someone who must have seen far more of it than has a country girl from a small village such as you see before you. Shall we go? I must warn you, however, I am known as much for my appetite as my dancing among the other women in my boarding house."

Lautrec laughed at her last remark in mutual recognition of his well-known affair with the star of the Moulin Rouge, *la* Goulue, which meant "the glutton". He extended his arm for her to take and led her to the entrance door and then out onto the street, where he quickly hailed a waiting hansom. Paulette could feel the eyes of the many passers-by staring at the oddly mismatched couple they made as he helped her step into the one-horse cab that would take them a few blocks to the small café. There, as she would learn in the days ahead, more than one well-known local artist kept a private dining room available in the back. The work of many of these men hung on the walls of the café, and a wide-eyed Paulette immediately felt drawn into the small, but exciting world she was entering for the first time. It was a world she had barely dreamed of becoming a part of herself, but was one she somehow sensed even that first evening would soon become far more important to her than her dancing ever could be.

That first evening was spent over a long, and exquisitely presented dinner, and Paulette and Henri spoke easily of many things. Their common knowledge of places both had visited near their child-hood homes made what might have been an otherwise awkward introduction for two such diverse strangers an easier task than Paulette would have anticipated. Henri had traveled widely, which she of course had not, and he seemed eager to impress her with his knowledge of faraway places and his acquaintance with some of the famous people he had encountered, including most of the well-known artists living in Paris at the time. He was apparently a close friend of Cézanne, a painter whose work Paulette often admired, and she could only imagine the conversations about their art that would transpire between two such gifted painters.

For his part, Henri was curious about how Paulette had found her way from the secluded Aveyron Gorge region to the bright lights of Paris, and equally, how she had obtained her skills, both as a dancer and as a budding artist. He was also full of questions about her life at the Moulin Rouge, and by the second bottle of wine she was reminding herself to be careful in responding to the many details and rumors about the personal lives of the various performers he seemed to have an insatiable desire to ask about.

Paulette soon lost all track of time, but she sensed it must be growing much later than she usually allowed herself to stay out on a night when she knew she must dance again the following day. Finally, Henri asked the waiter for a couple of small glasses, and when the man returned and placed them on the table Lautrec looked at her and said.

"My dear, mademoiselle, I cannot tell you how much I have enjoyed our conversations this evening. It is not often I have the privilege of speaking with someone from so near my home. It gives me a rare opportunity to recall more of the happy memories I still keep of those days. Unfortunately, I also have recollections which are much less enjoyable when they creep back unsummoned into my private thoughts. I much prefer the pleasant ones we have discussed together here this lovely evening.

"But the hour grows late, and I must apologize for keeping you out so long. As you can well imagine, it is most difficult for me to keep my movements in such a busy place as this part of Paris has become from the many eyes and wagging tongues which seem to be everywhere. It is my most sincere wish not to cause you any embarrassment for being seen at such an hour with a man who, shall we say, has a reputation that is not as salubrious as he would often like it to be. But then, I must also say much of the reason for these many unhappy rumors about me is they are sometimes quite well-founded."

At that, he grinned broadly and shrugged. Paulette could find nothing meaningful to say in return, except she was not worried about any such idle talk. He thanked her for her reply, and then reached for his cane, which was leaning against the wall close to his chair. However, instead of using it to help himself rise from his seat as Paulette assumed he was about to do, Henri began to twist the handle until it came off in his hand. Then, he surprised Paulette completely when he picked up one of the glasses that had been brought to the table earlier and filled it with a dark, amber liquid poured directly from the cane itself. He looked at a wide-eyed Paulette again, smiled, and said.

"Perhaps one final toast to our marvelous evening and the beginning of a new friendship, mademoiselle. That is, if you would care to join me? But I will completely understand if you do not. When I visited England for an extended stay with my parents some time back, I developed quite a taste for the fine whiskeys they produce on that fascinating island, particularly in those dreary lands of Scotland—the only useful thing I found there, I must say. Sadly, so many of the better cafés here have not yet decided to add these to their stocks, and I must carry my own supply about with me, as you can plainly see, if I wish to continue indulging my most recent addiction. I see you have a last drink of wine in your glass. Perhaps, you will still share a final toast with me, ehh."

Paulette happily lifted her glass to receive his toast, and they enjoyed their final drink of the evening far more quickly than they had the first one. When the glasses were set down, Henri replaced the head on his cane, even though Paulette could see he was sorely tempted to refill his glass once more. She had heard the rumors of his feats of drinking—as well as those of his other area of prowess—and she could not help but wonder why a man with such artistic gifts would need an additional escape from his obviously difficult reality when he had his painting to sustain him. However, Paulette was in those short hours in the company of this strange and unique little man already being irrevocably drawn to the amazing personality which was beginning to reveal itself to her. It was obvious their evening was coming to an end when Henri captured her eye with his intense gaze once again and spoke more directly than he had been.

"My dear, Paulette, if I might be so bold as to ask, it would give me great pleasure to see your sketchbook, which you spoke of earlier over dinner. I sense you have a talent sleeping within you that needs only the proper encouragement and guidance to awaken and burst forth. If I were to invite you to come to my studio, would you do me such an honor? I promise any stories or rumors you might have heard about me from others who have come there to act as a model or otherwise will in no way affect our purely professional relationship. I cannot believe myself for saying this to such a beautiful young woman as I see before me, but I would be most honored if you would consider me as a mentor or confidante, who desires only to see you grow in your budding talent. Please say you will allow me to assist you in any way I can."

This was such an amazing and unexpected offer Paulette did not need more than a few seconds to consider before readily accepting. She had told herself when she first mentioned the sketchbook earlier in the evening not to make it sound like she wanted him to see it, or even comment on it, even though she secretly knew this was, indeed, exactly what she wanted to happen. Now that it appeared her desire was coming to fruition, she willingly ignored all those rumors Henri had referred to, as well as more direct warnings she knew she would receive if she told any of her friends at the theater what she was going to do. Paulette sensed she would have to tread very carefully around this man, despite her eagerness to introduce herself into his fascinating world. She was also immensely curious about how the thoughts of a real artist motivated his work, just as she had always wondered about her own feelings, which so often compelled her to pick up her pencils and sketch pad. In the end, she eagerly agreed to show him her sketches whenever he could arrange to see them.

They left the café and he dropped her off at her rooming house well past any hour she had ever returned before. Even with the lateness, two other performers she knew were still sitting in the parlor of the large house when she came in, and she saw them whispering after she greeted them and quickly went up the stairs to her room. Paulette knew she would have a difficult time sleeping because she had so much to think about and many new memories to sort through and store in her mind. Before he dropped her off earlier, Henri had invited her on her next day off to come to the large flat where he lived and also maintained his primary studio. They set a time when he would send a cab and she would come with her artwork for him to see. He also invited her to dinner again for that same evening and this time she forced herself to think with a slightly clearer head than she had done earlier this same evening. Then, she had been so overwhelmed by his sudden introduction she could not have imagined turning him down. Now, however, she was beginning to wonder for the first time if she might be out of her depth with this little man and all he represented in her own hopes. Paulette finally resolved before she went to sleep that in the future she would proceed cautiously and with more self-control than she had exhibited since first meeting the famous Toulouse-Lautrec.

The next week passed rather slowly for Paulette as the excitement over her impending second meeting with Henri began to build. However, she made certain not to allow anything to affect her nightly performance. One evening two days before she was to go to his studio with her drawings she happened to glance beyond the gas footlights and across the audience to the small box she had noticed him sitting in once or twice before they met. He was there for the first time since their memorable meeting and he appeared to be standing and cheering as loudly as everyone else when the spirited performance of the cancan—the rousing conclusion to the nightly show—ended. When he saw he had caught her eye, he smiled and bowed very obviously in Paulette's direction as the line of dancers came forward to receive their applause, along with the usual flowers thrown their way by admiring "gentlemen" of all types, who she knew paid handsomely for their front row seats and the opportunity.

Two days later, she spent the morning trying to decide what to wear for her mid-afternoon appointment at the famous man's studio, which was not all that far away as it turned out. She assumed they would be dining once again in the same secluded little café as before and decided to do her hair in the similar fashion he had commented favorably upon during their first encounter. Finally, when she was as satisfied with her appearance as she could be, she grabbed her sketchbook and went down to the parlor to await the arrival of the cab Henri said he would send. The cab was late and she was beginning to think he must somehow have forgotten their appointment. After all, she started convincing herself, he may merely have been flattering her in an attempt to impress her in the same way he was famous for doing with so many other young women who performed in the theater. Her nerves were beginning to fray until finally she glanced out the window and saw an empty cab arriving. Paulette quickly brushed away her negative thoughts, stood, and headed for the carriage.

In what seemed like only a few minutes the cabbie pulled the glistening black horse to a stop in front of an elegant looking brick building on one of the wider streets in the Montmartre District. He helped Paulette out of the carriage, took his leave, and quickly disappeared, leaving her standing alone facing the door. She walked to it and saw just below a pull bell the entire second floor seemed to be assigned to M. Toulouse-Lautrec. She pulled the cord handle, heard a bell ring inside, and a short time later a well-dressed man appeared and escorted her to the stairs which would lead her to the studio and sleeping rooms at the top. Paulette hesitated for a moment, drew a deep breath as she clutched at her sketch book, and took the first step to climb toward whatever awaited her at the top of those stairs.

The door was ajar when she peered in and saw Henri alone and working busily on a painting near a window. The afternoon light was flooding in and illuminating his easel and he was dressed in a paint-splattered frock. When he didn't notice her arrival, Paulette hesitated a moment and then knocked softly on the partially opened door. He immediately turned and, seeing her, smiled, put down the brush he held in his hand, and walked to greet her as he spoke excitedly.

"Ahh, my dear Paulette, at last you arrive to brighten my dreary rooms. Come in, come in. I see you have brought your sketch book. I cannot wait to see what treasures it hides—waiting only to be revealed to an admiring eye. A glass of sherry, perhaps? Come, we will sit on the divan over there away from the paints and in this lovely afternoon light that has just arrived with you."

Henri pointed her to an overstuffed divan near a second window on the same side of the room where she had first seen him working. He removed his frock and went to a small table to pour two generous glasses from a bottle of sherry standing between a pair of whiskey bottles of a type Paulette did not recognize. Handing her one of the glasses, he sat down beside her, took the sketch-book which had been resting in her lap, and placed it in the small space on the divan between them. Paulette watched anxiously as Henri opened it to the first page. She watched his every eye movement intently as he began to sip his sherry perusing the first simple drawing of a stone barn; he then began slowly turning the pages and looking intently at each new drawing in turn, until he came to one of a horse hitched to a wagon. At that, he finally stopped, drained his glass before setting it on the small table next to the sofa, and spoke to a very nervous and barely breathing Paulette.

"Now this is more like what I wanted to see from you. These first drawings, I assume, were done when you were merely testing your newly discovered skills, *n'est-ce pas?* They show some promise but are stiff and almost like an attempt at one of those photographs which have become so popular, and which some say will soon put simple artists like me out of work. My friend Cézanne and I get drunk and argue about this very thing quite often. But in this horse you have drawn, Paulette, I see the beginning of something new and exciting coming through in your work. It is the awareness of capturing more than a single moment of movement—an instant in the life of a living and breathing thing. This is a gift only an artist can capture and reveal with the magical stroke of a brush, or the simple swirl of a pencil. No, my dear, here I see hope in your talent, and the affection you must feel for this animal is plain to see. Tell me, is there some special reason you chose this particular horse to attach to that old wagon, which is also quite well done, I must say."

"Why, yes, it is one of two horses we have on our farm. His name is *Bas Bas*. My mother named him that because of his two white forelegs, as you can see. He was her favorite horse and she often held me on him when she would ride him about the farm when I was a girl. After she died, my father used him mostly to pull the grape wagon in the vineyards or hitched with our other horse when he takes his wines to market. I always felt sorry afterward for poor *Bas Bas,* with no one to ride him or sing to him with a familiar voice."

"Of course, it is easy to see your love for the animal in the way you have turned his head toward you and the sadness I can almost see captured in his eye. Here for the first time, Paulette, you have drawn your feelings and not just what your eyes are seeing. It is the great gift which separates the mere painter of objects from the true artist. It is one I believe we can find a way together to help you learn to show in your work in the same way I saw in your sketch outside of Monsieur Oller's office. I am eager to look at what follows in your book; but before I turn the page there is something I want to show you."

Henri set down the sketch pad and stood up to cross the room to an old shelf upon which were various loose sheets and drawings of different sizes. He thumbed through a stack until he came to two he was searching for and then returned to the sofa to sit down once more. He showed first one and then the other of the two sketches to a curious Paulette. Each was a charcoal drawing of a horse hitched to a two-wheeled cart. In one of them the horse held an almost eerily similar pose to the one Paulette had done in the drawing Henri had just admired. She glanced up quickly at him and saw the broad smile on his face as he spoke.

"You see, my dear, you are not the only one who likes to draw horses. I have been using them as practice subjects since my earliest days. Just as for you, it was these noble beasts that helped me to first recognize my abilities, and my need to express something alive and vibrant in a lasting image. You must not tell anyone this, but I have used this same sketch of the old horse you see here in more than one of my finished paintings. In fact, I was always fascinated by them and they were often a subject I chose—before I came here and decided beautiful young women dancers were far more exciting as model subjects." He laughed, winked at Paulette, and then continued.

"This old horse you see here used to pull a cart near our home in Albi when I was a boy. I would wait for him with a carrot or an apple when he was pulled by our house by the old man who owned him and delivered small loads of wood. The horse was named *Bonaparte* and we became great friends, before I, well, had my accidents and my mother would not let me go into the streets so much.

Later, when he died, I went back and made these charcoals from my fond memories of him. Those drawings helped me realize perhaps I had something to reach out for and to contribute to the world at a time when the direction of my life was uncertain at best.

"You see, Paulette, when we draw the things we are emotionally connected to in some way, those feelings find their way from our head, and our heart, into our eyes and hands. Without that, we truly are little more than these photograph takers who capture an image frozen in one moment of time, without movement, without emotion, without love. It was your love for your mother you have no doubt expressed here in your vision of this horse you have drawn so well. I can see it, but more importantly I can feel it as well. Now then, I believe I will pour myself another glass of sherry and then we shall look at the rest of your drawings and see what else you have managed to learn on your own, before we start to see where we might go together—if that is your desire."

Indeed, that was truly Paulette's desire, and never more so than in that very second. However, she simply nodded and muttered a simple *'yes'* to his query and declined his offer of more sherry, as she suddenly took her first really long sip from the glass she had kept in her hand and tasted sparingly until just then. When Henri returned, he squeezed himself closer to her where they could balance the elongated sketch pad on both their laps at the same time. He began to turn the pages once more and make more specific comments about what he was seeing as he continued. The drawings of the farm animals in their various poses seemed to capture his interest the most, although he also commented favorably on her use of shading in one of her simple landscapes of the vineyards behind their barn. Finally, they finished and he carefully closed the book and looked at her.

"Mademoiselle, I believe you possess a rare and unexplored talent, which together we can help bring to bloom. As you must know, my own schedule is quite busy most days. However, if you wish, on days such as this when you have no dances to perform, and if I am available, I am most eager to assist you, but not as a formal student, simply as a compassionate friend who also enjoys your company. The only payment I would ask in return is you continue to have dinner with me, if I ask, or lunch perhaps if it is all we have time for that day, whenever you come here. I may, of course, also insist at some point you permit me to paint you, if you would be so kind as to model for my brush."

Henri laughed a little and Paulette felt herself blush slightly as she caught the possible hidden meaning of his last words—words he seemed to be acknowledging with the same laugh that he had used more than once in the past regarding some other young woman he wished to "sit" for him. However, Paulette believed what would ultimately prove to be correct, that Henri's main interest in her was based on friendship and mutual interest and was therefore different from the many temporary relationships for which he was so notorious among her dancer friends. She quickly agreed she was perfectly happy with such an arrangement. They spent the rest of what was early evening by that time looking about his studio, while he explained some of his work to her eager ears.

Finally, he excused himself to dress for dinner. He invited Paulette to wait for him and to feel free to pass the time looking at whatever of his many drawings and books she wished until he returned. Then he escorted her once more to the little café, where on this occasion Paulette enjoyed a much less stressful evening than she had the first time. Henri even introduced her to other friends of his in the café, and at one point thrilled her when he spoke of her to an artist whose name she recognized as his newest "protégé" and a young artist of promising talent. For Paulette, the evening ended far too soon this time, as she was barely aware of the lateness of the hour when he politely kissed her hand and dropped her off at her rooms.

Even then, she suspected the effervescent—and notorious— little artist's evening was not yet over, since she heard him direct the cabbie to an address other than his own, after she stepped out of the carriage and headed for the door of her boarding house. However, despite her eagerness to learn from the diminutive Master, Paulette already suspected she could never fully adapt her more reserved self to the kind of lifestyle she was apparently entering. When she made it to bed that night her mind continued to race from all she had experienced that marvelous day. The effects of the evening's last glass of wine finally subsided and she found the sleep she would need to resume the dancer's routine— one which would never again seem quite so normal—the following evening.

━━◁┼▷━━

Weeks soon passed into months as Paulette began her regular visits to work privately with Toulouse-Lautrec in his studio. At least those visits seemed regular to an always eager Paulette, even though she soon discovered it was impossible to maintain any kind of set schedule with the peripatetic little painter. In the beginning, at least, Henri made every effort to be available for her scheduled visits. However, she soon learned there would be days when she would arrive and he would be unavailable for one reason or another. If he was out of the city, she would still be shown to his studio, where she would work on her own on some drawing assignment he had set out for her earlier. She kept her art pad there as well, which made it easier for her to come and go unencumbered by it or the other items he frequently acquired and set up in his studio for her to draw.

On other occasions, the valet would simply say: *Monsieur is indisposed today and sends his apologies.* Paulette soon began to suspect on those days he was either still feeling the effects of too much alcohol from the night before, or was actually suffering from one of the several painful afflictions, which she had learned from their earlier conversations constantly interrupted his work, sometimes for days at a time. On those days she would usually politely decline the offer to ascend the stairs and work in the studio alone and would simply walk back to her room or take a stroll about, as she used to do on her days off when the weather was nice. Fortunately, she lived less than a ten-minute walk from his studio and any inconvenience she might have felt at his increasingly frequent bouts of being "indisposed" did not make her feel any less eager to continue their work together.

Despite such frequent distractions, Paulette felt she was making real progress in her ability to manipulate the various colors and perspectives about which he was always eager to instruct her. From their early conversations, she learned about the excellent professional art education he had been provided as a boy and young man, mainly through the auspices of his devoted mother. Henri came from a wealthy family and enjoyed all the privileges of his family's position that Paulette in her formative years had been denied. When she thought of how her mother had sacrificed just to get her simple dance lessons, she was envious of the opportunities Henri had been afforded. But she also soon realized, despite such things as only wealth and position could provide, she had enjoyed the far greater opportunities of good health and a stable home life, which were apparently not often present in her new friend's life.

Paulette could not help but believe she and Henri were becoming close in a way that was different from anything she could ever have anticipated between a man and a woman. It had not taken many visits of working quite literally hand-in-hand sometimes, until each began to openly confide personal aspects of their lives—both past and present—to one another. Until meeting Henri, Paulette had always viewed men as creatures with whom she needed to be cautious and protective of her own feelings. Even her difficult to understand relationship with Marcel, both before and since she left the farm, was nothing like the mutual confidences she soon found so easy to share with the little artist.

Perhaps, it was the tacit understanding with which they began: that in their relationship he would refrain from any untoward advances of the kind for which he was so notorious, which gave each of them the freedom to express his or her true thoughts and feelings. Each could speak entirely freely without any false efforts to hide themselves from one another or play at the emotionally charged games that more intimate relationships often required. Or possibly, it was the singular passion they shared for their art that overrode any potentially more personal entanglements in their deepening relationship. This shared passion allowed them to see each other almost as a "father confessor", someone who would make no value judgements, nor pass on anything spoken in confidence beyond the sanctuary walls of the artist's studio.

Before long Paulette began to learn some of the more important details about the famous artist's unique life, not the least aspect of which was his remarkable stature. Henri's particular affliction was somewhat unique, she learned, and was not something he had been born with as was the case for most people who suffered from some congenital form of dwarfism. At first, he had been reluctant to speak of his personal life and Paulette remained hesitant to ask about the obvious, even though she was immensely curious. Sometimes he would simply joke about the many disadvantages he constantly encountered because of his small stature, including such things as having to have his suits custom made even though he could easily wear normally sized men's short coats, shirts, or sweaters.

But Paulette could see beyond the laughter and attempts at humor over such things and note the hurt in his eyes and the real truth of his feelings when he mentioned something as simple as getting in or out of a carriage, particularly when in the company of a woman. Still, she was careful not to press him about such feelings until one day when he became frustrated with something he could not reach on a top shelf and she went to his aid without being asked. This seemed to upset him, and she immediately apologized for being thoughtless when she sensed her unsolicited help had caused him some embarrassment. However, he quickly regained his composure, and then it was he who apologized to her for his behavior. That seemed to break down any still remaining barrier in their relationship and he started that day to relate many of the more unusual details of his early life and very difficult childhood.

The Toulouse-Lautrec family name came from his father's family title referring to those locations in the south of France near their mutual homes. He came from a long line of counts, and the family in that region was still quite well-to-do. As often happened in such families in those days, his father had married a first cousin. In fact, as Henri joked more than once, it turned out his grandmothers were also sisters. When he was born, it soon became apparent he suffered from a defect of strength in his bones, which the doctors attributed to the fact his parents were too closely related by blood. The result was as a boy he had accidentally broken each of his thigh bones less than a year apart. Neither had healed properly because of his unusual condition, and the growth of his legs had virtually ceased as a result of those two traumatic events. However, the rest of his body had continued to develop normally, leaving him to endure the strange appearance he presented to the world from that point forward.

Henri began to speak often of his mother and how devoted she then became both to protecting him from unpleasantness others might inflict upon him because of his stature, and also to ensuring the talent her son exhibited from an early age received every opportunity to flourish. She soon arranged for Henri to study with a well-known artist and took him to Paris and later to England with the family to expose him to the Masters, past and present. He sometimes intimated to Paulette, however, that such attention and protectiveness eventually became oppressive and he inevitably began to rebel. Finally, he came to Paris to live and work on his own, although he still maintained a close and somewhat ambivalent relationship with his mother. Paulette could sense his notorious reputation for feats of drinking and his famous bordello escapades and other affairs—which Henri seemed to have little serious interest in keeping out of the public eye—must somehow be an attempt to remind his mother, perhaps, that he had actually made it on his own, that he was as "normal" as other men, and that he was resisting any further efforts by her to steer or dominate his life.

Paulette was also surprised to learn he had not immediately achieved success with his art when he first came to Paris. True, he had made friends with many of the new *Impressionist* painters, like his close acquaintance Cézanne; but he had chosen to pursue a more independent direction in his painting. It was not until he began to produce the colorful and extremely popular lithographs and posters of his work based on the dancers at the Moulin Rouge and the nightlife of Paris that he finally attracted the following which had thrust him to the pinnacle he had since achieved, especially in the busy artist community then centered in and around the cafés and boulevards of Montmartre.

For her part, Paulette reciprocated Henri's confidences by telling him about her relationship with her mother and how she had so influenced Paulette's earlier interest in dancing. She could see, too, they both had similar, more detached relationships with their fathers, if perhaps for different reasons. In Henri's case, his father seemed to have lost interest in his son's life when it became obvious Henri could not and would not assume the traditional role in his larger family his name and social standing required. For Paulette, her father seemed also unable to come to terms with her decision to determine her own course in life, especially after her mother's death removed the primary connection between them, thus allowing the different viewpoints of their equally strong personalities to emerge and diverge in their relationship with one another. Paulette was well aware she could be headstrong and even obstinate herself. But like many persons who exhibited those particular emotional traits, she frequently had a difficult time dealing with others, like Marcel, who behaved the same way toward her.

However, unlike Henri, Paulette always felt her father blamed her in some way for having, in his mind at least, stolen from him so much of his wife's time and affection before she had died far too soon. Now he would not have her to grow old with, nor would he have Paulette or anyone close with whom to share his beloved vineyards. His frustration with his daughter's attitude had pushed her away instead of drawing her closer at the critical moment in their relationship. Paulette was beginning to think more and more about the effects of her unhappy departure for a new life in Paris on her father's life whenever she received one of the letters that still regularly arrived from Marcel. Still, she managed to convince herself her father at least had Marcel with whom to share his love for his precious vines. She also suspected he was somehow still trying to manipulate her from afar by encouraging Marcel's constant requests for her to return, which came along with the repeated proclamations of his continued love for her with each new letter.

By this time, Paulette was shifting much of her focus to her art instruction. Each session with Henri seemed to open her eyes and mind to some new possibility which had been lying just beyond either her imagination or her ability to express it until then. Her dancing was becoming more of an outlet for her physical expression and energy than an emotional outlet, which it had always been in the past. Henri, as always, noticed this subtle change in her performance one evening, and chided her, even threatening to curtail her lessons if he noticed her not showing the same energy in her dancing, which he reminded her was what had drawn his attention to her in the first place. Paulette remained conflicted but vowed to renew her dedication to both aspects of her artistic life. After all, as Henri forcefully reminded her one afternoon, each was an aspect of her inner talent seeking a release and she needed the one to fully complement the other, if she was to continue to progress in the manner he kept predicting for her.

It was shortly after this conversation he told her it was time she was introduced to oil paints and the three dimensional possibilities they would unleash in the expression of her vision. Up to that point she had continued to sketch and draw in charcoal or the pastels she had come to love since the first time she was drawn to the bright colors and easy movements of the soft pencils upon the blank paper. Now, Henri wanted her to paint either on canvas or the smooth board surfaces he generally preferred in his own work. It was a momentous and revealing leap for an excited Paulette, and she dove into it with renewed energy, despite the awful mistakes Henri kept pointing out to her when her progress did not match either her, or his, lofty expectations.

Henri started her with simple objects, but soon suggested she use her sketch pad to select previous drawings or forms she was already familiar with and convert the soft pastel images to the heavier, yet equally vibrant colors he showed her how to mix. Inevitably, she finally came to her drawing of the horse, which had captured his imagination the first time he looked at the picture with her. Paulette immediately discovered the difficulties of revealing the same life-like features in the heavier oils, until after two discouraging failures Henri finally stepped in and guided her hand with the parts she was having the most difficulty with. That produced a moment of revelation of how she could combine different paints and textures on the same spot even to produce a new kind of image, one which had been well beyond her vision of her own capabilities until then.

When Paulette felt the soft touch of his hand grasping hers as he gently tried to guide it across the painted surface, she had for an instant experienced the strange feeling that she would not be unhappy if his hand had touched her in a more personal way. But that momentary feeling passed quickly when she realized Henri had been focused totally on the canvas in front of where she sat and on nothing else in that brief encounter. They had sometimes walked arm-in-arm together in the past on their dinner trips, or once even to a theater, or as he helped her in and out of carriages. But this was the first time the touch of his gifted fingers upon her skin had ever produced such a sensation rushing through Paulette, even if it was a fleeting one. That night, she lay awake in bed till well past midnight trying to deal with the strange feelings she had experienced that afternoon. In her heart, as well as her reason, she knew there could never be any true passion between herself and Henri. He had made that clear from the beginning, and she knew it was absolutely not in her plans to be pursued by him, or to pursue him in any way beyond their relationship of mutual admiration for each other's common talent and interests.

However, Paulette was becoming aware that something was missing in her life—something that neither her dancing, nor even her painting now, could ultimately provide. She began to wonder if, perhaps, the increasing frequency of Marcel's letters from home were not starting to have an effect on her longings for something beyond her life in Paris. Once she began to work so closely with Henri, she had decided to give up accepting occasional offers of an evening out with the many admiring men who always seemed to be begging one of the dancers for an evening's companionship.

At first, Paulette had taken the advice of one or two of her friends and occasionally accepted such invitations when it suited her, or even just for an exciting night on the town and a fine dinner in some trendy restaurant or café. For the men it was the opportunity to be seen in the company of a beautiful woman, perhaps even a recognized one, and this mutual, if brief, exchange carried little risk. However, Paulette soon learned it was best to avoid second or third such dates. Nor did she ever accept invitations from men she knew or believed to be married. She had seen firsthand the difficulties these less casual arrangements could lead to with more than one of her dancer friends and studiously avoided any such potentially disastrous entanglements in her already complicated life.

However, she had also seen two dancers during her time in the Revue leave to marry men whom they had met through their work at the theater. Whenever other girls spoke of such "opportunities" while they were eating or in the parlor together at the boarding house, or in the dressing rooms at the Moulin Rouge, the question came up of what the true motivations of these former companions might have been. Had it been love, or had it simply been the chance for a better life with a wealthy or doting husband motivating their decisions? It was a subject Paulette usually avoided when it came up among her friends, but was one she nevertheless thought about when she was alone with her many more disparate emotions of late.

By her third year Paulette was beginning to ask herself just what her own motivations were in continuing to pursue the difficult if often exciting and rewarding life of a stage dancer. The persistent loner in her personality kept Paulette from engaging in many of the hectic adventures of her few close friends. Many of these were activities she deemed too risky, or required she give up to someone else a piece of her individualism or privacy she did not wish to share just to attract the attentions of some man. When one of her friends would sometimes show her a nice little "gift" she had received from one of her "gentlemen friends", Paulette would just smile and refrain from asking what her friend had done to "earn" such a reward. She suffered no illusions about some of the things that went on behind the scenes at the theater, and Paulette often told herself she was no prude in her outlook about the intimacies that could easily develop in such an environment. However, from the beginning of her time there she had committed herself not to add such an unnecessary confusion, at least as she saw it, into her life of conflicting emotions and colliding ambitions.

Therefore, as she lay awake that night pondering the meaning of this sudden emotional need the mere touch of Henri's hand upon hers had revealed, Paulette came to the conclusion the absence of the kind of sensual expression Henri so obviously engaged in—and which she could sense the intimation of in Marcel's constant professions of his love for her in his letters—might be exactly what she felt she was missing and what her art was also beginning to demand from her. If she was ever to become an accomplished artist, like Henri and others, would she not have to completely break through any such unseen barrier still preventing her from mastering the techniques he was so willing to reveal to her, but which she felt were somehow beyond the skills he kept telling her she possessed?

It was a question that would begin to haunt Paulette regularly after that night and was one which would eventually throw her life into new turmoil and force her to a crossroads she must have known deep within from the beginning she would eventually have to face. In the meantime, however, she decided to commit herself again to Henri's instruction, even though for first one reason and then another the opportunities they had to work together were occurring less often. Still, on those less frequent occasions when he was available for her, he always seemed as eager as ever to explain patiently and help reveal to her new aspects of her talent of which she had previously been unaware.

Her abilities with oils finally began to develop exponentially, and these new abilities with the paints also helped to make the pastel sketches she continued to draw even easier and more fulfilling. Paulette was spending more time making those sketches at the theater, drawing her friends there and taking these to Henri's studio to convert under his watchful eye to a more exciting finished product she could never have imagined doing on her own before. If only she had more time—both hers and Henri's—she was certain she could develop her own unique style and perhaps achieve her place in the growing coterie of young artists she was beginning to see as her peers, even more so than she did her friends and fellow dancers at the famous theater. However, Henri's time—if not her own—was running out. Furthermore, as is always the case, and as Paulette was soon to learn, Real Life was to have its own idea about what direction her future might take.

AD 1899

All Paris buzzed with excitement at the approaching end of the Nineteenth Century and the hopes for a better world the new millennium seemed to promise. New technologies were appearing in every shop. Motor cars were replacing horse drawn carriages on the streets, and factories were sprouting up everywhere to turn out amazing new products to fire the imaginations of everyone from farmer to entrepreneur, and even those in the art world. The Moulin Rouge was packed for every performance as business men from around the world flocked to the City. In the ten years following the completion of the remarkable Eiffel Tower and the great World Exposition of 1889 for which it had been built, Paris had become not only the cultural, but now the entrepreneurial capitol of Europe.

It seemed to Paulette and the other dancers the men who attended their performances from often exotic places had never experienced anything like the now famous cancan, which highlighted each nightly performance at the Moulin Rouge. The great era of Cabaret Society and all it entailed was about to be unleashed on the world, just as it already had been in Paris. Europe's cultural energy which had been held somewhat in check during the now ending Victorian Age was quickly reviving. The raucous nightly performances were, however, becoming a drain on Paulette's energies, even though the dancers were making more money and receiving more "gifts" than ever before from the legions of new gentlemen admirers who descended on them from every corner of the world. These men would stand in line after the shows just for the opportunity to be seen having a drink or dinner with someone from the famous dance line, now the rage of all Paris and not just the boulevards around the Montmartre Hill.

Henri's health had also seemed to improve to the extent he was enjoying a new burst of energy which drove him to complete more paintings and drawings for his lithographs than even his usually prolific talents led him to do. As a result, Paulette found herself once again spending more time with him in his studio as he appeared once more to be eager to drive himself—and her—even harder than ever. The drinking that disturbed Paulette when she was alone with him continued unabated, however, and one day when he leaned over to examine her work and breathed heavily upon her, she could not refrain as she always managed to do before from saying something about it.

"Really, Henri, if you are going to fill your blood with drink so early in the day, must you breathe it into mine as well? I do so worry about you, and you know this is what causes you to be "indisposed" so often. Those of us who love you and respect you so much hate to see you continue to do this to yourself."

"Ahh, so now you must also be my mother—or is it my wife—dear Paulette, and echo the warnings of everyone else. Even Cézanne tells me I drink too much, and he is no slacker himself when a bottle is handy. You sound like my newest doctor, that awful pill-pusher. He tells me I will not make it to see the new century if I don't change my bad habits, and not just the drinking." Henri seemed to laugh a little, however, he moved back slightly from where he was standing.

"But he is not the first doctor to be wrong, I think. When I was a boy, I once overheard my mother talking with one of the doctors she used to employ to torment and prod me with their many instruments of torture. He told her he did not believe I would live to see my twenty-fifth year, because of my 'condition'. But I proved that one wrong, just as I intend to do with this new one. I have too much work yet to do, and the world and the new century we are about to enter are much too exciting to miss out on."

"Yes, Henri, they are. But the world will be an even more exciting place for the rest of us if you are still in it. I do wish you would take better care, and try to get more sleep—especially when it is actually still dark outside."

They both laughed and Paulette resumed her work on the painting of one of the dancers she had been working on for several sessions at the studio. A short while later, a more chastened Henri returned to critique her work as he often did, usually by pointing out some little detail she could add or another color she could bring out with a slight adjustment on her palette. At other times, he would simply watch her brush strokes without commenting or listen to her mindlessly humming a little waltz tune while she worked. This time, however, he noticed at the bottom of the easel a photograph she was using to get details of the costumes she knew so well just so for the painting, which was one of the most ambitious things she had yet attempted under his tutelage.

"Ahh, now I see it. That is Claire, the girl who always dances on your left. I see her face clearly now in the photograph you are using. Why, you have captured that little arm movement she always does just before she grasps her skirt and twirls those petticoats over her face. I can see it there just before it is about to happen. Wonderful, my dear, wonderful! You have captured her at the exact moment, and it is almost as if you have made a photograph on your canvas. In another instant her face will disappear, she will kick her leg, and all the young men standing in the back will shout *"Shu Shu"* just like they always do."

"My, my, Henri, you seem to know our dance routine about as well as we do. I have heard this being yelled above the music once or twice. What is *Shu Shu?*"

"Why Paulette, it is the name the regulars, the young men who stand in the back or can't afford a seat near the stage, have for your friend Claire. Most of the dancers have a favorite name among the men, if they have been in the line for a few months. I thought you all surely knew this, my dear."

"Well, we know about your good friend, *la Goulue*, of course, and a few others who have danced for a long time like *Grille d'Égout*, but I didn't know about Claire. Tell me, Henri, do *I* have such a name among all the young "gentlemen" who stand in the back and then wait for us after the show or send flowers to the dressing rooms all the time?"

"Perhaps, but not all have names, certainly not like my own sweet *la Goulue*, who has truly earned her nickname of "the Glutton"; but yes, dear Paulette, I have to say you have also earned one as well. You are known as *la Grande Orange* among the regulars who always stay for the final cancan. You are the tallest on your side of the line and that hair of yours, well, what else can I say, *chérie?*"

"So then, what else do you and your friends say about me and the others when we cannot hear for all the music and applause up front?" Paulette's face flushed a different shade of red than her hair just then, as she turned away after this reply while he attempted to change the subject.

"Oh, you know how young men are, my dear. It's the usual little wagers and guessing games about the number of petticoats or the turn of an exposed ankle. Of course, there are other things I shall not mention. After all, despite what you might believe, Paulette, there still remains in me some small shred of a "gentlemen's dignity", the appearance of which I still wish to maintain from time to time."

They both laughed again and Henri went back to making a suggestion or two for her painting. Then, he surprised her once more by bringing up a topic Paulette had begun to think upon herself, but had not yet made a decision about it.

"I can see this painting is almost finished. I must congratulate you, my dear. You have come a great distance in a short time. This is your best effort by far, and I have not needed to help you nearly as much as I have in the past. I think it is time for you to begin signing your paintings. Someday, a work by *Mademoiselle Paulette Gambeau* may be a prized item for any aspiring collector. Perhaps, in a few months, when you have built up a small portfolio of paintings, we will go to my dealer and together present to the world this exciting new 'discovery' of mine."

He laughed again as he touched her gently on the shoulder. However, this was no jesting matter for Paulette as she smiled and asked.

"Do you really think so, Henri? I have been thinking about this and have decided, at least at first, I wish to sign my paintings as *Pa. Gambeau* and not *Paulette.* I mean, I know it is difficult for a female artist to make it, and I have heard terrible jokes from some of your acquaintances when we are in the cafés about women who try to earn a name for themselves as artists, especially here in Paris. Don't you think it would be best to do it this way, at least until I sell a piece or two? I'm not sure I'm ready to see my work fail in a shop or gallery, just because it was done by a woman, even with your wonderful help."

"Perhaps you are right, my dear. But I think you undervalue your abilities. How would you feel if your paintings were bought only because someone thought it was a man who was signing them? We will wait until you are ready, and with my contacts, of course, I feel certain your work will be accepted either way. If not, then I will take my cane to any man who makes jokes about women artists. You must tell me who these scoundrels in the café are, and I will call them out and challenge them to a duel of paint brushes on the spot, ehh."

Henri laughed again at his little attempt at humor, but Paulette decided then and there it would be she who would determine when, or if, she chose how to reveal herself through her art to the public in the same way she had more easily done with her dancing. Her painting was far more personal and important to her now than it had been before, and she was not even sure she could continue with it without Henri's continued help and encouragement to advance her skills so far beyond her expectations in the ways he already had. However, by the end of that day she finished her painting and Henri watched with the pride of any successful teacher when she stroked the *Pa. Gambeau* in the bottom corner of the picture over the number 1899. They drank a toast of sherry to her first signed piece, and she left the studio that evening with a new spring in her step, along with the feeling she could almost have danced her way back to the boarding house.

Two more paintings of her friends dancing were completed in the following weeks, and the fall of the year was fast approaching. This would be Paulette's third winter in Paris and she knew in the coming New Year she would again have to face the difficult decision of whether to continue her dancing or strike out once more in a new direction, just as she had when she first came to Paris. Despite his constant encouragement and promises of help, Paulette was coming to the inevitable conclusion that Henri would not be around forever to guide her hand, or her career. His health continued to improve in short bursts, but then invariably a setback would occur—one from which his subsequent "recovery" never left him quite as well as he had been before. It pained her to see him declining so. However, the thought if she gave up her lucrative position at the theater she might soon have to support herself with only her art was even more frightening to an unsettled Paulette, more so even than the thought of being more alone than she already frequently felt.

Then one evening when she returned from the theater she found another letter from Marcel waiting for her at the boarding house. His letters usually arrived on a regular basis, and depending on her mood at the time, Paulette often did not open them at once. She knew they always contained the same sentiments, which increasingly threw her already troubled thoughts into more uncertainty. On this occasion, however, it was late, she was alone, and she decided to read the letter because it seemed to have been only a short time since the last one had arrived. The news from Marcel was not good. Her father's health had deteriorated considerably, and the doctor was saying his heart seemed to be failing rapidly beyond the point at which he could maintain much hope of even a brief recovery. Marcel explained how her father kept asking for her, and because of the doctor's prognosis he had decided he would come to Paris to bring her back, even if it was only for a temporary visit, as soon as he could arrange everything on the farm. Marcel would let her know by telegram when he would arrive in Paris in time for her to take the necessary steps to arrange her absence.

This was the message Paulette had been dreading for some time, the one she knew would cause her to face head on the dilemma she had felt building in her life for nearly a year. After a long night, she began the very next day to think seriously about what she must do to get ready for the trip back to the Aveyron Valley, and just what she could expect to happen once she was there. In addition to the disturbing news of her father's condition there would be Marcel to deal with, and Paulette sensed whatever decision she made this time would probably be the last one she would have to face in that regard. She needed someone to share this conflict with, but sharing her feelings with others had always been difficult for her. True, she had friends at the theater and there was

Julianne when she was in the City but there was no one to whom she felt close enough to confide her innermost feelings and whose counsel she could take to heart. At last, she decided to turn to the one person whom she felt would not judge her by any standard other than what he believed would be best for her.

Three days later she received Marcel's telegram that he would be arriving by train in the afternoon two days later. She had already begun her packing and even informed the Manager of the Theater she would need an extended absence and the reason for it. He reluctantly acquiesced, but asked only that she give him a couple of days' notice before her last performance prior to leaving and told her how she was to pick up her pay. It was not as if the people at the Moulin Rouge weren't used to losing performers in midseason from time to time. Besides, as Paulette knew well enough from her own experience, there was always some talented and eager young dancer waiting among the extras and back-ups to step into the main line and use her sudden break to launch her career. Still, the seriousness of Marcel's telegram, and what it would mean for the long avoided attempt at some brief, now possibly final, reconciliation with her father left Paulette dreading his arrival.

She went to Henri's studio early that same afternoon, something she never did on a day she knew she would be dancing later. She needed to retrieve her sketch book, finished drawings and paintings, and other supplies, as well as say some sort of good bye to the closest friend she had ever known. She knew this would be difficult, given the circumstances of Henri's own health and the bleak prospects for his future she was fully cognizant of in the last few months. When the valet answered the door, he responded that "Monsieur is indisposed", but when Paulette explained why she had come he told her to proceed on to the studio and he would inform Henri of her reason for being there. She climbed the stairs, went to the studio and quickly began assembling the things she wished to take with her when she left Paris. A few minutes later she heard some noise on the other side of the door connecting the studio with the bedroom beyond, followed by some loud coughing. A moment later she turned to see a dark-eyed Henri in a ridiculous looking dressing gown, which had been somehow altered to fit his unique stature, entering the room.

"My dear Paulette, Raymond tells me you are here to get your things and will soon be leaving us. Can this really be true? Surely, you cannot be thinking of giving up your work, when we have only begun to reveal your amazing talents. What shall I do without our afternoons together?"

"It is my *papa*, Henri. It seems the doctor has given up all hope for his recovery and my friend Marcel is arriving tomorrow to take me back to the Aveyron. Perhaps, I can return to Paris when things are settled, but for now, despite what I have told you about my relationship with my father, I really must go. I will take my work with me, Henri, and everything you have taught me will always be dear to me, no matter what comes next in my life."

"Ahh, I see. Then you must go, of course. But you know how I feel about doctors and their prognostications, ehh. I certainly wish I could meet this Marcel of yours, if you had more time. I should like to tell him he is a most fortunate man; because, my dear Paulette, I have seen into your heart, and I believe you will not be returning once you leave Paris with him."

Paulette could say nothing in response, although she felt herself blushing at Henri's somewhat strange and unexpected remark. She possessed so few even remotely close friends in her life. As such, she was never aware of how a true friend would be able to read her thoughts, when her words tried to hide them from the eyes of someone who might know her as well as she knew herself. She continued to pack her things and Henri helped her to choose some paints and other things he wished to give her. Finally, when it was clear she was nearly ready to leave, he surprised her once more.

"Paulette, my dear, you would do me a great honor if you would permit me to keep the three small paintings of your dancers here with me. I shall always cherish them as a reminder of the wonderful times we shared. Also, if you will allow me, I would like to give you something in return as a remembrance of me just in the event, you know, that your return to Paris should be significantly delayed and I am "out of town" so-to-speak when that day comes."

Paulette took his obvious meaning instantly, but before she could reply and offer him the three paintings she had already stacked with her portfolio, Henri turned and disappeared back into the bedroom. A moment or two later he returned carrying a small painting similar in size to the three he was requesting she leave behind. He walked over to where she stood with a questioning look on her face and handed it to her. Paulette took a look at what she held. Then her mouth dropped open and she stared back at his smiling face and exclaimed.

"Henri, when did you manage to do this? It is if I am looking in the mirror and watching myself about to do a quick turn on the dance floor. Really, it is wonderful, but how?"

"I have done it from memory, as any good artist can. You have certainly learned this lesson yourself already, my dear Paulette. Please accept it. I can do another, and it is a fair trade, I hope, for those three over there you will leave me as a remembrance. Is there anything else I can do for you before your unfortunate departure so soon, some money, perhaps? We could consider it a small loan against those paintings you are being more than generous to allow me to retain."

"No, dear friend. I cannot accept money for our friendship. This wonderful likeness of me is more than enough. I have saved a good deal of my earnings anyway. As you know, I am not exactly "the woman about town" as some of your other female friends from the theater are."

"Indeed, indeed." He laughed, bringing on another brief bout of coughing, which was the signal both of them were searching for to bring an end to the difficult farewell they were awkwardly engaged in. Paulette began to pick up her things. It would be a load to carry, and when Henri saw it, he called his valet and told him to go to the street and summon a cab for her. She thanked him, and their eyes met one final time, before he lowered his to prevent any more of his feelings from being obvious to her. She smiled and said.

"Dearest Henri, please promise to take better care of yourself. The world is a far better place with you in it. I shall miss you terribly. If I write to you, will you find the time to reply?"

He answered he most certainly would and he would be very interested to keep up with her career and that she simply must continue her art. He walked over to where she lowered her head so he could warmly kiss her on both cheeks. Then, he stepped back and was about to turn for his room when he offered one final bit of parting advice."

"You know, Paulette. Art is where you find it. A true artist need only look for it, and the subject will always find a way to reveal itself—man, woman, it does not matter. Just remember your sketch of the old horse, the one that first encouraged me to help you. You are good at your art, and never let anyone say you cannot succeed because it is not your destiny, or because you are a woman. Be happy above all, my dear. I will look forward to your first letter."

Then, they both heard the valet on the stairs coming to fetch her. Each turned away with a final smile for the other in nearly the same instant—to head off through different doorways, and to a different destiny.

Paulette spent most of the following day packing and saying her goodbyes to those she would perhaps not see again. Late in the afternoon the matron who oversaw the large boarding house appeared at her room and informed her that a gentleman caller by the name of Marcel Poincaré was downstairs asking for her. Paulette's hands trembled a bit as she took a deep breath, looked in her mirror to check her hair and the rest of her appearance, and then went down to greet the man she had not seen for nearly three years. His face beamed a wide smile as soon as he saw her on the stairs, and when she looked at him Paulette had the distinct impression Marcel had matured a great deal in those intervening years. His rugged good looks still caught her attention as they had the first time she had seen him, and a strange lump seemed to jump from her stomach to her throat in that moment of recognition. She immediately wondered what his view of the changes in her must be. When she got to him, she reached for his forearms without hesitation before he could react and kissed him quickly on each cheek. He did not draw away, and she decided she must let go of his arms before he grasped hers back and possibly returned her simple greeting with a more complicated one.

"Dear Paulette, I would hardly have recognized you. Somehow you seem taller, and your hair was never like this. You are more beautiful than even my fondest memories. I have long hoped our next reunion would be under far different circumstances than this one must be, but I fear we must get back home soon. I would like to stay in Paris tomorrow to rest from the journey and perhaps see a few places, if you are up to being my guide. I have not been here since I was a boy. I simply must see Monsieur Eiffel's marvelous tower. I caught a glimpse of the upper part on the way in through the train window. We can have lunch, and then we will speak of how soon we can leave."

"Of course, Marcel, I would be happy to spend the day with you. My packing is almost complete and I have said my farewells where I could. But I must tell you I still have to perform tonight, since I was already forced to give the theater such short notice of my leaving. I was hoping you would like to come and see me dance, and then we can have a late supper, if you can wait that long. I can get you a pass for the show and meet you backstage afterward. Do you have a room yet?"

"Yes, I found a small hotel between here and the train station. I must say the prices were rather shocking even there. But I would be delighted to come with you this evening. I would not think of missing your last performance here."

Marcel's use of the word *last* had carried a tone of finality Paulette had not much cared for; however, she said nothing. Instead, she replied she still had nearly two hours before she needed to go to the Moulin Rouge to prepare for the evening show. She invited him to go with her to a small café close by, where they could get some coffee and a light snack, which, as she explained, was her usual routine when she danced in the evening. He readily agreed and they were soon walking together the two blocks down the busy Boulevard de Clichy to their destination. Paulette refrained from taking his arm, and he did not offer it.

When they got to the café, they spoke mostly of her father's condition, the recent rapid deterioration of his health, and both the doctor's and the village priest's agreement with Marcel's urgency in bringing her home as soon as possible. The time passed rapidly, and Paulette soon began to become a little uneasy each time Marcel fixed her gaze with the intense stare she quickly recalled he often showed when he had talked with her in the past. After a quick stop at her rooms, she led him to the theater beneath the conspicuous windmill a few blocks away. She obtained a pass for him when she stopped by the office to pick up her final pay and say a heartfelt goodbye to the people who worked there. Then, she parted from him with another quick kiss on only one cheek this time as she told him where to wait for her when the show was over.

Much to her surprise, Paulette felt during the fast-paced show she was giving one of the best performances of her life that night.

Her energy seemed extraordinary and she made every spin and turn with a flair she had not recognized in her dancing for some time. She even heard a few of the shouts for "*la Grande Orange*" that came from the back and responded with even more effort on her next move. Finally, it was over; and an unexpected tear fell from her eye at the sudden realization this might truly be the last time she heard the loud cheers and applause to which she had grown so accustomed. She hastened to the dressing room to pack away her costume and some small remembrances she had accumulated in the last two days to take with her. Then she said goodbye to the two dressing room girls and left to meet a wide-eyed and strangely quiet Marcel a short time later.

They dined together that night in a little out of the way café the dancers frequented when they wished to avoid the crowds and men seeking their attentions or company. She introduced Marcel to a couple of her friends and they settled in for a quiet dinner before going back to their individual lodgings, until they would meet as they had agreed the following morning. Marcel said he would get up early to purchase her train ticket and they quickly settled the more mundane details of the trip back to the Aveyron. Finally, he set down his knife and fork, looked across the table where she sat trying not to watch him as if her thoughts were somewhere far away, and spoke more directly than he had done so far that afternoon and evening.

"Paulette, your dancing tonight was wonderful. I would never have recognized you up there if I did not know it was you. I could see how much you must love it—and the cheers and the applause all the dancers seemed to receive with such excitement. I see now that I have been mistaken all this time in believing I could lure you back to the farm to have you for myself with only the promise of my unending affection for you. And those men, of all ages but the young ones especially, the things they yelled at the stage and the awful suggestions and lewd remarks I heard. I could never imagine you in the kind of life you have here or the excitement it could provide. If this is the life you truly want, then I will not stand in your way as I now believe I have tried to do in the past. I can offer you nothing as exciting as what I saw tonight. When things are settled back in the Aveyron, and if you wish to come back to continue your dancing, then I can see it would be foolish for me to object any further."

Paulette had not been able to look him directly in the eye as he spoke to her for fear she could not control what her own glance might reveal. It was not exactly the speech she had been anticipating since his arrival, and she could sense the hurt in his voice and the difficulty he was having uttering the words. There were a hundred ways she wanted to respond, but she feared they would come out all wrong—or would reveal more of her conflicting emotions than she could control. Finally, she looked up, fixed his eye with hers, and smiled slightly as she began.

"My dear, sweet, Marcel. If I wanted any of those rich or exciting young men you saw tonight, I could have had one two years ago. There is a new gang of them it seems every night, and most of us either ignore them completely or use them for our amusement. It is true, I have known girls here who have chosen to throw themselves into that life of daily excitement, or even those who have looked for and found a man who could take care of their material needs far beyond what a poor girl from the countryside could ever hope for. But I am not one of those girls, Marcel. I came here to dance, and that is what I have done. You may have been right when you said tonight was my last performance. I cannot say or promise you otherwise at this moment. But if it was, then I wanted to do the best I could this evening and to have no regrets later, whatever comes. Let's finish our dinner, and then tomorrow I will show you around Paris. We will walk along the Seine, see the Tower, have a final dinner here together, and then we shall return to our home and let whatever happens next happen. But I can assure you I have made no decision about my life, or about you dear Marcel, that is beyond your hope."

The following day unfolded much as Paulette had foreseen. They walked along both banks, ascended the Eiffel Tower, and enjoyed a last dinner in Paris together. This time, Paulette did not refrain from taking his arm any time he offered it as they strolled along the Seine. Still, she thought of Henri and their time together whenever she saw the sketch artists and other aspiring painters set up under the trees along the river. She felt pain in her heart at probably having seen Henri for the last time whenever she thought of him and renewed her promise to herself to write him as soon as she came to a decision about her future. No matter what that should turn out to be, she knew her memories of his unique personality and talent would remain a part of her always.

Late the next morning Marcel arrived in a four wheel carriage to pick her up to go to the train station for their afternoon departure. He was surprised at the sight and weight of the trunk when he saw it, in addition to her large and small valise. But she laughed at his mock complaint about having to wrestle with it all the way back to the Aveyron Valley and simply replied it contained nearly three years of her life and what did he expect. Their train would be an overnight trip to Toulouse, with several major stops in between. However, Marcel informed her, they would be getting off at Montauban, the last stop before Toulouse. He had left the farm wagon and horses there to pick up on the way back. They would go part of the way to the farm with what time they had the next day, stay overnight in a small hotel he had arranged earlier when he delivered some cases of wine there on the way to the train north, and then arrive home sometime early the following day if all went well. Paulette purchased some food for them to eat on the train before they boarded for the long ride. They would have to sleep in their seats, but she knew that would probably not bother her; for she would find little sleep that night anyway in anticipation of all that would happen in the next few days—things that would undoubtedly change her life forever.

⊷⊹ ⊹⊷

Indeed, it proved to be a long train ride that evening and throughout the night. At one point Paulette must have fallen asleep for an hour or so, because when she awakened her head was resting against Marcel's shoulder. He said nothing when she stirred and resumed her normal position beside him in the uncomfortable seats. By daylight, the sights were becoming more familiar and old feelings began to stir in her when she watched the beautiful landscape of low hills, vineyards, and forests go speeding by. By noon they reached their departure station and Marcel saw to the unloading of their baggage. They decided to leave it at the station and find something to eat close by before he went to the livery where he had left the wagon and two horses a few days before. Afterward, Paulette returned to the station to wait for him to arrive with the wagon and team to begin the journey home. In less than an hour Marcel arrived, the trunk and other bags were loaded, and they set off for the short ride of a couple of hours to the small village, where he had previously arranged rooms for them for the night.

As soon as she was seated in the wagon beside Marcel with her parasol in her hand, Paulette asked the first of many difficult questions about things that might have changed in her absence, which she could not have anticipated before then. She immediately noticed an unfamiliar horse hitched to the wagon, the same one she had ridden in since she was a girl.

"Who is this new gray horse, Marcel? Please do not tell me my old friend *Bas Bas* has died. You said nothing of it in your letters. Was it just to spare me? At least *Babette* is still with us," she said as she whistled a familiar greeting to the smaller mare harnessed in front of them.

"No, no, old *Bas Bas* is still alive. I would have told you otherwise, since I know how special he was to you. But his legs got too weak to pull the carts up and down the vineyard slopes with the heavy loads. Your father sold him to old man Laplondes, who still owns the *boulangerie* in the village. Now *Bas Bas* pulls only a small wagon to deliver groceries in the town and up and down the nice level river road. I saw him only a week or so ago, and he recognized me when I passed him by, I'm sure. This new horse is only four years old, and he and *Babette* seem to get along and work well in harness together."

"Oh, I'm so glad old *Bas Bas* is still with us. *Mama* loved him so and raised him from a foal on the farm not so many years after I was born. Does this new horse have a name?"

"Why no, at least we did not hear of one when the man we bought him from sent him to us late last summer. I have not thought to call him anything yet but "the new horse", what with everything else that has been happening since we got him."

"That is so like you, Marcel," she laughed. "Then I shall name him *Bonaparte*, I think. When I have been home for a couple of days, Marcel, I shall go to the village and purchase *Bas Bas* back from Monsieur Laplondes. I cannot bear the thought of the poor old thing dropping dead in his harness all alone someday. I shall bring him back to the farm where he will never pull a cart again. Perhaps, he will allow me to ride him once more, like I did before I left. But he will be able to live out his days where he was born and then be put to rest near the big trees down by the road, where *Mama* and I used to ride him together sometimes and rest there to watch the river go by while we sang songs. Besides, I have my own money now, and that's what I want to do."

"I see you are as headstrong as ever, Paulette. Are you sure you don't want to change *Babette's* name to *Joséphine* while you are at it? But if you insist on this, will you at least let me go with you to bargain with old Laplondes? If he sees how much you want the horse back, he will surely drive up the price even higher than what he paid us for him not that long ago."

Paulette smiled and agreed. Marcel snapped the reins and clucked at the horses to start, and they were off on the last leg of their journey. Then, she took Marcel's arm in hers and wrapped her other arm around his briefly as well to pull herself as close as she had yet been to him. For the next two hours they rode along mostly in silence, speaking mainly of the things they were seeing and the changes Paulette could expect to notice when she got closer to home. There was still some daylight left when they arrived in the small town where they would spend the night. Marcel dropped her and their small valises off at the little hotel, where they would have separate rooms, while he stabled the horses close by. They enjoyed a simple dinner at the hotel, with a bottle of wine from their own vineyards, which Marcel seemed very proud to show off to her when it was delivered to their table. Paulette commented on the excellent taste, and Marcel replied their vineyard had been enjoying growing success locally in the last two years.

When they left to go to their adjacent rooms, he finally found the courage Paulette had been expecting, perhaps even hoping for, to kiss her softly on the cheek, before he released her for the night. *How refreshingly gallant,* Paulette thought at the sudden idea that most of the men she had encountered in the past years would have expected her to share a room with them, at the very least, after even only one or two evenings together. Marcel had not really changed all that much, she reminded herself, and quickly came to the conclusion this was not such a bad thing at all. Earlier, the ride on the familiar old wagon seat had jostled her close against him as they both talked of little things or spoke meaningless phrases to the two horses to encourage them along. Rather surprisingly, this gave Paulette the feeling that at least some of her Paris memories were already being stored in a place in her mind where she would not need to retrieve them quite as soon, or as often, as she would have believed only two days before.

They both slept a little later than planned the next morning to recover from the stresses and strains of the tiring trip down from Paris and the long two days there before they left. It was only another three hours or so by the wagon road to the farm, and Marcel decided to cross the Aveyron by the bridge in the town of Negrepelisse first thing before the gorge narrowed farther upriver. It was nearly midday when they finally passed through Montricoux and reached the turn-off that would take them a few minutes later to the family farm—a place Paulette had wondered on more than one occasion in the past three years if she would ever see again. Her nervousness increased dramatically over what was waiting to confront her as soon as she saw the neat rows of the familiar vineyards on the slope behind the old barn, and then a moment later the stone house of her birth. The wagon had barely been pulled to a stop in the front when the front door opened and a face Paulette did not recognize for an instant stepped outside.

"Oh, mademoiselle Paulette, praise God you have come at last. He asks if you have arrived yet the first thing every time he wakes up. I am so glad to see you both. I hope the trip was not too difficult, Marcel. I thought you might arrive yesterday."

"No, Madame Doucette, the trip was not too difficult. It just took an extra day to get away from Paris. We are both so grateful you could stay here while I was away. How is he today?"

"No better, I fear. The doctor was here two days ago to listen to his heart and was with him for a while. When he left, he said nothing to me except to try harder to get him to eat something. But I could see in his face and eyes that he is not hopeful. Should I get my things so you can take me home before you unhitch your team? I will speak with Mademoiselle while you unload your bags, and then we should go, if you do not mind. I told my daughter I would be home yesterday, and I'm sure she is getting worried about me by now."

Paulette went inside with the old woman, who lived on a farm a short distance away farther up the river road. It would not take Marcel more than an hour to deliver her and return, but Paulette was suddenly hesitant to be alone in the house with her father. Madame Doucette began giving her instructions, starting with some thin soup she kept warming on the stove and how she should to try to get her father to eat a few mouthfuls of it if possible. She said her father would ask for wine, no doubt, and the doctor permitted him a half glass in the evening, if he wanted it. But he was not eating much, she told Paulette, and it was difficult to even get him out of bed to use the water closet.

Finally, Paulette could tell the woman was getting anxious to leave, and when Marcel came in with the valises, Madam Doucette grabbed her own small bag and cloak and headed for the door. Paulette thanked her once more for her help, and a moment later she was alone in the familiar kitchen of her youth. She heard the wagon turn and head away as she decided to sit down at the table just to catch her breath and take stock of things. However, a few minutes later she heard some stirring followed by coughing on the other side of the nearest bedroom door, which instantly brought back another recent memory of a similar scene. She swallowed hard and got up to face the reunion she both secretly longed for but had equally come to dread. She opened the door and saw the instant look of recognition on her father's gaunt, ashen face.

"Dear Paulette, thank God you have come at last. Come, come here and sit beside me. Pull the chair over where I can see you in the light and touch your hand. Ahh, my dear, how you have changed! You look just like your mother did at your age when I first met her, except for the red hair, of course. That much of you belongs to me, at least."

He tried to laugh, but only another short cough came out. Without thinking about it, Paulette brought the chair close and reached for his hand where it lay outside the covers. Each of them could feel the slight trembling in the others', but no words passed between them for a short time. Then he fixed her eye and spoke to ask where Marcel was. She told him and said he would be back in about an hour.

"Ahh, that is good. We have much to talk about in a short time. I know it has been difficult for you, Paulette, and there have been times I wanted to write you, but I could never find the words. I know I behaved badly, perhaps, when you left; but I was in despair about your leaving, and you were as obstinate as ever in your desire to go. But Marcel spoke for me, as I am sure you understood from his letters, and he always read me yours, except for some parts he wished to keep to himself, I think. What are your plans now? Will you return to Paris, or will you think more seriously about staying here?"

"I am not certain, *Papa*. My mind is very confused and the last days have only added to that uncertainty. For now, I am here to see you and to stay until you get better, for as long as it takes. Then I will decide what I should do next."

"Pahh, to that my dear. I am no fool; neither is the doctor. Father Bernard has already come by with his purple vestment scarf and beads and said his final prayers for me. This is one decision, Paulette, which is not yours alone to make, as you told me when you left before. There are things you must know first, and then you can decide. I have made the arrangements and told Marcel if you leave and go back to Paris after I am gone, then the papers have been drawn that will pass the farm to him and not to you. He has been like a son to me these last years and has earned the right to stay here—one way or the other. The vineyards and our wines are succeeding mainly because of him and this has made me very proud as you must know. It was my fondest wish you would marry

Marcel and our family's long past would continue on here, where our ancestors have watered this land with their sweat, and yes, even their blood at times, over many generations. But I will not play the fool in such thinking any more with you, Paulette. If it is your choice to go, then that is what will happen. And that, my dear, *will be* your decision alone to make.

"But you should know Marcel is as good a man as any you will ever find, even in Paris I suspect. And besides, Paulette, he loves you as much now as he did when you left, the poor fool. I have seen him sit at the kitchen table just staring at the picture on the wall of you with your mother we had taken when you graduated from the *collège* not long before she left us. He would make you a fine husband and be a good father to your children. The farm is yours, of course, if you marry Marcel. However, it will still be his in any event if you do not. I am sorry to put things to you in such a way, but it is very important to me to see my work, and my father's work here before me, pass into the hands of someone who now has his own blood invested here and loves this bit of land as much as I have."

"I understand completely what you are saying, *Papa*. It is not as if I don't have a strong affection for Marcel. I know everything you are saying about him is true. But you were both wrong to think I left because I thought I could find someone better. That was never my intention. I had to go to find my own way, and to fulfill the confidence *Mama* always placed in me. I found more about myself, and my dreams, in Paris than I could ever have imagined for them without her encouragement. But in the last days, I have also come to see that what I discovered there was not really so much more than what I already had here, if I truly wished it."

"So then tell me, Paulette, what was it you found there? I could never understand this blind need of yours to pursue something beyond what you had right in front of you."

"I found my true talent, *Papa*. I am not the dancer *Mama* always wanted me to become. What I found was Art itself. I have a need to see what is inside everything I look upon and then to be able to express what it makes me feel on a piece of paper, or canvas, or whatever. I found out what made me truly happy was simply to create an image others could look at and know the same feeling it brought to me. It was like dancing, only it lasted forever. Most of all, I found a teacher who showed me how to look inside myself to find and know these things."

"Ahh, so you would be an artist now as well, ehh? Tell me then, Paulette. Can an artist not work as well in one place as in another? You know, once when you were young your mother and I were returning from a delivery I made up the Valley some distance. It was late in the day and the sun was bouncing off the clouds above a hillside and she said to me: *Oh, Paul isn't it beautiful, all the colors and everything, just like one of those paintings in the magazines.* I remember laughing at her and replying that yes, the vineyards on that hillside were in such neat rows and the grapes would soon ripen in the warm sun. I knew what she really meant then, but I liked to tease her sometimes when she spoke of such faraway things.

"I suppose what I am trying to say to you, Paulette, is what your mother might have said to you if she had lived in answer to what you just told me. Isn't Art where you look for it, and then what you make of it when you find it? She told me more than once she had learned to find her own happiness in singing a simple song about some place or some other thing she knew she would never see. Does a true artist really need to go to Paris or some far off place to make a painting, when the beauty surrounding us here in this valley is equal to anything you could find somewhere else? Can you not be just as happy right here, Paulette—if you set that strong mind and will of yours to it?"

It was the one question Paulette had been struggling with since she left Paris with Marcel, and even before then. She could almost hear the voice of Henri speaking directly to her once more in her father's surprisingly personal and meaningful words. She looked at him just as a tear formed in her eye and trickled down her cheek. She picked up his hand where he had laid it on the bed beside him and nestled it warmly in both of hers for an instant, and then a few more sobs erupted. He said nothing, but reached over with his other hand to stroke hers gently as well.

Finally, she regained control once more and the sudden realization her long struggle had never been against something, or even someone, but was only *for* something—the control of her own destiny. In that moment, she truly held it in her hands, perhaps for the first time with the self-assurance and awareness that whatever she did next should be because it was truly what she wanted, and not what she felt she needed to reveal about herself to others. She smiled meekly at last and saw an answering smile begin to form on her father's face as well.

"Yes, *Papa,* Art truly is wherever one looks for it. It started for me here, and there is no reason I cannot continue to search for it here as well. Marcel and I have grown much closer in the last few days in a way we never could have, if I had stayed here and married before I found what I was searching for in myself. If he asks me to marry him, I will say 'Yes', and be happy for it always I truly believe. That is *my* decision, *Papa,* and I think I was ready to make it even before I stepped through that door."

"My dear, sweet Paulette. Your mother would be so happy at this moment, and I wish more than anything she could be with us to hear your words. But I will tell her soon what a wonderful daughter we made together and how proud of her we both should be. You must listen for Marcel to return, and then bring him to me. I want to put your hands in his with my own and give you away with a father's blessing, as is my duty and my pleasure, while I still have the strength in them to do it.

"Now then, my dear, there is a bottle of wine over there on the dresser Madame Doucette has cleverly managed to keep in my sight, but beyond my reach. Would you get it and extra glasses from the kitchen so I can toast your future happiness? Then, when Marcel gets here we can have another and see if he is the man we both think he is and get him to propose. But you must not tell the doctor I had two glasses this evening, ehh. But who cares now; for I will have my daughter back, a son-in-law a man can be proud of, and a glass of my best vintage ever. After all, what is an extra day or two in this hard life to willingly exchange for such happiness at the end of it?"

AD 1948

"Oh, my dear Béatrice, we are all so glad you could come and stay, even if it is just for the two days. It's all so exciting with you performing in the concert in Albi on Sunday. Your *Papa* has borrowed a car to take us all, and your *Mama* has told everyone she knows about it. I'm afraid you may have your own little cheering section when the performance is over. She is so proud, as are we all. I do wish you could stay over longer; but your letter said the orchestra will all be leaving by bus afterward to go over to Montauban to take the train up to Limoges for your next performance. She hasn't told me where you will be going after that."

"Well, *grand-mère,* after the *cantata* at the cathedral on Sunday afternoon, we will have the performance in Limoges on Tuesday and then it's over to Bordeaux for three performances there before the orchestra returns to Toulouse in about ten days. Then we are done for the season and everyone can get back to their normal routines, I suppose. I haven't decided yet what I will be doing. There's the possibility of the local orchestra and a part-time teaching position, but a lot really depends on what Arnaud decides to do after we get back."

"Ahh, I see. So, tell me about your young man, Béatrice dear, just what are his intentions? I mean, you two have been keeping steady company for nearly two years. Your mother and I are getting very nervous about your prospects there."

"Oh *grand-mère,* such talk you two keep worrying me with. But Arnaud does seem rather more nervous and unsettled now that the tour is coming to an end than he has been. I suspect he has something "big" on his mind. You know, he is so uncertain of his own prospects right now. But things have not gone as well as we all have hoped since the War ended. I think he would love to propose, almost as much as I would love to accept, but he doesn't feel we can get a fair start until he has something more permanent to offer, a university position possibly, or something with a larger orchestra. I've told him it doesn't matter to me that much, but you know how men are about such things."

"Indeed, their male responsibility is a terrible burden for them at such an important time. First they say to you they just can't find the proper words to tell you how they feel about you, and then they can't stop blubbering about how *they will love you forever, if you will only give them the chance.* But it is plain to see you two would be so good together, I mean with your music and all, and he really is quite nice looking, Béatrice. You've made a fine choice and now you must convince him he has done the same and he needs to act in his best interest before some other young man steals you away."

"You're terrible, *grand-mère!* Is this some of the wisdom about men you learned those years you were in Paris with all those dashing bachelors and famous artists? *Papa* used to tell me some of the things about you he learned growing up. I don't think *Mama* believes the half of them, though. But I'm sure Arnaud will make his move as soon as he feels he is able. Still, a little shove to get him over the edge would not be such a bad thing either, perhaps, if I can just figure out how to do it."

"I'm glad you've mentioned that, my dear. There's something your parents and I have been discussing since you wrote about your visit and the concert in Albi. I've done a lot of thinking about what I'm going to tell you, and I believe both of them are in agreement with what I've already proposed to them. I don't believe your

Papa has told you any of this yet. The three of us decided not to mention it until I've had a chance to think more about it and speak to you first. In the last month he has received a serious offer to become the vineyard manager on a sizable estate winery just east of Bordeaux. He's tried to hide his excitement, but your *Mama* has told me this offer is like a dream come true for him. I have told him both his father and grandfather would be so proud of him; for everything he knows about his vines came through them and their hard work here on our own grapes. I only wish his *papa* was still here to share in Jean-Paul's wonderful achievement.

"But I know your father very well, Béatrice, and he is reluctant to leave me alone here with the farm. He also knows I would never leave it now to go with them, not with my dear Marcel and our sweet Bertrand resting side by side in the churchyard here. Of course, as you know, your sister has no real interest in it. Since she married and moved to Lyons we scarcely hear from her except on holidays and such. She hasn't visited for two years, and I haven't even seen my own great-grandson. Your poor mother is disgusted with her behavior, and now the possibility of this new opportunity which would take them even farther away has upset her more. But there is nothing we can do. Annette made the choice of that husband of hers during the War, and that's all there is to it.

"Anyway, Béatrice, I made a couple of calls just before you arrived to check on one or two possibilities. One of these was to the *Directeur* at the *Collège* up in Cassaude. That's only a twenty minute or so drive from here now with the newly paved road. He's a former student of mine and his wife is an old friend as well. He told me he is certain there will be an opening for a music teacher next term and he is also interested in starting a small orchestra at the school, with some additions from the community if needed. However, neither of his two possible applicants has any experience with running, much less developing, an orchestra. I just happened to mention I knew someone who might be both qualified and interested. He seemed excited and has agreed to hold off on hiring anyone, until he hears from me. But he also said he cannot wait much longer, because he has to submit his budget for the coming year soon.

"Now then, my dear, just this morning your father mentioned to me how taken he was with Arnaud's interest in the vineyards when he showed him around last evening after you arrived. He told me Arnaud had many good questions and seemed to know a lot about the grape varieties and even some of the more important vintages now being produced once again here in the south. I could tell he was starting to lean toward your *Mama's* and my point of view about our discussion earlier. I think he would agree to take the new position at this winery near Bordeaux, if he had someone he could trust to look after his vines here and share the farm with me. He would, of course, return a couple of times a year to see how things were going or to make recommendations. But if it could be you and Arnaud, Béatrice, I have no doubt he would be willing to clear the way for you to become sole heir someday, if that would be your wish. Of course, this could only happen if you and Arnaud stopped dancing around this ridiculous male pride of his and got married, like maybe when this tour is over."

"Oh, *grand-mère*, this is unbelievable. I mean it's so much more than I had ever even thought about. Arnaud would be a great teacher and he could continue to write his music, which is what he really wants to do. He also mentioned to me before he went into town with *Papa* and *Mama* this afternoon to drive the car back when they pick up the sedan father is borrowing for tomorrow how much he enjoyed his tour of the vineyards last evening. Arnaud fancies himself some sort of wine *connoisseur*, I think, you know the way most men who want to impress us always do. But he really does have an interest in it and has always told me when we get our own house he hopes we can afford enough ground for him to put in even one row of good grapes. I can't wait to talk to him as soon as they get back. I'm just thrilled he and *Papa* have hit it off so well. He never liked any of the boys I used to see when I was in school, you know."

"I was certain you would be happy about this, Béatrice dear. I told your *Mama* before they left earlier she should work on Jean-Paul when they are alone on the drive back here and convince him I would be perfectly happy to share the farm with you two for as long as both of them wanted to live over by Bordeaux. His position there would come with a nice house by the vineyards, and he would not even need his car, he said. I really don't want him to even think about using me or this place as a reason for not taking it. They both deserve the chance for some happiness, especially the way your sister treated them at the end of the War and has since, after she married that awful *Pétainist*. Now then, do you think you will be able to convince Arnaud his moment of opportunity has arrived? You know I cannot put my friend the *Directeur* off for very long."

"Oh yes, I will begin on poor Arnaud as soon as he gets back, and then we can all pounce on him together during dinner this evening. By the time we get to Albi tomorrow, he will be lucky if he can draw his bow across his violin without breaking the strings he will be so nervous. I'm glad I'll be sitting far behind him, just in case he misses his cues. I'm doing both French horn and oboe double duty for the concert tomorrow, which reminds me. I could even do lessons part time if he teaches at the *Collège* and can even help out in this little orchestra. Oh, it's going to be so wonderful, I just know it. Thank you, *grand-mère*! Thank you ever so much."

"Well, that's what family is for, Béatrice, and you do know you will still have to look after an aging and headstrong old grandmother, if you stay here, my dear. But I'm sure we will all get along just fine. Your parents and our young man will be returning soon, although your *Mama* wanted to stop at Monsieur Laplondes' to pick up some flowers for tomorrow when all the shops will be closed. Before they do, there is something in my room I want to show you. It's for your eyes only, Béatrice dear. Even your *Mama* has never seen these things, and I'm sure your father has long forgotten them from when he was a boy."

Paulette led her suddenly curious granddaughter to the smaller of the two bedrooms behind the kitchen. There she removed an old quilt which covered some sort of trunk at the foot of her bed. Béatrice looked at what appeared to be a well-used railway trunk of some sort, which was spotted with various faded travel stickers of different cities in Europe. She was surprised when her grandmother removed a small key from the pocket of the smock she was wearing, inserted it in the lock, and slowly forced open the lid of the trunk. *Why would she keep such a thing locked in her own house,* Béatrice wondered as she was beckoned over to where her grandmother had slowly lowered herself to her knees before the exposed interior of the old trunk? Béatrice quickly joined her. She looked at the strange smile on her grandmother's face as she ran her hand over one of the stickers of Paris and then spoke.

"Was this your trunk when you were a dancer in Paris, *grand-mère?*"

"Oh, my no, dear. I never got to travel to any of these places except for Paris, of course. This trunk belonged to a friend of mine from my early days there. Her name was Julianne and she gave it to me when I moved out of the rooms we shared when we were both struggling young dancers trying to make a place for ourselves in the great City back at that exciting time. Julianne was a better dancer than I ever was, and I moved out when her dance company was going on an extended tour and I was just getting started at the Moulin Rouge. She gave me this trunk to keep back then, because she needed to buy a bigger one for her tour and I had nothing. I've often wondered what happened to her. We stayed close while we were both in Paris, and then wrote back and forth afterward.

Then, the Great War came and I never heard from her after that. But then that war changed us all in so many ways. Who knows what became of her, but I still think of little Julianne when I look at this trunk. Maybe that's why I keep it covered because it saddens me so to think of what might have happened to her.

"But I want to show you the things inside and tell you what you must do with them when I am gone, because I am going to make all of this my legacy to you, Béatrice. Someday this trunk will be your responsibility and you must decide what is to become of it. I ask only that you think carefully about what you will learn here in the next minutes when the day comes you must make this decision and of what effect it might have on our family, which I fear you are now the last link to in a very long chain."

"You mean like the music box you gave me when I graduated from the conservatory, *grand- mère?* I still take it with me and listen to it every night before a performance. I have it upstairs and we could play it together once more this evening, if you would like."

"Perhaps, dear, that would be nice. But this is far more impor-tant than the music box, although you can't know how happy it makes me to hear you still treasure it so. Now, let's look at what's in here so you will know just exactly who your *grand-mère* truly was. Then you can be the one to decide what stories get passed to your children when I am gone."

Paulette started at the top of the trunk and revealed each layer of her life that was contained in the items she removed, until she came to the bottom and the painting by Toulouse-Lautrec and his letters. She talked of it and the content of the letters, but said she had not looked at them for many years and did not remove any of them from the ribbon still binding them together. Béatrice sat in rapt silence at each accompanying story she heard, as Paulette disclosed the amazing details of her early professional life and adventures in Paris to her granddaughter. More than an hour had rapidly passed when they heard the wheels of two cars on the gravel road coming up from the river to the house, and Béatrice quickly helped her grandmother repack the trunk. Paulette locked it and they covered it once more with the quilt just as the front door opened and her parents came in, closely followed by Arnaud. Béatrice left the bedroom first, and her mother quickly greeted her with a big smile. Then, she walked over and unexpectedly hugged her daughter and whispered something in her ear, which made Béatrice look at her and respond with a knowing smile in return.

Their dinner that evening had been late, which had given Béatrice time to be alone with Arnaud before they all sat down together to enjoy their last evening meal together, at least until the current orchestral tour Béatrice and Arnaud were on ended. However, by the end of that dinner there was little doubt Arnaud had been won over, first by Béatrice's earlier excited explanation of what her grandmother and mother had told her, and then by her father's formal offer at dinner. That night, as she lay awake in the tiny room upstairs while Arnaud slept alone on the old sofa in the front room of the small house, Béatrice thought about how much sooner than she ever could have hoped before that day they would be sleeping side by side in the bed her parents now occupied directly below her.

One of the things Béatrice had been told that afternoon while she sat on the floor by the old trunk, which was in response to her question about why her grandmother had kept these things to herself for so long, was the story of what had happened to her grandfather and her father's younger brother. Her father rarely spoke of these events and Béatrice could only recall a time or two when she was growing up and asked about them that he had ever wanted to speak of those events. Even her mother always seemed reluctant to talk of what must have happened in those days before they were married. It was almost as if she did not want to risk having her daughter know too much, because she might somehow inadvertently bring further hurt to her father or grandmother with an unwanted question, as children often do.

When Béatrice asked about the art instruction books in the trunk and wondered when *grand-mère Paulette* had been a teacher, she responded matter-of-factly it had been mostly before the First War. Béatrice casually asked why she had stopped teaching, since she could see from the drawings how accomplished she was and how much it must have meant to her. Her grandmother simply told her after the war she had lost all interest in art for many years. She became momentarily wistful at the recollection and even tearful, which caused Béatrice to regret having asked the question when she received the reply. Paulette explained when the war came she was so happy both her boys were too young and her husband was just barely too old to be taken as a soldier. When the awful deaths kept emptying the valleys around them of so many young men whom she had known or taught in school it was almost more than she could bear to think of back during those terrible years.

But when the Great War ended they had all felt relieved that unlike so many of their friends and neighbors their family came through it mostly unscathed. Jean-Paul was just turning seventeen and his younger brother Bertrand was eleven in 1918. However, as they would learn later, some soldiers who had been in German prisoner camps came back to the Valley and brought the horrible Spanish Influenza with them. First Europe and then much of the world began to suffer like some new Medieval Plague had been unleashed upon it, and millions died around the world before the deadly flu burned itself out.

Béatrice's grandfather had been stricken early on and Paulette and he quickly made arrangements to get both their sons to a relative of hers who lived on an isolated farm in the mountains a day's ride to the East. The night before Jean-Paul was to take his brother Bertrand there to escape the spreading sickness, which had already stricken their home, the boy showed the first symptoms himself.

Jean-Paul was sent on his own, and Paulette stayed to nurse not only her husband but her younger son. Somehow, she escaped the Influenza herself, but Marcel and Bertrand died within two days of each other. They were buried in the local churchyard with so many others who had fallen victim either to that terrible war, or to its unexpected and equally disastrous aftermath.

Paulette told Béatrice she could not even function for the first year or so afterward. Jean-Paul soon returned to look after the farm, but she had given up her teaching, and even the simple joys of her sketch pad and the music box. It had not been until Jean-Paul married Béatrice's mother and first Annette and then she was born before she could begin to resume her life once more. Even then, she never regained the desire to get as close to her students as she had before the War, only to see so many taken before their prime and before whatever talent she helped to awaken in them could come to fruition. *No,* she told Béatrice that afternoon, it always hurt too much to think about those days, and even the happier memories of Paris she was revealing to her granddaughter brought back so much she cherished but still wished to keep buried deep within herself. Béatrice could only respond that she understood and would do as she was being asked to preserve the memories within the trunk with the respect her grandmother was requesting from her in that special moment they were sharing.

Béatrice kept thinking about the many things her grandmother had revealed about her life to her that day and the heavy burden of responsibility for keeping those secrets, parts of which, including the letters, Paulette had never revealed to anyone before. When the day came that Béatrice would be in sole possession of them, she must make the decision about how and to whom the story of the trunk would be passed on in their family. Some of the things Paulette told her she had already known the main elements of from what her father had spoken of from time to time when Béatrice was younger. Other parts, particularly those dealing with her life in Paris beyond her well-known dancing at the famous Moulin Rouge for a short period were totally new to Béatrice. The stories and the visible proof of her brief life as a budding artist and her close association with the famous Toulouse-Lautrec were both new and in many ways shocking to Béatrice, who was somewhat confused by her grandmother's strong desire to maintain her distance from those memories—as well as her family's—at least until after she was gone. It would take Béatrice long after that still somewhat distant event to come to terms with what she herself would do about these things, until her own life had passed beyond the point where she even felt the need to reopen the old trunk and the memories of her beloved *grand-mère Paulette* that it contained.

The following morning they all rose early to prepare for the drive over to Albi and the concert scheduled there for mid-afternoon. An excited Béatrice and Arnaud packed their bags to leave with the rest of the orchestra afterward. Paulette convinced her son to leave early so she could show Béatrice and Arnaud around the Toulouse-Lautrec Museum in the old Bishop's Palace, which stood connected to the big Cathedral of Sainte Cécile where the concert was to be held. It had been several years since Paulette last visited the Museum, which Henri's mother had established to house as much of his artwork as she could assemble, not many years after the famous artist's death in late 1901. Arnaud's nervousness was plain to see, just as Béatrice had predicted, and she whispered to her mother as they were getting ready to leave she had every reason to expect she might receive his marriage proposal even before they left for Limoges.

The drive over took about an hour and a half, as Jean-Paul and Arnaud sat in the front of the big sedan, and the prospective father-in-law eagerly pointed out the virtues and the shortcomings of the various small vineyards they passed along the way. Paulette sat between Béatrice and her mother in the back and listened, until she finally told her son such talk was boring them all to tears and she began to speak of what she knew of the many picturesque villages they seemed to pass through every ten minutes or so. They arrived in time for an early lunch with more than an hour left to inspect the museum. Béatrice's parents decided to seek out an old friend of her mother who lived in town and whom she had promised to visit earlier, no doubt, as Paulette whispered to Béatrice, to brag on her daughter to someone who might somehow have miraculously escaped the knowledge of her participation in the concert by this time.

Paulette took Béatrice and Arnaud to the fortress-like Palace, the lower level of which contained the Toulouse-Lautrec works and others of some of his closer contemporaries and friends from those busy and important days back at the turn of the century. Henri had been a most prolific artist in his brief career, and even Paulette was amazed at how many of his works she had never seen before were now housed in the museum dedicated to him. Béatrice and Arnaud walked arm-in-arm as Paulette led them from painting to painting, often stopping to relate some little personal anecdote she suddenly seemed more willing to reveal and share.

Finally, the young couple told her they would move ahead because they must soon leave and join the other members of the orchestra to get ready for the concert. However, they had just gone around a corner and were out of sight of anyone else when Arnaud stopped, pulled Béatrice close, and asked the question she had been expecting, even if she was not anticipating it in such a strange setting. She replied immediately and they managed one quick kiss before they heard the sound of approaching feet coming through the narrow passage into the gallery they had just entered.

A short time later, they were walking back to say they were leaving when Béatrice saw her grandmother standing in front of a rather plain charcoal sketch of an old horse, head down in drudgery and pulling a broken-down looking wagon. Her grandmother's lips seemed to be moving as if she were talking to someone and Béatrice could see her reach up and apparently wipe a tear away from her eye. Arnaud was about to go over to announce they had to go and would see her after the concert before they left town when Béatrice gently grabbed his arm to restrain him and spoke softly to him.

"Come along, my love. Let's leave *grand-mère* alone with her memories. We can thank her once more and tell her the wonderful news after the concert. She will be sure to make it on time. I know she wouldn't miss it for anything. We have to go, but right now this is where she needs to be."

THE ARTIST

AD 2016

Almost three days had passed in a blur of excitement since Jason and Marie discovered the old trunk and its amazing contents shortly after they arrived at her grandmother's home in the Aveyron Valley. Marie's comment at the time that their lives were about to be changed forever was already proving to be a prescient one, beyond even anything they might have expected. After that first night of excited conversation and difficult sleep, Marie called the Toulouse-Lautrec Museum in the nearby city of Albi the next morning to talk to someone there about the spectacular discovery she was certain they had made the evening before.

At first it was difficult for her to get through to the right person. But after she left a message about the specifics of her finds and her location, only a few minutes passed before the Director of the Museum personally returned her call to confirm the details of what she was reporting having found. He made some phone calls and contacted them later that day to set up an appointment for two days later—the one from which they were now returning.

As it turned out, he had wanted to notify two other experts, one from Toulouse and one from Paris, about the possible significance of these new finds, and both men definitely wanted to be present to inspect the contents of the trunk when it was brought to the museum.

After they left the museum to begin the trip back to the farmhouse where the amazing events had started to unfold, Jason and Marie talked excitedly for a while about what had transpired during the meeting. As they got closer, however, Marie became very quiet and just stared out the side window at the familiar countryside as it went by. Jason could see she was lost in thought, and his own mind began to turn through the events of the past few hours, which were still playing out vividly in his mind. Much of it still seemed like a dream from which they simply had not yet been able to awaken and determine what parts of it were truly real.

The day before they had carefully repacked the contents of the trunk just the way they found them the previous evening in anticipation of taking it with them to Albi this morning. Jason removed only the page from the sketchbook Angélique had drawn on and they decided to let their daughter keep the pastel pencils she had been given earlier. Everything else was replaced as they found it. Marie finished reading the four letters and was convinced they were all from Lautrec to her great-great-grandmother and were apparently replies to letters he received from her, which dealt with experiences they had shared together earlier in Paris and events in her life since. Marie also notified Jean-Pierre of what they had found the next evening when they went to his place for dinner. He had also been very surprised and excited at what they found. He and his wife agreed to keep Angélique while Marie and Jason took the trunk to the museum in Albi and to host them again for supper when they returned that same day with word of what they learned.

They had arrived at the museum early where three men greeted them: two senior officials from the museum and the professor from Toulouse. The art expert from Paris was late but expected soon. They helped to unload the old trunk and then Jason left to find a place to park the car. When he returned, one of the museum people showed Jason and Marie around the galleries while they waited. Jason was surprised when he saw it was housed in the Thirteenth Century Bishop's Palace, which was connected to the spectacular structure of the Cathedral of Sainte Cécile, which he quickly learned was the largest brick church in Europe and possibly the largest in the world with over a million bricks. The cathedral itself had taken over two hundred years to complete, and with the fortress-like bishop's palace attached, the entire structure with its beautiful, walled gardens as it looked down over the Tarn River below was in Jason's opinion very impressive. At one point he had been reading a description of Toulouse-Lautrec's life and pointed out to Marie with a grin that the artist's first middle name had also been *Marie*. She was unfamiliar with the fact, and it gave them both a quick chuckle.

By the time they were finished with their brief tour and had viewed many of the impressive Toulouse-Lautrec paintings in particular, Jason's and Marie's level of excitement and expectation was beginning to rise significantly. They could sense the museum people were becoming very impatient to see the contents of the truck, and they all hastened back to where it had been taken as soon as they received word the man from Paris had finally arrived. They were led to a conference room where the inspection was to take place, and the contents of the trunk were soon being spread on a large table.

The excitement of the four men was palpable and Jason quickly settled in to pick up as much of the rapid exchange of French conversation as he could absorb. He watched quietly while Marie confidently handled the excitement of the four men, who seemed amid the rapid exchanges passing back and forth to want to know everything and every detail they could about her family. The ten o'clock appointment had soon become one in the afternoon before someone thought to send out for a quick lunch of sandwiches and what Jason quickly noticed were a couple of particularly nice bottles of wine. It had been nearly three before the men agreed to let the two of them repack the trunk to return to the Aveyron Valley. Just before that, there was a short conference over the wine about the significance of their important find and the possible directions Jason and Marie might decide to take with it.

The art professor from Paris, a recognized Toulouse-Lautrec expert, seemed to be the most excited and was able to supply information none of the others appeared to possess. However, all four men readily agreed, as soon as all the contents had been individually examined, that, indeed, everything was most certainly genuine and constituted a major new find for the art world in general and for Toulouse-Lautrec enthusiasts in particular. The museum people had been positively giddy and Jason could quickly see they were already concerned with how their institution might be able to acquire the entire collection. One of them kept stressing how important it was that *"grand-mère Paulette"*, as he was soon calling her, was from the local area, just as Toulouse-Lautrec had been, and how these finds deserved to stay in the region. The Toulouse art expert and the Paris professor seemed less enthusiastic about that prospect, however.

The man from Paris was particularly excited about the artwork of Paulette Gambeau, far more so than the other three. He finally told them that in his extensive research with Lautrec's papers and other personal effects over the years, he had become aware of three paintings in the collection no one had ever been able to properly attribute. They were in the Lautrec style and most Lautrec experts had come to believe they were probably the work of some unknown student of the Master. All three were signed in the same fashion as the ones from the trunk as *Pa.Gambeau* and dated 1899. No one, he said, had ever been able to find such an artist. However, as he quickly made it clear, they had always assumed "Pa." referred to the name Paul and no one apparently ever thought to look for a woman with a similar attribution.

Marie simply smiled politely at his remark, but Jason noted both her pride and a little pique of disgust at the man's sexist comment when she replied perhaps that was a mistake which should not have been made, even a hundred years ago. Jason then casually mentioned how on the previous day while looking through the old show bills and theater announcements used in the trunk for packing, he had found the name of Paulette Gambeau listed more than once among the featured dancers. Marie smiled back and winked as if to say: *Why couldn't someone else have taken such an obvious step over the years?*

There was also no doubt among all six persons present the woman in the original Lautrec oil on board painting was positively *grand-mère Paulette,* based on the photo of her in her costume. This, as they quickly pointed out, would make the four letters even more important and create a new stir about a possible romantic involvement with one of the most written about artists of the turn of the last century—a man who was well-known for his many romantic affairs, bordello escapades, and other sexual liaisons. Marie quickly pointed out, however, there was, in fact, no direct evidence of such an intimacy in the letters. Jason immediately sensed his wife was determined to protect her ancestor's, and her family's, reputation from any such unfounded and salacious conclusions if she could, just as her grandmother Beatrice had apparently wanted to do for all those years. All four men also agreed the drawings and sketches of Paulette Gambeau with this Lautrec connection, if confirmed by more thorough analysis, would constitute an important find in and of themselves and add a new artist, and more particularly a woman artist, to those from that major and influential period at the turn of the twentieth century.

Finally, just before they began repacking the trunk, the four men held a private conference to discuss possible disposition alternatives to recommend. The man from Paris wanted to contact an important art dealer there to come down to the farm and look at the paintings and drawings in person and to offer possible sales recommendations and appraisals. The professor from Toulouse and the museum administrators were more inclined to wait to feel out other people among their art world contacts and to wait for more scientific analysis of the artwork and letters before making the announcement of this major new find to the public. Marie and Jason held their own quick little head-to-head while this was going on and soon agreed not to allow themselves to be bound by any sudden decisions, but to permit all parties to have access where possible to present their recommendations and proposals. As soon as the men finished and gave their points of view and Marie informed them of her family's desire to make no immediate decision, she raised the matter of value, since it was obvious by then all the men were reluctant to be the first to establish some benchmark the others might find out of line.

The man from Toulouse and the professor from Paris conferred with the other two, who then informed them they all agreed that, if and when the entire collection was absolutely authenticated by the necessary further scientific tests and other experts, and was offered together as one lot, it would undoubtedly increase the interest in the letters and Paulette's drawings. As such, they were fully confident a starting bid of three to five million at a well-advertised auction at that time, which this would certainly become, would not be an unreasonable starting point. The man from Paris quickly added in the last twenty years two works by Toulouse Lautrec had brought fifteen and twenty million dollars respectively at auction, the one as recently as ten years or so earlier.

Additionally, given the volatile and excitable state of the international art world just then, a new painting with a well-known subject by a recognized Master, as this was, might start a bidding frenzy that could lead an opening bid to some unforeseeable conclusion well above that amount. The man from Toulouse also raised the possibility that separating the Lautrec painting from Paulette's work and offering her collection as a separate lot might be even more financially rewarding, given the circumstances involved with the signed letters. Either way, the decisions Marie and Jason would soon have to make would have a profound effect on their futures. Of that, all six people in attendance were in happy agreement.

Somehow, the two of them managed to maintain their relative calm until the trunk was repacked and Jason brought the car around to reload it for their return trip. They did not talk much until Jason managed to clear the busy late-afternoon traffic heading out of Albi and regained control over his shaking hands. Marie was quite excited as well, but was far more restrained than he would have expected, given her excitement since discovering the trunk's contents two days ago. For the first thirty minutes or so they talked mostly about the events of the meeting, while Marie filled him in on those parts of the conversations he had not understood or been able to keep up with.

By the time they turned to head back into the low hills leading to the Aveyron Valley they both realized they would soon have to face important decisions about their immediate future well beyond any financial windfall which might occur. Both became quiet and Jason supposed the familiar surroundings of her youth were probably reviving many memories for Marie during the last few days. He glanced ahead and saw a sight that was familiar to him, too. It was the beautiful little walled, hilltop village of Puycelsi, one of the most picturesque villages in all of southern France; or so he had been told when he visited it when he first came here to meet Marie's family, back before they were married. He recalled the day of that visit well, looked at his wife, who was also staring that way just then, and said.

"I remember the day when we came here with your grandmother Béatrice, just after our first time down from Paris. I thought the view from up there was one of the loveliest I had seen in all my time in France. I can still recall how impressed I was with the place; you know, the old church with the beautiful wood carvings, the swallows swirling on the steeple, and the veteran's memorial in the little park near the edge of the hill looking up toward the valley you're from. I remember I couldn't believe there were over fifty names, just from World War One on that monument. God! How awful such a tremendous loss must have been to endure for such a small place as this back in those days."

"Yes, it was, and there are monuments like that in nearly every little village in France, you know. As I recall, *Mamie Béa* pointed out a couple of distant cousins or uncles of hers whose names were carved on that monument. She took me there a few times when I spent the summers with her and we would go to visit an old friend of hers who lived up there in the village. The view from on top is pretty spectacular. See that rock cliff up ahead we're about to pass by. It's the entrance to the Aveyron Gorge area—sort of like a gateway into my family's past. There's also a Paleolithic campsite that was excavated some years back just below the cliffs over there somewhere. That 'old' church you mentioned is not as old as others hereabouts, but there was an older one once and the town was walled about then because it was involved in all that Cathar and Albigensian heresy trouble of the time, I believe. Before that, I think it went all the way back to a fortified Roman camp, as were so many other hilltop towns around here from even earlier, just after the time of Christ. You can't scratch the surface anywhere in this part of France without uncovering some major historical event, or some family's unique story. Time always seems to stand still—or at least passes more slowly—in these old, isolated valleys and tiny villages. So much history seems to flow west with every little river around here, I think.

"I learned all this history of the Valley in school the one year I was fourteen when I lived here, right after my father died and while mother got herself situated. That was when we had been living in Toulouse and *Mama* decided to relocate to Paris, but had to leave me behind until she found work. Losing my brother, and then my father not long after that, was really hard on her. I've never criticized *Mama* for any of the difficult decisions she made at that time. *Mamie Béa,* however, was pretty upset about it back then. I figured it all out later, when *Mama* apparently sent for me to join her a lot sooner than she told my grandmother she planned, I think. I don't believe their relationship ever got any better after that. Those were hard times for our little family back then, and I'm sure with me being a teenager I probably didn't make things any easier on either one of them."

They both fell silent again for a while until Marie turned to her husband and spoke. It was the first exchange in a conversation Jason had been reluctantly expecting, because he knew it would lead to the questions facing them each was probably unwilling to confront until absolutely necessary.

"You know, Jason, there just isn't any way I can bring myself to sell the farm now with all that has happened. It wouldn't feel right after everything those people have done for us. I think it would be for the best, after what we've heard today and with all that's still going to happen, if I stayed behind here when you have to leave. I also think it might be better if Angélique stayed also. Her school term has only just started back in New York, and I could enroll her in the local primary school here right away. Jean-Pierre happened to mention the other evening he has an old Renault he can loan me, if I decide to stay for a while, or at least till we make some more permanent decisions. I know this will be really rough on you, but I can't see any other logical alternative to what we are going to have to deal with in the next couple of months or so. What do you think?"

This was the question Jason had been both dreading, yet secretly hoping for at the same time. It meant he would not have to be the one to bring up the difficult subject of his business situation and try to put it into some context that didn't sound like he was making a decision without her input. Actually, he quickly realized, this might be just the solution he had been dancing around with himself for the last three days in the blind hope some outside force beyond his control might yank him out of his dilemma.

"Well, I've certainly been giving a lot of thought to what needs to happen here in the coming days and weeks, at least insofar as it affects our little family. Being scattered several thousand miles apart though, I must say, is not the situation I envisioned when we opened that trunk the other evening. Look, Marie, there's something I've been wanting to talk to you about for the past few weeks but couldn't find the right time—or the words, I guess—to bring it up, especially after we decided to come over here and all that's happened as a result. I'm afraid our business has not been going so well in the last few months and something major is going to have to be done. Most of the problem is on this end, I'm convinced; for it seems our old friend and partner, André, is neither the great— nor the honest—businessman we were both led to believe when we hooked up with him.

"I've been thinking about some major changes in the business here in France in the last several days and would like to refocus much of it on some new areas I've seen this week I think might allow us to recover and even expand. But I would have to take direct charge over here myself, if my ideas are to pan out. Maybe all this business with the farm is just the opportunity I was struggling to find to have an excuse to make the big changes I was reluctant to mention to you until all this happened. You know, I think I could make Ed Davis an offer he'd accept to run the New York end of the business, at least until things got really firmed up on this end. Maybe I should just plan to stay here myself until things get straightened out, which will have to start with our saying "*au revoir*" once and for all to André. What do you think about that, my love?"

"Oh, Jason! Do you really mean it? It would be so wonderful if we could all stay here together, at least until the artwork thing is cleared up. You'll love the Valley once you've been here for a while. The people are all so great and you'll fit in so well, I just know you will. Then, maybe we can decide we might stay beyond that. We could fix up the farm, or turn it into a couple of *gîtes* for the rental business. With the money from the sale of the paintings we could even build our own place. There's a spot down closer to the road where the big linden trees are I've always thought would be a beautiful place for a house. *Mamie Béa* used to think so, too, but she would just laugh at me when I told her I would like to live there some day."

"Hey now, let's not get too carried away just yet. I still have to reshape this business and my new ideas into something that will allow us to live here more permanently. We can't just live on *grand-mère Paulette's* legacy forever, you know. I'm not the "kept man" type, my dear; or don't want to be anyway. Besides, there's just the three of us and a new house at this point seems a bit of a reach."

Jason looked over at an excited Marie and laughed slightly at his own joke about being a kept man—and in his relief for having finally been able to find a way to get the other difficult subject out into the open. Marie grinned back at him, lowered her eyes, and turned to look back out the front windshield once more. After a couple of quiet moments she spoke.

"Well, since we're both in the "confession" mood here, Jason, there's something I've been meaning to tell you, also, since right before we left New York. Then, all this other excitement descended on us and made it a difficult thing to bring up. I also didn't know what effect it would have on Angélique, what with the death of *Mamie Béa* and now this business of having to take her out of school and away from her friends to start all over here. I guess the best way to say it is just to blurt it out. I've been fairly certain for the last three weeks I'm pregnant."

Jason jerked his head away from the road to where Marie had turned toward him with a new, wider smile on her face. He grinned back and then refocused his eyes, if not his mind, on the road ahead once more. Just as they passed by the towering stone cliff to head back toward the little valley, which would now be their home as it had been to so many before them, Jason instinctively eased back on the gas when they came to a small village just beyond the narrow entrance leading to the Aveyron Gorge. Marie, who had turned back to look out the side window, faced toward him again, smiled, and said.

"If it's a girl, I'd like to name her Béatrice, Béatrice Paulette. What do you think?"

"Well, I suppose we owe them both at least that much. What if it's a boy?" Jason winked and grinned.

"Oh, I don't know. How do you feel about Antoine? It's a name I've always liked. Got any other suggestions, or a middle name from your family, perhaps?"

"Uhh, I don't think I've had quite as much time to think about all this as you have. But Antoine, has a nice ring to it, I suppose. There are a bunch of "Tony's" on my mother's side. You know all those Italians. Maybe we should ask Angélique what she might like as a middle name. After all, if it is a boy she'll be putting up with him a lot more than we will, and for a lot longer. Just so long as she doesn't want to name him *Matisse* or after one of her other dog friends, or even some other artist. Although, I suppose *Henri* would certainly not be too out of line at this point, ehh."

They both laughed at his comment and agreed getting Angelique's input was a good idea. Marie said it was important their daughter be kept in the whole process as soon as she could be told what was going to happen. Then they fell silent again, until Marie finally looked out the window once more and said somewhat matter-of-factly.

"I don't think I mentioned this earlier, but Jean-Pierre told me last evening after dinner he was fairly certain there was an old man named Louis Gambeau who lived in this little village we're passing by. He was also pretty sure this old fellow once kept a wood working shop hereabouts and had a good reputation locally as a master carver and cabinet maker. Jean-Pierre didn't know if he might be related to *grand-mere* Paulette somehow; but I think I'll drive back over here as soon as things settle down a bit and see if he might be some long-lost family member. Want to come along?"

"Sure. Sounds good," Jason replied with a nod. Then he glanced quickly over at Marie, smiled broadly, and said. "I wonder if the old gent has red hair by any chance."

They both laughed openly at the thought and all it might mean. Marie looked back through the side window in silence once more, and Jason soon began to hum the little French tune Angélique always sang to herself when she was having happy thoughts—thoughts that were hers alone to keep and cherish.